JACK BE NIMBLE

BOOK 1: GARGOYLE

by BEN ENGLISH

"Just as much appeal to me as the Dan Brown books I have read. International settings, technology, and a mystery to solve.

... an appeal to young adults that like reading about more adult things ... give it a try!"

— *Tales from the Shelves*

"The author describes the events vividly and spares no detail. In books containing any mystery, the reader needs to feel as if he/she understands the whole plot; with this book, the reader will find satisfaction.

— *Live to Read*

"The writing is amazing. Intense action scenes ... English paints vivid pictures with his words and they are a joy to imagine ... fell in love with the characters ... would like to go back and read the first part of the book again. It's so much fun!"

— *Six Mixed Reviews*

Jack Be Nimble: Gargoyle
Ben English

This is a work of fiction. Names, characters, places, and incidents either are products of the author's imagination or are used fictitiously. Any resemblance to actual events or locales or persons, living, dead, undead, or wandering the streets of San Francisco, would be pretty amazing, now, wouldn't it?

Second edition, published in the United States of America.

Cover art modified, original photo by Brian Jeffery Beggerly. View west over the city of Paris from the Galerie des Chimères of Notre-Dame de Paris. Licensed under the Creative Commons Attribution 2.0 generic license.

English, Ben E. (Ben Emery), 1971 -
Jack Be Nimble: Gargoyle / Ben English -1st ed.
1. Novelists—Fiction. 2. Crime—Fiction. I-Title.
ISBN-978-1463680893
ISBN-1463680899
ebook ISBN - 978-1-4524-2207-7

Visit the author's website: www.BenEnglishAuthor.com

Contents

This one's for Gilen.

Ben English

Trade Secrets

"Art lies in its concealment."
–Cicero

She struggled through mountains of falling rain, until her own bright reflection resolved itself on the skin of the train before her.

It was barely a short dash then from the depot to the open train door, and Mercedes ran as quickly as her skirt allowed, thrusting her briefcase ahead of her. Maybe it's just me, she thought, but why does it always seem to be raining in Seattle? Droplets of moisture fell underneath the swing of her hair. It hadn't exactly been a perfect day. Men had tried to pick her up in what seemed like every airport in the country; every single one of her flights had been delayed; and the final one, from Seattle to Spokane, Washington, had been canceled outright because of the relentless storm.

In Seattle, things had gone from bad to worse. While she didn't relish the idea of driving five hours through the rain in a rented car, Mercedes was sure she was having a nightmare when the rental agent informed her all the cars had been taken for the evening, and would she care for a motorcycle?

She refused to take a bus, not for all the teacups in China.

Mercedes had been sitting in the airport restaurant, fighting jet lag and combating her hunger with a disgusting salad, when salvation had come in the form of a short, bright-eyed waiter. "Sounds terrible, ma'am. Me, I always check my horoscope and have my palm read before I travel. Hey, why not try the new bullet train? It'll get you there in almost an hour, and they have these great all-glass observation cabins on top of the regular cars. You should give it a try."

Sure, Mercedes thought, it'll be an adventure. I'll just sit back and read a good book. On her way to the ticket counter she picked up the latest paperback bestseller from the book stand.

So, after ignoring the roving eyes of the herd of commuting businessmen in the lower cabin, Mercedes forced herself up the stairs and found she was alone on the spacious deck. Wearily she sank down into one of the plush chairs and dropped her briefcase and purse at her feet. Even her eyelids were tired. She closed them and listened to the soothing thrum of the rain on all the yards of glass stretching over her. The track lighting was dim, and she felt the strain and tension from a day of maddening inconveniences and petty frustrations slip away. For the first time in three time zones she didn't worry about her extremely unpressed suit or smudged makeup.

A heavy step on the stairs broke Mercedes from her meditation. Irritated, she sat up and peered through the gloom at the stairwell, where a man's head and shoulders loomed unsteadily.

Mercedes took him in instantly, her photographer's eye clicking away: a thirtysomething businessman in a cheap suit, not quite done digesting his liquid lunch. The toupee probably cost more than the ring he surreptitiously twisted off his left hand and dropped in his pocket. Mercedes had faced this a hundred times before; she knew exactly what this guy was going to—

"Say! Hello! The name's Miles, and I couldn't help but notice you walk in." This one was smooth, or at least thought he was, straightening his tie and gesturing expansively at the same time. Probably in advertising, Mercedes thought. "So I said to myself, Miles, you old dog, you've met this fine woman before somehow, why not grab the opportunity to reintroduce—"

Mercedes wasn't exactly sure what happened next, only that it happened fast. Something bumped into Miles from behind as he was about halfway up the stairs; hit him hard enough to actually knock him off balance. He whipped his arms around a few times before the toupee slid down over his eyes and he fell backwards onto the carpeted floor below. Mercedes winced at the heavy thud, then blinked in surprise at the cheery voice from below.

"Dreadful sorry about that, my dear lad, hope you don't have a concussion, The old eyesight isn't exactly all it used to be, what? Didn't even see you loafing on the stairs like that. Oh, my, you did hit your head a bit, didn't you?"

"Urkl," replied Miles.

"I say, that's a lovely hairpiece." Mercedes placed the speaker's age somewhere between seventy and eighty. She had to suppress a smile as the old man wheezed to the top of the stairs. He turned once again and called out to the foot of the stairs. "I'd lose the tie—if I were you."

As he turned back and caught sight of Mercedes, his whole face lit up. Mercedes was unable to withhold her grin, and his face brightened even more. As he slowly hobbled closer, his warmth seemed to flow outward and wash over her, and she gestured to the seat across from her own. "Thank you, my dear," he said as he settled himself in, leaning his umbrella against a large black suitcase and removing his hat. The shock of hair was brilliantly white, matching his bushy eyebrows. The old fellow was dressed in a worn black suit that had undoubtedly seen as many miles as the battered suitcase. He was tall but a bit stooped, and his smiling face was a maze of wrinkles. A fresh-picked rose sprouted from his buttonhole. Mercedes couldn't decide which was more striking—his flaming red cheeks and beaklike nose, or the outrageous tie he wore. It was vividly colored and crafted to resemble a fish.

Oblivious to her scrutiny, the old man placed the suitcase on his lap, opened it a crack, and withdrew a steaming china cup. "Would you care for some hot chocolate, my dear? No? Well, pardon me, but it is, after all, high tea." She watched with growing disbelief as he pulled a spoon from an inner pocket of his suit and stirred the drink a few times. "My-my-my. Terrible rain, what?" He stopped stirring and leaned the spoon against the outer rim of the cup. As he brought the cup to his lips, the spoon swung around and hit a flank of his great nose.

Calmly he set the cup down and moved the spoon back to its original position, then attempted to drink. As the cup tilted, the spoon hit him again. The sheer delicacy of his manner was ludicrous. Again he attempted to drink, and with the same result. He set the cup down and glared at the offending spoon.

Mercedes let a giggle escape her, and the old man's frown turned instantly to a smile. Mercedes knew the battle was lost. Her laughter joined his wheezing chuckle in the cabin.

Presently he handed her a frog-embroidered handkerchief, and as she dabbed her eyes, he spoke. "Sorry about that, my dear, but you looked a bit sad, and I simply can't bear the thought of a young person depressed. Please allow me to introduce myself." He bowed slightly from his chair. "Gil Deguiser, professional salesman." It sounded like 'Geel.' Probably French.

He sat and Mercedes handed him his handkerchief, shaking his hand. "Mercedes Adams, professional photographer." Her smile remained. "What do you sell?"

Deguiser's dark eyes twinkled as he sat back. "Look in your briefcase, my dear." He sipped the hot chocolate delicately. "And don't look so confused, you'll give yourself unsightly wrinkles."

Mercedes set the briefcase on her knees and dialed in the lock's combination. The old man was absorbed with his drink. There, on top of her photograph folders and next to her new paperback was a little white business card. Mercedes set her open briefcase on the adjacent seat and read aloud.

"'Gilitano Deguiser, Gower Street 007. Magic tricks for every occasion you can probably think of.' Now, how did you do that?"

He set a gnarled finger against his lips. "Trade secret. Are those photos of yours?" He gestured with the spoon.

"Yes. I shot the ceremony in Cuba yesterday as President Espinosa took the oath of office."

The old man finished his drink and set the cup down. "Dangerous work, that."

"Yes," she said. "I do my share of ducking bullets." It didn't quite sound ironic, saying it aloud.

"What's that book you have there?"

Mercedes followed his gaze to the paperback she had bought to distract herself with on the trip. *Half to Death*, by Fletcher Engstrom. "Oh, I bought this just to take up the time. It's part of a series— very good, or so I've heard. They're supposed to be making it into a movie or something. The fellow that writes them used to be a friend of mine. He writes under the name Fletcher Engstrom but his real name's Jack Flynn."

"No, really?" He was incredulous. "You don't mean the actor, Jack Flynn." Mercedes nodded. "Fascinating! And you know him! Tell me, what's he like? I'll bet his life story would sell for a pretty penny. Where's he from, pray tell."

Mercedes thought for a moment. She sure was talking a lot with this old gentleman. He had that quality about him, though, that

15

made you want to open up. She decided she liked the old fellow. She began. "I haven't seen or heard from him in years, but I knew him fairly well when we were younger. Jack was from Forge, Idaho—"

"Amazing! I used to sell from Post Falls to Boise! Quite a piece of country, I—pardon me, I'm stealing your story."

But Mercedes had seen the light come into the old man's eyes as he had slipped back along the tracks to the past. "No, please go on, that's all right. What were you going to say?"

"Just that there were quite a number of athletes to come out of that area back then." Deguiser could see she was interested, so he continued. "One year in particular, I remember the whole town of Boise turned out to watch the state swimming championships. Seemed like the whole town, anyway. Not a lot of people in Idaho, you know. At any rate, there I was, working the crowd, and enjoying the free show. There was one race in particular where a certain young man stood up on the blocks and the whole crowd from Northern Idaho went wild. Good looking fellow, too. Blond. He never seemed to notice the crowd, just kept staring at the water. All the time his hand was making these odd little gestures. Sign language, that's what it was, yes! A boy next to me read sign, and as he watched he asked his mother why the young man on the starting block was spelling out the name of an imported car—"

Now it was Mercedes turn to interrupt. "It was Jack! You saw Jack!" Mercedes opened her purse and felt around inside as he went on.

"I did? Can't seem to remember the name. Marvelous swimmer, though. What a race! Bless my soul, I think he won."

As the words died out Mercedes held up a gleaming golden disk. "Kind of a . . . good luck charm. Been in there awhile."

The old man turned the bright metal over and over in his gnarled hands. "I'm an old fool. Name of a car, indeed. The boy was spelling your name over and over, wasn't he?"

Mercedes nodded, slipping the gold medal back into a sleeve of her wallet. "He never told me that."

*

Deguiser exhaled deeply, running a hand through his tangled explosion of white hair. The sound of rain on the glass dome had almost ceased. The train seemed to be outrunning the storm.

*

"Did you love that boy?" he asked.

Mercedes searched for the right words. "I thought so," she said slowly. "Jack was my first real boyfriend, I guess. Before I knew what boyfriends really were." She had to smile. "You wouldn't believe some of the crazy things he would do." She glanced at the old man. He answered with the ghost of a grin. "I could never tell if he was serious about anything. He met my family dressed as the Bike Gang Member from Hell. No one ever figured out exactly how he managed it, but once he filled the school swimming pool with Jell-O and spelled my name with a million M&Ms. He'd make up terrible poems that wouldn't rhyme, but would write me something new every day. Just the sort of person you'd expect to grow up and become a movie star."

The old man leaned forward and spoke softly. "He sounds as though he loved you very much."

Mercedes nodded, letting a few stray wisps of hair drift over her face. She could feel a tear starting to build despite herself. "He did. A little while after the race you saw, I got—I wasn't well. He couldn't believe that I didn't want to see him or his letters. I suppose I was unfair to him. I mean, he tried to be understanding, but I never gave him much of a chance. And he was busy with his own life. Trying to figure himself out.

"Jack went on a religious mission to Eastern Europe for two straight years. I got better and went to college. By the time he got home I had changed addresses so many times he couldn't find me."

The old man was spellbound. "Why? Why did you do it?"

"All the time I was sick I kept thinking how little control I had over my own life. Jack was the only guy I had ever really dated. As fun as he was, there had to have been someone better. I had to find out if there was someone I could love more. There wasn't anything wrong with Jack, but I didn't know if he was 'the one,' you see?"

"Did you ever find 'the one'?" Deguiser asked.

"No, not yet."

"Did you ever find anyone you loved more than Jack?"

"No."

Her new friend frowned. "Then I'm afraid I don't see." Deguiser leaned forward, his aged face a crease of concern. "You had true love in your hands, and you threw it away? Do you realize how fantastically rare a gift that is? Oh, my dear." The old man pulled out his frog handkerchief and wiped his eyes. "Did you ever see him again?"

"There were rumors that he'd gotten married, but Jack was too superior to come to his high school reunion. I went to the premier of one of his movies a few years back and saw him there with some red-headed actress, but he didn't see me."

"Are you sure?"

"Positive. Jack's the kind of guy who'd have leaped out of

the balcony, slid down the curtains, and had me in his arms before I could've gotten away. Besides," she smirked, "That redhead had his full attention."

"What if you saw him again, my dear? Could you still love him, do you think?"

Mercedes had something in her eye. "Could I borrow your handkerchief?"

A soft pinging filled the cabin as the train hummed to a stop, and once again the sound of rain danced on the glass dome. "Ah," sighed the old man, with the air of someone who has come home. "I wonder why it always seems to be raining in Spokane?" Leaning heavily on his walking stick, he pushed himself to his feet. Luggage in hand, he and Mercedes walked down the stairs together, arm in arm. "It's been wonderful talking with you," he said. "I feel fifty years younger. Good luck with your photography.

"Oh, and before I forget, take my umbrella." Mercedes tried to refuse, but the old man was adamant. "It's not every day an old fellow like myself gets the chance to be a real gentleman."

Mercedes reluctantly took the umbrella and turned to one of the doors. "I'm sure I'll never forget this," she began, struggling to get the ancient umbrella open.

"I hope you never do, my dear."

Mercedes forced the battered umbrella open above her head and was showered in a deluge of red and pink roses. The scent of fresh roses and new rain filled the cabin as Mercedes whirled to face the old man. He was gone. Peering out the door, she could barely discern his looming bulk as it faded into the swirling rain and fog. The wild elements seemed to have added to his size, somehow. Like an old battleship, he plodded on through a huge puddle. "How did you do that?" she yelled into the rain and wind.

He kept walking. "Trade secret, my dear!" Mercedes laughed. She felt very warm.

*

The old man crossed the gray street and slipped into the passenger side of a waiting limo. The driver chuckled and accelerated away from the train station. It was the same bright-eyed waiter that had advised Mercedes to take the train in Seattle. There was a paperback book on the dashboard, another by Fletcher Engstrom. The passenger picked it up. "You really read this stuff, Alonzo?"

"Somebody's got to keep you from starving to death, pal." The short man concentrated on the road ahead. "So, was she worth it?"

Jack Flynn pulled the last of the rubber makeup and about 40 years away from his face. "Yeah, she's great. As–as incredible as ever. I'm afraid I still love her, Alonzo."

Alonzo swore under his breath. "Here we go," he muttered.

Now, let's take a few steps back –

JACK BE NIMBLE

BOOK ONE: GARGOYLE

The only cure for grief is action.
—George Henry Lewis

To sing, to laugh, to dream,
To walk in my own way and be alone,
Free, with an eye to see things as they really are,
A voice that means manhood—
To fight—or write. To travel any road
Under the sun, under the stars, nor doubt
If fame or fortune lies beyond the bourne—
Never to make a line I have not heard in my own heart.
You ask why, my dear, against one singer they sent a
hundred swords?

Because
They know this one man for a friend of mine!
—Cyrano de Bergerac

Home

San Francisco Peninsula, California, USA
8PM

Think big, then think little. That's what his father told him.

The sky hung red, dead motionless in the sunset over the San Francisco Bay. The plain man kept his back to the dying light. Fog sloped into the grooved hills as he drove further and further south of the city on Highway 101, a muted smile on his face and stark secrets on his mind.

It had been three years since he'd driven himself anywhere, and a decade more since Alex Raines last came all the way home, but he knew what lay ahead as sure as he felt gravity bind him to the earth. Ramps and freeway patterns might change, but the man behind the wheel followed a pattern set deeply enough in his own heart and mind that he knew he was far, far past making a mistake of any kind.

Blinking hazard lights a few miles south of San Francisco International pulled at him as well, and before he knew what he was doing he found himself pulling onto the shoulder and killing the engine. A shabby, sad-looking car sat halfway on and halfway off the shoulder.

He checked his watch. Time enough.

"Are you alright, ma'am?" he asked the startled middle-aged woman alone in the dented Altima. "I'm Alex." He offered his hand and she cracked the window open. They looked to be almost the same age.

"The police'll be along shortly," she said, eyeing his clothes and face. The passenger side and rear of the car were filled with brown paper bags full of ice cream. From somewhere under all the dairy, a small dog squeaked. Alex saw her cell phone, saw the dark display screen, and knew she was lying. He knew the designer of that phone; more to the point, he knew the *design*, and that particular brand of phone always stayed lighted if the battery held a sufficient charge. He decided a white lie of his own might balance things out.

"I used to work on this kind of car," he said. "If you pop the hood, I might be able to help." She held to her suspicion. Raines sighed, grinned, and fished a key ring out of his pocket. "Here," he said. "Why don't you hold on to my keys while I take a look." She hesitated for a moment, then accepted the keys through the cracked window, and released the hood.

Raines chuckled to himself as he rounded the front of the car. Couldn't blame her, really. The world these days was getting more and more and more frightening. Trust had to be earned, even by the trustworthy. He found a penlight in another pocket and clicked it on. Raines freely admitted himself a gadget junkie, and actually had another, brighter light with him— he'd built his own, with a brilliant microlamp hardwired into the case—but it was attached to the keys he'd surrendered. At least he had a Swiss Army knife in his pocket.

Truth be told, Raines could have diagnosed the engine in the dark, practically by touch, but he didn't want to spook the woman, and from the looks of all that ice cream, Raines wasn't the only one on a timetable.

He was glad for the distraction. Raines had been almost hoping for a blow tire of his own, anything really, as long as it held an opportunity to fix something mechanical. He was good at that kind of thing, and it was the kind of small, manageable victory in which he always took joy. His rented sedan was disappointingly sturdy.

A snapped belt. Raines sighed, and checked over the engine again, pulling the dipstick and checking for bubbles in the oil. Too simple.

"Ma'am? It's just one of your belts." He held up the frayed rubber for her to see. "I hope you don't think me too forward, but I could give you a temporary fix."

Her expression softened somewhat, but the wide brown eyes still didn't trust him completely. Raines couldn't blame her, given the circumstances.

"It looks like you are coming from the store; I wonder if you might have bought a pair of ladies' stockings?" She had, and Raines rejoiced. Luck or God smiling down, and all that. The stockings in question were thick enough to do the trick. "I can get you a fix good for ten miles or so, but see you drive straight to the shop tomorrow and get this properly replaced."

"I'll have one of my boys look at it first thing," she said. A trace of a Louisiana accent, and he was starting to win her over.

Raines measured the stockings by eye and by touch, knotted them expertly and snipped the ends clean with the scissors blade of his knife.

"Go ahead and try it now," he said, and the engine roared to life. Her alternator sounded like it had about two weeks left to go, and he told her so.

"My but aren't you clever," she said, smiling for the first time. Her name was Angela Weidermeyer, and Raines decided she was a warm person after all, mostly untouched by what a dangerous, nasty place the world could be. She produced a tiny poodle dog and he shook its paw.

"That's a lot of ice cream you've got there," he said.

"A little something for my boys. I was sure it would all melt before anyone stopped to help." She didn't admit that her cell phone was dead, and Raines didn't bring it up. He listened instead to the good-natured relation of her night's trials and minor victories. Putting the bits and pieces together, Raines gathered that she ran the Eleven o' Clock Club, a small home for runaways and children seeking legal emancipation from their parents, and had just gotten a license of some sort from the state. This was all very nice, but he could feel the weight of time beginning to press, and he altered his posture and responses accordingly.

"Oh, but I'll talk your ear off, you give me half a chance. Thank you so much." When she tried to offer him money, Raines steadfastly refused, but still stood awkwardly, rooted to the spot. "Is there something else then, dear?"

He stood sheepishly in the light fog, traffic brushing by a dozen feet away, and said, "You've still got my keys."

She laughed and handed them over, then he waived her on her way when the freeway cleared. Moments later he was back in his own car, slicing south again through thin traffic.

Raines picked up his own phone and pushed a single button. "Update, please" he said, checking his watch. Still three hours until sunrise in the United Kingdom. "Good, now: There's a woman named Angela Weidermeyer who lives somewhere on the peninsula. Runs a service for children who get away from their parents, or who request emancipation. Tomorrow she is to receive a new Lexus and a passenger van. Take special care with the stereo and theater systems, as if these were for your own children. One million and eleven dollars are to be deposited in her business account at precisely eleven o'clock. Bear in mind," he added, "this is to be strictly anonymous. She didn't recognize me, and as far as anyone is to know I'm still touring factories outside of Prague."

Raines disconnected the call, and concentrated on his driving. Traffic wasn't as bad as he remembered. He doubted he'd find another stranded traveler, though fixing their car would prove depressingly easy as well. Pistons to microchips, he could fix any part of any vehicle he had ever seen, given a few simple tools.

He loved to fix the broken things around him.

He made this discovery at age nine, when his parents forced him to come to this horrible place, made him fit in with the miserable children who only spoke English. With no friends, Raines spent his youth taking things apart, breaking them down as far as they would go. Finding their inner operating principle. Thinking big, and then thinking little.

He remembered now he enjoyed driving. Usually a bodyguard or one of the secretaries escorted him, but a single night alone was something Raines promised himself years ago—decades before anyone ever heard of Raines Dynamic. Ages before the money. What a journey it had been.

He left the freeway for Redwood City. West on Whipple Avenue, past Pizza Hut and Jiffy Lube and a dozen other monuments to the long-standing inertia and mediocrity of the old neighborhood. The streets at this hour should have been busy, but were vacant, swept clean.

All too quickly, he arrived at the house on the right, nearly unchanged. A stucco two-story, with brick at the corners and a cedar-shake roof. He'd forgotten there were two chimneys. The hedge had grown, despite his strict orders to the gardeners, and Raines wondered what other orders the caretaker staff had ignored. No one had dared take down the basketball hoop his father had nailed above the driveway.

Basketball was supposed to be fun. The kind of thing American fathers do with their American sons. It was the one action in the man's life that had been free of rigorous logic, and Raines remembered feeling a strange tinge to his curiosity towards the father buried somewhere within the scientist, perhaps hope at last. But they never played basketball.

As Raines stepped onto the walkway leading to the front door, a car door behind him opened. He turned to find a startled-looking young man, a sharp-dressed fellow with eager eyes, charging across the lawn.

"Mr. Raines? Mr. Raines, is that you?" The youth was beside himself. Behind him a girl emerged from their car. She was using a cell phone, which would not do.

Raines reached in his coat and tapped one of the many devices he habitually carried. Immediately, the young woman jerked her head away from the phone, as if shocked.

"Mr. Raines, thank—ah, sorry. This is such an honor." The young man looked like he wanted to either shake hands or actually hug. Raines palmed another of his gadgets and switched hands before extending an open hand.

"Are you student?" The girl paused at the sidewalk, obviously still stunned by her phone shorting out. She was pretty, much like the girls had been when he himself was in graduate school, like this unsure boy stepping from foot to foot before him.

"Heather, this is him, this is really the guy! She smiled vaguely. The boy frowned at her, embarrassed. "He was on the cover of Newsweek last month. Mr. Raines, it is such an honor to meet you, sir!" He pumped Raines' hand. To the girl he added, "The new engineering wing is named after him."

As if on cue, the floodlights over the garage and front porch came on, and they all heard the sounds of the front door unlocking.

"Is this a smart house?" the young man asked.

"One of the first I ever built," Raines admitted. "Experimented on, really. Before I learned how to make things really small." Technical staff from one of the companies under the Raines Dynamic umbrella came by once a week, not only to dust but to run system diagnostics as well. It wasn't unlike the master to come quickly and unannounced to any part of his kingdom.

"Yes sir! Remember Heather, he spoke to our class last fall at Stanford? The billionaire," he added, sotto voce.

"Thank you. I remember the speech. How did you manage to stay awake?" The boy laughed, a little too loudly. Glancing up and down the street, Raines added, "and how did you know I would be here tonight?"

"Oh sir, I drive past your house every night. The dean pointed it out to me my very first week. I want to continue your work, sir. I'm one of your scholarship students."

Raines smiled. "You'd be Robert Hampton, then, wouldn't you?"

The youth was dumbstruck. "You actually know my name?"

"Of course." His secretary had mentioned the name nearly a year ago. Ah, and now the young lady was coming into the light. Yes, she was prettier than he originally thought. Blond, fairly athletic, but not much facial expression. Intense sensations might help her discover new ways of expression. Raines could work on such a canvas.

He touched another device in his coat. "We'll have cappuccino for three in, say, 2 minutes?"

The young man was beside himself. All the way up the walk he sputtered about his physics classes and nanotechnology theory; undergraduate stuff, pedantic. Barely a child in the wading pool, thought Raines. To think he'd almost fallen into a life of teaching these whelk. "Are you an engineer as well?" He asked the girl.

She responded no, that she was pre-med. For her part, the girl didn't seem to know who he was, or for that matter, have decided how to act around a rich, rich man. She allowed herself to be led up the stairs at her boyfriend's elbow. So much the better.

Thanks to another of the devices he carried, the house's security system recognized Raines and deactivated the front door as they approached. Lights winked on through the downstairs foyer, and music began to play softly. The furniture was twenty years' old, but well cared-for.

"This is nice," said the girl, as Raines closed the door. The boy was asking some question or another about microscopic power supplies and heat transfer when Raines, smiling, pressed a device into the inside of his arm.

The meaty sound of his body hitting the parquet floor caused her to turn, and Raines brushed a hand, featherlight, over her neck as well. Heather started to scream, and Raines allowed this. The outer walls were soundproof. Heather backed away, then twisted and fell against the wall, clutching at herself. Under her skin, her muscles writhed and coiled. "Bobby!" She screamed again. "Bobby!"

"You really shouldn't have recognized me." Raines pocketed the injection device, trading it for a tablet computer, and turned his attention to the boy. The youth had managed to turn himself over on his side, and blood ran freely from his face. He'd most likely broken his nose during the fall. The girl sobbed behind them, and whimpered when she saw the boy's greasy, white face. "Cold," he said, and then only his eyes moved freely. The girl turned and tried to run, but her body only obeyed her halfway. Her limbs tensed and relaxed, then tensed again. She jerked in the air like a marionette, screaming all the while. She kept screaming even after her body went completely slack and collapsed at the base of the stairs. She took in great, gasping lungfulls of air, and wailed for help.

The computer readout jumped. "Interesting," said Raines. He watched the display for several seconds, then removed the young man's wallet. Behind him, the girl continued to scream.

Confusion and fear and panic, delicious panic shone brightly on her features. Her breath rasped. "Please. Please don't hurt him."

Raines propped the boy up so he could see everything.

Her change was progressing. The devices were moving through her almost as quickly as they'd taken the boy. Raines tapped out a few commands on his computer, and made a few modifications to the program, and watched it run.

"You're pre-med? You should take some satisfaction in tonight, my dear." He gestured with the computer. "The information I'm collecting on you right now will one day make it possible for tiny, tiny machines to cure specific anomalies in the human body. Because of you, other people might just live forever."

She closed her eyes and shuddered.

"There's something wonderful in you right now, moving through your circulatory system. Think of the way Alka-Seltzer dissolves in water. Getting smaller and smaller, riding your blood, then riding the electric currents and tides within your cells. But you'll stay awake. I wanted you to experience this fully."

"You put something inside me," she said.

"Many thousands of tiny, tiny things, actually. By now they've started building a nest near your brain stem. It's easy for them to do. They have no natural predator." He could just turn them off, but Raines saw no need to burden her with unnecessary hope.

"Why can't I move?"

Raines considered the many ways to explain the effect. There must be a context that she would understand. "Have you ever become weak after being tickled?"

She stared at him.

"Lost your strength after you've laughed very, very hard. It's called 'cataplexy'—a sudden loss of muscle strength caused by an extreme emotional response. The delivery agent blocks the neurological pathway that causes your muscles to contract."

Raines nodded dismissively to the corpse on the floor. "I could have just shut you off, like Bobby."

"Don't you say his name," she seethed. "I don't care how much you hurt me."

"Hurt you? No." Raines tapped the screen and a few moments later she moaned, then gasped, then groaned again with her whole voice.

"I'm going to take you past the limits of what you thought you could feel."

The girl wailed again in the throes of reckless ecstasy, and bit her lip against what Raines guessed was pleasure. Raines sat down to wait and observe. Her body would ride out the bliss sooner than she thought. She made little animal sounds deep in her throat, and her face and neck perspired enough to puddle against the floor, mixing with blood from her lip.

He turned it off. After a moment, she whimpered with disappointment.

If the eyes were any indication, she didn't know where she was. Raines waited, eyes on the screen, watching the progress of the other agents he'd injected into her. Apparently she didn't smoke or do any of the drugs young people were so fond of these days.

Eventually she reclaimed enough of herself to pant, "How can it— feel so —uhh! What are you doing to me?"

Raines moved nearer her head. "Have you ever heard that old joke about the man who bled from every pore? See, men of science, like Robert over there, would tell you that bleeding from every pore is impossible. A question of blood volume, for one thing, but actually because of the way our nerves work, bleeding like that would generate too much pain. A living creature would reach a physiological limit, and pass out. Part of our defense mechanism, I suppose. Simply speaking, I've removed your limits. You'll be surprised at the length and breadth of what you can feel now, and remain conscious.

"Now what you and I just did was establish a baseline, my dear. Everything that happens to you tonight, you're going to be able to compare to those few moments of pleasure a moment ago. And unless you swallow your tongue and asphyxiate, you'll experience it all without losing consciousness."

He leaned very close. "Remember how it felt, just now?"

She retched, and began to weep. Raines delicately touched his finger to the smooth screen.

Much later, Raines held the family Bible comfortably in the crook of his arm as he crept down the hall. The suite of rooms on the upper was quiet in a soft, expectant manner. The girl below was beyond the ability of making any noise, and Raines felt quite alone. He wandered through the rooms, smiling slightly to himself. The silence seemed almost anticipatory, just like in the hushed moments before a snowstorm. He looked around aimlessly, letting his gaze sweep over the simple desks his parents worked at. "I'm home," he announced.

"Prometheus In Our Day", the article in *Time* had said. "Paragon of the Modern Man," as he'd been proclaimed on the cover of *Pop Science*. He set a copy of each on their desks.

Raines came to a stop before a portrait of his parents, done in oils. He'd commissioned it a few years previous to their deaths. It was illuminated by several tiny cunningly placed spotlights. His parents still looked healthy, happy together, dressed in the simple clothes they'd favored since their days in Europe, before the money came. Their smiles were equally simple, belying the latent intelligence they'd harbored and passed on to their only child.

They had taught him well. Had seen to his further education when his own mind grew beyond their ability and inclination to teach. They had opened up the world of information to Raines, and let him devour it whole. They had done their best to teach him about God. They'd let him discover the Devil on his own.

Eyes on his parents' faces, Raines slipped his personal computer from an inner pocket of his linen suit. He opened it, and watched as it linked, instantly and invisibly, with the network in the house, then negotiated the local networks until it touched a node of the Raines Dynamic extranet. He saw it was one o'clock in rural Scotland.

Glancing once again at his parents, Raines tapped a simple prearranged code on the miniature keyboard. He paused, then pressed a final key.

Closing the small device, he crossed the room and opened a cabinet filled with decanters of wine and various liquors. Raines hummed to himself as he walked around the room emptying each bottle on the baseboards near the walls, the curtains, and finally pouring an entire carafe on the Louis IV sideboard underneath the portrait of his parents.

Calmly he walked to the door. He turned on the threshold, Bible in hand, allowing it to open to the first page. The names of his family for three generations lay inscribed there. There was no Alex Raines on the page.

He roughly tore it out. Looking across the room at the picture of his parents, bathed in golden light, Raines struck a match and set it to the corner of the yellowed paper. It caught quickly, and he released it, watching briefly as it drifted toward a dark stain of wine. Then Raines swiftly, silently eased the door shut and walked away.

An End

Balmoral, Scotland
4 AM

The figure in murky fatigues crouched silently on the precipice, watching the cloudbank close around the moon like a giant, smoky blue fist. He was poised at the edge of one of the many rocky hills overlooking the castle nearly a kilometer away. Beside him sat a portable radio, protected from the occasional spatter of rain by a nonreflective tarp. The fields and lower hills below reflected varying shades of the black night, relieved only by the weak lights proclaiming the castle's perimeter.

"Sleep tight, your Highness," muttered the night watcher, raising a monocular and scanning far to the left. At least the early spring storm hadn't drummed up any fog yet. Several hundred meters away a second man-shaped slice of darkness raised his hand, looking straight into the night vision's crosshairs.

The first figure glanced around the small clearing, then looked far to the right, where another man stood with his own NG-45 night vision spyglass. The signal was passed on. Outer ring clear.

The watcher panned his night scope across the scrubby hills, locating the lightly-glowing forms of three of his teammates in their places of concealment. That was odd. There was a jumpy, static-like corona around each of the men as he zoomed in on them. He adjusted the miniature focus wheel on his monocular. "Built by the lowest bidder," he muttered.

Above, the clouds were suddenly backlit by a series of staccato flashes. Misshapen shadows played weirdly along the watcher's peripheral vision. The forest was silent, almost holding its breath.

The radio clicked a few moments later, the transmission relayed automatically to the earpiece of the watcher on the rock. "Balmoral security detail 1, all clear. Logged at four o'clock."

The crackling reply came from the duty officer at the nearby Royal Navy base. "You blokes better get out your slickers, looks to be a real howler tonight. Weatherscouts missed this one, eh?"

"Thanks for the heads-up, chief. So much for a quiet night in bonny Scotland, lads."

The radio went silent.

Wind rushed suddenly through the upswept branches of the conifers behind and to the sides of him, a many-surfaced ripple. Storms often came pushing down the slopes of the Lochnagar mountains, casting up huge waves and angry surf against the shores of Loch Muich. Not a fit night to be about.

Reaching back underneath the tarpaulin, the watcher extracted a neatly folded rain cloth, allowing it unravel down the cliff face before pulling it on, then paused. *Idiot. Rebuckle your weapons over the rain gear, couldn't you remember the first lesson of all-weather training?*

He released the catches on his vest, then quickly slid out of it. The first few troublesome winds racing before the approaching squall caught the rain slicker as he bent for it, catching its hood and billowing the entire affair out above his head. *This is not exactly what I needed tonight.* He set his rifle down and forced both arms up through the slicker. *Finally.*

Without warning, the slicker was jerked halfway from his arms as a jagged triangle of holes suddenly punched themselves through the back of the hood. The guard sensed more than heard the furtive movement from the treeline at his back as he clumsily scrabbled for his weapon. He felt himself struck as if by blows from a savage, invisible opponent.

Then the nerves all along his left side lit up with searing pain, and before he could scream he felt himself dashed from his perch on the rock. Down he went, tumbling headfirst in a miniature avalanche toward the talus below. He knew, even as he fell toward death, that at least one bullet had entered his body through the chinks created in his body armor when he had raised his arms up through the rain slicker. His free arm gyrated wildly, hampered on the nearly sheer slope by the unbuckled vest.

Just as his body cleared an overhang his groping hand managed to find a space–some sort of uneven crevice in the rock. Without thinking he wedged as much of his arm as he could into the crack as he slid over it, then choked in white agony as the tendons and bones in his elbow wrenched and separated. He writhed against the pain, twisting completely out of the heavy vest and rain gear. Before he could scream he slammed into the mossy wall, the impact flush on his shoulder blades, driving the breath from his lungs.

He dangled there for a long moment, gagging silently through the crashing waves of pain, wondering what kept him from completely passing out. His right heel somehow found support against a knob of rock.

The guard allowed his head to sag forward an inch, until he could see his gear at the bottom of the ridge. The vest and jacket were almost invisible where they had landed, splayed against a clump of the long grass, blood-red in the feeble light. He strained against the night and against the numbing agony, but heard nothing. Only the low, wordless whisper of the chill breeze off the North Sea fifty kilometers away.

The sky above the stepped gables and turrets of the white granite castle suddenly flared a harsh greenish-blue, backlighting the cloudbank strangely. From the promontory above the guard came a quick half-dozen *chuffs* like the sound made by a metal brush against a piece of finished lumber, and the pile of gear below jumped as the suppressed rounds swatted into it. Then a brief scrape on the rock above and afterward, silence.

With difficulty the wounded man reattached his radio's earpiece, then felt for the control switch. A dull hiss issued from the earpiece. Whoever it was at the top hadn't even touched his radio, that was strange. The first law of armed assault was to take out your enemy's communications. Something else was wrong. The line was simply dead. He cycled through the other dozen channels fruitlessly, receiving only snatches of static. Damn storm. He closed his eyes as dizziness and nausea washed over him, then forced them open again when the sensation doubled.

The sky above was a whirling, nightmarish kaleidoscope of lambent energy. Strange how the lightning was unaccompanied by any thunder, he thought, then grimaced at his own obvious delirium. Still, odd. He'd expect thunder to roll down from all sides of the long valley.

Straining, he managed to unsnap a vest pocket and retrieve his night vision monocular. There were no signs of his companion watchers at their posts in either field to the right or left. Nothing. The guard swore softly as his spyglass fell from nerveless fingers. Everything he looked at was framed by a swimming, brown-black haze. He didn't even have the strength to shout a warning he knew at such distance would be futile. The castle lights below gleamed bravely against the black night; innocent, unaware. The last lingering image in the guard's field of vision was a group of dark figures rising up slowly out of the field near the castle wall, stark and jagged against the light.

The Banked Light

Paris, France
6 PM

Jack looked up suddenly from the café table as wind shook the panes of glass a few feet from his head. The gusting beyond the glass transferred a portion of the night's chill into him, etched an icy sharpness down his spine. It was only a matter of minutes before the storm would decide to begin in earnest, gashing down through the City of Light, carving at it with knives of lightning and rain.

Twilight always took too long in Paris. If he took the time, Jack could actually see darkness creep out from the heads of the alleys down Montmartre, could watch the shadows steal out from behind the statuary in the Luxembourg Gardens, could glance up in time to grasp the gathering gloom underneath the cornices and balustrades. Jack didn't have to look at the sky to feel the skein of dusk draw over the city at the approach of night, the approach of the storm, but he could, if he took the time. Twilight always took too long in Paris.

The table before him was littered with a dozen tightly-bound manuscripts; sheaves of a hundred and twenty words apiece baled with bright, heavy cardstock covers and filled with sparse, widely-spaced type. The white spaces between the lines seemed enormous and stark to Jack; too empty. He shook his head and closed the screenplay, turning once again to contemplate the hurtling, intransigent approach of night.

He sat there at the window, pensive and unconsoled, feeling a thousand dark eyes upon him. He'd dressed carefully, in what he'd come to consider his armor against the night. Jeans and a loose sweater always allowed him to move quickly if circumstance demanded, and he didn't feel so much like a ridiculous American. You could always tell the American tourists in Paris, if not by their baseball caps and ill-fitting pants, then in their guarded, slightly self-conscious gait, as if they were inwardly cradling some fragile bits and pieces of home. Almost all of his countrymen he'd met on their first visit to Paris showed the same inconsequential discomforts. They always looked distracted; they always spoke just too loudly, and they always ordered too much food.

It wasn't a matter of pride, but Jack could silently acknowledge the fact that he'd never needed such personal reassurances. It used to privately please him that he found himself comfortable anywhere he found himself in the world, though he'd never felt it was a point of personal arrogance. He was merely comfortable. Jack's adaptability, the ductile, elastic disposition he counted as his greatest gift, usually afforded him a sort of peace. Even so, that night in Paris, in the Helmut Lang jeans and Prada sweater that had become his agile armor, he felt as if his body was shod in unfeeling lead. He pushed the pile of screenplays away from him.

Victoria would have laughed at that. She would have smiled and shoved the whole bulk of paper back into his lap, told him to choose a good one this time; think three movies ahead because you never knew where your career was headed and (smirk) she didn't want to leave him for a more glamorous star. And Jack would have picked another great one, and Victoria would have said she picked that one too, how strange.

He couldn't do it anymore; couldn't fill up the gaping spaces in a movie script with his own life, his own essence–transform the blocky words on the page into something that beat and sang and shouted with a life of its own, even if only on dry film.

She was gone, and he couldn't do it anymore. She was gone.

*

Carly Bateman paused a moment as she exited the women's restroom, and looked across the busy café at her friend. As always, Jack fit in without really blending into the background–the cant of his head, the line of his shoulders, the way he lifted his thick-glassed cup for a sip of chocolate, and a thousand other little details–she could almost believe he'd lived the entire span of his life here in Paris, perhaps selling bolts of bright cloth on the street near the Sant-Pierre market, or sketching famous skylines from the Place Emile-Goudeau, arguing shading and angles with the ghosts of Picasso, Braque, and Matisse. She smiled at the thought.

Jack was, as always, delicious to the eyes. As she'd noticed with many of the people in his line of work, once he had your attention it was actually difficult to look away from Jack. Just last month Entertainment Weekly had devoted an issue to the "science" of physical beauty, and the section on smoothness of action and symmetry of facial features focused on her friend Jack. She'd thrown it in her bag along with the scripts she would show him, thinking he"d get a good laugh out of it.

Jack always maintained that real beauty and classic appeal was found in how people recognized their imperfections, which she thought was funny. Jack was perhaps the most physically peerless man Carly had ever met, and that was saying a lot for a woman whose business life revolved as much around the buying and selling of an actor's image as much as it did his or her talent.

He possessed both talent and image, though those weren't the reasons Carly counted Jack her friend. From the moment she met him, his genuineness had captivated her. It had surprised her how–it seemed a lifetime ago, now–he listened to her, honestly listened. From the moment she'd met him—

*

San Francisco, California

She leaned against the bar with her arms, careful to keep the weight off her burgeoning abdomen. Slowly, Carly pushed up until she was standing completely on her toes. Even in her bigger pointe shoes, it was so hard. Her leotard was too tight; she could barely breathe, and every movement caused her shoulder straps to gouge painfully into her skin. She pushed away from the bar and tottered to the center of the practice hall. Carefully, carefully, Carly settled all her weight on one foot, squaring her shoulders and extending both arms and her free leg into an arabesque. Slow, even piano music filled the room and echoed off the polished floor.

She faced away from the door; away from the bank of mirrors along that wall. She had no desire to glimpse her bloated, pimpled face. Mark had told her once that her face was like a painting by Raphael. Mark's hands, tracing along her cheek. Mark's hands . . .

Carly spun, floating into a pirouette. She was weightless. She was an angel again. Her eyes slipped shut as she took the small steps that would lead into a pas de bourrée couru—

Abruptly, the baby within her shifted, throwing its strange compactness against her ribs, and she stumbled to the side, falling, to slow to save herself, slipping, too slow again to get her feet under herself, trying desperately to twist to keep the weight off the baby, but falling–

And then she felt lithe hands around her, under her, and arms that were strong enough to catch her up and set her again on her feet. Carly gasped with relief as the room righted itself and resolved into a blond young man. His face was tinged with guilt and concern.

"I'm so sorry, I didn't mean to sneak up on you like that!" He helped her into a chair. "The music was so loud, and you looked so — well, you looked like something out of heaven, to tell the truth. Sorry. Are you Caroline? The girl at the front said you were Victoria Moran's roommate, and you'd know where she's at. I'm so sorry to startle you like that."

"Not your fault," she wheezed. "Lucky I didn't roll an ankle. Stupid, stupid!"

"Maybe," he conceded. "But at least you know you can actually do it." She looked up at him, confused. He smiled. "You can still dance, Caroline."

*

Jack was different this time; quieter. Oh, he'd greeted her warmly enough yesterday at the airport, and during their cab ride into the city he'd been his usual talkative self, telling her the same jokes he'd been repeating since the day they met—but something was definitely amiss. If she hadn't known him so well or so long, Carly wouldn't have seen that his joviality and utterly *normal* composure was merely a veneer, a sheen Jack had decided to cast up between the world and whatever demons rode his soul.

"Well, so, Jack?" Carly slid into the seat across from him and swept the scripts into a tighter pile, smiling as she rearranged them. "Next time the waiter comes by, order me another cappuccino. Should keep me awake till I get on the plane."

He nodded at the scripts. "Plenty of money sitting there, Carly, but I'm not sure. How many historical dramas are they planning on doing this year? Don't take this the wrong way, but seems like everything you send me lately is either a remake of something that was already done right in the first place, or so morally bankrupt I can't even ask my friends to watch it and still keep a straight face." He stirred his chocolate absently, frowning. "I know it's not your fault, but really, why all the junk lately?"

Carly spoke briefly with a waiter, then said, "Jack, you should see the garbage I don't even show you. Any given week, I have to throw out maybe eighty percent of the stuff that comes into the office. Almost everything here is from other agents. There's a couple you should look at, anyway.

"The one with the blue cover, the Celtic thing, is already in preproduction. Branaugh is lined up to direct, and Schramer's going to edit it. I told them you'd come on–*if* you come on–in two weeks or so, now that Cyrano's done over here."

She held up another. "He knows you're a big fan, and Dean Koontz called a few days ago about *Lightning.* You're a few years young, but he wants you to play Stefan." Carly smiled. "You shouldn't have told him so much about your childhood. He asked me when you were going to have a phone installed over here."

"Okay, those two are pretty good, but—you're right, Carly, I'm being picky. My writing's taking up too much time lately, and with Cyrano finishing up—"

"What are you writing about these days? I read your one about the guy coming back from the dead to protect his girlfriend." Carly saw a glimmer of something—amusement, maybe?–across Jack's countenance.

"Something along those lines. I don't think I'm ever going to have a hardcover bestseller. My prose is too goofy. And I can't help but slip in the action scenes."

She picked up her white napkin and began rolling up an edge as she spoke. "I keep wondering how a nice guy like you knows so much about exotic poisons and military weapons and things like that." She began rolling another edge of the napkin.

"It's not that hard. I read a lot. The thing is—well, it's the same with these scripts, Carly. I'm just—I have a tough time making myself believe the way all these stories wind up. So trite. I mean, can all the problems in life tie themselves up and get solved within a few chapters, a couple of hours?

"Everybody needs a break from reality now and then, but—"

Carly smiled and touched his hand. "You don't need to explain it to me, we've been friends long enough. Look, you know how good this stuff is." She tapped the stack of scripts. "Everybody back home knows I came over to try to get you back in the business *in front* of the camera instead of just as a writer, but that's got to be up to you. You don't just quit after five great movies in five good years, not counting that documentary that the Academy liked so much." The waiter brought her a large cup crowned with froth, and Carly took a sip before continuing.

"I think it's great that your over here, that an Idaho boy is doing Cyrano in Paris–in *Paris*, for crying out loud–and you've got a book on the bestseller's list, but Jack, enough of this business of reinventing yourself European. When are you going to come home?"

Jack pressed his hands hard into the tabletop. "Home?" An brittle slice of bitterness crept around the edges of his voice. "And where is that exactly, Caroline? Rodeo Drive? Hollywood and Vine? Do I even–ah, sorry." He looked away. "This isn't me. This isn't the person I want to be. Sorry."

Carly covered his hand again with hers. "Jack. Jack, I'm going to keep coming around. Don't worry about me."

He looked back at her, silent. Listening.

"I'm one of the people who owes you, whether you like it or not."

Jack flinched a little around the eyes. "For Victoria's sake."

"No, not just for Toria—Lord, she married somebody as mulehead-stubborn as she was." She signaled for the check. "Either of you get an idea in your head and forget to eat or sleep until you've made it real. Not that we ever had the money for food in those days."

The haunted look in his eyes was quickened by a flicker of merriment. "I remember when you two were living on Gatorade and those checks sent by the phone company."

"And you had to give blood so you could afford to take us to dinner!"

She watched him start to smile, but joy had no momentum within Jack, and the smile never quite came together. Carly gathered the scripts together and filed them into her leather bag. "I had copies of all these sent to your apartment. Take your time." She sipped her cappuccino. "Call me if you find a project you like, Jack, but even if you don't, call me. It never used to bother me when you'd disappear for a month or two, or when you'd take Toria with you wherever, but lately—" Her eyes, deep and liquid, filled with concern. "You seem like you're looking for . . . trouble."

He shifted in his chair. "Don't worry, Carly. Thanks. I'll be careful. And I'll read some of these, too, I promise," he added. "We'd better call a taxi, if you want to make your flight home." Jack paused and considered her. "You're a good friend, you know that?"

Carly smirked. "I'm a good *agent*, Jack. I'm a *better* friend."

Jack used his phone to called for a cab as they stepped out. A brisk wind, a harbinger of the storm to come, snapped at the edges of their coats. Carly turned up her collar and threaded her arm through Jack's. "What about that girl I heard you were with? The blond?"

45

Jack leaned close, the inconstant wind snatching at his words. "Isabelle? She just needed someone to listen to her while she worked out a few things. Last boyfriend was an idiot. There's nothing between us—and seeing as how she was up for the part of Roxanne, we tried to avoid problems."

Carly frowned slightly. "Jack, you're still too much of a nice guy. Problems, hah!" Then she went softly serious. "It's been more than a year since Toria, Jack. Don't you ever, you know, miss having—a physical relationship?"

He thought for a minute. "I get invited to parties and make the rounds, but I have to admit, the old routine of meaningful glances and raised eyebrows across the crowded room—just doesn't do it anymore. I was awfully naive before I met Victoria."

She poked him playfully in the side. "I know."

The taxicab pulled up, and she found herself hesitating.

Jack embraced her, slowly, then fiercely. "Thank you, Carly. Be safe. Oh, I almost forgot!" He pulled a small, brightly-wrapped package from his pocket. "This is for Kelly's collection. It's from Istanbul. Tell her it's two hundred years old; maybe she'll take care of this one."

"Oh, Jack, that girl has enough spoons. And you're only spoiling her."

He hugged her again. "I thought that's what godfathers did. Take care, Carly. Call me when you're home safe."

There was only room for one more in the cab. Her overnight bag snug at her feet, Carly turned and watched Jack's face as he lingered at the curb, and sighed. A kind of slippery depression was stealing over her. Her friend was seriously in trouble. She hadn't broken through, she was sure.

He'd read the scripts, smile at the article in Entertainment Weekly, and that would be about it. Jack needed to heal. He needed the kind of peace a woman could provide–Carly caught herself in the thought. *Way too melodramatic,* she thought. But what else could there be for Jack? He hadn't retreated from his career, that was certain. In all honesty, his acting had improved, gained a bit of a desperate edge. The critics, unaware of his personal loss (Jack was so careful about that) had nearly enshrined him last week, despite his absence at the opening of *And Caesar Whispered*, for his performance as a young Douglas MacArthur. He could very well get another Oscar nomination, poor guy.

Jack could be so infuriating. He didn't drink, except during a filming when his character required him to as part of a scene, and that was just apple juice. He didn't smoke, except herbal cigarettes and the like, and again, that was only when the demands of a particular role called for it. During a shooting he didn't hide in his trailer, argue dialogue and motivation with the director, or throw chairs and farm animals through windows. To the best of her knowledge, he'd never tried to fool around with any of the other cast members, not even his leading ladies in the name of "getting more realism into their on-screen romance." If not for his disarming friendliness and reputation as a bit of an on-set practical joker, Jack would probably be the most peaceful, centered, boring person in Hollywood. But lately . . . Carly sighed again. What else could she do? He'd managed to graciously turn down the numbers of half-a-dozen good, expensive therapists since Toria died.

Since Victoria had died.

Carly leaned back in her seat, trying vainly to relax. Orly International Airport was more than half an hour away yet, in this traffic. She put Jack's gift to her daughter in her overnight bag, and wondered.

What to do for Jack?

He watched the tail lights of the cab submerge into the thick, darkening maelstrom of Parisian traffic, then slowly began walking south toward the Seine.

The light had narrowed into a sullen, red finality to the west. Jack hunched his shoulders slightly in the cool breeze, sinking deeper into his long jacket. He was thinking consciously in French again, musing over Carly's offer to stay with him. It seemed like only a few days ago they'd been at the hospital, she swearing like a sailor at the nurses while he scribbled at the paperwork, and him claiming vociferously that he was her husband and they better damn *well* let him in the delivery room. He smiled. Sometimes the line between acting and a boldfaced lie was a little too thin. Nonexistent, in fact.

Jack walked briskly, choosing the less-frequented alleys and byways in his haste to get back to his apartment on the Left Bank. If he hurried, he'd get home in time to write another chapter or two. He didn't enjoy Paris at night as much as he once had.

It already seemed an entire life ago he'd wandered through the heart of the city with his wife, exploring every artery and vein it offered. One of their favorite places had been Chinatown; the portion located near the lower end of the 13th arrondissement. In fact, they'd once gotten lost in the triangle between the avenues de Choisy and Ivry, down to the boulevard Masséna. With the high buildings and clamor it could have been a housing development in Hong Kong or Manila; lacking only the thick smell of a harbor.

He and Toria used to sit for hours at random outdoor cafés, right at the edge of the street, and watch the tide of humanity sweep by. She loved making up stories about the people hurrying along under the ethereal, billowing canopy of light above the city.

Jack didn't dare look up, not now. He kept his eyes at ground level. Better to ignore the great, vaulted emptiness overhead. Right about now, he thought, Carly's no doubt mulling over ways to help poor, wretched Jack.

No, not poor Jack. Never poor Jack.

The wind tore at him, even in the narrower streets, pulling up the ancient smells of coming rain from the worn, blunted cobblestones. No moisture yet, but soon. All the more reason to get inside quickly. As he passed a narrow, greasy-black passage between two high blocks of apartments, the wind seemed to leave his shoulder and caroom off into those depths, snatching and scrabbling at the curled husks of unswept leaves which littered the passageway. Their dry rasp echoed heavily in the confined space, and Jack was struck instantly by the image of a game of dice; of devils in some acrid corner of Hell throwing dice for men's souls, casting them against some desiccated, chitinous wall that was terribly neither hot nor cold.

He took a quick turn down an alley and glanced back up his own path. The street was empty, soundless but for the wind. A sudden prickling twisted up the nape of his neck, and he increased his pace. This was what he disliked about the city, he thought. Not like the deep woods at all. Harder to tell if you were being hunted. In the forest, at least, impending violence could be heralded by utter silence. Nature's alarm system. Here in the city it was harder to trust instinct. No wildlife other than the uncountable pigeons to give warning. Not even one damn cricket.

At that moment Jack desperately missed the wildness he'd known as a boy and then as a young man, the close connection with the inhuman and the untamable. Now, in a city that had been mankind's bastion and refuge for two and a half millennia, he felt disarmed and defenseless.

49

A man-shaped cleft of lighter darkness resolved itself before him, and Jack involuntarily drew back, a challenge at his lips before he realized it was merely part of a stone figure, a weathered, crumbling gargoyle that had either fallen into the alley and lodged against the wall, or had been hauled there and left to disintegrate. It was still fearsome; though webbed with cracks its visage–that of a monstrous feline–had grown angular against the elements and assumed an enraged, almost frustrated aspect. It seemed to fix Jack with its eyes; bind him in its Gorgonian stare as he passed.

He looked behind himself again, then paused at the arched entrance to a longer section of alley. Jack knew he was being foolish, but he stared for a long moment into the gaping maw of the lane, his neck and shoulders crawling with dread. Nothing was there. At least, nothing he could see. The angle of the entranceway was off slightly; inset against the gray, crumbling mortar so that the diluted illumination from the streetlamp behind him did not penetrate. Jack paused before that complete, Stygian darkness, imagining within for a moment shapes and movements unhuman.

Something was stalking him, all right, running him down, closing in unstoppably from the inside out. Something in his own soul.

He stepped through the archway on cat's feet.

It was one of those alleys leftover from before the time of Haussmann and Napoleon III, who'd both been so eager to lift Paris into the modern age of the 1850's by doing away with its tangled web of sidestreets and narrow, suffocating byways. A cobblestone gutter ran down the middle, and the high, barred window casements seemed to look down at odd angles. Scraps of papers and other unidentifiables littered the corners and clogged the bone-dry gutter. Jack stepped around the wooden shambles of what may have once been a piece of furniture, and walked softly down the alleyway. This zigzagging route was the quickest way to the river, and then his apartment. The best way to avoid the city crowds and steer clear of the humid mass of humanity.

But not all of them. He heard a dry, muted crackle, as if someone had stepped on a cardboard box. Jack froze, motionless, as a bulky shape crossed the alley not fifty feet before him, moving quickly, scuttling from shadow to shadow. Jack had the impression the man was large, though the shrouds of gloom obscured his actual size. The shadowed figure lurched into a doorway just barely within Jack's field of view, a few steps down an intersecting lane. It wasn't the man"s furtive movements that gave Jack pause, nor his silent, even stare back down the alley, toward voices that even now drew closer.

It was a dull glimmer, like off a shard of dirty ice, that reflected against the knife in the man's hand.

Jack eased closer, clinging to the wall nearest the thug. He was taller than Jack by a few inches under his porkpie hat, and considerably thicker; though his face was soft, he had the stance and posture of someone who spent considerable time with weights of one kind or another. A ratty-looking overcoat hung open at his chest, and Jack could see the man was shirtless. Some kind of winding tattoo down one shoulder and across his chest. The man even appeared to be holding his breath, intent as he was on the approaching voices. He sunk back into the contours of the doorway, until Jack could barely make out his profile. If he hadn't known the man was already there–

He turned slightly, mindful to keep the whole of his body in the angle of darker gloom out of the thug's view. A couple was strolling towards the intersection, the man gesturing rapidly at an unfolded length of paper–a map—and speaking in a frustrated tone to his companion, who suddenly detached herself from his arm. Americans, Jack thought, from the snatches of English that carried through the hot, still air.

The woman stopped, hands at her waist, and the man allowed his momentum to carry him a few steps farther before turning, exasperated. "Listen, Debbie, it's not *my* fault this street isn't on the map! You're the one who wanted to get to Notre Dame fast."

"Mike, you always put it back on me." Her voice was soft, Jack thought, though strained by a day's worth of walking and no doubt by more than a little irritation at finding herself straying so far askew from the Approved Tourist Version of Paris.

"Well, dear, I don't see anybody else here to blame, do you? You and your midnight Mass! It's going to be too dark to see the stained glass, anyway."

"I just wish you hadn't asked directions from that guy in the ugly hat," she said.

The man sighed explosively. "You're the one who's always telling me I never ask directions enough as it is."

Jack started to ease back down the alleyway, back the way he had come, then stopped himself. *You leaving?* a dry inner voice chided him. *Not my fight,* he silently responded. The man had already taken his wife by her arm, and was gently trying to propel her further down the passageway. He was speaking softer now, apologizing. They drew nearer, and Jack saw that the man was in fair shape, probably able to handle the assailant by himself. The woman walked more guardedly, with her purse strap diagonally across the whole of her body instead of dangling loosely from one shoulder. Good for her. At least she was following the advice in the tourist books, he thought. Both were in their late twenties, with faces aged only by fatigue and the long-exhausted enthusiasm of adventure in a new city. The young man wore a yellow t-shirt and tan chinos. Both had on new Reebok cross-trainers, the laces twice-tied. *He's not ready for this,* Jack realized. The lank-haired young man, smiling now as he whispered something into his companion's ear, was blithely unaware of the impending confrontation, of the dirty knife in the doorway's penumbra. Only a half-dozen more steps.

Whose fight, then?

Jack grimaced, nearly swearing aloud. Even as his eyes scoured the narrow alley, he inwardly cursed himself. Why's it always have to be this way, he thought, then found a rough chunk of pottery, a nearly-intact flower pot turned over against the wall a few steps away. The grainy jaggedness bit into his hand as he hefted it. How many more times could he be expected to do this, he wondered, then his mind snatched itself away like it always did, plotting, planning, projecting angles, amounts of force; summing up position and aspect of possible outcome. It took less than a second, and he was ready by the time the young couple took their first step into the intersection. The woman's hair was as yellow and straight as fine straw, Jack noted, and then he moved.

The thug flinched beneath the hurtling pottery, throwing himself out of the confined entry as the pot exploded and showered him with dust and blunt shrapnel. He didn't even see Jack, who erupted into him a moment later, slapping aside the knife and landing six open-handed blows from his kidney up along his tattoo of a writhing, many-legged serpent to his right temple. He hit the ground at nearly the same time as his shapeless hat.

A slight scrabble behind him was all the warning Jack had as a second thug launched himself out of the doorway across from where his cohort had hidden. He ducked, and the man's leather kosh only glanced the back of his neck. Jack stumbled under the blow, pushing himself off his assailant's body towards the wall. The man swung again, and numbing fire took the place of Jack's right arm from the shoulder down. His opponent stepped back slightly for a better swing, and Jack's eyes focused on a prognathous jawline almost basaltic in its thickness and texture, a clipped, ragged slash of a mouth over mismatched teeth, and a bony forehead. One single eyebrow jerked like a bolt of bristling lightning over intelligent, deep set eyes.

As the man leaned forward, shifting all his weight into his stroke, Jack snapped his leg up and in, then violently out and into his opponent's solar plexus. The impact sent Jack into the opposite wall, and threw the other man straight backward into the doorway, where his head rebounded wetly against the jamb.

As the man slid moaning and nerveless towards the ground, Jack hit him along the left temple, then again, harder. He sagged into the doorjamb, breathing heavily, vision swimming. Up! he thought. Up, there might be more of them!

Belatedly, the woman screamed. A figure loomed close, but it was only her husband, jabbering rapidly and reaching out to help Jack up. He pushed the American back, using the wall behind him to lever himself all the way to a standing position.

"Are you two okay?" he asked. Feeling was beginning to return to his arm, and painful as it was he flexed his fingers and rotated his wrist and elbow. Nothing broken. The fellow was still chattering at Jack, trying to offer money, still speaking in broken, tourist French, and Jack switched to English. "Be quiet! There may be more of them close by."

A point which eluded you a few moments ago, idiot, he chided himself silently. But his returning senses brought no warning, no precursor of attack.

Jack bent over each of the assailants, patting them down for identification as he listened to their breathing. He thumbed their eyelids up, checking for the uneven dilation that would indicate concussion or brain injury. Both would wake with considerable discomfort, but at least they would wake.

"What are you doing, um, now?" asked the American.

Jack flipped through the cards in the larger man's wallet. "See all these Visas?" In addition, he found what must have been over three hundred dollars in American and British currency, which he pocketed, and two more knives. The thin man also carried a snub-nosed revolver, dark with grease. Jack threw the weapons down a nearby sewer.

The baffled tourist, Mike, returned to his wife and held her until she quieted, then the three of them made their way out of the rubbish-filled labyrinth, Jack in the lead.

They were out under the streetlights near the Seine when the man decided to speak again. He'd had a bit of time to think, Jack noted, and even the man's posture had changed. He now stood nearer to his wife, within easy distance. Indeed, from time to time Mike would reach out to touch his wife's hair or hold her arm, and he was particularly solicitous toward her as the three of them maneuvered to a well-illuminated park where a pair of benches faced each other above the river. They spoke quietly for a few moments, Jack pointing out the lights of Notre Dame a few hundred yards down the river before warning them against taking any more shortcuts. Mike and Debbie were from Tennessee, recently married and celebrating their new Master's degrees. A nice enough couple, Jack thought.

"Well, my apartment is only a few blocks up, and I'm sure you'll want to get down to the cathedral. I bet you'd like the archeological exhibits underneath, too. And, Mike, no more shortcuts! Debbie, don't let him talk you into swimming the Seine, or anything like that."

They laughed, and then Debbie said. "You know, you look an awful lot like the guy in that movie we saw on the plane–what was his name, honey? The guy in *The Walking Drum*."

Jack nodded, letting an ounce of chagrin steal into his voice. "Yeah,

I hear that a lot. Wish I made *his* kind of money, eh?" Mike nodded.
"And that reminds me," said Jack, fishing out the wad of money he'd
taken off the two thugs. "You look like a couple who could find a way
to use this."

They tried to refuse, but Jack pressed the money into their hands,
anyway. "Courtesy of the Paris underworld, or something. Take it.
Ride in taxis. Go to EuroDisney–no, never mind; you want to have a
good time, don't you?" This elicited another laugh. "Enjoy yourselves.
Stay in love."

They parted company with enough handshakes for a crowd of twice
as many. Jack walked a dozen steps before turning to watch the young
couple, strolling away through the pools of amber light. They walked,
heads close together, arm in arm, Mike now considerably more watchful,
which pleased Jack. Debbie was leaning into her husband more than she
had in the alley; allowing him to cradle her to a greater degree. Jack
looked after them until the sweep of the river carried them out of his
line of sight. Odd. Only a few years separated them, yet Jack felt ancient
compared to the young couple. Older by eons.

Yet maybe he could survive this.

He looked across the bridge, and could almost see her coming to
him through the gathering gloom. Almond-shaped eyes, lustrous dark
hair as pure as a raven's wing, and a gypsy's smile. A Black Irish girl.

But no form carved itself out of the glittering night. Jack sighed,
rubbing at his temple briefly. Time to go back to pretending you have a
normal life, he thought. He looked once more down the Seine, toward
young love, and then stalked briskly into the Parisian night.

Girl in a Berkeley Sweater

Forge, Idaho, United States of America
7 AM

Garret leaned through the doorway, arms against either jamb, and felt the muscles across his chest tighten as he looked out at the pool. It was already half awash in the slanting sunlight of early morning, as placid as the surface of any mirror. Garret had been a lifeguard at the Forge city park for two years—had practically lived at the pool every summer, as far back as his memory ran—and the sight of the L-shaped pool motionless against the morning light always somehow reminded him of a great, sunken slab of lime Jell-o.

He wiped the last of the sleep from his eyes and stepped, barefoot, onto the concrete deck. It was cold, as usual, and its dry porosity clutched at his feet as he made his way to the centermost guard tower. He swung his steel whistle around his wrist by its lanyard until it slapped against his arm, then reversed the swing, keeping time with his slow, unhurried stride across the deck. Though it was still early, he slipped on his sunglasses.

The steel gates leading to the locker rooms creaked open, emitting the half-dozen patrons that forced Garret out of bed at this ungodly hour. He swung his long, lean body up the brief ladder of his tower, then sat on its edge, watching as the elderly women arranged their paraphernalia on the benches at the shallow end of the pool. One of them smiled at Garret and waved as she tucked a loaf of blue hair into the side of her equally blue swimming cap. He waved back.

The Fish family (if *that* wasn't ironic, Garret didn't know the meaning of the word) came nearly every day. If the yelling in the dressing rooms was any indication, the kids had arrived. Their parents were religious swimmers, absolutely addicted to the water. They kept their children in the water nearly all day, starting with lap swim, then lessons, through two swim team practices, and then picking them up at 7:30 at night, after open swim. Garret smiled. Pretty smart parents. No doubt the chronically hyperactive kids fell over themselves trying to get to bed.

The morning shift wasn't so bad. Between the older ladies who drifted, jellyfish-like, from one end of the pool to the other, and the thrice-weekly triathlon maniacs who showed up an hour before lessons started to grimly thrash out their two miles, Garret had an easy time of it.

And the past few days, one visitor in particular had made it even better.

He yawned, this time in earnest, closing his eyes and tilting his head back until it felt like he was flexing his entire face. The sun had eased up over two-thirds of the pool now, and small curls of steam began to appear above the water, quaking now as the ladies edged into the pool.

"Gets colder every day!" one of them said.

Another, submerged up to her waist, shot back, "The city ought to pay its electric bill!" They all laughed. Part of the morning ritual. They chattered among themselves like they did every morning, commiserating their fate and admiring their collective willpower at being able to withstand the frigid water. Listen to them, he thought, you'd almost expect to see chunks of ice floating in the water around them.

Ripples spread out across the pool, deepening as they widened.

The city pool stood on a small hill in the center of the park. From his vantage point, Garret could see over the fence and down into most of the wooded, terraced grounds. The sunlight was still caught in the tops of the trees; it hadn't yet found its way down onto the jogging paths and brown benches. As he watched, half of the sprinklers shut off and the other half sprang on, sweeping fine, pale arcs of mist across the meandering footpaths.

Any minute now.

Garret had been manning the till at the front counter a few days ago when the woman had first come to the pool. An older guard, a college guy named Tommy, had nudged Garret aside when she stepped up to the counter and asked if a week's pass to the pool still cost ten dollars. Even Tommy had swallowed before he could reply, though Garret had to hand it to the older guard; he'd recovered far better than Garret had. His brain felt like a movie projector that had run out of film and left the ragged end of celluloid flapping noisily against its own apparatus.

She'd been wearing loose shorts and an old Berkley sweatshirt, but that hadn't been the kicker. Days later, when he tried to recall the exact details of the woman's features, he was left with only a vague impression of a tanned face framed by hair that looked like liquid gold. What lodged in his mind's eye most firmly; the memory that reached out and shook him nearly every time he'd thought of her since, were the woman's eyes. She'd looked at Garret over Tommy's shoulder as the older guard had begun to turn on the charm, had winked when Tommy looked away briefly to check his hair or whatever in a nearby mirror.

What cobalt did for the color blue, her eyes did for green. Even that dusty morning, in the washed-out blue of the pool building's office, she had been luminous.

Garret remembered the feeling of his cheeks beginning to burn, and he quickly busied himself with counting quarters in the change drawer. He noticed in passing as the other lifeguard explained the pool's hours that he'd tightened his own pecs and stomach the instant the woman had walked in.

Tommy had finished his baritone rendition of the pool's features and paused, trying himself for eye contact before delivering the punch line. "So if you're new in the area I could maybe show you around town. Forge isn't that big, but we've got a lot to offer in local color, y' know?"

She'd begun to fill out the application form as he'd spoken, smiling faintly to herself. She kept Tommy there at the counter until he'd begun to fidget. Garret couldn't tell how old she was, he realized. She looked to be close to Tommy's age, maybe a year or two older.

"So what about it," Tommy said. "Want to get some coffee or something?"

Those green eyes flashed up again, sparkling. She smiled as she handed back the clipboard. "Thanks, but I don't date lifeguards anymore."

Then she'd paid her bill and left, Tommy still leaning against the countertop.

As soon as she'd turned the corner they both had lunged for the clipboard on which her application lay. "Definitely not a local," Tommy said. "Idaho couldn't be so lucky."

She was staying with her cousin, Diane Bergstrom. Garret's neighbor, and a pool regular for years. She'd left a number for a satellite phone, proof positive of her exotic nature. And the name at the top of the application for a week's pass to the Forge pool was like something off a movie poster.

Mercedes Adams.

And that's why Garret had learned to love the early morning shift at the pool. He watched, rapt, as she appeared out of the trees, jogging evenly across the manicured grass. She scorned the footpaths, but always approached the pool from the same route, apparently choosing the steepest path up the little hill towards the entrance. She ran in blue cotton shorts and a matching tank, her hair pulled back in a thick ponytail, bouncing loosely against a small backpack. She doesn't know how good she looks, he thought.

She slowed to a walk and circled the fence once, breathing deeply. Garret heard the hollow *slap-slap* of her steps on the wooden deck that wound from the parking lot into the locker rooms.

The Fish kids–only two boys and a girl, but loud enough for a crowd of ten—ran out onto the deck. Howling from the cold cement, they cannonballed into the six-foot area. Man, but they were noisy, Garret thought, but at least polite enough that they kept their early-morning hijinks out of everybody else's lane. One by one they broke through the surface and began splashing one another. Garret swung his whistle up into his hand, but let it fall again. They weren't hurting anything, and their parents would appear shortly enough and set them all to doing laps. Assuming, of course, they hadn't drowned themselves, lost their goggles in the drain, or given each other concussions on the pool bottom by that time.

Garret's thoughts were interrupted when she stepped out onto the deck. She wore her pink suit today, he noted. It was a sturdy two-piece that showed off her tight stomach. She passed his lifeguard tower on her way to the broader section of the pool deck, over the drain tank, where the sun had been warming the cement the longest. "'Morning, Garret," she smiled up at him good-naturedly, dripping. Garret managed a wave he hoped was nonchalant. He never had found out how she knew his name.

Her back to him, the woman shook out a long towel and set about her daily routine of lower body stretches. On her first morning at the pool, before making her appearance on deck she'd taken the obligatory shower, even though there had still been a sharp chill in the air. This surprised Garret, as most people ignored the shower rule, and the lifeguards were always ambivalent about enforcing it with anyone over the age of thirteen. Garret noticed that she never deviated from her routine, nor did she seem the least bit uncomfortable or self-conscious as she worked the lactic acid from her jog out of thighs and calves that looked like they belonged on a model runway somewhere.

Even safe behind his sunglasses, Garret felt a bit like a voyeur. This is my job, he thought furtively, but all the same he had to glance away as she stretched her hamstrings. She's so fluid, he thought, checking over the bevy of elderly women trolling blissfully toward the shallow end.

He looked back in time to see her reach back to tighten the ponytail, and admired her deltoids, like arrowheads pointing from her shoulders down either arm. She reached up and grasped the top edge of the Coke machine, leaning into a full stretch, and Garret saw her whole body ripple, from her exquisite pecs down around the sheaves of muscles that wrapped themselves about her entire frame. He wondered, as he had every morning since she appeared, why a woman so good-looking to begin with would take the time to further buff herself up. Her undeniably feminine layer of fat was a thin sheath overlaying more resilient muscle. Garret wasn't complaining, but he had to wonder why. Why did she do it?

*

Mercedes bounced a few times on the balls of her feet, enjoying the pleasant tightening along the lines of her calves. She could feel the sun on her back. This was the best part of the ugly morning jog, she thought, stepping to the side of the pool. The indented gutter below made a rhythmic slurp-slurping sound. She slipped in, and the water was a warm envelope sliding over her chilled skin. Mmmm. Too bad Diane and Alice wouldn't try this. Couldn't get the girls out of bed before sunrise with a six-alarm fire, unless maybe Zac Efron, or Ryan Reynolds, or maybe Jack Flynn–hah!—was the lead fireman. Even so.

She pushed away from the gutter and stroked past the turbulent children. The oldest, a freckled, blond imp with a face reminiscent of a happy crocodile, paused long enough to let her pass before slapping a spray of water into his brother's face.

Mercedes reached the deep end and began to tread water. The sky above was a perfect, cerulean dome framed by the spruces, Doug firs, and evergreens that limned the deep, wide valley. She glanced at the timing clock at the pool's edge, and lifted her arms out of the water. One full minute of this ought to be a good start, she thought, kicking hard. She lashed over to where a small outlet valve would wash cycled water over her legs and keep them cool. Mercedes knew this pool well.

As she surrendered to the habits of exercise she'd forced her body to accept, she found her mind wandering. That was one aspect of her programmed workout patterns she never had particularly liked; the tendency of her thoughts to occasionally ramble off by themselves instead of staying on the neat little paths she preferred.

The Senator would be back in town later today and wanted her to call; she and the girls would have lunch with the old man and show him her latest batch of photographs. Mercedes counted herself lucky that her grandfather had been fishing buddies with one of the richest men in the region. When Sean Lyons had gotten fed up with the status quo and decided to run for State representative years ago, he'd asked a young Mercedes to take his campaign photos. She'd assumed he was just being solicitous, but the shots had turned out well enough. To hear old Sean talk, you'd think he'd won the election on her photographs alone, never mind the fact that the incumbent had conspicuously leached money from the county during his 16-year reign.

Lyons had always shown a sincere interest in Mercedes, and when he campaigned for U.S. Senator, he'd irritated some members of his staff by asking Mercedes–an amateur, worse yet: a political nonperson—to coordinate the photography end of his campaign. Again, she'd done well–well enough that her candid pictures of the Senator-to-be down on his knees in his garden had caught the eye of a magazine editor.

Such are the things of which careers are made.

Nature shots weren't her specialty, but no doubt she'd find more than one meadow or vista to capture during the drive out to his property. Northern Idaho was so pretty in the spring: stately trees lining the blacktop like twin colonnades, hidden lakes lying along arms of the mountains like huge shards of the sky fallen and come to rest. Deep, thick forest. She'd have to be careful, Mercedes reminded herself, to watch for deer and other critters on the road. The thing she liked best, the hallmark of Forge she thought of when she was on assignment for Conde Nast, whether on a llama's back in the Andes or riding on a barge in the Yangtse River delta, was the profound, almost primeval quiet.

Forge had sprung into its existence from a single blacksmith shop staked out in 1863 at the headwaters of the Clearwater River. The convergence of several small tributaries had been the ideal spot for trappers and prospectors to resupply, trade wampum with the Nez Perce Indians, and have their mules reshod. Alternately converging and forking rivers with their shoals and shifting sandbars had marked the furthest incursion of steamboats that had come up the Columbia River past Lewiston, the original state capital. Lewis and Clark themselves had been the first recorded white savages to winter on the banks of the

Clearwater and carve out huge canoes from the great bull pines they found, nearly three quarters of a century before the first steamboat shattered its paddle on the rocky river bed and been turned into Forge's first semi-floating hotel, just down the new street from the smithy and across Oro Fino Creek from the Chinese laundry.

Forge had eventually been reincarnated from a gold-mining boomtown to a logging capital. Mercedes had often heard her grandfather tell about his first summer job as a poleman on a log drive. He and his friends had come up from California one spring and been dumbfounded to see the great Clearwater River nearly choked by a great, shivering jam of lumber. They'd lent a hand, prying the freshly-hewn and strangely naked-looking logs off the banks of the Clearwater, and ended up riding the jam itself all the forty miles to the cedar mill. Max Adams and his companions were hired on and spent the rest of that summer and two succeeding on the river, herding tons of bobbing, new lumber toward its destiny in the various mills which dotted the wide banks. His last year before heading off to college in San Francisco, Max and his brother Harry had been assistant cooks on a floating chuckwagon, a prefabricated mess hall with a pair of outboards that traveled with the log drive from the logging camp all the way to the mill.

A chunk of this rough, raw wilderness had settled solidly into Max's soul. He'd fallen in love with the wide, green valleys from his very first summer, and Max twice made good on his promise to return. Once to marry Britta Bergstrom, the daughter of an immigrant Swedish farmer he'd stayed with when he wasn't cooking flapjacks for the smelly, bristling loggers. Again when his last child, Mercedes' father, had left the nest for college. Max and Britta had retired from California as fast as they could pack their station wagon, and come back to the quiet.

As much as Mercedes was a product of one of the most boisterous, blaring, overflowingly Italian families of San Francisco, she had equally deep and reverberating roots here, in Forge, Idaho. A fact that she'd only begun to discover the summer she was seventeen, when the general course of her life and of everything else around her had nearly convinced her that life was over.

Mercedes allowed her arms to drop back into the water and began sculling with her hands, moving her elbows and wrists in a snap-glide-snap that reminded her of the fake salutations of parading prom queens. Her calves ached. Slowly she began to turn, the jet of water velvet smooth against her flushed skin.

The little boys playing at the end of the pool seemed to have reached the limits of pleasure that mere splashing could provide. She watched as the smaller one reached out and grabbed his brother's goggles by the thin band of plastic that connected the two lenses, and soundly snapped them across the bridge of the larger boy's nose. The older brother squawked and reeled back. "Ow, Donald!" Mercedes winced. The only kids she'd seen play like this had been Alice and Diane's little brothers. The lifeguard on the tower across from them just laughed and twirled his whistle by its nylon tether.

Mercedes switched her kick style, whirling her legs beneath her, twisting slightly from side to side. Maybe I should step in before one of the little tykes ends up in the hospital, she thought. As she began to move towards them, the older boy ripped the goggles completely off his brother's head, then, jumping purely for height, threw the rubber-bound goggles over the smaller boy into the gutter. "There, that's what you get!"

Yelping, Donald pounced to the side of the pool, his arm shooting into the covered trough that gurgled greedily. The bright blue lenses sailed on, borne away on a wave from their owner's splashy approach. He almost snagged the slithering end of the rubber strap before it slipped away down the drain. Red-faced, he aimed himself at his crocodile-grinning brother. Before the lifeguard could blow his whistle, Donald had surged over his snickering brother in a rush of miniature breakers and chlorinated froth.

Mercedes looked up at Garret before turning back to the empty deep end. Better leave this to the proper authorities, she thought as she listened to the lifeguard's dictates over the now-silent boys.

During the brief show she had never stopped treading water, and as she lifted her elbows once again out of the water, Mercedes found herself looking towards the widest spread of the concrete pool deck, where she'd spread her towel earlier, between the fence and the Coke machine, next to the square blue trapdoor, locked now, that accessed the pool's surge tank. Before passing through the entire filtration system, the goggles would no doubt go there, along with all the other detritus that was washed down the drains.

The young lifeguard, Garret, had climbed down off his tower and was now quietly berating the boys, who stood shivering before him, bouncing on the deck, their arms firmly clapped around their tanned middles.

Mercedes kicked the water with greater ferocity, groaning softly as she forced herself to work. Lines of white fire now drew themselves across her legs, winding from her buttocks down around to her inner calves. Thirty seconds more. She managed to lift herself out of the water nearly midway up the slopes of her breasts before she gave out, her arms collapsing into the water and immediately working to support her. A rivulet of perspiration ran into her eye, and she leaned back, dipping her face backwards into the cool, cool water before lifting her legs up as well. Gradually, Mercedes arched into a back float.

She began to breathe deeply, letting her body know to begin its cooldown. Years of this type of exercise had thoroughly programmed her metabolism, had managed to educated the mysterious workings of a body that had so often and so thoroughly turned traitor to her. When it came to exercise, at least, her body now seemed to know precisely when to flex itself into something taut and hard and when to relax.

Mercedes felt like she was weightless; floating almost without effort, and she could imagine the pool bottom more than twenty feet behind her and below, herself buoyed above.

This was the best part, she thought. She wondered if her doctor had known he would turn her into an endorphin junkie by prescribing such a rigorous exercise schedule. A gentle warmth was spreading through her entire body. It filled up the hollow, aching chambers in her legs and lower abdomen. Overflowed the bounds of her body. Wrapped her in a tender heat.

And there, floating, almost levitating blissfully on a wave of buoyant emotion, Mercedes found her thoughts once more spiraling in reverse, down through the history of Forge; not that dry commentary friendly to any museum chronicle, but the story of her own first coming to Forge. That miserable, torturous, deliriously happy summer when she was seventeen.

Forge

When she was seventeen

Mercedes leaned back into the leather upholstery and closed her eyes, trying to listen to her grandfather whistle through his teeth in syncopation with the jazz piano gliding from his CD player. She could feel him glance her way occasionally as he drove the white LeBaron through blades of sunlight and shadow cast by the pine trees lining the sides of the road. The top was down, and the tires themselves were singing on the blacktop, a monotone background note to the music from her grandfather's CD player.

She could smell Grampa Max's cologne. Her whole life, the scent of Brut aftershave had been one of the fine constants she marked time by. To her it was the essence of her grampa, of summer afternoons hiking with him in the hills, of her first memory of being pushed gently on a toddler swing and then turning to recognize the raw, handsome Swedish masculinity of her grandfather. To her, he'd never changed. She recalled the sheer delight she'd felt as a young, young girl when she realized for the first time that her eyes were exactly the same shade of green as those of Grampa Max.

Eyes closed now, she imagined her surroundings: the wide, green Clearwater River slipping by on the left, headed in the opposite direction. Beyond it, the steepening, boulder-studded cliffs that reached up to the sky. On her right, greener hills with miniature valleys of their own; wooded and rolling hills that eventually led (she'd seen from the airplane) to a bright yellow prairie, and then more mountains. It would be nice to capture the view somehow.

So far, Idaho wasn't that different from the hills and parks north of Oakland, where her grandfather had taught her how to fish when she had been a little girl and before he and Grandma Brit retired.

He was looking at her again, stealing glances away from the unwinding black ribbon of highway. "Merc, you're being awfully quiet on me. Hardly said a word since you got off the plane." He tried to sound jovial, but Mercedes knew him well enough to hear behind the forced gallantry of his concern. She might be losing a father, but the old man next to her was losing a child. Maybe. Not for sure. Even the doctors didn't know for sure.

"Sorry, Grampa." She managed to smile. "I was just thinking 'bout Dad."

"Me, too, plum." His thick finger stabbed at the CD control, and the sharp-edged, opening chords of a rolling blues piece filled the brief pocket of air in the convertible. "But I'm sure glad you could come up and see us. I ever tell you you're my favorite granddaughter?"

Mercedes laughed. "I'm your only granddaughter."

"That's right! Uncontested champion of that department." He leaned slightly as they rounded a tighter, sloping corner. "Say, you don't think your aunt Sylvia will have any kids and upset the apple cart, do you?"

Sylvia was her father's older sister, a professor of English at Berkley and a pronounced feminist. Mercedes didn't know how to respond to that one. She'd never been sure exactly what her grandparents thought of their outspoken daughter. It had upset them terribly when Sylvia had decided to become a Mormon a few years ago, which was odd, since their daughter had already swung along the complete pendulum of radical, left-thinking politics. Once Mercedes overheard the neighborhood gossip chattering on and on about how Max and Britta were leaving the state so they wouldn't have to spend their retirement money bailing their daughter out of jail. "Such an irresponsible dreamer, that girl. An embarrassment to her family."

But it had been Sylvia who'd paid for Mercedes' plane ticket to Idaho, and Sylvia who'd moved in with her brother to help him take care of his wife during her final months. Just over a year had passed since illness killed Mercedes' mother in tiny, quick degrees, grinding her down, shredding the delicate protective sheaths around her nerves. The doctors couldn't even agree on a diagnosis of the symptoms, aside from terminal myelin degeneration.

Neither her fierce Italian blood nor the resounding adjuration of a thousand Hail Marys had stemmed the tide inexorably turning against Mercedes' mother.

Sylvia arrived on their doorstep–broken into the house through a window, actually–and took charge. By that time, Mercedes was accustomed to staying home from school three days out of five to care for her mother. Even with Sylvia's timely advent, Mercedes barely made it through the semester.

Now it was Sylvia who stayed by her father's side while he was recovering (he *was* recovering) from the removal of some kind of cyst or growth that had attached itself to his intestines. Sylvia would take care of him long enough to give Mercedes a kind of vacation. Sylvia had a good heart.

"I hope she has kids, Grampa," Mercedes said, squeezing his knee. "But we both know who'll always be your favorite, right?"

He smiled and patted her hand. "That's right." Max tapped the volume on the CD player, and driving, focused piano filled the car. The music was upbeat, seamless, and Mercedes simply couldn't imagine anyone's fingers moving that fast across a keyboard. During a measure's worth of drum solo, Max said, "Can you name the piano here, Merc? Remember anything I taught you?"

"Let's see. Sounds a little like Duke Ellington, but more . . . careful about his notes." She thought. "Smooth, like Michel Petrucciani, but—"

"Listen to the tone."

She snapped her fingers. "Benny Green!"

"Good girl." Max slapped the steering wheel. She could tell he was pleased. "Okay, honey, we're coming up on the town. Tell me honestly if you've ever seen a prettier sight."

The trees had begun to thin out somewhat, and Mercedes had noticed the occasional house nestled in among the lush, leafy green boughs. The valley itself had widened out, as if someone had scooped a miniature plain out of the smooth, lime-colored hills. The mountains themselves began to look more sculpted, more graceful, though occasionally the ridges were broken by craggy outcroppings of rock that looked like an exposed backbone of some great prehistoric beast.

They crossed a bridge, then another, then a third, and then, as Max pointed, Mercedes saw the great white dam, far up one of the canyons, extending almost from peak to peak. "Water in the reservoir is almost high enough," Max said. "Spring runoff was good this year. Another week or so and she should be warm enough to ski in. You ever waterski?"

Mercedes shook her head.

"That reminds me," Max said. "Your grandmother and I take turns taking her sister's grandkids to the city pool, but today we're both strapped. They've got lessons at eleven, and then we usually let them swim the whole afternoon. Would you mind?"

"Taking them to the pool? Easy." Mercedes looked out at the widening valley. Whole neighborhoods now stretched from the highway to the foot of the mountains, and not a mini-mall in sight.

"Are you sure? Not too tired from your flight?"

"No problem, Grampa. How old are they?"

"Alice is seven, and the twins are, oh, I don't know—nine or ten.

Oh, and you'll want to meet Irene and Diane; they're your age. Diane gets her license in the fall, and Irene–who usually drives–just had her's suspended for the summer. Broke her heart."

"Why's that?"

"Mercedes, in a town like this, a teenager without a license is like a blindfolded parachutist–frustrated, irritable, but with a vague idea that something exciting is just about to happen. You've got to have freedom in a place as little as Forge, but a little discipline, too. The kids here can go crazy from boredom if there's nothing to do. Poor Irene. That girl's got a mischievous streak—reminds me of you. Are you sure you want to be a chauffer? You're supposed to be relaxing up here. If your dad knew we'd put you to work right away, he'd give me hell."

"'S' alright, Grampa. I can't just sit around. Wouldn't want me turning into a blindfolded parachutist, now, right? Hey, what's that?" She pointed at a rambling two-story building across the river, about halfway up the rolling hills. It had been painted a stark, jarring blue, unnerving against the dun hillside.

Max laughed. "That there's the high school. Another reason for the kids in Forge to go a little crazy sometimes."

They left the highway and crossed another bridge. As they wound through town, Mercedes was struck by the fact that she couldn't see a single stoplight. One movie theater, a single screen. A modern-looking library, across from the ancient brick junior high school her father had attended for part of a year. It was so quiet.

"Not much to look at," her grandfather said lowly, smiling and waving at a passing motorist. "Not exactly Chinatown or Market Street, is it?"

"Oh, I don't know. It's peaceful, kind of nice. Relaxing."

Her grandfather looked across at her. "Good. Relax, Mercedes."

They pulled into an elm-lined neighborhood. Max's house was

larger than Mercedes expected, and as the car purred to a stop in the short driveway, the side door opened with a bang and out came Britta, trailed by three girls. Mercedes' grandmother was a blond giant in a flour-covered apron, and she trundled forth, kneading small bits of dough out from between her fingers.

"Hey," was all Mercedes could say by way of greeting before she was swept up in a hug. She wondered if her smile would one day be as beautiful as her grandmother's; framed by jowls as pink as a baby's.

Max took care of the luggage while Mercedes was bustled inside, borne on a wave of her grandmother's exuberant chatter. The house smelled of cinnamon rolls; absolutely redolent with the aroma of whatever spicy was simmering in a huge black pot on the stove. She was introduced to her cousins: Diane, Irene, and Alice, who each had mahogany-colored hair and deep-set eyes to match.

"We didn't know you were so pretty," blurted Alice.

"What, me?" Mercedes set her suitcase on the big bed that would be hers for two months. She noticed with pleasure that the second story offered a view. "You're the ones who are pretty." She cupped Alice's chin in her hand. "Absolutely a little doll! Tell me," she sat on the bed. "How many boyfriends do you have?"

The little girl blushed, and Irene said, "Tell her about Tommy!" Alice blushed an even deeper shade of red. "You'll see him when we go swimming this afternoon. We are going swimming, aren't we? Right?" All four laughed.

Diane, the tallest, sat down on a cedar chest that poked out of the closet. "Aunt Sylvia called about an hour ago, asking if you'd gotten here yet. I think she's going to call the airline and complain. Oh, she also told us that you should look in your suitcase the minute you got here, and that we should watch."

Puzzled, Mercedes stood and began dialing in the combination on her suitcase. She was pleased her cousins had turned out to be so nice. Of course, they would know Sylvia, too. Mercedes kept forgetting they were all members of the same family, the same clan. It felt good to be in a normal house, with normal people for once. So what if Forge was a minuscule town, a dot on the map. Maybe she needed a good, healthy dose of *normal*, boring life. "Did she tell you what it was?" she asked, unsnapping the lock.

"Aunt Sylvia said it was something that would help you take it easy while you were here. She said it would help you make friends or something."

Mercedes opened her suitcase and choked on a very unladylike guffaw. It was a black Jantzen bikini.

She held it up by its underwire for the girls to see. Except for Alice, they were speechless. "That looks like underwear," she said.

Mercedes smirked. "Anybody got a real suit that I can borrow?"

*

The pool was actually pretty nice, she decided one swimsuit later, as they waited in line outside. From the street she'd been impressed with the surrounding park and the ten-meter platform that rose above the pool like a monument to some techno-aquatic god. The other side of the fence was a maelstrom of color and noise, shouting and splashing supplicants at the temple of summer. Mercedes felt vaguely disjointed in the summer heat, but not uncomfortable. Part of her couldn't believe she'd actually left home. She was sure she'd blink and find she was still in California.

Everything looked new, and she said as much to Irene. "Pretty nice for a one-horse burg like Forge."

Irene's voice was muffled by the pile of towels she carried. "New pool. It was a donation by one of Grandpa Max's friends, Sean Lyons–I think he's an architect." She went on to explain how the pool had become *the* place to hang out, at least until the water in the reservoir warmed up.

Inside, the little kids made straight for the water, while Mercedes followed Irene and Diane as they hunted for a dry place to spread the towels. If there was anything lacking in the pool, it was deck space. They finally laid down next to some other high school students on a wide square of concrete awash in hard sunlight. Her cousins' friends were a pretty clean-cut bunch. "Mercedes, this is Ryan, Chad, Ken, Lani, Neal, . . ." Irene's list went on and on. Mercedes went through the motions of saying hi to one and all. Not much use. The heat was like a solid presence, a thick, humid quilt blanketing one and all. The monolithic diving platform stood unused.

Mercedes found a spot between a Coke machine and a blue iron trapdoor about two feet across. The trapdoor was open, and two little boys crouched over it, squinting down into the blackness. They were in her way.

"You guys mind?" Mercedes made as if to unfurl her towel over them, and they scuttled halfway out from under it, embarrassed. She was beginning to get annoyed. Little boys. They were just sitting there, like they were fishing or something. "Hey, *amigos! Habla ingles?* Move over."

"Duane!" Diane said, reprovingly. "Close the door and give us some room, will you? Don't make us call a lifeguard!"

The little blond boy stuck his tongue at her and swatted his companion. "Come on, Abe." They left.

The water in the surge tank below them gurgled. Sunlight slanting inward refused to illuminate more than a narrow rectangle. No telling how deep or wide the dark chamber was.

It took Mercedes and Irene together to lift the edge of the trapdoor.

None of the sunglass-veiled guys laying out a few feet away offered to help. As they tipped the heavy door over, Mercedes caught a glimpse of the murky water below. The smell of chlorine and other chemicals was intense. The door shut snug with a flat clang–

–and almost immediately swung open again. Mercedes and Irene stepped back, startled, as a figure emerged from the dark tank, streaming water. One palm flat on the trapdoor, the other gripping the side of the gaping hole, the young man shook water from his eyes and levered himself out of the miniature abyss. He stood just over six feet tall, a good four inches over Mercedes, and he was covered in paint chips, bits of plastic, and strands of hair from the tank. In his hand he held a pair of goggles tangled with hair.

"Excuse me," he said, and moved to the side, ostensibly so as not to drip on Mercedes' towel. He closed the trapdoor and walked to the outdoor shower, puzzling over the enshrouded goggles.

"Hey, Jack," said a few of the other kids. "Way to go, man," added another. Jack nodded and smiled, still blinking. He wore a black racing suit. Sitting, Mercedes watched as he yanked the silver chain and embraced the sparkling cascade of water.

Nice.

The hot summer sun streamed over him as if he were a part of it, not glaringly down as it did upon the layabouts on the deck, but seeming to favor him, accenting the glow of his tan and the glimmering shine of the water as flooded through the deep grooves in his arms, back, and legs. His hair was blond with a dark coppery luster; burnished by the summer sun. As he turned and directed the shower onto his back, Mercedes watched the water shed off the line of his jaw and cheekbones. He was still smiling, but it was a slow, simple smile, as if he was relieved to be out of the dank, black surge tank to which she'd nearly consigned him.

Mercedes had the funniest, prickly feeling then, as if she alone could see his smile; almost like he was smiling just for her and no one else, though plenty of eyes had riveted on him, no doubt, as he had sauntered across the deck.

He leaned back, and the spray pummeled his hair, his shoulders, his raised arms, his soft smile. Then he opened his eyes.

She'd been expecting arrogance, or at least a vague sort of haughtiness that would indicate vanity, but Mercedes was surprised by the expression and depth his eyes lent his sharp face. His eyes were uncommonly fierce. They looked directly, easily into her own.

She smiled back.

The young man, now water-blasted clean, turned off the shower and strolled over to where the tow-headed boy was playing. "Here, Abe. Next time, keep them on your head." Mercedes watched as he slipped a pair of dry shorts over his suit, then grabbed sunglasses and a whistle before heading for the lifeguard tower at the farther, shallow end of the pool.

"Hey, knock it off!" Mercedes twisted on her towel to see another boy, a newcomer, bending over Irene, shaking water from his thick, black hair. Droplets flew everywhere. One girl, sheltering the paperback book she'd been reading, called out playfully, "Kyle, you look just like a dog." A few of the others laughed and stirred briefly in the hot sun, squirming around to watch.

Kyle crouched down on his haunches in front of Mercedes and Irene. He had a swarthy, ragged look about him, but his lips were heavy and delicate, like a woman's. The rest of him was a solid knot of muscle. "Hey, babe, you didn't call me last night. S'problem?" His hand snaked out and snatched Irene's sunglasses before she could stop him, then dodged back as she tried to reach for them. He laughed loudly and grabbed her leg, just above the knee.

Mercedes was not impressed. She'd seen this kind of beach-thug

78

act before; heck, half the guys she went to high school with acted this way. The small-town punk version was a new one on her, however. She looked at Irene as the bigger boy began to speak. Her cousin drew her knees up, quivering, indecisive, and as Mercedes watched, something like fear and uncertainty passed briefly beneath her chestnut eyes. The skin on her leg immediately around his thick fingers was white under her tan. Irene hesitated, then opened her mouth to speak, but Mercedes heard her own voice.

"S'cuse me, you want to give my cousin back her shades, acne-boy, or what?" What? Mercedes couldn't believe she'd actually said that. The self-satisfied smirk on his face wavered for a minute, though, and his attention turned fully to Mercedes. He sneered.

"You got something to say, milk-cow, you need to speak up."

They'd drawn the attention of pretty much everybody on the deck. A few of Kyle's buddies (same shaggy hair, same vacuous expression) propped themselves up on the side of the pool. Ah, well, out of the frying pan . . . "You got a face underneath all those pimples, or does your mama just read your collar to remember your name, you pus-faced mistake."

Kyle looked at Irene, sticking his thumb at Mercedes. "Who the hell is this?"

Diane was a bit dumbstruck. "My, um, cousin. Mercedes."

His eyebrows waggled. "Mercedes, hunh? Like to take *you* for a test drive."

Mercedes sniffed. "You get that line from a Corey Feldman movie, or what? Pathetic. Listen, loser: there's nothing here for you, get it? Don't call my cousin anymore, *capisce*? Not—going—to—score—to-day. Too many syllables for you?" Mercedes felt her face harden with each word. What was she doing? She'd never gone looking for trouble before, and definitely not like this, with some ignorant, hopelessly clichéd, shovel-faced punk. Yet the anger was *right there*, not coming in a slow rise at all like she'd read about in books, but right there, *right here*, blue-hot bright and at the surface.

She ripped the sunglasses off his face, nearly slapping him, startling the older boy.

"We pay to come in here and lay out, not to be hassled by some overworked farm boy. Why don't you go on down to the gym and pump yourself, little farm boy?"

He was red-faced and breathing hard, and his eyes were two coal-black ingots of hate. Kyle grimaced as laughter bubbled through the crowd. His hand twitched off the pool deck, then relaxed as a lifeguard walked by, swinging her whistle. It was half past the hour; time for all the guards to rotate to a new tower.

Abruptly Kyle got to his feet, sneering at Mercedes. As the others watched, he strode to the base of the diving platform and mounted the ladder. At the top he took one look around, one pointedly toward Mercedes, then threw himself off the lip of concrete, crashing into the water nearly a second later. Afterward, he and three of his lookalikes pulled themselves from the water and walked out with nary a glance in their direction.

Mercedes had already put her arm around Irene's thin shoulders. "Are you all right?"

The other girl shuddered once, and said, "I can't believe you said those things to him, right to his face. Are *you* okay?" Irene was absently rubbing her leg where he'd latched on.

"Hey, don't mess with the Italian chick, know what I mean?" she replied, dipping deep into the accent. Mercedes smiled and shook her cousin's shoulders. "That was dinner-table conversation for my Mom's family. The kind of chit-chat the ladies engage in while knitting in the sewing room. Or sewing in the knitting room. Which is it?"

"Sewing room," supplied a grinning Diane. Slowly, they managed to coax a smile into Irene's face. Mercedes continued talking to her cousin in subdued, relaxed tones, but underneath her placid exterior she was boiling with anger and something of surprise. Why did men have to act like this? Kyle's assumption of unequivocal *ownership* of Irene sickened her to the point of fury, while her own reaction to him, despite what she'd said about her Italian family, had been completely uncharacteristic of her.

During the past year since her mother's death Mercedes had felt the wide, hollow chambers of her heart fill at times with sadness, with despondency, and with frustration. She hadn't realized until now that those black emotions were merely the surface, like thin films of oil atop a deeper, murkier intensity. Mercedes felt like a liar now, mouthing platitudes to her shaking cousin. She wondered if there were any tenderness left in her at all.

Irene looked up into Mercedes' face. "He's very popular."

Diane spoke up. "He's a jerk."

"Amen," said Mercedes. "Did you see the way he was looking at us?"

"Eww," Diane made a face. "Good thing you didn't wear your bikini after all, Mercedes."

"So now what? Do you want to leave?"

Mercedes shook her head. Her insides were still a Gordian knot of anger and indignation. Kyle had fled, but the flat, acrid taste of the confrontation lingered in the back of her mouth. "No. Let me borrow a hair tie." She pulled her hair back into a ponytail. "You got anybody around here who knows how to use that thing?" she asked, indicating the diving platform.

"Why," asked Diane, "You gonna—that's right! Aunt Sylvia said you did gymnastics and stuff."

"Not anymore," said Mercedes, standing. "Not since my mom got sick."

The others watched as Mercedes climbed the platform and steadied herself on the railing at the top. The pool seemed farther away than thirty feet–an illusion, she knew, caused by her own height of nearly six feet. She looked around, feeling her body calm itself and get ready for the dive. The strange rage inside her began to subside, to wisp away in the slight breeze she felt at the top of the tower. Her anger seemed so odd, so completely disproportionate now to the boy's clumsy offense. In the heat at the apex of summer, Mercedes shivered, then stepped cleanly off and into suddenly rushing air.

*

That night, Mercedes could barely keep her eyes open at the dinner table. Despite Max's attempts to draw her into a conversation, Mercedes found that a basic combination of the sun, the heat, and her flight on the airplane was working its subtle magic on her. Sleep was a second guest at the Adam's table that night.

Britta noticed her granddaughter's drowsiness, and made a point of firmly taking the meal's dishes out of Mercedes' hands when she silently began clearing the table. "No, dear, go keep your grandpa company. I'll do these. I need to get my hands clean, anyway."

So she dragged herself across the hall and sunk into the overstuffed chair across from the old man, who was just in the act of putting on a pair of half-glasses to read the cover of a CD case. He paused and considered her. Max looked at home here in his pine-paneled den. A trophy steelhead trout graced one wall, next to a grandfather clock and a sideboard that looked like it had been whittled from a single piece of cedar.

Bookshelves covered the other walls. Mercedes had always been proud of her family's immense appetite for good books. It was the one characteristic identical to both her mother's and father's clans.

Max cleared his throat. "Sylvia wanted you to call before you went to bed, but if you'd rather wait 'til morning—"

"I'll be okay, Grandpa. Just too much good food." That makes two identical characteristics, she amended. "Do you think Grandma Britt and my Mom's mother made a bet when I was born to see which of them could get the most food into me?"

Max laughed. "You've stumbled on the great conspiracy of all grandmothers, plum. We grandpa's have something along those lines, but it has to do more with pocket change and loose dollar bills." His eyes twinkled.

Her smile turned into a yawn. "Sorry; I don't know what's wrong with me. I'm usually up way past this, back home."

"Your dad says you do all the housecleaning and other chores at night."

"Yeah. It's the only time I've got, with school and all."

Her grandfather put down his book. "Merc, I sure hope you can take it easy while you're with us. You know, you can do whatever you want while you are here. Britta's anxious to have you help in the garden, but I told your dad we would show you the town first, maybe help you meet some of the kids your age."

Mercedes shifted in the chair, throwing one leg over a hassock. "I saw some at the pool today, Grandpa. Except for Diane and Alice, they're a pretty stiff bunch."

"I know what you mean. Take a few days before you make up your mind, though. Go skiing on the lake. Relax, Merc. Don't worry about anything."

She knew her grandpa loved her. It told in the way he watched her and nothing else in the room; in the total attention he paid. "Who knows, you might find a guy or two you like, and—"

Mercedes flushed. "Grandpa Max! I'm not going to find a *boyfriend* in *Forge*, Idaho!"

Max laughed. "Better watch what you predict, plum. Going to break a few hearts in that swimsuit Sylvia sent you. Now, are you going to get on up to bed before you fall asleep there, or you going to make me carry you upstairs? I'm not as spry as I used to be, you know."

"Just a few more minutes, Grandpa. It's not even dark yet. Can we listen to some more Benny Green?"

And she sat back there in the lassitude of a full, complete day, listening to Benny's slow, sweet piano, feeling a little guilty she wasn't scrubbing pots, scouring floors, or sorting sheets in a big house nearly a thousand miles away. And she did fall asleep there in the big chair, and her grandfather carried her upstairs to bed, resting a slender sprig of new jasmine on the pillow next to her.

*

Mercedes woke with a gasp and a small cry, folding over herself in the big bed. She clutched at her stomach, but the phantom pain had flickered away before she could be sure it was real. Her disorientation lasted a few seconds more, before she could remember where she was. The unfamiliar slant of the ceiling above her and the alien position of the window lent her a disjointed feeling. She swung her feet to the floor and sat up in the dark, further surprised to find herself still in her clothes from the night before.

She dreaded dreaming about her parents. She was a little girl again, standing in front of their big new house in Palo Alto, the house they'd moved into just after her mom and dad had received their last, big raises together at the lab. Everything was identical to the day they'd moved in except that she was too young by several years. That was how her dreams usually went.

Mercedes the child stood on the front step, clutching her stuffed cat doll, and watched as smoke and clouds roared over the house, seemingly just a few feet above the peak of the roof. In the sudden twilight, she'd noticed that there were no lights on in the house. She ran from window to window, and from door to door, but the big house was as black and unrelenting inside as a tomb.

In the dream, a heavy ache had suddenly blossomed in her middle, and when she woke up and seen the canted, shadowed ceiling above, she'd thought for one irrational second she'd awakened inside that stark, black house of her dream.

She rolled toward the lighter rectangle of darkness that marked the window, and pushed it open. The fresh, slightly chilly air washed over her pale face; fingered through the sweat-damp hair at the base of her neck. A tiny, white light winked into existence out in the night. It blinked twice at her, then grew in intensity before subsiding to a thin beacon.

Mercedes reached for the lamp, then decided against it. The backlit hands of her watch showed it was only a few minutes after four o'clock. In the darkness she found her suitcase and put on her light denim jacket. Mercedes needed to get out of that bedroom, get out of her grandparents' house, if only for a few minutes.

Her head was almost clear by the time she eased out the front door. Not even locked, she noticed with a smile. Her white sneakers were silent on the black pavement. Mercedes made her way toward the little light she'd seen come on over the dark slanting roofs of the subdivision. It was a beautiful neighborhood, compact and green. Broad, tree-lined streets like you'd expect to see in a Norman Rockwell painting. Everything hushed. She realized she felt like she needed to whisper.

When she reached the park a few blocks away, Mercedes aimed for the broad, manicured fields where soccer was played, and for the flat baseball diamond instead of the clustered trees. Even if nobody locked their doors in Forge, it went totally against Mercedes' grain to even consider strolling through the patches of dark green dimness where the feeble park lights stood eclipsed.

The light was coming from the pool on the hill at the center of the park. As Mercedes drew closer, she saw that someone had set a spotlight on the top of the platform, and had angled it and taped it so that it shone down in a slanting, elongated strip of incandescent light on the water below. Someone was swimming.

Lap after lap his stroke never slowed. Instead of gripping the rough gutter at the pool's edge to haul himself around, the young man did a quick flipturn, somersaulting with barely a splash and tapping his feet on the wall just long enough to rocket back in the opposite direction. Mercedes almost walked on past the park, but then realized the young man was swimming alone. What an idiot. If something were to happen to him, like a cramp or if he hit his head on the wall—great. Mercedes had had enough of babysitting for one day; she didn't need this. Better to walk on, she told herself, maybe think further about the meaning of her dream.

But as she passed the single small pickup truck in the parking lot, she found herself turning and walking to the front entrance of the pool building. If he's locked himself in, she thought, there's nothing I can do.

To her chagrin, the door stood wide open.

This is dumb, she thought, walking through the darkened dressing room. Just an embarrassment to herself and whoever this was who'd decided to take a moonlit, excuse me, *spot*lit swim in the middle of the night.

He'd rolled back one of the plastic insulation covers, and thick steam boiled up in his wake. There was a grace to his long, sharp strokes, and the smooth rotation of his shoulders bespoke an economy of movement common to those who spend most of their summers staring at the bottom of a pool. Mercedes sat on a folding chair and watched him swim. He cut precisely down the middle of the bright pathway delineated by the light above him. Mercedes noticed his hands entered and left the water at exactly the same angle each time.

Against the rhythmic patterns of the young man's strokes, Mercedes realized she could hear—music? It was a muffled, throbbing beat, interspersed with jangling guitar. She looked for nearly a minute before noticing the source of the garbled, almost inaudible tone. There at the edge of the water, next to a digital clock, lay a small MP3 player wrapped in a ziplock bag and duct tape. A thick cord ran from the bag into the water. Now I know this guy's an idiot, she thought. Headline: Illegal swimmer electrocutes self with digital audio player, Death by U2.

At the far end of the pool, he stopped, bobbing slightly as his own wake caught up with him. Before Mercedes could think of an excuse for being on the deck with him at four in the morning ('Excuse me, sir, I was looking for my pet octopus, Oscar.' Or, 'Pardon me, didn't notice you were here?') he gripped the edge of a diving block and drew himself out of the water. At the edge of the light, the young man looked more unreal; unearthly. He snatched up a small box and stood on the block. As he curled his toes over the edge and flexed his arms down around the block, the light shone down on his wet skin and limned him in platinum fire. He looked perfect. Half silver and half black. He tucked his head and tightened down into a racing start, and the grooves appeared again across his back. Pockets of smooth shadow.

Mercedes had never been so fully, completely aware of another human being in her entire life. A pearly, feathery sheen shimmered across him as he inhaled, then, as he evenly blew the air out, shimmered back again. Water dropped from him like glittering bits of diamond.

He leaned forward, then erupted from his racing start, body tensing and releasing in a wonderful arch that carried him across the water and then down into it. He'd flung his head up as he dove, and Mercedes was sure he'd seen her.

A low beep issued from the digital clock at the edge of the pool, and the yellow-green numbers began marching up from zero.

Mercedes smiled, realizing she'd been holding her breath.   S h e stood, and watched as he rippled like a shadow beneath the surface. He came up after nearly half the length of the pool, swimming breaststroke, gathering great armfuls of water to himself and pushing them behind with a powerful, sweeping kick. There was more strength than grace in his stroke, but Mercedes couldn't help but notice the sinuous symmetry in his reaching arms and bending shoulders. Four laps, and his speed increased with each. As he rebounded from the wall nearest her, Mercedes stood and walked along the edge of the deck, keeping pace with him.

At the far end he gave one last lunge, then reach-slammed into the gray pad affixed to the wall. Breathing hard, he twisted in his wake and looked to the digital clock. "Ah, man," he exhaled. He slipped his goggles off and glared at the clock again, muttering to himself.

Mercedes smiled. "Not fast enough?"

He still looked toward the clock. "Not quite, no. I've got to shave off another two-and-a-half seconds, at least; maybe if I pop my start more, instead of leaning out, or hold the streamline off my turns. It's a shortcourse meet, so–hey!" His eyes snapped up, and he gulped air. "What–who are you doing here?"

His astonishment nearly made her laugh aloud. "Huh? Could you repeat the question?" As he hauled himself from the water she handed him the towel she'd found. "You left the door open, and anyway, you're not supposed to swim alone. What kind of lifeguard are you? I'll bet you didn't even shower before going in."

The young man started to say something, then blinked at her. He took a step back. Mercedes liked his dark eyes; they seemed to twinkle-glitter in the half-light, and she could tell he was thinking at a tremendous rate. He wiped the water from his hand, then extended it.

"Let's try that again. My name's Jack." White, straight teeth on the horizon of his smile.

Mercedes took his hand firmly. It was softer than she had expected. "Nice to meet you, Jack."

And that was the first time she met Jack Flynn.

Miklos

Washington D.C.
6PM

Gary Gledhill loosened his tie as soon as he crossed the threshold and closed the door at his back. There were always more reporters. Some days crossing the street from the Capitol to the Dirksen Building was as close to a marathon as he could come after 13 years in office. After today's farce in the Senate, the newsboys and-girls hadn't let up.

So what if the administration was funneling more money into the Central American and Caribbean projects? Did that idiot from the *Post* expect him to stop and explain the math every time?

His staff was all at lunch. Gledhill found the sandwiches and Aquafina in the little refrigerator under one corner of his desk, and planted them next to the stack of the afternoon's reading material. His newer office was smaller than the old, chilly rooms in the Hart building but even so, the senator found it harder to keep track of paperwork. At least he didn't have to walk past that horrible Mountains and Clouds sculpture in the Hart atrium anymore.

There was a brief he needed to go over before the day was gone, a situation paper on the Caribbean emailed to him earlier in the day by someone's aid over at the Center for Strategic and International Studies. Gledhill liked the CSIS situation reports, they always felt less watered-down, less secondhand than info passed to him by the State Department. This one was more money for Cuba, essentially. No matter what economic strategy Gledhill and his office proposed, the island would never really be self-sustaining. Miguel Espinosa had only held office 4 years, and everyone expected him to create money from thin air. Cuba was still Cuba. Baseball players and cigars, another beach on which American's could cook themselves and spend money. It was always the money—almost always. Odd how most people forgot that it was Espinosa himself who'd come to attention for his economic juggling— the *Post* called it compassion—in 1998, thanks to a tropical storm. He'd been the junior bureaucrat responsible for Cuba forgiving the 50 million dollar's worth of foreign debt that Honduras owed when that country was devastated by Hurricane Mitch, even though the countries were both rivals at the time.

Why did one country's mercy invariably cost the U.S. hard cash?

The economist leaned into his desk, stretched his back—better do those exercises for the sciatic, like he was supposed to—but he sat and began reviewing the proposed changes to the Afganistan aid package. A good warmup to his work on the Cuba file, the far larger stack on his desk.

Gledhill didn't simply love his work, he let it nourish him, feed his passion like only anonymous service could, to those who understood it. He spoke to his two children—both in the throes of college—every night, but he saw them rarely. The work, you see, the work. He'd have time for them when the work was done.

The outer offices were so quiet, he almost didn't hear his office door open. Gledhill mentally placed a bookmark on the column of numbers and glanced up at the solemn stranger.

A question on his lips, Gledhill gasped as the spare, grey man raised a weapon, the sharp intake of breath covering a whispering report. He felt a hot-then-cold sting at the base of his throat, almost like a touch of a cool hand, and shot to his feet—

—and fell, all muscles unclenching at once, into his chair.

Gary Gledhill struggled to breath as the tall stranger approached the desk. The intruder didn't even bother to close the door, even though broad daylight streamed through the hallway behind him.

I should be able to see that light, he thought, but even keeping the thought coherent was effort. Below his throat, his body rebelled. Shards of glass, no, ice in his veins.

Another figure entered the room. A woman, by the sound of her voice. "Anything we missed?"

The first man, now a collection of grey angles to Gary, spoke from somewhere close. "No. The rest of the staff knows better than to disturb his work. The wife passed away eight years ago. No . . . intern. He's logged in; get the package."

The subordinate went to work on the computer as Gary's chair was moved away from the desk. Something slowed the chair, and he realized his slack heels might be touching the carpet.

The credenza, and pictures of his kids, swam into view briefly, then Gary's face was caught in a steel vice; no a hand, and he found the original intruder staring into his eyes.

His face was sharp and strong and utterly empty of anything. Sharp cheekbones framed by long, lank hair the color of dust. In another life, Gary might have remembered his face from somewhere, but that didn't matter now. The face spoke. "Isn't it nice? Isn't it liberating, the lack of feeling?" A wisp of curiosity. "Are you afraid?"

Gary struggled to speak, to want to speak.

"Could you be trying to pray?" The face drew nearer, the voice lower, chiding "Why?"

Gledhill found himself, his sense of self, tattering away. He edged his eyes past the ghostly features over him and focused on the pictures of his son, his daughter, and his wife.

His breath ebbed, thinned, trickled away.

Too Far Broken

London, England
8 AM

Minute by minute, the sense of powerlessness was driving him mad. William the Fifth bowed his head, leaning into the mantle above the fireplace, and thanked God for the sedative that was allowing his wife to sleep in the next room. He'd brushed aside any such suggestions for himself, preferring for the moment a rather bleak reality to the chance that he'd be in some drugged, stuporous sleep when they found his daughter.

When they bloody well found his daughter.

William Arthur Philip Louis (Mountbatten) Windsor, His Majesty the Lion of Britain pried his fingers from the mantlepiece and turned to face the cluster of uniformed men seated in his study. Instantly they stopped talking amongst themselves and settled into their chairs. It wasn't their usual Tuesday meeting, and the Joint Intelligence Committee, consisting of the heads of SIS, MI5, GCHQ Cheltham, and the Defense Intelligence Staff each looked uncomfortable in each other's presence. The figure furthest from the king, a short, blond-haired fellow, leaned back into a corner nearest the window, fully into the wash of late afternoon radiance.

Like the shattering blue sky over London, the newcomer himself was an oddity. He remained apart from the others, pointedly ignoring their attention. There was an edginess about him, an anxious sincerity reflected in the way he ran his fingers along the border of the mullioned window.   William had no doubt the section heads guessed he was an American. He could only hope that fact remained the extent of their knowledge. Heavens knew they had plenty of other things to discuss.

The king coughed quietly. "I really must ask you gentlemen to lower your voices. My wife is attempting to sleep in the adjoining room." With difficulty, he sat at his desk. "Strine, you're saying that the Navy has found nothing?"

"Dash it all, your Majesty," the round-faced man shook his head. "The coastline is clean, as are each of our northern ports. The outlying radar stations were rendered useless by the storms, even our redundant systems. We're coordinating with the Americans, sir, as their equipment is superior at the moment to anything we have ready to deploy into the North Atlantic."

The head of Diplomatic Service spoke up. "But they haven't been informed specifically whom we are looking for, your Majesty. As decided, the identity of the princess is being kept from all possible avenues to the media."

William nodded and turned to face another section head. "Timmon, you are certain she couldn't have been brought into the city?"

The mustached man shifted under his king's scrutiny while the others in the room traded dubious glances. "Yes, your Majesty, we have been over this. The discreet checkpoints established by D-11 and the Metropolitan Police this morning disrupted several illegal shipments of drugs and other illicit material, but found not a trace of Her Highness. Sir, if I may, none of the groups who could be responsible would secrete the princess here, under our noses. It's out of the question, your Majesty. Doesn't make sense," he added.

The others in the room made general signs of agreement and sipped their tea. William nodded and sighed. "Quite. Very well, you all know your business. I'll expect another report in two hours. That is all. Thank you, gentlemen." Much to their surprise, the young king stood and shook hands with every man as he filed from the room.

When each had left, William exhaled and drew his fingertips across aching temples. "Leave us, Bethers," he said to the suited man near the door. The guard, one of two Scotland Yard detectives detailed to the king, nodded curtly and stepped out, not quite closing the door behind him. William sighed again.

And that constituted as much privacy as he was likely to receive. He turned to the blond man near the window. "Bethers has been watching over me for years, nearly since that nasty business when I first met Jack." Voice pitched low, he walked to the casement. "Whole bloody lot of them are walking on eggshells around their 'boy king,'" he said sarcastically.

The other man's lips curled as if he would speak, then he merely nodded. He was a short, hard fellow whose physique would have made him Herculean had he grown an additional six inches. As it stood, Alonzo Noel was a remarkable character. Bright, quick Latino eyes belied the leanness and angle of cheek and jaw more common among the peoples of Northern Europe. His posture indicated confidence and self-possession; it was the stance of a much larger, more imposing man, yet for Alonzo, it seemed to fit.

He pushed a handful of pale hair back from his forehead and said, "I'm so sorry, your Majesty. My clothes—I came as fast—"

William roughly embraced the other man, then released him. "I don't care about any of that, Alonzo. Can you get her back for us?"

Alonzo blinked and licked his lips. "With all respect, sir, I've read the dossier and heard most of the report your men just gave. If Christine was taken out of the country, then their plans are technically—"

Again the king cut him short, grasping his shoulder, then the nape of his neck. "I think she's here, in London." He leaned close. "Somewhere in the city. Damn their plans and their 'special contingencies,' Alonzo. My *daughter's* been taken."

The shorter man hesitated before the king's intensity. "What makes you think the kidnapers brought her into London? Like the chief, or whatever you call him over here, said, 'doesn't make sense.'" He turned to face the window, squinting against the unseasonable brightness.

Windsor walked to a recessed bar and mixed a drink. "Several months ago one of my subordinates passed a document to me, concerning some sort of plot. Came out of South America; Colombia or some such place. No, I don't usually take notice of that rubbish, unless the Yard draws it to my attention," he said in response to Alonzo's unspoken question. "But my mother's name was in it several times."

The king continued. "The plot, or plan or whatever, had been passed over as nonsense, even though it was remarkably detailed."

"Assassination?"

"Not only that, no. It called for the 'elimination of national trust.' There were a number of actions listed–assassinations among them–specific acts aimed at undermining a people's trust in their national leaders and, I suppose, in the ideals of their culture."

"Sounds ridiculous."

"I thought so, too, until I read the entire document. Think a moment, how your own country was affected by that sordid business with your President a few years ago? I've studied the American Founding Fathers, Alonzo; how many of your countrymen truly understand what a President is anymore? Do you recall the concurrent problems in your stock market? In your military's credibility?

William gestured helplessly. "So much of the workings of a

country depend upon ethereal things. 'Faith in democracy' is not just a cliche, my friend. You may not recall, but England suffered a similar demoralization at the death of my mother." He took a drink from the tumbler in his hand.

Alonzo was visibly shocked. "She was a target?"

"She was—a case study of some sort." Windsor steadied himself against the bar, and returned to the window. "'The true aim of any terrorist is the destruction of a belief system, of confidence in a way of life.' Jack told me that once."

The man at the window nodded. "That's how they operate; instill fear at whatever level necessary to make people meet their demands. Their victims fold essentially because of fear, which is the essence of outright coercion."

"My people, my subjects love Christine. The overall plan outlines the elimination of certain people and institutions which represent the faith of certain countries. My daughter was one. The Cuban president, Espinosa, is another."

"Do you still have the report?"

"No, I passed the original on to the head of Six, months ago, and now he's got no bloody idea where it is. Vanished from the archives, or mistakenly shredded. He never read it. I believe the Yard kept a copy of the targets for assassination." William finished his drink in a single swallow. "Some of it was ranting, also. Ravings of a lunatic, decrying Western culture, the Arab nations, others. There was also some nonsense about an enormous electrical weapon. Pure science fiction.

"None of the others will act on this, Alonzo."

"Doesn't fit the profiles or scenarios their intelligence-weenies work so hard on, does it?"

"You're perceptive."

Alonzo's nose twitched. "And in this plan you read, Christine was to be brought into London." When Windsor nodded in affirmation, he continued. "Basically, you want me to contact Jack and try to find your daughter before whoever's kidnapped her decides to kill her in the most demoralizing manner possible, to break the British psyche or whatever."

"You put it so succinctly."

The American looked away. William could see he was thinking ferociously.

"I'll be frank, your Majesty. Jack—I doubt Jack will help. Since the accident last year—"

"He must. Make no mistake, Alonzo, you two are my last personal option. Jack must do this for me." He clenched his teeth and swallowed, fighting the sudden wave of emotion that carried his heart up into his throat. William was so tired, so utterly empty.

He caught Alonzo watching him, and stiffened. Before he could open his mouth again, the small man spoke. "I'll try. Comes to Jack, that's all I can promise." He walked to the door. "If he won't help, I'll come back and tear down this whole damn city myself, William–your Majesty."

The king had regained his composure. "I've had a diplomatic liaison assigned to you." He took a deep breath. "To keep me appraised more than anything else, though she's supposed to be a crack shot. She'll get you through customs with any equipment or weapons, and provide you with whatever you need."

Alonzo fished in a deep pocket of his coat and withdrew an old leatherbound notebook. "I want a computer with anonymous 'Net access, first of all. And a copy of whatever assassination wish list your people copied from the original record. If Jack's in on this, he's got weapons in Paris we can use. If that's not enough we can always hit a POMCUS."

"A what?"

"Ordnance that's Prepositioned Outside Military Custody of the U.S., your Majesty. Caches of military equipment–weapons, ammo, trucks, all sorts of stuff hidden in special bunkers or civilian storage facilities around Europe. Very handy. They were originally put in place to resupply NATO for a month in case of a Soviet attack. Kept up ever since." Alonzo zipped up his jacket. "I'm sure your country has something similar." He was at the door.

"Quite. Godspeed, Alonzo."

The other man nodded pensively and exited the room. William heard him muttering to himself as he paged through the notebook. "Going to need some of the team," he said. "The thief, the magician, the ogre, and the woodsman, at the very least. Maybe even the vampire."

The king looked immediately to the clock. With any luck he was wrong, the aching suspicion that Christine was somewhere in the city would prove false, and she'd be found. A scrap of evidence, a hint, a ransom note, something. He added fresh ice and poured himself another drink.

The last time anything like this had happened, he'd been fortunate beyond belief. Could it be too much to hope for another miracle, such as he'd seen all those years ago?

*

Young William hunched his shoulders and bolted for the alley, the heavy clatter of automatic weapons deafening him, shaking his bones. All his papers and art books from St. Andrew's lay scattered on the wet cobblestones, some drenched in bright scarlet from his bodyguard's wounds. The old man turned and fired once more back toward the figures on the other side of the Rolls, then was simply obliterated in a cloud of ruby red.

"Keep running!" the big American shoved him from behind again, and

both young men entered the alley a split-second before the Rolls Royce Phantom IV exploded. The shockwave pitched them to the alley's other end, and both managed to scramble to their feet before the first bullet ricocheted down the narrow walls.

The American's jacket was burning, and he threw himself backward against a wall, smothering the flames and cursing. He'd picked up a handgun somewhere, and began to fire around the corner, loosing a dozen unaimed shots so quickly they sounded as though they came from a fully automatic weapon. The prince shook his head and tried vainly to think. His hands were sticky. Where was so much blood coming from? What was wrong with his mind?

Then movement from the far end of the lane caught his eye. More grim-faced assailants.

The American saw them, too. "Um, here!" He thrust the hot gun into William's hands, and reached down to pry at a sewer access.

"What are you about?" The prince demanded. He'd had plenty of practice with pistols and managed a shot at the approaching gunmen.

His companion grunted and pulled at the manhole. "Can you swim?"

He wrenched the heavy slat up and half-pulled, half-dragged William down. The prince dropped the gun, slipping awkwardly into the gaping hole. There were stairs; no, a ladder of some sort, and William stuttered down it until he was standing in calf-deep water.

Above, the blond American curled into a ball, bracing against the edge of the sewer access and the half-open manhole. The thick metal bucked and screeched suddenly, and Wills heard the caroom of light caliber rounds echoing in the narrow lane. Then the American dropped into the sewer, pulling the manhole shut behind him.

In the half-light, William watched as the American whipped off his own belt and shoved it first under a rung of the ladder, then knotted it through some sort of handle on the manhole's underside. No sooner had he finished than a heavy footfall resounded against the steel slab.

There was barely enough light slipping in around the edges of the manhole to see the expression on the American's face as he joined William in the tunnel. "I'm Jack. You hurt?" he asked, frisking William awkwardly.

The metal above groaned and a sliver of brighter light sliced down the access shaft. The belt was stretching.

A muzzle of a gun jabbed into the thin opening, and both young men moved. William was taller by an inch or so, but Jack was thicker, more heavily muscled. He led the way. As they slogged off down the dark tunnel toward a spot of wavering, green light, William was positive he heard him speak.

"I'm getting good at this," Jack muttered. "I can't believe I'm actually getting good at this."

*

William Windsor was a decade past that tragedy, a full ten years past that harrowing ordeal the papers had called an adventure, and he could still feel the cold, dark insistence of all that water. At least he hadn't faced it alone, though his companion had been nearly as bewildered as the prince himself.

Would Jack fix this, or was he too far broken himself?

"God give us all grace equal to our day." The king bowed his head and began to pray.

Her Father's Notes

Forge, Idaho

8 AM

The cool morning breeze carried intimations of jasmine and pine needles through the open back door. Mercedes sat at the table in what had been her grandmother's kitchen, peeling an orange and laying the triangles of curling rind on the marbled Formica. If she ducked her head just so, she could see into a robin's nest outside the window. There were two light blue eggs in the nest, the parents flitting anxiously from branch to branch nearby.

Just then Diane came through the kitchen on her way to the pantry, a load of laundry balanced before her. "'Morning," she said brightly. Diane's hair was still in curlers. "Oh, did Harry leave this open?" She set the laundry basket on her hip and levered the door shut.

"Sorry, Diane; I kept it open after he left. Can I give you a hand?" Mercedes started to rise.

"That's all right, love," Diane set the basket on the white drier that sat adjacent to the washing machine and came back into the kitchen. She wore a faded blue bathrobe and matching slippers. One toe peeked from a hole in her footwear. "I'll get to these clothes later. I've got a house to show this afternoon before Neal gets home from work, then we're taking you out to eat. Can't let you and Irene waste away on vacation."

Her cousin had become modestly successful as a real estate agent; Mercedes imagined that her salary, combined with her husband's earnings as an engineer at the local power company, placed Diane's family in the town's upper middle class. You wouldn't know it to look at her. She was still the same cousin. Same threadbare slippers.

A third voice sounded from the stairs. "Who's wasting away? You cook as much as Grandma Britt." Irene, still in her thick cotton pajamas, stepped into the room and folded herself into a chair. She took a section of orange. "You're going to have me getting up before the roosters, like Mercedes here, to run off all the fat. Honestly," she glanced at Mercedes. "Is this a vacation?" Under her breath she added, "Any luck at finding me a Starbuck's while you were out running around?"

Diane set two plates in front of them. "Listen to that, Mercedes. My sister; she grows up to become a cop, marries a guy from L.A., and forgets how to have a real breakfast. Waffles, eggs, and bacon for the both of you!" It sounded like a threat.

Mercedes laughed. "I boiled myself some eggs while you were out, and Harry shared a bowl of oatmeal with me before he went to t-ball." She handed her cousin a section of orange.

"You early risers," Diane smiled, ripping a section of paper towel off the rack for their cousin. "Did you sleep okay?"

Irene shook her head. "Hard to get to sleep without a husband and a bed full of kids kicking around all night."

It was Diane's turn to laugh. I'll send Harry and the baby in with you then tonight. I'm keeping my husband, though." She took a sip of juice. "Serves you right for going on vacation without your family. How about you, Merc?"

"Like a rock. You guys put a new mattress on the old bed, didn't you?"

Diane took an orange from the bowl on the table and began to work her thumbnail into the pored, pitted skin. "Neal and I bought a bunch of things for the place after Grandpa Max passed away."

Though their relationship was a bit farther removed than grandparent and grandchild, Diane and Irene, like all the Bergstrom children, referred to Max Adams by the title he liked best.

"That reminds me," Diane said. "We found some of your dad's papers in the study, in Grandpa Max's old desk. They were still in the FedEx box they came in."

"Really?" Mercedes finished the orange and swept the peelings onto the paper towel. "A whole box worth?"

"Yeah. Neal went through them all; he said they were research or something. Maybe notes from when they taught at college."

"Dad told me he sent a bunch of his notes and white papers up here for safe keeping. I must've forgotten." She thought for a moment. One of her father's old friends back in California might have a use for them. Mercedes didn't care all that much for pieces of her parents' professional lives. It had been the research, she sometimes told herself, the particle research and all the stray radiation that had caused her family's health problems. Problems, hell; the weird, secret experiments for the government in lab after nameless lab had taken her parents and damn near killed her.

Mercedes gritted her teeth and then smiled. "Probably notes for their classes. I wish Mom and Dad had just stayed with the university."

Irene made a sympathetic face and added Mercedes' orange peelings to her own, sweeping the lot up and depositing them in the yellow trashcan beneath the sink. She worried at her lip with her teeth, and began pulling the curlers from her sister's hair. "If they'd just been teachers you wouldn't have to worry so much about your inheritance."

"Oh, I don't worry. My lawyer told me anything I inherited— including all the money the government forked over when Mom and Dad died—can't be touched as long as I keep it in trust."

"That probably made Bryce a little crazy," Diane said.

Mercedes grimaced at the name of her ex husband. "He was a little crazy to begin with." She'd been divorced nearly eight months. "But my trust fund wasn't much compared with the allowance and portfolio his parents gave him. What bothered him most was the fact that I didn't want any of *his* money when we split. *That* made him a little crazy." Mercedes slipped her feet out of her sandals and put them up on the chair opposite her.

Irene stood. "I've heard this part of the story. Want some tea, Diane?" She fished a copper teakettle off its hook by the stove and began filling it with water.

Diane took a piece of the orange. "Sure. Get Merc some too."

Mercedes held up her hand. "No thanks."

Diane was curious. "I always thought Bryce married you for money. Isn't that the way rich people think?"

"My inheritance was small potatoes compared with his family's money. He liked to think he was taking care of me, even when he'd be gone for days, sailing. All the time I'd be gone on a photo shoot, or running around L.A. setting up business, he'd be out on his boat with whatever silicone-pumped bimbo he could pick up. He never figured I'd start having enough success taking pictures that I wouldn't have to rely on him."

Diane shook her head. "But with the money your parents left you, that'd never be the case." She took another piece of orange. "So he honestly figured you for the 'defenseless little wife?'"

"That's where Bryce was odd. Always two versions of reality. I still think he doesn't know I found out how much he was sleeping around."

Irene brought her sister a steaming cup. "How *did* you find out?"

Mercedes smiled humorlessly. "I actually dreamed about it. Then he left some stuff at home one day when a shoot was canceled, and I followed him." The smile dropped from her face. "When I tried talking to him about it, he . . . started yelling. Broke a lamp, then he started hitting me." Before her cousin could say anything, Mercedes looked up fiercely. "Irene knows. I filed a police report through her when it happened. You're the only other person I'd tell this to, Diane."

The other woman bit her lip, orange forgotten. "I'm so sorry." She seemed about to ask a question, then thought better of it. "But you were okay. He didn't—"

Now Irene grinned. "She gave him a black eye, honey."

They both laughed. Mercedes found she couldn't join them.

"I had a doctor's appointment a few days afterward, and had him check my ribs and arm. He said I was all right."

They were quiet a moment. Mercedes placed a section of fruit in her mouth and chewed slowly. Irene finally spoke up. "It was bizarre to see how quickly Bryce changed after that."

"Yes, he seemed to be happy for the divorce. Anything to get me in a courtroom and drag out a simple procedure. I'm sure he thought I'd try to punish him somehow, and he'd get a chance to sic his lawyers on me, have them paint me as a gold-digging harpy."

"Harpy?" Diane raised her eyebrows.

"His word, not mine. You should have seen his face when we met with our lawyers–so they could at least make this pitiful offer to settle— and I turned down everything. Alimony, the works–except for my house in Studio City. I was entitled to more under California's community-property laws–half of what we made together while we were married."

"And that was a lot?"

"Enough to matter to Bryce, and he's always been bored with money. Between his portfolio and my business, we did pretty well."

Irene frowned. "I remember when you called last month, right after you'd been on the phone with him." She looked at Diane. "It's why I asked Mercedes to come up here with me." To Mercedes she added, "You really needed a vacation from that guy."

"Yeah, it's pathetic. He still keeps trying to get us back together. Our old friends do, too."

Diane said, "He's a pretty big guy to be calling pathetic. I still say you should get a restraining order."

"Maybe," she conceded. "I just don't want to be one of those women they find murdered with their restraining order the only thing still in their purse."

The teakettle whistled, steam escaping. Diane, closer to the range, moved to get it. "Are you sure you don't want some tea or coffee?"

"No, thanks," Mercedes also stood, smoothing nonexistent wrinkles out of her blue t-shirt and jeans. "Not supposed to drink coffee. Doctor's orders. 'Sides, I don't think I should think about Bryce and have a bunch of caffeine racing around inside me. I might do something desperate."

Irene met her grin. "I've always thought of you as a desperate woman. Your dad's papers are on the desk in Grandpa's study."

*

He'd been such a careful man. It was so like her dad to have sent copies of his research to his own father for safekeeping. Mercedes read through the titles: "Wave Stochasticity and Linear Plasma-Maser Effect." "Electromagnetic Forces on Plasma Particles in the Presence of Controlled Resonant Plasma Turbulence." Et cetera. Mercedes would need a doctorate in physics herself just to understand the titles.

That wasn't entirely true. As the only child of two brilliant minds, Mercedes had picked up quite a bit. Her parents had never been reticent about their work in front of their daughter, and had always treated her as if no subject was beyond her comprehension. The three of them had discussed everything from whether or not a certain purple dinosaur had three green spots or four to the basics of superconductivity.

She knew her father had received his greatest acclaim for inventing a method for feeding energy to satellites from the earth's surface. The patent for that contraption had taken care of college and the down payment on Mercedes' bungalow in Studio City. Though she'd donated most of her parents' white papers and research documents to people who could actually make use of them, such as the men and women at California's Intercampus Institute for the Research of Particle Acceleration, she kept a few—for nostalgia, if not for recreational reading. From time to time one or another of her parents' colleagues would call and ask to review a fine point of data. She'd kept all their phone numbers, with a promise to pass along anything new she discovered.

"Let's see," Mercedes said to herself, flipping through pages of her address book. "Vernon Eby, Manal Teobi, or Mitch Fenn."

She decided on the latter. With his floppy haircut and dimpled chin, Mitch reminded her of the actor Chevy Chase. Fenn had been as close a friend as any to her family, and still sent her a card with a handwritten note every Christmas.

Mercedes picked up the phone.

Team

London, England

Alonzo **looked hard at** the phone before him, nonplussed. It lay on the desk, between computer and the ancient, leatherbound notebook. He'd done this before without Jack, but never without Jack's knowledge.

Thief, ogre, woodsman, magician, and vampire. The entire team included other people, other specialized skill sets, but these five might respond in time. According to his notes, Brad, Sol, and Steve we're all in Europe at the moment. Ian stayed in Chicago these days, when he wasn't traveling with his new wife. And Pete, the vampire, reliably haunted San Francisco.

No, best leave Pete out of it for the time being. Alonzo imagined himself explaining to Jack why he called up the team without warning. He wondered how on Earth he was going to speak to Jack, never mind get him to join.

Well. He'd burn that bridge when he came to it. Alonzo pushed the phone aside, flipped to a specific page in the notebook, and began typing on the computer. He copied the long string of characters directly into the browser's URL line. A moment later, the screen bathed the room in deep blue light.

"Here we go," he said

The Thief in Bohemia

Southern Bohemian Region, Czech Republic
5 PM

It had taken Brad a long time to get good at this, and it was finally beginning to pay off.

A heron sailed by, veering away from the willow tree and the knot of concealed men, crossing over the river. Lights from the shadowy compound glimmered sullenly across the steel-gray skin of the waterway.

Brad leaned into the sway of the willow and raised his head up just enough to see over the crumbling stone-and-mortar wall. He moved with painstaking caution, though the security guard strolling along the inside of the modern fence two hundred yards away was looking at his feet and no doubt anxious to finish his last sweep of the perimeter. It had been over four hours since the guard's last break, and only two minutes remained until shift change, when he could finally go home. Night was falling, quicker than usual, thanks to the storm clouds in the western sky.

The guard—Brad searched his memory for a name; Vaclav—was visibly tired and riding the careless line of boredom. Brad pushed a black strand of hair back under his hood and watched the man stumble. He was perfect.

"This country's version of Rent-a-Cop," he whispered unnecessarily to Gan, motionless against the next tree. Gan, also dressed completely in black, responded with the barest of raised eyebrows, then thumbed the switch on his radio.

"Begin, Marko."

Brad immediately turned his attention towards the purling river, though it would be another five minutes yet before any change would become apparent. "This will go well. Tomorrow you will have vacation for the rest of your life."

His older brother responded in their native Mandarin. "Just watch yourself, Zhihuan."

Brad returned to his contemplation of the guard, but inwardly frowned. No one but Gan called him by that name anymore. He checked the straps securing all the equipment to his narrow, whip-thin body. *That* name. He hadn't been that person in a long time. Not since their mother and eldest brother had died under a tank's tread in the spiritual center of a country they'd called home.

Gan was too sentimental, and too ill-timed. Foolish of his brother to remind him of the past when they were on the brink of a job.

"We will yet drink tea together," Brad whispered back in the same language, then dropped from the tree.

Behind him, four other men also began to move. He and Gan, with the help of their other brother, Li, who was back in the truck babysitting the computer expert, had hand-picked this little group out of the best the Prague underbelly had to offer. They'd chosen their Czech accomplices carefully, not only for their expertise at breaking-and-entering, but for their popularity with the local police. With any luck, the discernible style, techniques, and overall flavor of the larceny would be so marked by the mannerisms of their Czech comrades that the three brothers could slip away unnoticed. Despite the old cop adage about criminals always making at least one mistake, the brothers stood a good chance of going 100% undetected, as long as one of their local friends wasn't caught and forced to sing.

Which was unlikely, as their target in this remote corner of the Southern Bohemian forest was, for all its secrecy, a branch plant of an American corporation currently out of favor with Czech officials. Why should the police care? The obscure location and the fact that nearly everyone at the plant were American nationals virtually guaranteed a sluggish response by the local constabulary. The Americans were scientists, engineers; technocrats who snootily kept to themselves in their rented compound in the nearby city of Brno. Come Monday morning their first reaction would be disbelief, then shock that their technology had betrayed them. Heh. Brad had thought of everything.

Industrial espionage could be such fun.

Before him, beyond the ancient, pitted stone wall and another sloping 100 yards or so of low brush lay the Czech campus of DynaSynth, Inc., manufacturer of synthetic diamond. One huge, red-brick building laid down in an L-shape, at least three stories tall, with segmented steel bay doors at either end that extended nearly to the roof. From his research into the industry, Brad knew the enormous doors were necessary to bring in the twenty-ton presses that would force graphite dust into diamond. The steel presses themselves–machined in America–were worth several million apiece. Brad was after something considerably smaller, however since he'd begun planning the theft five months previously he'd occasionally wondered what it would be like to steal one of the gargantuan, octagonal presses.

The wind blew down river, cool against Brad's face as he ran against it. He pulled up the mask portion of his cowl. The thickly-woven ninja suit combined with the greasepaint under his eyes kept him warm enough. He led the four men at a brisk, silent run across ground that had once been a mass grave, a boneyard of a medieval war.

Brad had studied the territory, memorized everything about the factory he could lay his hands on.

112

DynaSynth fabricated synthetic diamond, specifically the small, cylindrical diamond-tipped inserts that fit on the ends of drill bits used in mining oil and natural gas. With drilling still a staple industry in Eastern Europe, the U.S.-based company had recently opened this plant, to better service their customers in the area. According to stateside accounting files that a friend of his had cracked into last week, DynaSynth recently received seven million dollars worth of orders from the Ukraine and Eastern Russia. Business was booming and the stockholders were delirious.

Another heron flapped by overhead.

Brad had no compunction about stealing from large corporations. His target had nothing to do with the main supply of revenue for DynaSynth, and the tiny diamond inserts were such a specialized product that he could only fence them to the original customer. No, what he was going to take physically amounted to only a few thousand dollars at best, and that paltry sum was more than covered by the company's insurance, swallowed up in the morass of accounting procedures that went along with such a large company. Nearly a year earlier, DynaSynth stock had been quietly bought up by the Raines Dynamic, a development firm with resources that were—for all intents and purposes conceivable— bottomless.

And bottomless bureaucracies made the best targets.

He reached the base of the old wall and turned slightly, jumping and then kicking back off one of the supporting pillars. The apex of his rebound gave him enough height to snatch the edge at the top of the wall and swing himself over, smooth as glass. Under his balaclava, Brad grinned. His heart was pounding, and he felt effortless, light as a feather despite the twenty-five pounds of gear distributed in the various pockets of his black ninja suit. He moved to the side as the second man came

113

over the wall. *Ninja, that's a good one, 'cept those guys were Japanese.*
Not that the guards inside the fence would know the difference.

Two months earlier in Las Vegas he'd had a similar thought, sitting
at a blackjack table across from the sweating, chubby man who would
soon be plant manager of DynaSynth-Czech. Roland Mmar was built
like an apple: a thick-lipped, multi-chinned chap with a mop of thick,
greasy blond hair and a ridiculously tiny waist. By the time Brad joined
him at the table, Mmar had downed at least five Manhattans and lost
upwards of twelve thousand dollars, though as he'd informed his new
Asian friend, "Blackjack is my game. I own it." Then he'd given Brad
what he obviously considered a traditional Japanese greeting by bowing
until he fell heavily from his stool.

"Bet you Japsters do that all the time."

The man was a boor. Over the course of the evening, Brad arrived
at a new respect for the fierceness with which he could come to loathe
another human being in so short a time. As he coaxed and cajoled the
man into revealing details about the Czech plant, he learned to dislike
Mmar's gibbering laugh and sloppy table manners. The fat man actually
won a few hands, but lost his biggest payoff when he spilled a drink all
over his ace of diamonds and nine of spades, and quit the table to get a
new Manhattan.

And although the man obviously managed his employees as bit of
a tin-god tyrant, Brad discovered Mmar knew surprisingly little about
his own plant. He and Gan had found out much more by enlisting
another sometimes-business partner, a computer specialist named
Steve Fisbeck, to help them research the site. The actual security
computers, like many of the systems inside the plant, were stand-alone
and therefore unreachable over the 'Net, but the strict accounting
documents Mmar insisted on were easily cracked into. The files in the

computer of DynaSynth's receiving department, when added to copies of the blueprints and the ramblings of a slightly drunk plant manager told the team of burglars everything they needed to know.

Brad led his four companions at a quick pace through the maze of brush and long grass. The plant was build on a swell of ground, over the battered ruins of a castle erected, according to local belief, by the Knight Templars. The foundation was the same, still capable of supporting several tons of steel machinery after a thousand years.

An added inducement to the plant's construction was the nearby river, from which the designers planned to siphon off enough water to cool the various grinding machines in use, piped in through the old moat bed. The new brick building above looked just as bleak as the castle probably had, squat yet looming on its extended knoll.

By the time they reached the river, the water level had dropped remarkably. The black-clad figure in the lead smiled again to himself as he began leaping from stone to stone towards the open drain on the other bank. Gan was a genius. Damming the water upstream just enough to expose the inlet tunnel had been his idea from the start.

Brush on the steep hill above shielded them from discovery due to an unscheduled pass by the guard, though Gan would have radioed a warning if that happened, or if the regular activities at the plant differed in any way from what they had observed over the past week.

Brad was certain his little band was in no danger from the motion detectors set outside the fence or from the two cameras sweeping the wide, manicured grounds.

That was another thing. The three brothers hadn't had any trouble finding the factory. DynaSyth had hired a local landscaping company out of Prague, and the finely-trimmed trees and perfect lawns stuck out as much in the scrubby, overgrown forest as the corpulent Roland Mmar had in that casino in Vegas. Brad and Li had spotted it in their first sweep over the timberland by helicopter nearly two weeks previous. The Southern Bohemian forest *was* four thousand square kilometers of trees and scrub, but DynaSynth was no needle in a haystack.

Brad paused at the tunnel's mouth and allowed one of the hired hands from Prague to lead the way. Paulos, the smart one, held a flat, narrow bar of instruments ahead of him as he walked, scanning for infrared or ultraviolet sensors. Ahead echoed the scraping, grinding hum of heavy machinery.

It wasn't a long walk in the dark, just a straight shot through to the open-ended filtration system. Unlike his companions, Brad could manage to stand completely upright and sidestep the shallow pools that had gathered here and there in depressions along the pipe's length. The cobblestones underfoot and overhead were smooth–a thousand-year flow.

Paulos already had the grate unhooked by the time the others reached the end. Brad took the lead now, stepping out into an open steel tank. The air was dusty, gray, dull against the blunt concrete walls. Several sealed bins were lined up against the wall of the long, narrow chamber, labeled in Czech. The room was empty but for the noisy filtration machinery at the far end. Three grimy doors led into the grinding area, where specific angles were abraded into the synthetic surface. The group walked past an open trough filled with black, frothy sludge and passed cautiously around a bend, into a wide storage area.

They were following the general L-shape of the building, moving away from the part of the building where Brad knew all the employees would be gathering before they left work. During his conversation with Mmar, he'd learned that all the plant workers had to submit to a physical security check before they were allowed to leave. Brad shook his head. What a fascist.

Another filthy door led them into the plant proper, though this area of the manufacturing floor was dark and as yet unused. Stacks of unopened equipment and crates of parts rose thirty feet to the roof. This part of the plant, at least, was clean. Each man wiped the soles of his feet with an absorbent cloth. Footprints wouldn't do, here. One of them stifled a cough, and Brad nearly did the same. The filtered air had a strange, slightly acrid taste, as artificial as the pale concrete wall around them.

With a wave from Brad, the men divided to their various assignments. Their primary goal lay directly ahead of them, up a flight of stairs to the engineering offices, but Brad was a firm believer in always having a plan B.

Having a plan B had gotten their family out of Tiananmen Square. Most of their family.

Brad slipped soundlessly down the side of the cavernous hallway towards the building's center, stopping underneath an open exhaust port for the ventilation system, some thirty feet from the gray double doors leading to the guardroom.

Eyes on the small rectangle of wired glass, Brad withdrew two small boxes and affixed them to the wall above an exit sign–another American affectation that provided an ample enough base to aim each at the door. Thank the heavens for small favors.

The first container was actually a minuscule camera and transmitter, barely the size of a sugar cube. Guess the Japanese were good for something, Brad thought for the thousandth time in his career. Gan's voice was a clear whisper in his ear. "I have the picture. Link the camera to the launcher."

The next box, about the size of a pack of cigarettes, went just above the camera. Brad carefully directed the battery-powered mini-launcher

117

towards the door, and extended the six exhaust barrels. Now, in the event of a security alert, his brother had the ability to ensure that the guards dashing out the door would be met by half-a-dozen screaming, exploding rockets.

Brad retraced his steps to the stairwell door. The anti-theft measures outside the factory walls were adequate; par for the course, at least–but the security within was ludicrous. Good thing Mmar was in charge. He almost wished he could send the man a thank-you note.

The fusebox and backup battery were under the stairs, exactly where the blueprints called for them. Underneath each Brad pressed a strip of Semtex, then gingerly attached two radio-controlled detonators between them. One should be enough, but even plan B called for a contingency. He paused for a moment to blot the perspiration from above his eyes. Ironic somehow that an American factory on Czech soil was in danger from a Chinese national using the Czech version of American C-4 plastic explosive.

And the French version of the FBI's electronic pick gun, he thought a minute later as he pressed the tip of the narrow, undersized pistol against the keyhole on the second floor. He pulled the trigger, and thin, narrow needles licked from the gun into the inner lock at over a dozen times a second. The door was open by the time Brad's companions joined him.

Quickly they fanned out into the carpeted space beyond, removing their flat backpacks as they did so. Wide windows on one side of the dim room admitted a tinted version of the gathering night, while identical panes on the other side looked down on the dim manufacturing floor. Besides the dozen monitors scattered around the room in various cubicles, the only real light came from a hallway opposite the stairs they'd just made use of.

This was the first job the three brothers had undertaken together in Europe, and they'd orchestrated it well. "Down to the last wave of the conductor's hand on the last train out of town," as a certain ersatz music professor would have said. Brad loved American musicals, and *The Music Man* was his favorite by far.

"We are in," Brad said to Gan over his lip-mounted microphone, then clenched his jaw at the sound of movement in a corner of the room.

Each of the men jerked involuntarily into a crouch, then froze. "Wait," Brad whispered over the line to his brother. No one moved, though Brad was itching toward the rubber grip of his weapon. He had a narrow, many-barreled concussion gun in a sheath on his pack, loaded to fire dozens of packets of mini-explosives designed to stun and disable.

Instead, Brad drew out a narrow aerosol cannister and removed the safety pin, then went motionless again at the unmistakable sound movement.

Thirty seconds ticked by. It seemed like nearly an hour to Brad, and he wondered if the other men felt the same. No one moved. They could have been mannequins, he decided, in some spy-fetish shop.

If whoever it was had been lying in wait for them, or were alerted somehow, they certainly would have made themselves known by now. Patience. Brad allowed another minute to ooze by, then crept toward irregular noise. He worked his way around several workstations, each monitor projecting a different, mindless screensaver. Good, they left their computers up and running all the time; that would make things easier. Assuming the men could deal decisively with whatever was making the noise that was grating across his nerves like sandpaper on Swiss cheese.

Squeak, pop-pop-pop. Squeak.

Metal coils–a chair? Brad leaned his head around a corner and saw the source. One of the guards leaned back in an office chair, his feet propped up on a desk, balanced by his head, resting against a file cabinet. As he watched, the man began to snore lightly, then shifted, eliciting another muted squeal from the chair's base.

The guard had fallen asleep despite the screensaver he'd sat to watch, which depicted several thong-clad women frolicking on a beach.

A less professional man would have been tempted to laugh. Instead, Brad crept closer, closer, until he was positioned right above the man's open mouth. As the guard inhaled, Brad leaned away and sprayed a tiny portion of the aerosol can's contents into his face.

The man tensed under the cold mist, one hand going to the baton at his belt, then immediately relaxed, sagging further into the chair's ample padding.

Brad stood up then, squeezing the tension out of the back of his neck with one hand. "Let's go, everyone."

One of the hired hands from Prague took up his position as lookout near the door and eyed the guard. "He is dead?" he asked in his thick English.

"No," Brad replied. "Just napping." He pantomimed sleep. According to his security badge the guard's name was Glevanik. Brad checked the list he'd brought, then nodded in satisfaction. The guard in question had begun his shift a short time ago; they had over an hour before he was scheduled to relieve another post. Plenty of time for the job, and just about enough time for the chemical to wear off and the man's sleep to return to normal. Brad replaced the safety pin on the aerosol can and returned it to the proper pocket. Nice to see the stuff really worked.

The guard was under the effects of a specialized version of ether. It was amazing the things one could synthesize out of common automotive chemicals.

As the other men were setting up, positioning themselves behind workstations in certain cubicles and removing their tools, Brad took a moment to look over Glevanik's equipment. Interesting that the guards outside carried guns, while the one's inside were armed with . . . 17-inch stun batons. Hmm. Take away their two 9-volt batteries and you'd even the playing field somewhat.

Brad sat behind a PC and spoke into his mike. "Gan, we are all set up and ready to go. Steve? You there?"

"Yeah, but I still don't know what I'm doing here." The voice in Brad's ear sounded thready and indistinct despite the digital connection. "You've got Jack's software in there with you. Is it working?"

"Shaking hands with the security system now."

"CastleBreaker should get you in and find whatever you're digging for," Steve said, around a mouthful of something. "I'm an unwilling accomplice here, remember."

Brad allowed himself a smirk as he inserted a flash drive and introduced it to the computer. For all his love of techno-gadgets, Steve Fisbeck would never trust his own digital encryption systems. Wouldn't implicate himself over a safe line. "You're here because you wrote the program, Steve; Jack just came up with the ideas." A command box came up on the screen, and Brad clicked on an option. "Besides, who knows if *he* will ever use this stuff again? Nobody's heard from Jack in months." It was as though their friend had fallen off the face of the earth. If something went wrong; if the program couldn't withdraw the proper files, Steve was just as good.

"Even so," the other man replied. "You know how mad Jack'll be if he ever finds out what we're doing with his program."

Brad drummed his gloved fingers lightly on the desk. That couldn't be helped. In the cubicle next to his, someone dropped a screw. Brad grimaced and suppressed an expletive. He supposed that also couldn't be helped. Even though the men had practiced this one task to distraction over the past few months, they were operating under tremendous pressure and working in near-total darkness. Couldn't be easy for anyone.

And when all was said and done, Brad's was the easier task. He grinned as a list of files appeared on the screen. CastleBreaker was an amazing program; rather, a cluster of programs. Brad didn't understand much of how the software worked; it was far too baroque for him.

But he would trust its creators with his life, and more, if it came to that.

"Ah, jackpot, Mr. Mmar." The computer Brad accessed contained a directory of all the projects the plant was working on–the actual information was broken up, encrypted, and spread throughout the other computers in the Research and Development office, for that is where the burglars were and whose computers they were cracking.

"This is good, this is good." He couldn't help rub his palms together as he began copying the directories and addresses for the information he sought. There were half-a-dozen good projects in the works at DynaSynth, but Brad only needed a quick look at each. He was taking them all, anyway.

R&D had recently developed a way to grow diamonds using laser technology–the focused light could map out and speed up the progress of crystal formation. With the information he was *at that very moment stealing* (and the thought rewarded him with a little thrill of adrenaline)–a similar company could build a machine that would manufacture jewel-quality diamonds for about five cents a karat. In a few years the prices for diamond applications would fall rather dramatically. Industry leaders like DeBeers and G.E. would feel it, though not before three brothers from China had a chance to cash in. Big.

Brad copied a few more files, pulling the designs for the nanotransistors used in the instrument that would fine-tune the direction of the laser. Amazing idea (he'd read about it in a *Popular Science* magazine), but still fairly crude. It was just too hard to engineer something measured in billionths of meters.

His friends from Prague were about halfway through their assignments, Brad judged. They worked fast, but still took time to double check the fittings on each of the computer casings when they were done. Brad had a few more minutes to himself. He took a sip from his water bottle and wondered which of the files before him he should partake of next.

Then he noticed that Castlebreaker was still running, still decoding. "Hey, Steve,"

"Yeah. You got it yet?"

Brad frowned. "I believe so, but the program is still working. How long does it usually take?"

Steve cleared his throat. This time he was chewing on something wet. "Well, Jack and I tested it on some NSA stuff at Fort Meade and it chomped through their light-to-medium security material in just over thirty seconds." He laughed. "You should have seen the look on their—"

Brad licked his lips before interrupting. "Has it ever taken more than five minutes?"

He waited.

When Steve spoke again, it was with his mouth empty. "What are you talking about? It gave you the files we're after, didn't it?"

"Yes, but it is still trying to decipher something. Could there be a problem?" Brad moved the mouse, and the pointer on the screen hovered over the command to cancel.

The response was immediate. "If it says it's still digging for something, then there's something buried under another encryption layer. Let it dig." Brad noted the odd note in the creator's voice. Steve had always been the nervous type, but had seemed fine earlier in the van, huddled over his laptop and bag of candy bars in the middle of the Bohemian forest.

While the other men worked feverishly away around him, Brad deliberated. It was an unusual activity for him in the middle of a job—usually he tried to clear his mind, practicing a meditation trick he'd learned as a child that kept his thoughts orderly, his pulse slow.

It wasn't working at the moment.

DynaSynth's R&D department had a state-of-the-art security system on a stand-alone network. They'd split up their sensitive files, probably assigning different files to engineers according to their individual speciality and contributions to the projects. All the files were physically present, so to speak, on the various hard drives in the room. Yet Castlebreaker had found something else, a file cached and coded so that its pieces were located within pieces of each of the other files.

Like a jigsaw puzzle made from fragments of the scattered pieces of a dozen other jigsaw puzzles.

Brad could feel a headache building behind his right eye.

The men were almost done with their tasks, maybe he should just–and then the screen before him changed, and Brad found himself staring at a single folder, headlined by a Czech word he was unfamiliar with. "Hey, Karel," he whispered to the guard near the door. "In your language what does 'hradek' mean?"

The other man never took his eyes from the hallway. "It is a small castle."

"Castle?" Brad tapped a few keys, connected a spare flash drive he'd brought along for this very contingency, and copied the entire file, more than a gigabyte's worth of space. While it was copying, he clicked open the first file and found himself looking at the detailed schematics for— some kind of building. Architectural blueprints, for something big and sophisticated.

After that came a shock: more notes on nanotransistors, but from what Brad could glean from the plans, these microscopic circuits were far more elegant and efficient that those he'd copied a few minutes before. At least a generation ahead of the other R&D material.

Brad wished he could have brought some kind of nano-electrician in with him, or even Steve. Fisbeck probably could have translated some of what he was seeing into terms that Brad could have understood–at least in terms of dollar value.

The next screen showed him the plans for a kind of fiber optic line, using–what?–some sort of synthetic diamond filament to conduct signals. Brad shook his head. Was that possible? Mentally he went down the list of possible buyers for this odd tidbit of technology, then found himself wondering. Brad certainly was no engineer, but what on earth did high-density fiber optics have to do with plans for . . . a castle?

Time to go. Brad backed CastleBreaker out of the system, allowing the pirating program to clean up after itself and remove all the evidence of its incursion. By the time he pocketed his flash drives, the monitor had already returned to its screenshots of mountain lakes and wildlife.

His companions made a quick sweep of the room, returning chairs to their original angles and running the heads of small, silent vacuums across seats and carpets they'd touched. The breath of the guard bore no trace of the foul-smelling residue usually left by the ether.

Brad was the last to exit the room, re-engaging the lock as he did so. Swiftly the men backtracked through the plant, retrieving the plastic explosives and other gadgets they'd positioned earlier.

Across from the guardroom, Brad pulled his gadgets from the wall, frowning at the slight, pale smudge left by the resin he'd used to affix the mini-launcher. Have to remember to fix that, he thought.

The door at the terminus of the hallway opened suddenly, and Brad leaped straight up into the shadowy maw of the air shaft, gritting his teeth as he dragged himself upward with his arms. Bracing himself upside-down with his feet, the young man locked his elbows and arched his back until he was looking overhead at the ground below.

Two uniformed watchmen strode by below, their hard soles tap-tapping against the cold concrete. Given a spare hand, Brad could have reached down and snatched a hat as they passed. Instead, he worked his neck and flexed his legs to offset the rush of blood that was threatening to make him pass out.

When the footsteps had fully faded, Brad took a deep breath and pushed off with his feet, turning and twisting as he fell, then cursing the noisy slap his feet made on the smooth floor. Too close.

The evening shift was starting up at the plant, and twice Brad had to conceal himself, fitting into unlikely wedges of shadow while precious seconds ticked past. By the time he reached the filter inlet, the other men had all gone but for Paulos, who snapped the grill back into place as soon as his employer passed. Brad slapped the larger man on the back before jogging up the tunnel towards the river, where the other men waited.

They lingered on the bank for another three minutes, hunkering in the mouth of the moat shaft while a guard wandered by not five meters above them.

Finally, Gan's voice sounded the all-clear in each of their ears, and they retreated back over the crumbling wall. Each of the Czechs wore a broad smile as they ran through the trees, their backs to the factory.

It wasn't until they reached a dirt road on the other side of the hill and piled into the dark, unmarked van that Brad allowed himself to relax.

Hradek, whatever it was, stood to be electrical somehow. He'd have to talk to Gan about consulting an engineer before deciding if they could salvage anything from the plans. A fiber optic line made from flexible, synthesized diamond? It sounded too bizarre. The nanotechnology involved in making high-density cabling on the diagrams he'd seen was light years beyond anything that DynaSynth could do, judging from the other projects they'd stolen.

The van grumbled to life and began moving down the dirt road. At the rear of the open van, Brad's youngest brother Li turned the valve on a fifty-gallon tank, then directed a high-pressure stream of water and air back and forth onto the ground behind them. The tracks of the van were obliterated under the heavy stream.

No chances. No trace.

One by one the men removed their gear and handed their backpacks over to Steve. The portly American took each in turn, gently slotting them in a foam rubber storage bin. As the lock clicked on the trunk, each man breathed an individual sigh of relief. Someone laughed, and Paulos flipped open a small cooler filled with Becherovka beer. Later, there would be plum brandy.

As the men began to unwind and recount their adventure, comparing the theft with some of their other exploits, real or otherwise, Brad leaned back against the cool metal wall and forced himself to relax. "Who's got my hat?" Someone handed him his Stetson. They still had a considerable amount of work before them, and hours before he could truly rest.

Each backpack contained three hard drives taken from DynaSynth's R&D department. Actually taking the hard drives was quicker than copying all the information to another drive, and besides, there were myriad security programs that made copying impractical–the most common of which caused some part of the program to be copied incorrectly, thus rendering the entire file incomprehensible.

Since procurement records were kept on the company's worldwide network, the brothers (with Steve's help) had spent only an hour the previous month going through DynaSynth's Material Receiving notes. They learned the vendor, the size of each hard drive, even the serial numbers etched on the individual mechanisms within each drive. Again, Brad had to thank the single admirable trait of his good friend Roland Mmar: obsessive recordkeeping.

Obtaining exact copies of each hard drive and training the men in a little "aggressive maintenance" had been relatively easy. Now, when the engineers at DynaSynth attempted to access their information, they would universally get an unpleasant message–the disks functioned perfectly well but were empty, and the computer would register any request for information as an error. Heh.

Initial bafflement would give way to casting blame within the department as quickly as possible, then most would shrug and access the backup information. Everything they worked on was stored weekly at the plant's mirror location in central Utah, anyway. Brad grinned. With just a bit of luck, the plant manager would try to muffle the report to his superiors, or downplay it at the very least. From the fat man's mumblings in Nevada, Brad gathered that Mmar had a basic distrust of technology, and was loath to claim responsibility for anything he couldn't understand. His transfer to the Czech plant was in part an opportunity to redeem himself for some past error–Brad supposed that Mmar had ignored the chance to take advantage of some new technology while employed as the manager of the Utah factory, and as a result the company had lost ground. The marketplace for synthetic diamonds was quietly vicious, he had learned.

Brad sniffed, picturing the watery-eyed, cherubic face. So many shortcomings in security. Distrust of technology. Intellectually, Mmar traveled in a covered wagon while everyone subordinate to him drove Porsches. In his arrogance, the man painted himself as a target.

That made something Darwinian about the whole heist.

But Brad was too fatigued to pursue the thought. Fifteen minutes of rest, and then he, his brothers, and Steve would be in a helicopter flying up the Jihlava river and then across the Austrian border. By the time the darkness had gathered itself into true night, they would be in Vienna, calling buyers for the information they'd taken, and Steve could figure out how to make money off Hradek, whatever that was—all those blueprints . . .

Brad slipped off to sleep, his mind's eye overshadowed by mortar ramparts and the statuary of some vast, menacing fortress, topped by a fluttering scarlet flag.

The Gentle Ogre

Central Germany

Solomon Keyes quietly closed the door of the private office adjoining his classroom, his thick, dark hands shaking slightly. Of the four English teachers on the high school staff of Wiesbaden Air Base, he alone had been given a personal room–albeit minuscule, considering his physical size—to use as an office. A few members of the faculty had been surprised at this indulgence, and attributed his special treatment to the fact that the enormous man was a minority: his features spoke thickly of South Pacific Islander-African American heritage. Others said the man had recently been in some branch of the service himself. The wildest rumor placed him as a sniper, whose quiet assignment to the American base, home of the 221st BSB, in the middle of Germany nearly two years previous had been a reward of sorts for a black operation that had gone particularly well. Truth of the matter was, he *did* spend an inordinate amount of time on the base's shooting range, and sometimes left the base with little warning and often as not in the middle of the night. Odd for a full-time teacher, and often problematic for the principal who had to cover the classes, but no one thought to press Solomon for clues as to his disappearance.

He was such a nice man.

Solomon Keyes was overpoweringly gentle. Despite his formidable appearance, children took to the great dark slab of a man, instinctively trusting to his strength and kindly, crinkled face. Adults who knew

Solomon found him quietly opinionated but never overbearing; articulate but never verbose. He was the kind of person who radiated a tremendous intellect and physical power but none of the arrogance so common to men graced with such presence. Besides, how do you label a man whose tastes in clothing included bright bowties and fresh carnations in his buttonhole? Dapper would not be too strong a word.

Those also stationed at Wiesbaden would have been surprised to see Solomon's mahogany hands, gnarled wedges of sinew, trembling faintly as he turned to face his classroom. The single student, slouched at his desk near the back and closest to the window, hardly glanced up from his book.

Solomon opened his briefcase and returned the thin computer to its pocket in the lining. A garment bag he kept ready at his small house contained everything he'd need for a three- or four-day jaunt to who-knew-where. Paris, first of all. He curled one hand into a blocky fist.

He knew he was not a handsome man. Even as a child growing up in American Samoa, Solomon had been large and unwieldy, as if the competing bloodlines of his ancestors were vying for superiority within him. Adults had been mistaken about his age since just after his twelfth birthday, when his family had emigrated to Hawaii. "Angry spirits fight inside you, make you grow too big," his grandmother said. Though she'd fallen in love with an American serviceman with skin as dark as her own, his grandmother had never approved of her son marrying a Tongan woman. Samoan son and a daughter of Tonga? The old woman spent as much time clicking her teeth in disapproval as she did fussing over Solomon and his brothers and sisters.

One last thing to tie up before he left.

The young man drooped over his textbook sighed noisily and slapped his book shut. "This is a waste of time," he said. He was a study in slovenliness. Everything about him, from the angle of his baseball cap to the slack lines of his shoelaces, showed a careful, studied, purposeful sloppiness. His t-shirt proclaimed the slogan: Pave the Planet. "Why're you making me read this?" His eyes roamed the room as he addressed Solomon. "Nothing but garbage, anyway."

"You really think so, Carl?" Solomon closed his briefcase and sat on the edge of his desk. It groaned underneath him.

"Yeah, I do." It was as close as Carl would get to challenging the massive Mr. Keyes. Solomon knew this young man had problems with authority, a record of minor offenses–pointless, half-hearted vandalism, firecrackers in the toilets (did anybody really do that anymore?) at the other bases his father had been assigned; that sort of thing. According to Carl Marcussen's school file, previous administrators were concerned that the boy's lack of a mother might lead to overaggression and self-destructive behavior.

When they had arrived at the base four months ago, both Carl and his father processed through the Army's F.L.A.G. (Families Learning About Germany) program, spending two days learning about their new surroundings, including attending Wiesbaden's fabled "Great Start" Welcoming Forum. Nothing had eased Carl's abrasiveness or his adjustment to the new surroundings, and the coordinator over the base's Relocation Assistance Program had approached Solomon personally, warning him about the boy's excoriating personality. According to his file, Carl had been forced to see four Army psychiatrists. Each had taken note of his hostility and "resistance to conform to the therapeutic process." Solomon thanked God the boy seemed to like English. Books often served as a way out for children. Adults, too–though Carl seemed to be lodged somewhere between child and adult. Somewhere painful.

"I don't see why I gotta read this stuff. You don't make anybody else. This is a book for college students."

"You understand it well enough though, don't you?"

"Of course." He seemed annoyed by the implication that he might not.

"Good, then you can humor me for a few moments. I'm going away for a few days and I wanted to share something with you before I left. Open your book. Back to page 729."

"This is nothing. Who the hell is Gerard Manley Hopkins, anyway? Depressing. You trying to drag me down, man? My dad say's you're a spy or a killer or something. You a wet boy once upon a time?"

"Page 729, Mr. Marcussen."

Solomon stood and took a few thoughtful steps before the windows. In the distance, sunlight sheeted greenly off the Taunus Mountains.

"Read the first part, out loud."

The young man sighed noisily again, then began. Even considering his professed distaste, he read with vigor and unconscious passion.

"'*The world is charged with the grandeur of God.*

It will flame out, like shining from shook foil;

It gathers to a greatness, like the ooze of oil

Crushed. Why do men then now not reck his rod?

Generations have trod, have trod, have trod;

And all is seared with trade; bleared, smeared with toil;

And wears man's smudge and shares man's smell: the soil

Is bare now, nor can foot feel, being shod.'" He paused. "'Reck his rod?'"

Solomon did not turn from the window. "To obey, Mr. Marcussen. To obey the commandments of God. What do you see in the poem?"

"I see words, old guy."

Solomon's expression changed not a whit. "What do the words mean? To you?"

"Well, the dude who wrote this uses parallel alliteration and assonance in line four, when he says, 'Why do men then now not reck his rod?'"

"Very good. What's the poem about?"

A long pause. "With all the generations of men, I guess with all the people on the earth, everything is covered by our trash. There's no more beauty, at least that anybody can appreciate. 'Nor can foot feel, being shod.' The whole human race is numb. I guess we can't feel anything anymore. "

"Good guess. I suppose that's exactly what the author meant to say." Solomon eased his bulk into a nearby desk.

The boy was quiet, looking intently at the page. Gerard Manley Hopkins had taken hold. "This is true, Mr. Keyes." He sounded surprised. "The world really does suck."

"Go on and read me the last portion."

The boy's voice was even more hushed as he read.

"And for all this, nature is never spent;
There lives the dearest freshness deep down in things;
And though the last lights off the black West went
Oh, morning, at the brown brink eastward, springs—
Because the Holy Ghost over the bent
World broods with warm breast and with ah! bright wings."

Now the pause lasted even longer. "I don't get the part about a warm breast and bright wings. What's that mean?"

"The Holy Ghost is sometimes symbolized by a dove. For some religions, the Holy Spirit Himself, in turn, is a manifestation and symbol of God's love and grace extended toward us."

"You believe in this stuff?"

Solomon smiled. "I'm a Baptist, boy. 'There are more things in heaven and earth, Horatio—'"

"'–than are found in your philosophy.'" The boy smiled, a completely unselfconscious expression. "But this guy says that evil, darkness, and sin, like, cover the world, bury all the good stuff."

Solomon nodded. "He also says that despite the numbing drudgery of evil, we still have reason for hope. The longer you live, Carl, the more you'll see what Hopkins means." He leaned close, hurrying before the boy had a chance to shut himself off again. "You've had a rough life, son." He swallowed. "Mother gone; your father away much of the time; always moving around just because he's on the fast track; hard to make friends.

"To be honest with you, considering your high intelligence, your grades, and your chosen attitude, the statistics point you in one of two ways."

The boy appeared curious, a response new to Solomon, and he continued. "In ten years you will either be serving hard time in a prison, incarcerated for committing a felony—a failure. Or tremendously successful in whatever field you choose to pursue. You have the drive and the charisma, but your wise-ass, tough guy act prevents everyone from getting to know who you really are, including yourself.

"Keep your eyes open, and you'll see that however horrible, however terrifying the *bad* in your life can become, it is nothing more than a layer over a core of essential good. Evil wins some big battles, son, maybe most—but it never wins the war. That's a fact that exists separately from you and me, Carl. You'll see it when you've lived long enough; the goodness in the world triumphs."

Carl Marcussen blinked rapidly, looking away from his teacher. Solomon could see thoughts piling up like bright clouds behind the boy's eyes. "Stay here as long as you like, son. No one is scheduled to use this room for the rest of the night." He stood. The tremors had left his hands. They would not return for the duration of whatever mission lay ahead. "I'll check back with you when I can."

Solomon sighed inwardly. He knew he hadn't solved all the boy's problems, or even treated the sad symptoms of the heartache which kept him alone. But a chink in the armor? Perhaps.

Carl pulled his baseball cap around to a more conventional angle and straightened the book before him. "Hey, Mr. Keyes."

"Yes?"

"You going to do some more secret spy stuff? Blow up some exotic doomsday device and save the world?" The boy smiled.

Solomon returned the expression. Instead of answering immediately, he said, "Did you really flush a cherry bomb down the toilet when your father was assigned to Fort Stewart?"

His grin widened. "I sure did."

"Where did you get it?"

"I made it myself."

Solomon laughed, a rich baritone. "Good for you. And Carl, don't kid yourself. All those doomsday devices are never that exotic." He closed the door, leaving Hopkins' poem open beneath his student's eyes.

The Artful Woodsman

Chicago, Illinois
4PM

Ambrose Delgado touched his flawless hair furtively and stepped through the doorway to the staccato strobelights of the Chicago press. Overcast afternoon; the background lighting would be just about sinister enough.

Beautiful.

Twelve years on the force had blessed him with being on a first-name basis with several of the reporters now waiting to greet him below the steps that led up to the old brownstone. As he exited the apartment he managed to turn his head *just so* in time to furnish a pensive profile shot for the popping flashbulbs. Ah, yes. They'd been good to him ever since he made detective.

Delgado loved the press. He was especially good friends with two of the journalists he saw–Browning and Edelblute from the Sun-Times and Tribune, respectively— in the clamoring crowd that awaited him outside the old building. Work this right and his picture would be all over the front of the Sun-Times tomorrow. He even had a prop–the blood-soaked T-shirt the killer had been wearing now clenched tightly—vindictively, some might say—in Ambrose's fist. He didn"t want to get any of the man's filth on his silk suit.

Pity only one camera crew had arrived so far. The news of the capture of Hubert Caulfield was still breaking, though. There would be more newsmen by and by, and at least two more television crews, then Ambrose would be invited to appear on the local NBC affiliate; perhaps even be offered the coveted position of violent crimes consultant for the network. It was about time. About time he got his due.

The crowd parted slightly, and Ambrose halted on the lowest step, raising his palms against the clamor. As it lessened he smiled patiently, timing the flashbulbs. "Hubert James Caulfield was taken into custody at 5:45 p.m. with no loss of life." He paused, raising his hand and allowing the foul rag he held to unfurl. "He won't be stalking any more residents of the Windy City."

Though most in the crowd were seasoned reporters of one magnitude or another, a hearty cheer went up at the sight of the bloody cloth. Ambrose shook it once for effect, then slipped into his gravest expression as the first question was asked.

"Can you describe the raid, Mr. Delgado?"

Ambrose took on a more serious mien even though inside he was nearly giddy with pleasure. They knew his name! "Certainly, gentlemen. I found several forty-five caliber handguns and more than two hundred rounds of ammunition on the coffee table in Caulfied's room. Since Caulfield is a proven sharpshooter, it was touch and go from the moment we entered the building. He'd also booby-trapped the entrance to his apartment."

"If you call tin cans and baling wire a booby trap." The newcomer, a stout, hard man in jeans and a plaid chambray shirt, had just exited the building. His eyes were bright behind gold-rimmed glasses, and in his boots he looked as though he'd recently hiked down out of the woods somewhere. In sharp contrast to Delgado's dapper appearance, the new man seemed steadier, made smooth by much use like a rock in a riverbed. He was also obviously near exhaustion despite his glaring eyes; several days' worth of beard overlaid his moustache.

Instantly, the spotlight shifted. "Can you explain that further, sir? Would you describe Hubert James Caulfield as a loner? Mr. . . ."

"I'd have to say Caulfield is more of a loser, actually. Please, no pictures," he said to a photographer.

Edelblute from the Tribune shouted from the front. "What about the weapons? Did he put up a struggle?"

"No, we found him hiding under his bed, wrapped in a Star Wars bedsheet." A murmur of laughter ran through the assembled reporters. One near the rear raised his hand.

"So you don't see him capable of succeeding in the assassinations he threatened?"

He plucked at his new beard. "I doubt it, honestly. He's never succeeded at anything else." More laughter.

"Sir!" It was Edelblute, again. "How is the suspect being held at this time? What sort of security precautions are—"

The bearded man laughed right back at them. "Right now, Caulfield is handcuffed to a rusty pipe in the alley out back. He's being watched by a single guard, Officer Nebecker." His eyes were gleaming with suppressed mirth as he looked across at Delgado. "*Maureen* Nebecker."

Ambrose flushed. It wouldn't take the newsboys long to find out Nebecker was the smallest, frailest-looking officer in the city.

"Now, if you gentlemen and ladies will permit me," the newcomer continued., "I'd like to speak off the record for just a moment." He waited until cameras were lowered and pencils slowed. When he had their attention, the bearded man took a deep breath and spoke.

"Hubert Caulfield, as you all know, stalked half-a-dozen media figures in California and here in Illinois before he shot out the windows of the mayor's car two days ago. No doubt each of you are going to go back to your desks tonight and write about the 'meticulous plans' he made and carried out, or maybe take shots of him being escorted away tonight by federal officers, or," here he gestured to the cameramen, "get footage of the helicopter coming to pick him up. It'll make for some great reporting, that's for sure; but would-be assassins provide great material, isn't that right? And you can say whatever you want. Hell, it's not like Caulfield's going to sue you, is it?"

He waited while the scattered laughter trailed off. "What's your point, sir?" asked a junior newspaperman from the Tribune.

"Point is, that's what Caulfield's been after all along, just like ninety-six percent of the losers who try what he did," the bearded man shot back. "His fifteen seconds or whatever in the spotlight. Just like anybody, he wants recognition, acknowledgment–even if he can't get acceptance.

"He wouldn't articulate it in those words, but that's been his core motivation all along, ever since he saw Hinckley take his shots at Reagan back in the 80's. You make that video showing Caulfield, the criminal mastermind, you're making a commercial for assassination and half-a-dozen other major crimes." He poked a thumb back towards the building. "The 'meticulous plans' you'll write about included Caulfield amassing a library of media stories about murderers. He's got notes galore on all the hoopla that television and newspapers kick up whenever some nutcase does what he tried to do. He's got your name, Bob," here he pointed at a local television reporter, "on his telephone's auto-dial.

"Think, for a minute, about what you folks do that encourages behavior like Caulfield's. A friend of mine once told me the media actually encourages domestic terrorism, the sort of thing Caulfield and people like him try to do." He paused, as if gauging his audience. They were actually listening.

Ambrose Delgado never would have said anything like this.

"Terrorism is a crime, consisting of an intentional act of political violence specifically designed to create an atmosphere of fear. Acts of terrorism are premeditated by their perpetrators and are conspiratorial in nature. Terrorists conspire their acts of terror to generate fear. Even if fear isn't the main purpose of the terrorist, our society is often completely consumed by it.

"It is our responsibility to secure society from this threat, from attacks against our faith in society. From attacks against our morality. Too much fear and doubt can cripple us."

One of the reporters started to object, but he continued. "All I'm saying is, think twice about how you're going to present this man. Don't glorify him, if you can help it."

Bob Browning nodded curtly, then scowled. "But the first amendment—"

"The first amendment doesn't provide for putting the Unabomber's face on the front of Time, Newsweek–twice—and U.S. News and World Report, then describing him in each of the cover texts as a 'genius.'" The man on the steps was near exhaustion but spoke evenly and with an air of good-natured reason. "Why is it, Bob, that regular guys get to be known by their full name only when they've somehow qualified themselves as someone to be feared? That's an invention of the media. Assassins never use their triple names in their pre-attack lives. Mark Chapman, Lee Oswald, John Booth? Doesn't sound so intimidating, does it? Doesn't sound nearly as powerful." He sighed, and seemed to collapse in upon himself somewhat. "Just a suggestion, folks. You never know when lightning will strike. Don't feed the latent ambitions of those out there who might, one day, point a gun at your head. Or your husband's or wife's." The crowd before him was silent. He turned to go.

"Sir, what do you suggest we call him, then?"

The man in the rumpled chambray shirt made as if to shrug, then smirked. "Hubert Caulfield was called 'Screwie Huey' in high school. Good luck with that one."

*

Ian Whitaker reentered into the brownstone, gently pressing his temples. Let that nozzle Delgado have his moment now that he'd at least made an attempt to deflect the press. It was one of two things he disliked about his profile work for the Bureau: the fact that many of the criminals he met were sustained, even nourished by the media as much as they fed off their victim's fear.

And Ian got the opportunity to ride along with them, a passenger on their often twisted, much-tangled trains of thought. Getting into their minds was what he'd been trained to do, what he was good at. As a watcher, however, as someone who predicted what would happen next, Ian was often just hours too late to prevent the crimes he envisioned through the mind's eye of the killers.

That fact was the second thing he hated about his job. You couldn't save everybody; hell, you'd be lucky to save yourself. Ian knew his own psyche well enough to say he didn't have a hero complex, but even still. He should have been able to do more.

Everybody wants to make a difference.

He met briefly with the head of the SWAT team that had taken point earlier in the evening, then placed a call to his superior in Washington. "Agent Whitaker!" Martin Schlass' voice was a cheery rasp over the connection. "Good work on the Caulfield wrap up. Just about to call you; listen, boy. After all this mess you deserve some time off, and you'll get it, with pay, but—"

"But?" Ian couldn't believe his ears.

"I just got a notice from the Director himself. Remember the unique instructions you used to get from time to time?"

"Yes sir, of course." What was this? He hadn't operated under the special directive for nearly a year yet, not since Victoria—

By the sound of his voice, Martin Schlass was intensely curious. "You timed the ending of the Caulfield case just right, Whitaker. All I'm supposed to tell you is, get on the internet as soon as you can. You're authorized, of course, to take as much time away from your regular duties as you'll need. Looks like I'll have to wait for your report on Caulfield. Just like before, this comes all the way from the top, far as I can tell."

Ian knew what thoughts chased themselves 'round in Schlass' head. Hah. The curiosity is killing him. "Yes, sir."

"You'll tell me all about this someday, won't you, boy?"

"As much as I can, sir."

"Right, then. I'm going to dinner. Whatever it is, take care of yourself, Ian."

The line went dead.

Ian rested his head against the dingy red wall. He had the option of refusing the assignment, of course. He'd never done so before, but then again, he hadn't been married then, either. After a whole year? Hmm. He'd warned Rachel this day might come. Schlass had already approved vacation with pay afterward, and–but what was this? Was he actually talking himself into it?

Whitaker punched a new combination of numbers into the phone he held.

"Hello?" The voice of an angel on the other end of the line.

He explained the situation, and felt a thin pang of regret. She was disappointed. "Well, Ian. We planned for this, just in case, didn't we? I'll have your bag packed—a week?"

"Sweetheart, I don't even know yet where I'll be going, and Jack always gives us a couple hours to get ready." There would already be tickets for him at the airport. "I'm at the corner of Bryn Mawr and Wayne Avenue right now; there's an I-net café down on North Clark. I'll know more then, after I get online. I'll be home in an hour."

Rachel exhaled. "My husband the spy." Even over the phone he could tell she was smiling. "I-net, huh? Bring me back some of their garlic chicken pizza."

They lingered over the phone a few minutes more, and by the time he'd hung up, Ian felt rejuvenated. It amazed him how rested he felt, after just a few moments of verbal contact with his wife. They complimented each other so well. That instant's recuperation was one of the many fringe benefits of marriage he'd never suspected as a bachelor.

Her face still filled his imagination as he drove to the internet café. WXLC blared on the radio, drowning out the gush of air from the heating vents with a diatribe against the Cubs. Chicago was experiencing an unseasonably cold spring. Maybe he'd be sent someplace warm this time, someplace tropical. Maybe for a change he wouldn't have to blow anything up, and he and Rachel–

Quit dreaming, he told himself, pulling the wheel around onto North Clark. Jack needed him.

Ian paid the $5.00 fee for an hour on the 'Net, though he wouldn't be on for more than half that. He took a console with his back to the candy-apple red wall and logged in. The screen filled with the deep, patterned blue that had always preceded a coded transmission, and it finally seemed real. Ian took another deep breath. Jack needed him again. He grinned in anticipation.

A chance to make a difference. Something he was really good at.

The Apprentice Magician

Vienna, Austria
11PM

Steve rubbed his eyes and reached across the table, brushing aside a tangle of cables for his bag of Snickers. Better make these last. Expensive in this part of Europe.

He peeled the brown wrapper back as he returned to his monitor, part of three full-sized systems arranged around him. The hotel had prepared the room exactly to his specifications, setting two executive-sized desks together in an L-shape and providing multiple 'Net connections. A bag of Snickers had even greeted Steve upon his arrival, no doubt according to long-standing instructions from Jack Flynn or Alonzo Noel.

Which both amused and intrigued the engineer. Jack's team hadn't used the Ana Grand Hotel Wien as a base of operations for—oh, it must be sixteen months, yet when Steve phoned in reservations using the credit card and corresponding alias set up for him a year and a half ago, the staff had responded with breathless efficiency. What a facility. Oriental carpets, a grand staircase, and brass enclosed elevators. Steve liked the 24-hour restaurant the best, though the chef's bratwurst and angel-flake streusel always made him feel a little guilty he never used the free health club.

Everything he needed had been laid out upon his arrival–twenty minutes after opening the first sealed case, Steve's entire system was humming away, not only plugged into the 'Net and local police and news networks, but the building's internal security system as well. His eyes and ears.

Steve had long ago admitted to himself that he was a bit of an introvert. Seven years at MIT hadn't erased the closet hacker or the recent escapee from a solitary adolescence. Even at his job with the NSA Steve generally found it difficult to make friends, until Jack Flynn and Alonzo Noel.

*

Southwestern Yemen

Steve stood in the open doorway, nearly dropping his computer in fright as the two light-haired men, guns drawn, wheeled on him. The smaller one, jagged with fatigue, snarled something in Russian and shoved the barrel of his pistol neatly around Steve's Adam's apple.

The other man intervened, whispering back in the same language, then, "Hold off, Al; he's not with security." The speaker's face also showed the marks of exhaustion, but his actions were quick, his eyes curious.

Steve found his tongue. "I've been watching you. Mr. Noel and Mr. Flynn. Ah, I'm with the Agency–NSA. I can't believe I actually found you."

The shorter man jerked his pistol away, then looked both directions down the passageway. "How the hell—"

"You guys leave an electronic trail a mile wide!" Steve smacked his lips, then jumped on with the rest of the speech he'd memorized on the plane from Maryland. "You're like ghosts when you're in the middle of an operation, but the minute you use an ATM–bam!"

"We caught part of the message you encrypted and sent from Beijing about five months ago, right before somebody snatched the Prime

146

Minister." *Their eyes widening, he continued. "Nobody believed you guys were doing all that stuff and you weren't with any agency. Just out there on your own!" He knew his enthusiasm was evident, but he didn't care. "The top brass told us to keep you secret, but, I mean, how the hell do you classify something when it isn't even a part of the U.S. government, any government?*

"So I was assigned to watch you, keep the file. The last couple months, I think I know about it all. The French Air Force guy you got out of Tehran, the hostages in Belfast, even the drug lords you scared out of Cuba. Yesterday I read a scanned copy of the thank-you note sent to the U.S. president by Castro's successor, Espinosa himself."

Now came the hard part. "You guys are good, probably the best freelancers in the business, but you need somebody on the electronic end." Time to drop the other shoe.

"Somebody like me."

The explosive Mr. Noel raised his pistol, but was again waved down by his larger companion. "Wait a sec. You've been watching us. How'd you get this far inside the installation?"

Steve patted his computer. "I've got the blueprints for the whole place right here. Hooked into the security cameras by remote. And," he hesitated. "I've always been pretty good at staying away from people."

The smaller man grudgingly nodded. "And you can show us where the mullah keeps his bio-weapons vault, can't you?" he completed.

His companion spoke. "Get us there and we'll talk about what comes next." His gun switched hands. "I'm Jack, this is Alonzo."

*

This is Alonzo. It had been Alonzo eighteen months ago who set up Steve's credit cards and alias in Vienna, and no doubt left standing instructions to keep a bag of candy bars on hand. Much like Flynn himself, Alonzo had proved to be a resourceful ally and a good friend. They'd had some interesting times.

Too bad neither was around to help with the present puzzle.

Two of his monitors were filled by the schematics from the extra files Brad had discovered. The programmer had been very clever, Steve noted, masking such a vast amount of information behind and within layers of extraneous material–other projects, personal emails within the company, somebody's score on an old Duke Nukem game. Piecing everything together out of it all had turned into the computerized equivalent of rummaging through a bin of red herring. Looking for a pink herring.

Steve rubbed his eyes. Again with the fish metaphors. He really needed some sleep.

But the schematics before him all added up to something, didn't they? These new, high-density fiber optic lines, well, no telling how much information they could transmit in the form of light energy. But why hard-wire so many of them into the structure of a building, big as it was?

Ah, well, he'd figure out what the castle-thing was supposed to be later, after a good night's rest. Those high-density lines, though . . . Steve pounded the heel of his hand heavily against the edge of the desk. He was so close.

10:48 p.m. in Vienna–almost quitting time on the east coast of the U.S. Steve instructed his computer to dial a phone number and adjusted the microphone on his headset. The line rang twice.

"Hello, this is Doug Gale." The voice was clipped, efficient. Bureaucratic to the hilt.

Steve cleared his throat. "Hello Dr. Gale, this is Steve Fisbeck."

Pause. "Steve! How are you? Anything you need?" Of all his instructors at MIT, Doug Gale had been the one who'd imparted the most to Steve. A practical man as well as a tireless promoter of his students, Gale had been the first to recommend the young, bashful programmer to the National Security Agency recruiters.

"Actually, I'm working through something right now I thought you'd be interested in."

Silence, followed by a short laugh. "You're stuck, aren't you?" Gale chuckled. "My security clearance expired with the last President, Steve; I'm afraid I can't help you hack anything more complex than the ingredients in a candy bar. Or have you conquered that particular addition?" For several years Gale had worked at Lincoln Laboratory, the off-campus facility where MIT sent all its classified work.

"Oh, no sir, this doesn't have anything to do with work. I've sort of stumbled onto a design for a high-density kind of cable . . ."

Steve went on for several minutes, picturing his teacher nodding and bobbing back and forth over his desk in that cubbyhole of an office back in the States. Thanks to Steve's status at the NSA, Gale wouldn't think twice about divulging information to his former student.

"I see," said Gale presently. "Could you describe the chips set along the cable at intervals, again? Small, you said."

Steve did so. "I could email the file, if you'd like."

That caught the old man by surprise. "That would be best, my boy. Give me a chance to look at it here, perhaps pass a few of the ideas on to a few of the other members of the faculty. We're publishing a few papers on nanotechnology, but nothing like what you just described to me. Good heavens."

Gale's tone lightened. "Come to think of it, old Charlie Townes might get a kick out of this."

Charles Townes had been appointed provost and professor of physics at MIT back during Gale's graduate studies. The man could walk on water, at least that was the conclusion Steve had drawn after several hours' worth of Dr. Gale's anecdotes and tangents during class. Townes' pinnacle contribution to the world had been the invention of the maser, a device that amplified electromagnetic waves and created a means for the sensitive reception of communications and for precise navigation. Gale clicked his tongue and continued.

"I could be wrong, but it sounds like you've unearthed a device for transmitting, if not outright controlling, energy on a molecular level. NMR technology."

This wasn't what Steve expected. "How's that again?"

"Solid state nuclear magnetic resonance. Electromagnetic radiation. Tell you what," Papers shuffled on a desk thousands of miles away. "I've got a friend, a colleague actually, in California. Working on much the same thing. Mitchell Fenn, a good man. Examines synthetic fuels, that sort." More paper shuffling. "He's attached to the Intercampus Institute for the Research of Particle Acceleration. This is right up his alley. Let me give you his number."

Steve copied it down. "Thanks, Dr. Gale. I'll email you what I've got here."

"Splendid. Now I really must be off, Steve. Damn faculty meeting in a few minutes. Wouldn't think of starting without me. You'll be stopping in the next time your in Boston?"

Steve smiled. A few more pleasantries, and both men hung up. He pushed himself back from the desk and knotted his fingers against the base of his neck, almost surprised to find himself back in his Austrian hotel room. He rubbed his eyes, and yawned, then stopped short. Magnetic resonance. Controlling electrons–electricity, *lightning*–on a molecular level.

What had he found? What was the application of this technology?

One thing was for sure: this was light years beyond anything *anybody* at DynaSynth could have in their pocket. This was way beyond them.

—or above? What was the parent company, the conglomerate that had bought out DynaSynth stock a year previous? Raines Dynamic.

Raines Dynamic. Not so much a consortium as a benevolent dictatorship, a development firm with heavy—though vague—interests in research and application of new technology. Steve looked once again at the dizzying field of blueprints.

Could they be—

Steve laughed out loud and rubbed his eyes again. "Watching too many X-files reruns, Stevie," he said, imitating the Australian accent that Jack had done so well. He spun in his chair toward the bedroom and stood.

Abruptly his three computer screens blazed a too-bright blue, then filled with a pattern of algorithms that were alarmingly familiar. Steve jumped and started away from the desk, his first reaction sheer disbelief, then trepidation.

Jack?

Steve reached for a chocolate bar, fumbled with the wrapper. Had his vanished friend discovered their illicit use of CastleBreaker?

Steve dropped the candy bar and grabbed his notepad as a coded transmission swam up out of the morass of letters and digits on the screen. A minute later, he was grinning and punching up numbers on his phone.

At last.

"Brad? This is Steve. No, shut up, I don't care. Sell it when we get back. Paris. Jack wants us to set up shop tonight, now, as soon as possible. Paris, yeah!" Steve paused, tapping his knuckles against the

151

hardwood desk. "No." Pause. "I don't know, some kind of kidnapping thing. Meet you at the airport. No, you get the tickets this time."

Steve pressed a button to terminate the call and looked around quickly at his system. It had taken him twenty minutes to set it all up. He'd have it cased in ten.

Interception

The Illuminatus Tower, London
Midnight

My apologies for calling you so late, Mr. Raines."

"Nonsense, Michael. What is it? What do you see?"

The muscular Asian in the pinstriped Saville Row suit looked carefully at the screen before him. "A copy of one of our files was sent a few moments ago through the Internet to an email address at the Massachusetts' Institute of Technology. The complete Hradek file, sir, unencrypted."

"Not encrypted? Then, not transferred to one of our people."

"That's correct, sir."

"The origin?"

"I— I'm still working on that, sir. I'm—"

"No need to apologize, Michael. Clean it up as soon as possible. Use the teams already in play. I believe Mr. Thiel and Mr. Krest are in that area tonight, if they haven't gone to Paris already."

"Thank you, sir."

"Sleep well, Michael. Tomorrow, the world will be a new place."

Erasure

Massachusetts Institute of Technology

Boston

2 AM

Middle of the night, bless his heart, the little man was still at work. Erma approved of Douglas Gale. She'd gotten on as a temp cleaner in the library back when Dr. Gale had been something of a temp himself, fresh at MIT, lecturing on the Dibner Fellowship Program. In the early days he was one of Charles Townes' favorites, and he had the old man's gift of a gracious gesture. She and Dr. Gale both started full time at The Tech, together, and Erma cleaned his small office ever since.

She preferred nights. The doctor always emptied his wastebasket himself; the worst she faced in his office was the occasional spilled coffee, not counting the candy bar wrappers left almost every night for 3 years by a student under Gale's wing, but that was several years ago.

The lights were left on in the hall as a matter of course. But wasn't that a light under Dr. Gale's door? Not much of one, just the washed-out dishwater light from a computer monitor. Erma was close enough to hear someone at work on the keyboard.

As quietly as she could, Erma retreated to the teacher's lounge to pour a cup of coffee. He liked one sugar and no cream. By the time she returned to Gale's office, the coffee's heat was reaching through the Styrofoam and her plastic gloves—she hated the clammy things, but regulations at The Tech were practically from the mouth of God.

The typing continued, unabated. She eased the door open.

"'Toiling upward in the gloom,' Doct—" But the two men in the office didn't belong there, didn't belong anywhere in Erma's world, and as they both turned—the older, bearded one in front of the computer and the younger, blond, *angry* boy. "What are you doing in Dr. Gale's office?" She demanded hotly. The older man, who she now saw wore tight dark gloves as he typed, simply shrugged, while the youngster, also in black, practically bared his fangs as he flowed at her from an open filing cabinet.

Her breath suddenly catching in her throat, Erma hastily stepped back, jerking the coffee at him, and ran for the exit. Their dark clothes, the dead, furious look in the younger one's face, this was worse than no good, this never happened on campus, never—

She was five feet from her janitor's cart when the sharp, cold pressure hit the back of her neck. Reflexively her hand went there, brushing something small and hot from her skin even as spots of frost swirled around her. No, *within* her. The door was a dozen steps away, then three, then one. Erma shuffled to a stop, her momentum carrying her into the door jamb next to the fire alarm. What was wrong with her eyes? How could it be this cold?

Her arms didn't move where she wanted them. She managed to twist around, actually falling at an angle, fingers, legs, face shaking uncontrollably. "What did you do to me? What is this?" She croaked at the young man in black, standing a few feet away. She tried to say more, but her throat was slack, shapeless. She didn't even have the strength to work her mouth, or blink away the rushing cold, the insensibility of it all. This wasn't right. She had a family to get back to, her Paul at home in bed, waiting for her, ingredients for a roast in the kitchen. In the . . . kitchen. Where?

Erma found herself trying to pray, but it was suddenly pointless, as if her soul were frostbitten through. Sensation ended, free will danced like a spark in the wind, and vanished. All sense of meaning, simply . . . not.

Eyes unseeing, Erma nevertheless felt the young man drawing near. She felt like she should envy him his life, his warmth, but there was simply nothing left to feel anymore. She knew he watched her die, and then even that thought wavered like a quick candle and was gone.

Nimble

Forge, Idaho
7 AM

Mercedes came awake with a feeling of epiphany, quickly, surrounded by the laughter of children. Echoes bounced around the bedroom at the peak of the house, and fell like the sunlight coming through the open window. "Wake up, Aunt Mercedes, wake up!" they shouted, running around the edge of the bed. "You're going to miss the plane!"

"Whose kids are these?" Mercedes yelled, and threw the covers over their heads. "Help, somebody, save me! I'm being attacked by Oompa-Loompas!"

Diane's youngest three laughed uproariously and squirmed out from under the blanket. Each under the age of ten, they had their mother's straight brown hair. "Mom says you're going home today," said the oldest, Gretchen.

"Why do you have to go today?" asked Marla.

Mercedes kissed her nose. "Some birds need me back in California."

"Birds." Chris had a mischievous look to him. Mercedes swore he inherited it from his Aunt Irene. "Birds need you?"

Mercedes thought a moment. "These are birds that people think are disappearing. I'm going to take their picture as their babies hatch, sometime in the next few days."

Gretchen, excited, caught on immediately. "They're going extinct?"

"That's what some people think."

Marla didn't get it. "But you'll take their picture and then they won't stink?"

Chris leaned into his little sister. "Ex-tinct, Marla. Not smelly."

Now Marla nodded. "Like Dad said you'd be if he caught you riding your bike in the house again." She wiped her mouth with the back of her hand, coming away with a handful of eggs. "Mama says you have to eat a big breakfast before you go."

Gretchen broke in. "Aunt Irene already ate four eggs and six pancakes!"

That was in character. Mercedes nodded. "She's got to keep up her strength," she agreed. "Her kids are going to want to play when we get back to L.A."

"And she's got a tough job," added Gretchen. "California is full of criminals she has to catch."

Chris sat on the wide windowsill. "Aunt Irene said you help her sometimes by taking pictures where bad guys do things." He mimed clicking a camera.

"When she needs me to, honey."

Something else occurred to Chris. "I thought you're going to stay and go swimming with us in the lake," he said.

Gretchen pushed her brother in the arm. "Not yet, Chris. The water's not warm enough yet."

Mercedes nodded solemnly. "Gretchen's right. The lake won't be warm enough to swim in for at least another month. It's because of all the melting snow."

Chris frowned and pulled at the covers. "We know *that*," he said. "Maybe you can come back when it's warm enough. Aunt Irene's coming back this summer, and she's bringing everybody back!"

Marla and Gretchen spoke together. "Can you come too, Aunt Mercedes?"

"Yeah, come on! Vacation's just getting started!"

She laughed. "I'm not even going to make it out of this bed if you guys don't give me some privacy! Shoo! I've got to get dressed! Aunt Irene's going to eat all my pancakes!"

That got them out of the room. Mercedes laughed. Irene's kids in Orange were the same, always wanting her to stay. She liked being the fun aunt, Mercedes had to admit. It was the best way she knew to get rid of all the sweets in her house and the loose dollar bills in her wallet.

She loved her cousin's kids.

Mercedes stretched and collected her things from the adjoining bathroom. Jasmine still overgrew the arbor beneath the bedroom window. Mercedes breathed as deeply as she could, then yanked the sheets and blankets from the bed and dropped them on the floor. Pillowcases next, then she got dressed herself, pulling on jeans and a green-blue shirt the color of her eyes.

Mercedes sat on the bed and wiggled her toes on the windowsill. Everything beyond the window burned brilliant green. In a winterbound place like Forge, springtime must seem like a miracle. Everything grew again, everything could breathe. She loved this place.

Ever since she'd been a little girl Mercedes had felt a funny kind of expectation when the calendar swung 'round to spring; an odd, implacable epiphany, a hint that something wonderful was about to happen. She'd lost that feeling for a while after her parents died, and during the last year or so with Bryce. But this year—she grinned. She wasn't too old, after all, to feel that everything was going to turn out better than she had reason to expect.

She placed a hand on the wall and leaned out the window, wondering if the new growth on the trees covered the view of the swimming pool.

"You going to jump?" said a voice behind her.

Mercedes turned, faster than she intended. It was Irene at the threshold, still in her robe.

"What did you say?"

"Thought you were pining away for your squandered vacation," her cousin said, "The kids are trying to convince me to abduct you when we all come back in August."

"I might try to convince you myself." Mercedes handed Irene her duffel bag. "They all promised me they'd know how to swim by then."

Irene found her cousin's hair brush in the duffel and dropped the bag. "You should come then, if you can get away." She began brushing her hair. "Forge is really pretty in late summer."

Mercedes looked out and down at the jasmine draping the arbor below. "Yeah. I remember."

*

She and Irene made a clean getaway right after the kids left for their morning lessons at the pool. Diane let her sister drive, and Irene piloted them through Forge's back streets at a leisurely pace; they had more than two hours before the plane left from the airport in Lewiston.

Once she made it to the car, Mercedes activated her phone, hesitated, and thumbed the key to check her messages. In the seat next to her, Irene was looking guardedly at her own phone. They'd made a pact together, a solemn vacation vow, not to listen to their voicemail while on vacation—was this an admission, then, that vacation was really over? Mercedes listened to her neighbor, Sylfa, report on the health of her indoor plants. Lord, it was too mundane.

"Want to hear my life?" Mercedes asked her cousins, and plugged the phone into the car's speaker system. The next message voice on the

160

phone was low and smoky. "Yeah, Mercy, hello. I just got the loft laid out, we're all stocked up here for a *thing* on the 15th. Want to stop by and chew some meat and cheese?" Mercedes' cousins made appreciative sounds, but quietly, so they could listen to the voice. "Don't worry about bringing anything, see, there's a guy I want you to meet. He owns a couple of vineyards up in Sonoma. Let me know."

"That one sounds good," said Diane.

"Sure, that's all I need," Mercedes said. "Brian tries to set me up with these guys all the time, these sensitive 21st century-types. It's always a guy with a winery, or a health club chain, or some kind of working farm. He's hoping I marry rich again so he can freeload off us."

"What about this guy? Brian? He's got kind of a sexy voice."

Mercedes smiled, biting her lip. "Here's the thing: Brian's gay." The other two women blinked, in unison. "I'm his guy test, Mercedes added, "if they can go out with me and 'not have their ignition turn over', he says, then they must be for him."

"Oh. Sure."

Irene spoke up. "Is this the one that dresses funny?"

"Like a picnic table."

"Gotcha."

The next few messages were similarly short. One was from a reedy-voiced woman asking Mercedes' advice on whether or not she should volunteer her blind dog for experimental vision surgery. The next was from a comedienne friend saying that she was moving back to San Francisco. "At least there, people think I'm funny. Check this out: " You have to love the carpool lane. One of the best things about California, get somebody in the car with you and blaze past traffic. But what about hearses? Do hearses get to drive in the carpool lane? I mean, it's not like the guy in back is really in a hurry to get anywhere, is it?' So what do you think, is that funny? '" Mercedes clicked off that with a smile.

A few business calls made it through to Mercedes' private line, both from her assistant, Marty. She jotted the details in a little spiral notebook before instructing her phone to save them to her home computer. "It's not real until you write it down," she said to her cousins.

"You'd make a great homicide detective, Merc," Irene said, and Mercedes waited five whole seconds before her two cousins broke up, laughing.

Mercedes shook her head and looked across at Irene. "I still think you're crazy for going on vacation without Barry and the kids."

"Oh, we do this every year," she replied. "He get a few days in Las Vegas with his high school buddies, I get a few weeks of peace and quiet by myself. I'm glad you could come up with me."

Now it was Mercedes turn to laugh. "A few days in Vegas equals two weeks in Idaho? That's about right."

"Separate vacations can be good," said Diane. "'Absence makes the heart grow fonder', and all that. That's the way a man's brain works, right?"

Irene smirked. "Sure gives Barry what he's missing."

A few moments later in the car, Irene spoke up. "Maybe it's not really the guys fault that they've got such one-track minds. Maybe we just need to get them out of their element, you know, get them out of their comfort zone and see how they deal. Some guys completely change when you give them a good whack in the head." She pulled the wheel, and the car jumped out onto the town's main drag.

Mercedes couldn't resist. "So where do you take Barry to 'whack him'?"

Her cousin's smile showed her teeth. "Hawaii. There's this place on the Big Island called Punalu'u. They have black sand beaches there, big, glossy dunes underneath the palm trees, and it feels so good to lay on.

The sand's softer, like baby powder, and pitch black." Her voice started to drift. "At night, when there's no lights but the stars, you feel like you're floating up in the sky, way up there, and it's like there's just two of you in the whole universe."

"Okay, still driving here, Irene!" Diane giggled as Irene blinked back toward reality, shaking her head as if she'd been stunned. She flushed.

"Must be some place," Mercedes said.

Irene kept her mouth shut, smiling tightly at the road ahead. From the back seat, Diane spoke in *sotto voce*, "You know, all her kids' middle names are Hawaiian." Laughter *popped* from Mercedes, and Diane smiled broadly at the other two women. "Yup. Get a guy on a beach in Hawaii. A vacation like that sticks with you a while."

Mercedes noticed that Irene was driving faster now, concentrating more fully on the road. There was a man who loved her at the other end.

They passed the park and the long road to the pool, and a few seconds later the library. It was the only building Mercedes could see with a new addition; everything looked remarkably as she remembered.

"It really hasn't changed much, has it?" she said.

"Not as much as you'd think," Irene said. "The best parts are the same."

A beat. "He still comes around here," Diane added, offhand.

After a moment, Mercedes cleared her throat. "I bet." She folded her hands softly, precisely in her lap. There was a clearing on the hill high above them, where two towering bull pines stood. "'Home town boy makes good', right? They give him the keys to the city?"

"Nothing like that. He's really low-key; just wants to hang out. What's funny is, he's given a lot of money to the town—rebuilt the pool, donated computers to the schools, that sort of thing—but he didn't want anybody to know. All these checks coming in to the building and

163

planning committee and the school district offices signed by 'Fletcher Z. Engstrom,' I mean, come on. The town's only so big." Irene guided the car over the bridge and turned onto the highway. "So when he comes around, everybody keeps mum, plays like they don't know. Unspoken agreement."

"You're kidding. Fletcher Engstrom? Same as the writer?"

"A lot of people here think he *is* the writer."

Irene spoke up. "Back in high school he used that name to write letters to the editor of the paper. He thinks he's pulling a fast one on the whole town, and we all let him."

Mercedes folded her hands again. "I wonder what his angle is."

Irene glanced over. "Hunh?"

"Don't you think he's doing it for a reason?"

"Sure," Diane replied. "He wants to help out."

"Ah, I don't know."

Irene frowned. Before she could speak, Mercedes added, "Come on, we both know people in the business. I work with a lot of these Hollywood types, I live close to some of them." She knew she wasn't saying what her cousins wanted to hear, but she went on. "Bryce has a lot of friends in the business; everybody's on some kind of wheel-and-deal. There are some decent people, too, but when it comes down to it, they all make money off the . . . weird ideas people have about them. If he's become anything like some of the guys I've met, he'll milk this somehow, when he needs it—he'll use his charity involvement to kick up good press as soon as he makes a movie that sinks. I've seen it before. I've made pictures of it happening before."

Diane and Irene didn't seem to know what to say to that, so they kept quiet for a while. The wide river kept pace on their right. Mercedes opened her mouth to add something, or maybe to apologize, then promptly shut it again. There had been too many parties on Bryce's boat, too many sozzled musicians and almost-actors in their condo, too much all-gloss happiness and chemical bliss passing by or passing out in front of her those years. "Sorry," she finally said. "I shouldn't have said that. I don't even know the guy anymore."

Diane and Irene shrugged it off, and the conversation turned to the scenery that was flashing by them. All three women had been girls on the same grandfather's knee, and heard stories about the Clearwater River. It had grown into a family legend the size and breadth of Griffin Bunyan himself. "Remember when Grandpa'd tell about the fish he caught by the Indian caves?" asked Mercedes.

"Or when he and Grandma Britt's brothers broke the log jam and saved the town from flooding?" Diane rejoined. "There's a picture of that in the old museum, you know."

"It really happened? I've got to see that museum one of these days."

Irene cleared her throat. "See, you've got to come back this summer. Your photo studio runs itself now, you know you can swing the time off."

"We'll see." Mercedes felt a strange disquiet grow within her at the thought of work. "Do you really think you can get the time off to come up again so soon?"

Irene nodded confidently. "I'll just arrange for all the homicidal investigations in the greater L.A. area to be wrapped up nicely before the third week of July, and I'm sure everybody can behave themselves for a few weeks. Might have to go on channel 5 and explain the situation."

The river was as perfect as Mercedes remembered. She spoke without thinking. "If I had a place like this to come to, I doubt I'd ever want to leave. That's how I felt, the first time I was here."

Diane was quiet for a few minutes, then cleared her throat gently. "Do you think things might have turned out differently if you hadn't gotten so sick that summer?"

Mercedes watched the river run beside them. "Probably. Yeah. Hell, yes." Her hands knotted themselves. "For a little while, like a minute, my life was perfect, and he was all the future I could see.

"Look, it took me a long time before I didn't think about that every day. What kind of a person I would have turned into, what kind of man he would ha—but it was just a fluke, that summer. It was what I needed then in my life, a fun time. A wonderful, fun time, but we were kids. I don't look back and I don't wonder."

Irene spoke knowingly from the driver's side. "You guys were good, though, weren't you?"

"There wasn't a scale that could measure it."

In unison her cousins reached across and squeezed Mercedes' hand. "I'm glad you came up here with me," Irene said. "Hope this vacation sticks with you a long time."

Mercedes returned the squeeze. The fine taste of epiphany, the impression that something wonderful was about to happen, billowed up again. She looked out the window again as Forge slipped back behind her. There were no ghosts here. Just epiphany on the horizon. Something good bound to happen.

*

The trip back to L.A. was like any other, she and Irene transferred to a larger plane in Seattle and flew down the coast between the ocean and the mountains. Hard to believe, she thought, a whole vacation already behind me. The week in Forge had been a great rest, but she found it left her feeling off-kilter somehow, tense in a way, as if she'd left something undone. Was it the vacation? She hadn't really taken a break since she started taking pictures—the last time she'd taken a day off she'd found her husband in someone else's bed—and not counting her the days she'd met with Bryce's lawyers, Mercedes worked pretty much straight through. Maybe the vacation threw me off balance, she thought, but there was more to it than that.

The business was doing as well as she'd ever dreamed. Running her own studio was as challenging and fun as she'd ever imagined, but if she was going to be completely honest with herself, photography didn't leave her as giddy as it once did.

Not that she'd had her fill of adventure. When she began, Mercedes had thrown herself into photography with everything she could come up with, and it was almost shocking to find that other people would actually pay her to jump out of a plane with a camera, or eat rice in spicy parts of the world while trying to un-extinct certain animals. She'd never shot anything worthy of a Pulitzer, though she carried the extra film when Big John Holdaway made the pictures of Indonesian rebels firing rocket-propelled grenades into a Red Cross helicopter. That was usually the way things went career-wise in photography; she'd learned the craft with Big John in her early 20's and then widened her own reputation into a solo career that turned profitable just before her thirtieth birthday. Three thousand dollars a day was pretty good. Bryce's connections had gotten her into fashion and the celebrity wedding-and-bar mitzvah set, but Mercedes really lived for the obscure jobs. Every time she went into the shark cage, Mercedes knew Big John would approve.

Yet, what was this strange disquiet?

Mount Ranier slid glacially by to the left of the plane, white and blue under the spring sun. Irene typed merrily away on her computer. Mercedes sighed and settle back into her seat.

Thinking she would be anxious to get back to work right away, before she left for Idaho she set contracts for jobs in southern California; big-money weddings and a trip into the sequoias for the Raptor Center at U.C. Davis to shoot golden eagles right after they hatched. Mercedes was excited to get the jobs, but now . . . maybe she'd give the job to her assistants—partners, really.

No, she'd keep the golden eagle gig, that would be worth it. Let the kids take care of the weddings. The San Jacinto Mountains were beautiful this time of year, and after northern Idaho, Mercedes decided she wasn't quite ready to come out of the woods.

There it was again, that odd feeling of expectancy. Something about to change. Mercedes frowned. Why should anything in her life need changing? Things were finally settling into place. She lived in a nice house, full of books and windows. She did her best to be a good neighbor; the kids on her street knew they were welcome in her pool. The business was all but running itself, so much so she could walk away for a month. That was the idea from the beginning, wasn't it? Set it up and live on a beach somewhere? Punalu'u?

Mercedes had worked very hard for several years, even admitting the terrific luck she'd been handed from time to time, but now her baby didn't need her quite as much. She'd earned freedom.

So why balk at epiphany? Was she souring at the idea that she couldn't enjoy success, or was there something else wrong, missing, lost? She'd worked hard building the studio, even during the divorce, and at the time the superficial regret she felt at failing "until death do you part" was overwhelmed by relief at not being trapped in a marriage with a man determined to stay fifteen years old the rest of his life. Thank God she'd sidestepped that freight train. She told herself *that* prison would be a greater harm than divorce; she should be glad to escape, that a lingering sense of betrayal was an easy price for her own selfishness. She touched her empty ring finger. Mercedes would never understand her own heart. She had never told anyone, not even Diane, but the hardest nights since the divorce, maybe half a dozen nights, she'd wake up sometime in the middle of the night, curled into herself, surprised to find herself weeping.

But she woke up in the morning stronger. Sometimes alone and not lonely is the strongest place a woman can be.

Mercedes didn't have anything against epiphany, she just didn't trust it. Epiphany had yet to prove worthy of her faith. If anything miraculous was about to happen, it would only come out of her brains and sweat. She settled back into her seat and tried to breathe. This was too much introspection for one day; she needed to get back to work. People think themselves into craziness this way. Better keep the world as solid as possible, and leave fantasy and fairy tale to children. Solid was best. Solid was best.

But it was tempting to remember.

*

When she was seventeen

The wind tumbled gently across each of the overlapping canopies of leaves that hung above the street. Below, a boy and a girl walked slowly down the middle of the pavement, heads together, whispering in hushed, conspiratorial tones. They drifted through each pool of warm radiance cast by the odd porch light that had been left on, or by the occasional hooded floodlight that marked the beginning of one of the short driveways. They clung to each other, deliberately treading in sync with the slow, inevitable rhythms of the night, of each other.

Jack held his tennis racket and the tube of bright yellow balls loosely in the crook of his other arm, smiling vaguely across at her. "I've really got to thank you for the tennis lesson," he began in that offhand, barely flamboyant manner she'd begun to recognize as a prelude to something more serious.

She swatted him lightly in the stomach with her racket. "Well, I thought at least we'd get past figuring out how to hang the net. And here all my cousins told me what a Boy Scout you are." She batted at him again.

Jack doubled over slightly, puffing out his cheeks, feigning injury. Mercedes laughed as his eyes widened and he mocked gasping for air. Sagging to his knees, Jack clutched a handful of her cuff. "Bury me with my racket," he croaked, then sprawled backwards into the street.

Mercedes waited a moment, then stepped back, clapping. "Bravo, bravo, bellissimo! Molto bene!"

Jack opened his eyes. "Bellissimo? Molto benny? You're making up words now?"

She brandished her racket threateningly, trying for a grim glare, but her smile managed to crumble in around the edges.

Jack raised his hands, then covered his stomach. "No, please, no more, I beg you. I—retract—or something like that." He was beginning to laugh, too. "I've always loved you Italian people. What with your leaning towers and brass knuckles and all." His eyes widened again as she raised the tennis racket over her head. "And the whole Venice idea; great, really great! Who would have thought to build a whole city so it would sink into the sea? Ugh!" The racket thumped home, but lightly.

Mercedes giggled again. She could never hurt Jack. "Ooh, poor baby," she cooed, bending and patting him on the stomach. He was solid, firm. She never *could* hurt Jack. Mercedes set the racket across her knees and rested her elbows on it. "I hope you'll live 'til tomorrow. Should I call the paramedics, or is there something I can do right here to make it better?"

He looked at her askance. "How much better?"

Mercedes blinked. Before she could think of a reply, the porch light behind her blazed on. "You kids get *home!*" The man behind the screen whisper-shouted. "It's almost five o'clock in the blessed morning! Folks are trying to sleep." He shook his fist. "Just wait 'til you have to work a nine to five," he muttered, then more loudly, "And you, you bully! Quit picking on him! Knock him down in the middle of the . . . Five o'clock—" The heavy door banged shut, the scowling man still grumbling to himself.

Mercedes gave Jack a hand up, and both hurried down the street as two other porch lights blinked on behind them.

By the time they reached the house, they'd gone from muffled snickering to full-blown laughter. "Did you see that guy's face?" Jack choked, "And what was he wearing?"

"I think maybe it was a toga." She was out of breath, too. They both took a few hesitant steps down the short sidewalk. It was a pale, grainy gray against the dark of the grass.

Jack shook his head. "Know what, Mercedes? I'm never going to work a nine-to-five." He was serious.

Mercedes leaned on him, breathing hard while she adjusted the heel of her shoe. "Why's that?" They had almost returned to a whisper.

"At the rate these tennis lessons are going, we won't have time!" They were both seized by fresh gales of laughter. Mercedes couldn't help herself. Part of the reason she laughed was knowing how *unfunny* the joke was. She wiped a tear from her eye. The other part was, Jack knew it too.

They held each other tightly through the laughter, swaying slightly, half for support, then, when the hilarity of the moment trailed off, tighter still. Mercedes found it surprising that Jack didn't immediately release

her. Greater yet was her surprise when she realized she didn't want to be
let go, not just yet. Her hands found each other in the small of his back,
underneath his jacket. He chuckled, and she felt the warm vibration of
his voice spread through his chest at the same time his breath stirred
across her face. Mercedes rested her head on the pad of muscle drawn
tight at the junction of Jack's arm and shoulder, and smiled up at him.
"Jack?"

"Mmmhmm?"

"You ever notice how they always name the good guys 'Jack?' I
mean, in that movie last night, wasn't that the hero's name?"

He had an infectious smile. "And don't forget Jack and the
Beanstalk—"

"Or Jack the Giant Killer. 'Seven at one blow!'"

"Or Jack and Jill." The boy was quiet for a moment. Then, "Mercedes,
does this feel as good to you as it does to me?"

It did. Their bodies fit together like pieces of the same puzzle. It was
miraculous, wonderful. Mercedes had never felt anything like it before.
She couldn't tell exactly where she left off and he began. As a cool
spring breeze flickered over her, she became aware of the tremendous
heat growing between them, as if two candles had been lit and placed
flame to flame, and she felt the strangest impression that the two of them
were melting somehow, thawing and dissolving into one another. Any
minute now, and they would meld and fuse into something even more
wonderful, more refined. Looking up at his face, she knew he could feel
it, too, at least some of it. She settled her weight on her toes, and leaned
up–

And then Jack broke away. "Hang on a sec, Mercedes." He looked
up, over her shoulder, chagrined. Then Mercedes became aware of the
rhythmic squeak-screech of a bicycle being peddled up the quiet street,
and the soft, rustling thud of newspapers landing on cement.

They stood perfectly still, Jack's hands in the groove of her waist, as the paperboy trundled past them on the street. Without a glance towards the couple, the younger boy whipped a wrapped newspaper deftly at the front stoop. Jack nudged her hip, gently turning himself into the path of the paper. It slapped the side of his head and fell to the grass. He winced.

Mercedes put a hand to her mouth as if impressed. "Jack," she breathed. "You took a newspaper for me."

"Well. Not like it was a Sunday edition or anything." he said as he rubbed his neck. "They really told you I was a Boy Scout?"

She grinned. "Yeah." Mercedes hesitated a moment. She was a little dizzy. "Thanks a lot, Jack." She gave him a quick peck on the cheek. "Now, get home, you whippersnapper!" She mimicked the whisper-shout of the irate man in the bedsheet.

Mercedes turned and stepped up to the door. It was unlocked. She could feel Jack's eyes on her, and she looked back as she eased the door open. He stood in the wash of light, smiling, waiting until she was safely inside.

"Whew!" Mercedes pushed the door shut and leaned there a moment, letting her breath out in a long puff. In the illumination cast by the lamp in the den to her left she could clearly see the brass hands on the old mahogany clock in the far corner: sure enough, 5:05. The light further revealed a set of feet protruding over the edge of the sofa. One of the socks was missing a big toe: that would be her grandfather.

She peeked over the sofa's back. She knew she was being unnecessarily quiet–the Swedish side of her family could sleep through a brass band. Grandpa Max looked younger, like a little boy. He wore sweats and an old flannel shirt. The lines on his face were perceptibly smoother. He seemed to be smiling slightly. Mercedes carefully shed her jacket and draped it over his chest. The long, deep breathing never changed tempo.

173

Despite the hour, Mercedes felt wide awake; more awake, even, than she would be during the day. She silently took the stairs two at a time, unbuttoning her blouse. Strange how spending the whole evening talking had left her more energized. In the dark at the head of the stairs, she paused, her hand on the newel, and shivered deliciously.

She still felt his arms around her.

In the spare bedroom, she stepped out of her shoes and moved to the window. It was open a crack, and the room had gently filled with the scent of jasmine from the arbor below. Her grandfather had been in the process of changing the storm windows when she arrived; the mesh screen was probably still in the garage. Mercedes sighed as she sat on the old-fashioned wide windowsill.

Life was so much simpler here than at home.

Everything in this little town was so predictable, so fresh and appealing for its expectancy. She loved falling asleep in the big, cool bed, sleeping soundly until her eyes popped open by themselves. She loved waking up to the smell of her grandmother's baking. She loathed admitting it, but Mercedes was beginning to enjoy the routine of taking her little cousins to their swimming lessons every morning, then bringing them here and fixing lunch. She was actually finding joy in baloney sandwiches, apples, and Kool-aid. The daily predictability was so calming.

She loved it.

And what she liked best of all was, by no stretch of the imagination, predictable. She spied Jack out on the road, near his little Toyota truck. His back was to her, he seemed to be thinking.

Mercedes shouldered the window all the way open and leaned out. "Hey!" she hissed. "Hey, mister!"

Jack turned around, looking up at her window. Slowly he jogged

174

over. "Hey yourself! Holy cow, Mercedes, cover up or something. You can get arrested in this town for that kind of exposure!"

She glanced down, then drew her shirt closed with one hand. What was the big deal? He couldn't see anything from all the way down there. She had a bra on, anyway.

Jack stood for a moment with his back to the fence, a dark shape against the short white posts. "I forgot to give back your tennis balls," he whispered. "Here, catch."

He lofted them up, and she caught them. "Thanks."

Jack waited, delicately fingering a pale spray of jasmine on the trellis next to him, then said, "I forgot something else, too."

He took a few steps backwards and sat on the fence, then stood on it. Mercedes watched in amazement as Jack, his tongue clenched firmly between his teeth, bounded across and up to the center support of the jasmine arbor, then abruptly spun and *dove* at the side of the house.

It was an angling leap, and it brought him just below the window. His hands found the edge of the sill, and he managed to pull himself up slightly as the rest of his body glanced off the white siding just below.

The impact wasn't overly loud, and Mercedes knew her grandfather would sleep through it. She was speechless, as Jack, flushed and grinning, hooked his hands over the inner sill and drew himself up to her. Their lips met, and she placed her hands lightly on either side of his face. He was smiling through the whole kiss.

When they at last parted, both were breathless, and Jack was beginning to tremble. "Thank you so much," he said. "Thank you for being here right now, I just can't . . ."

Mercedes brushed his hair from his forehead. "Jack, you're the most amazing person I've ever met."

He glowed back at her for one second more, then released his grip on the window sill. He twisted as he fell away from the building, and landed heavily, facing away from her, letting his body contract to absorb the impact on the grass below.

Pushing himself slowly to his feet, Jack returned her gaze. "Know what, Mercedes?" His voice held a note of undeniable earnestness and sincerity.

"I'll be a lot better when I'm older."

Jack jogged back to his truck at the curb, and was about to get in when Mercedes yelled down to him. "Jack!"

He raised his head. "Yes?"

Mercedes waved. "Be nimble!"

She laughed softly to herself and closed the window.

The Stone

The two boys rested, panting in yesterday's sunshine. They lay near the gap-toothed grin of a boarded-up shaft. "I can't believe it," said the smaller one. He only had one shoe. "I thought I was a goner!"

The other boy shrugged and said "I saw you running across the field and then you just, like, whoosh, disappeared! I figured you didn't know about the old mine, and maybe the boards broke."

"Yeah," said the first boy. "I forgot about it. Hey, what's your name, kid?"

"Jack. I'm new. My uncle told me all about the mine."

"I'm Alonzo. You always pull people out of mine shafts, Jack?"

"Hey, what are friends for?"

"Friends, then."

"Yeah, friends. 'Sides, you'd do it for me, right?"

*

Paris

8 AM

Why did it always have to start like this? Alonzo wondered. Hours of nothing—waiting for a woman, nonetheless—and then a few insane moments of action. He needed a new line of work. This just wasn't healthy. Look what you've gotten me into, Jack.

She was taking too long. Alonzo leaned back once again into the bridge, unconsciously sliding closer to the leering gargoyle that shared his view down the Seine. Anything to block the bloody frigid wind. It

177

wafted along just above the water below him, stealing up occasionally like a thief, or like one of the ghosts that walked this town.

"I hate Paris," he muttered against the rough cloth of his scarf. Too cold in the morning, and twice again too loud in the afternoon, when half the inhabitants managed to shake themselves out of their collective hangover. The fact that the other half of the population was female was the city's only redeeming value, he decided. He watched a particular ripple spread as it moved down the river, past the sleepy barges and leashed watercraft, until it became indiscernible from the rest of the mass of silent, muddy water. He continued to stare at that particular spot of water as it passed under another bridge, then curved with its mother river around the bank to the left. He could barely see the spires of Notre Dame. About two-and-a-half minutes, he decided, and his personal ripple would pass the Arc du Triomphe, then the Eiffel Tower.

Too bad you couldn't predict people the same way as you could the path of a mass of shapeless river.

"We're waiting for *whom*?" Her voice was harsh. Strong, even attractive, but harsh.

Alonzo turned to the British woman patiently. "Eliane. The girl who sells flowers here." Outwardly he was passive, almost sullen in his calmness, while inwardly he could hear his own dry chuckle as he considered Major Griffin. He wasn't about to divulge the fact that the waiting was driving him crazy as well. You just had to be patient. The woman from the Royal Air Force had no idea how these things were handled.

"You simply have no idea how this sort of thing is handled, do you?" Her voice had gotten a notch more irritating, he decided. Understandable, considering what–*who*–was at stake. The woman continued, half to herself. "Why His Majesty requested this, this bunch of—"

"Vagabonds?" he supplied helpfully.

"No."

"Troublemakers?"

"No!"

He thought a moment. "Miscreants?"

"You're getting closer." she said, almost smiling despite herself. "I suppose there's not much else to do while your man researches. Do you really think he can do any good?"

Alonzo raised his collar to the wind. "Steve is the best in the world at computer sleuthing. The little girl's only been gone two days, but I'd lay odds on the hacker geek."

"But you need this other man, this Jack Flynn, before you can do anything. He mu st be very important to your group."

He *did* like her accent. And her hair was just the right shade of red-brown. Auburn, that was the word. "Did you know he's Christine's godfather?" Alonzo asked.

"His Majesty did mention that. You are a very strange man, Mr. Noel. Your little group is very strange. What is it exactly you do?"

He looked her dead in the eye. "I'm an interior decorator."

Major Griffin exhaled deeply and crossed her arms again. "I still don't understand why you need a flower girl to simply go talk to this man Flynn."

"Every door has its key, Major." Yeah, he added silently, and 'this man Flynn' would probably be just as happy if I were burning in hell. Alonzo wished he had a cigar. Something to warm him up, anyway.

Alonzo gazed left and up at the twelve-story apartment building two blocks away. All the lights in the top two stories had been on since their arrival nearly an hour before. Squinting against a sudden gust, Alonzo thought he could almost see someone there through the bars of the balcony and behind the floor-to-ceiling windows. Does he ever sleep? he wondered silently.

Soon the sun would be up in earnest. Already it was smudging the grey Paris skyline into a blushing pink. At least the wind would be gone, he thought.

"Sorry Major Griffin. Until she gets here, I'm afraid it's just you, me, and old Floyd here." He indicated the gargoyle looming over them. "Wonder what these things are for, anyway? Too much art in this city, if you ask me."

She sniffed. "Americans." He smiled pointedly. "If you must know, they were supposed to keep watch, to keep guard against evil." She shook her head. "I'm going to get out of this wind. Good luck."

Alonzo watched her retreat to her car, an ugly Peugot. Nice legs, he thought. "What do you think, Floyd?"

The gargoyle wasn't disclosing his opinions. At least Major Allison Griffin was safely out of the way. Another minor problem fixed. Alonzo had always considered himself to be a bit of a mechanic.

A dog barked in the distance, and then as if on cue, church bells began to ring from somewhere far behind the short man. Alonzo burrowed deeper into his long coat, shivering despite the warmth and light spreading across his back. A few Parisians passed him, nodding amiably. On their way to Mass, no doubt. What would the priest say to him now, Alonzo wondered, a smile brushing at the corners of his mouth. Better yet, he mused, reaching through the narrow slit he had cut into his right coat pocket, what would he say to the priest? Bless me, Father, for I've run out of bullets? He touched the Glock 19 in the ballistic nylon holster strapped to his thigh. No, it would be a long time before he was out of bullets. A Mass would be nice, though. Too bad he was beginning to understand French, otherwise he could pretend it was being given in Latin.

He relaxed visibly as a young woman in a blue cardigan and a Detroit Tigers baseball cap rounded the usual corner with her small wheelbarrow full of flowers. She smiled familiarly at him as he pushed himself off the wall and quickly stepped to intercept her. "Bonjour, mademoiselle," he said with mock severity as he took over the task of pushing the enormous bouquet. "Combien pour toutes les fleurs?"

"Ah!—Monsieur Alonzo, I cannot let you buy all of them before I have even set up my business!" she responded in English. She half-skipped beside him as he pushed the wheelbarrow to her usual spot near the bridge, next to a man who was already setting up his easels and half-drawn sketches. Later, Alonzo knew, the man would fill in the blank spots on his canvas with the features of tourists who wanted to take home a painting of themselves by the Seine.

"Alright, Eliane, just one bouquet this morning, but it's got to be the most expensive." Alonzo's Spanish eyes narrowed into twinkling obsidian. "And I need a new phrase along with the flowers. Come on, teach me something new."

Eliane leaned over her stand of bouquets conspiratorially and whispered "Why is it you wait for me in the morning to buy these flowers, hmm? Whose woman's heart are you buying your way into before the sun rises?"

"Only yours, mademoiselle. Can you doubt it?" Alonzo's grin was sharp and lean, like the rest of his face. It was an honest smile.

Eliane smiled back. Americans were such fun to tease. "Bon. Here is your flowers, and here is your phrase: J'adore la fleuriste. There. Tell this to the one you give the flowers to. They will be most impressed, I guarantee to you."

He paid for the bouquet and crossed the bridge.

Alonzo eyed the building as he drew abreast of it. The browner sections of mortar looked like dried mud in the rising light. Here and there along its river-facing side the upper face was pitted and slightly charred. The corners of the building itself gave greater testimony to the ravages of the last war: German and then Allied shells had bitten chunks out of the edges of the building, and lighter patches of the wall showed where newer, cheaper cement had been used like an antiseptic over the scars of machine gun fire.

Alonzo walked past the main entrance to the apartments and turned down a steep flight of stairs just beyond. The air in the narrow alleyway was already redolent with the aroma of frying sausage. Pausing before the door he heard a woman's scolding voice upbraiding a man in German. He couldn't speak German; couldn't tell how far along they were in their argument, but he rapped on the door regardless. "Greta! Franz!" he called out.

The old woman who came to the door always reminded Alonzo of his third grade teacher for some reason. The eyes, the lips, even the ears seemed drawn together slightly and pinched. Her face, comfortably fat like the rest of her, creased into a maze of smiles at the sight of the visitor and the huge bouquet he proffered her. "Ah, Alonzo!" The English was heavily accented. "Come in, come in. You get here in time for bratwurst, good boy." She took the flowers and stepped back, welcoming him into the apartment.

"Sorry, Greta, but I'm really in a hurry this morning. You don't suppose you could do me a little favor?"

She eyed him suspiciously through a wisp of iron grey hair. "You want to go up and see Jackie boy, do you?"

He nodded.

"He tells us to let no one to see him, that he doesn't want any company, even you. Told us when he helped Franz bring in the new furnace. Since you came last—when? Three weeks now he's seen nobody but that American woman, the movie woman. Doesn't go out for groceries. The other tenants, they complain that his lights are on all night! Never mind he's the one who owns the building, but we have to explain to Madame de la Grande Bouche why her neighbor is moving furniture at three o'clock in the morning? No, this is not work fit for old people like me and my Franz." She was really getting herself worked up, Alonzo thought.

"Greta, sweetheart," he broke in. "You have known me for what now, two years—"

"Since Jackie and—since Jackie boy moved in."

"Yeah, now, I can tell you're worried about him, especially now. Why not let me up to talk with him? He'll see it's me and lock out the elevator if I go in through the front or through the garage." Alonzo gave her his confident, good-looks-and-clean living-will-get-me-through-this grin.

Greta clutched the flowers tighter to her chest, eyeing him. "But he said not—"

"Greta girl, let the boy up to see his friend!" The owner of the gruff voice loomed at his wife's side. "Hello, Alonzo, come in."

"Franz." Alonzo stepped in and shook the huge German's hand firmly. Even in his sixties, Franz was a bear. A grizzly, Alonzo decided.

Greta eyed her flowers. "These are very nice, and probably very expensive. What is it that you do for a living?"

"I sell hats." Alonzo said.

"Ah. Hats. Well," She gave him another long stare. "Franz, show him to the elevator."

The two men made their way through the knicknack-bejeweled

183

apartment, into a maintenance room, where Franz pressed the button for the elevator. "Forgive my wife. She has doted on those two since the day they moved in and bought this place from us. She fears for Jack. When Victoria died, it was like we had lost a daughter. Jack is... not himself."

Alonzo looked away bleakly, wishing the elevator would hurry, willing it down the shaft to the basement. He turned back to Franz as the door slid open. "To be honest, I'm not sure exactly what I'm going to say to him." He tried for a smile, and stepped inside the mahogany-paneled compartment.

The old man moved forward, placing his hand lightly on Alonzo's arm. "No matter. You are his best, true friend. Inspiration will come to you for what to say." The old man paused, as if suddenly very tired. "No one should lose his wife." Before Alonzo could reply Franz stepped back and the doors slid shut.

Alonzo's caught himself before he pushed the button for the twelfth floor. Turning, he reached up behind the light fixture, disabling the alarm. He hesitated for a moment, then stabbed the button. He and Jack had climbed all through the interior of the building, the first time to check its integrity before Jack bought it, then subsequently to do a little home renovation of their own. For instance, pressing either the eleventh- or the twelfth- floor button would send a visitor to the eleventh floor, where there were no features to tell you exactly what floor you were on, while an alarm sounded in the main suite on the twelfth floor. That had been Alonzo's idea. He was very proud of it. Jack and Toria always had liked their privacy.

The elevator doors sighed open and Alonzo stepped out into a Roman hallway. High, arching ceilings were lost in the feeble light let in by the tall, wide window at the end. The tile gleamed. At least he's managed to look after the place, Alonzo thought. He stepped around the small table and walked the length of the hallway, ignoring the gaze of the Greek statues in alcoves to either side. There was something spooky about them now. At the end of the hall on the left was a door; stairs on the other side led up and around to the master apartment. Alonzo turned to the right and stepped inside an empty alcove, hands questing for a slight unevenness in the curving plaster.

A click, and he was in.

Whatever original use the builders of the old apartment had in mind was long since forgotten by its latest owner. The first room held little more than a table, some empty shelves, and a miniature refrigerator. *She'd always have sandwiches waiting for us when we came in*, Alonzo recalled against his will. *He'd forgotten that.* A weak, sickly light trickled in through frosted windows spaced evenly along the wall. He listened, and thought he heard his own heartbeat echo back at him. The whole place was as silent as a tomb. He got the sense the air hadn't been disturbed in a long time. Not by the living, anyway.

The hallway beyond led past three rooms, each filled with its own curiosity. Peering into the first, Alonzo saw a mass of circuit boards, all state of the art and all in various stages of assembly. It looked as though someone were trying to build something fantastically high-tech but couldn't decide exactly what it was going to be. The morass of electronic equipment looked . . . pointless. He shrugged his shoulders and moved on.

Water leaked under the next door, which Alonzo thought was slightly ajar until he drew abreast of it. He swore softly. The two-inch hardwood had been slammed, perhaps kicked, off its hinges, then replaced almost as an afterthought. He looked in, and saw splinters on the floor around what had once been a martial arts practice dummy, a thick wooden opponent made to spin and fashioned with wooden "arms" that had stuck out at right angles. It lay in four pieces. Jack had built it himself, spending hours tightly wrapping coarse rope around it.

Beside the dummy sagged the remains of two punching bags, one made of horsehide leather and inner nylon filler, the other one of the new, water-filled bags. *She'd* given it to Jack as a present. The water Alonzo was now standing in had come from its inner bladder bursting. Alonzo had never seen a ruptured punching bag.

*

"If you have to confront a kickboxer, always watch his feet," the tall man told the two of them. "You can always tell right before they attack by the position of their feet."

Jack turned to Alonzo, grinning. "I'm going to learn this stuff."

"Think you'll ever need to use it?" Alonzo was almost kidding.

"Nah!" Jack caught the joke. "But Toria will think it's cool!"

*

The small man blinked at the wreckage, biting his lower lip, then moved on. Following the building, the hallway angled sharply, and Alonzo breathed a sigh of relief when he turned with it.

For all the furniture piled in front of it, he could barely see the door. A gigantic armoire was the biggest piece, supplemented by an old French stove, a fire-blackened safe, and two heavy chairs. How'd he manage to move all this, Alonzo wondered. He squeezed around the blockage, then stooped when he saw a dull, golden glimmer. A broken key, smashed with a hammer, and beside it the torn splinters of a more modern, credit card-type key. He looked at the door, and felt more than heard the thrum of the technology beyond it. At least the weapons room was safe, he thought.

The next two rooms were storage for food and such, and Alonzo passed them without a thought. At the end of the hall a narrow spiral staircase wound up briefly to a trapdoor. Now he was really putting his head into the lion's mouth, he realized. He set his jaw, and pushed the trapdoor open. He could reach his gun quickly if he had to.

The top level was much more lavish. The ceilings were half again as high, and artwork graced the walls. He moved soundlessly down a hallway, pausing to straighten a picture of himself and Jack and two huge fish. Sturgeon. Other pictures followed, all dusty: Jack smiling tiredly, framed by a magnificent Himalayan vista; Jack in a tuxedo sheepishly raising a golden statue; and finally, Jack and a strikingly beautiful dark-haired woman, both in camping gear, frying fish over an open fire.

The wooden floors were clean but beginning to lose their polish. Somewhere, probably in the living room, slow, moody jazz was playing on a stereo. Alonzo's eyes darted back and forth, past the pantry and the guest bedroom. He could hear the alto sax and the piano accompaniment. No one in the dining room. Someone should definitely dust that chandelier.

An old laptop had been left open and on in the adjoining kitchen. Alonzo bent over it, curious. It was one of Jack's novels. I wonder if I'm in this one, he thought, skimming over it. He wrinkled his nose. The story, from what he could get of it, was hopelessly maudlin. Something about vampires and lost loves. The last line on the screen caught his eye. It had nothing to do with the mysterious nighttime guest that had loomed in the helpless heroine's bedroom for the past few paragraphs. It read, 'My aching heart.'

Alonzo sniffed and stood. The place was still quiet, but over the sax he thought he heard the sound of someone tapping away on another keyboard.

Alonzo felt a breeze move through the penthouse. That left one place.

Alonzo stepped around the corner and into the light. Jack sat behind a desk at the end of the library, his face angled away from the growing light that shone in through the open balcony doors. A plate of half-eaten bread and a laptop computer sat before him, set unceremoniously on a layer of official-looking documents. He looked thinner, but that was just in the careless way he sat. Alonzo hadn't seen Jack in jeans and a flannel shirt for years, and they now seemed to hang on him in tatters. His hair had become an afterthought. Jack had shaved, but not recently. His face was drawn. Lines that normally appeared only when he smiled now knifed down the sides of his face. The skin under his eyes was as hard and gray as Paris stone. Jack looked up from the laptop. His eyes—

"How the hell did you get in here." Not necessarily a question, but . . .

Alonzo tried for nonchalance. "Somebody left the back door open, and I was passing by—" So much for inspiration, Franz, he thought.

"Why'd you come? Trying to cheer me up?" Jack's voice was raw, as if he'd been shouting for hours.

*

The mineshaft was dark, and the dust burned Alonzo's eyes and throat. His ears rang from his own screams, his breathing ragged. He hated his ten-year old arms for not being able to pull himself up out of the hole he'd fallen in. Why couldn't he be bigger? This wasn't like Tom Sawyer at all!

His feet windmilled against the shaft's wall, and he lost a shoe for his trouble. It splashed into the water far below.

His arms felt like hot lead, and he could feel his grip weakening with each hesitating thud of his heart. **Hail Mary, full of grace.** *Nobody was coming.* **Mother of God, pray for us sinners, now and at the hour of our death.** *Nobody was there to–*

"I've gotcha."

The hands that wrapped themselves around his wrists weren't much bigger than his own, but they were full of warm strength. All Alonzo could see was the top of a blond head against the clear blue sky. He couldn't believe it.

"Hey, stupid, let go of the beam so I can pull you up. What a moron." *Definitely not an angel. The other boy, legs planted against the edges of the mine shaft, gave a tremendous heave, and then another, arching his back, and then both boys were out of the hole, the dry grass of late summer pricking their skin.* **The Lord is with thee.**

All Alonzo could think to say was "Thanks...a lot." **Amen.**

His rescuer smiled lopsidedly, also panting from the exertion. "You're welcome. You're the first person I've met around here. My name is Jack."

"You always pull people out of mine shafts, Jack?" *Alonzo asked when he had rested a bit.*

"Hey, what are—"

*

"—friends for?" Alonzo said.

Jack stared at him. Alonzo could see conflict in his friend's eyes. Jack's hand darted across the desk, and Alonzo almost went for his gun right there, but Jack merely tapped a key on the laptop, then rocked back into his chair. It was a match for the other two used in the barricade downstairs.

"What do you want? It's not another job, is it?" Alonzo had expected him to be tired, empty. Instead he got the distinct impression of a restless panther, pacing beyond Jack's dark eyes.

Alonzo walked slowly to the desk, taking a circuitous route around the furniture. Calm was the operant word here. He unbuttoned his coat and draped it over the back of the couch, watching Jack's eyes flicker to the gun. Alonzo tried again for a smile. "Nobody's heard from you in weeks; Solomon bet me ten bucks you'd be sacked out up here with a bottle of tequila." He leaned against the windowsill.

"Looks like you win again."

Alonzo looked at his friend. "I know you better than—"

"Yeah, you know me, all right." His voice was like a razor. "You've got a pretty good idea what I'll do to you if you don't turn around and get your—"

"Listen, we haven't much time," Alonzo began tersely. "There's been an incident, a kidnapping."

"I don't care."

"Solomon, Steve, and Brad came in from Vienna, you know the drill. I called Pete and Ian and a couple of the others back in the States; Ian's flight arrives this afternoon. And there's this woman who thinks she's calling the shots, this Major—"

You don't get it, do you? Jack's not playing anymore. I'm out. Done!" Jack's eyes were stark, inhumanly fierce as he rose from his chair. He continued in a hoarse whisper. "You were there when it happened, and you have the *nerve* to come up here and ask me—"

"People need you, Jack!" Alonzo shot back. He took a step back, suddenly confused, disbelieving. This wasn't how he'd imagined it at all.

He saw guilt pass briefly behind his friend's eyes as Jack began to turn away. "Just go . . ."

No.

Without warning, Alonzo launched himself from the wall, covering the distance between them in an instant. Jack stumbled up and back, stunned, as the smaller man raked his arm across the desk, scattering papers and shards of china. Furious, Alonzo swept up the laptop and hurled it against the glass window. The big pane trembled under the impact, and the screen snapped off with an electronic squeal. Alonzo whirled back to face the desk, slamming his palms down with a sharp, loud crack like a pistol shot. He leaned against it, as if to pin his friend behind it with a shove. Jack raised his hands against the attack. Alonzo looked him in the eye, matching madness for madness.

"I miss her too!" He bellowed. He held Jack against the wall by the sheer force of his gaze. Both men were panting slightly, breathing through their teeth.

Jack's arms fell to his sides. He regarded Alonzo curiously, almost desperately. The smaller man seemed to relax and fall inward slightly as he stepped back from the desk. He slowly moved to the balcony doors, massaging his neck with one hand. Crossing the threshold, he almost didn't hear Jack's whisper.

"What?" Alonzo turned.

"I never thought it would turn out this way." Jack stepped dazedly toward his friend on the balcony, squinting against the swelling light. "Do you know what it feels like, Alonzo? Do you? Do you really know?"

Alonzo nodded, not in affirmation, merely to keep the other man talking.

Jack looked slowly around himself. He stared at his apartment, not letting his gaze rest on any one thing. "You live your life," he said. "You live your life a certain way, and you obey the rules, you...eat the right stuff, you do the right thing. You . . . stop at the yellow light, and you think you're safe."

191

Jack began to pace. "It feels like I've forgotten something. Every day I wake up and I try to live, to get back to what my life was, but...but I can't shake the feeling like I'm overlooking something, some important detail I've lost or misplaced, or...forgotten." He plucked at his shirt absently. "I locked all my guns downstairs and destroyed the key–you don't know the dreams I've had, I mean, if it were just a matter of finding something to make the pain go away, or losing myself in work. But it's all—it's ashes. Nothing feels good anymore.

"And I keep telling myself that it wasn't my fault, that it wasn't the job, or you, or anybody's fault." He spoke somberly, slowly. "But that doesn't help when I wake up fast in the night, reaching for her–like, if I can just reach out quick enough and far enough, I can catch her before she falls away into the dark.

"And leaves me all alone."

He shuddered as Alonzo's hands rested on his shoulders. The smaller man turned him about, and led him onto the balcony. Jack let out a jagged sob as he leaned into the balustrade. The sunlight trembled as it touched his hair.

Alonzo gripped his shoulder firmly. Below, on the street, he could see Major Griffin marching purposefully toward the apartment's entrance. She was carrying a briefcase or bag of some kind. He squeezed Jack's shoulder tightly. "You'll be all right, my friend."

He watched Jack shake there for a few minutes. He never moved from his friend's side. Nothing he thought of to say would be the right, exact thing, Alonzo knew.

Finally, Jack shrugged away from the stone railing and walked back into the house. Alonzo followed him to the couch, where Jack sat, staring at a small crystal bird on the coffee table before him. At length he turned. "What sort of job did you say it was? A kidnapping?" His voice sounded a shade closer to normal.

Alonzo pursed his lips. "Christine Windsor's been abducted."

He couldn't have gotten a stronger effect had he dashed a pail of water upon his friend. Their eyes locked over the couch, Alonzo actually *saw* the moment when Jack's mental wheels shrieked back into operation.

The other man was instantly electrified. His eyes darted around the room. His hands clenched. Alonzo could almost hear Jack take a slow, small step back from whatever precipice on which he'd been balancing.

"You said . . ." He swallowed. Began again. "Who's our tech?"

"Steve."

"Materiel?"

"Ian."

"Sniper?"

"Sol."

"Medic?"

"Also Sol." Alonzo hesitated. "Brad's the other sniper."

"His father won't like that."

"When was the last time you visited the Joss House to ask permission?"

Jack made a face. "You said something about Pete?"

Alonzo nodded. "He's on the West Coast. This thing is going to get wider."

"Let's go," Jack said. He stood, unevenly, reaching for the closet. "You still a fair lockpick?"

The smaller man grinned tentatively. "You still the world's worst pistol shot?"

Jack almost smiled, but it never got as far as the corners of his eyes. He shrugged into his jacket. "This is terrible. How's her father?"

"Will's frantic, but he's sure she never left England. Everybody else thinks otherwise, that's why he called for me, for us—for you."

"Well, come on then, help me break into my own house." The two men walked briskly toward the trapdoor. Jack stopped halfway and turned toward his friend. His eyes were still haunted, but he was closer to an honest smile. "You brought Greta flowers, didn't you?"

Alonzo smiled, more to himself, and kept walking. He felt like he'd just pulled the sword from the stone.

Into the Woods

Studio City, California
11AM

Mercedes heard the truck coming long before it made an appearance in front of her quiet, shaded house. Climbing gear, water, and snack bars went into a small backpack, along with extra batteries and memory for the cameras. She picked her favorite digital, a Nikon D3X, and an old-school non-digital as well. Some of the best shots came from the old film cameras.

Her luggage sat unpacked on her bedroom floor. It would have to wait a day; the raptor center called while she and Irene were still in the airport, fishing for their suitcases. The golden eagle chicks were starting to hatch, and the young ornithologists currently on-site were beside themselves. Mercedes was going to have to sprint—literally—if she was going to make any pictures of the event.

Not that she would mind; the plane ride left kinks and knots in her legs that only a good hard run could work out. Mercedes set her cross-trainers next to her climbing shoes, and wriggled into a pair of thick canvas pants that could take a thorn or a rock's edge well enough. Must remember to dress in layers, she thought, pulling on a fleece top. The San Jacintos could still freeze this late in the spring; she wedged a set of Softsilk thermal underwear into the backpack.

With any luck, she wouldn't need to stay in the mountains overnight. The Raptor Center at the University of California, Davis, had a helicopter pilot coming down-state with a load of professional birdwatchers, and she could catch a ride back into the city before midnight.

She hesitated over her cell phone. There wasn't room for it in the pack, and the battery charge was two weeks old. Besides, she was going into the woods, and Mercedes doubted the Forest Service had gotten around to installing cell towers in the San Jacintos.

Nobody besides Irene and the kids at the studio knew she was back in town, anyway.

Marty's Ford Bronco rumbled to a stop in front of her house. Didn't she pay him enough to buy a new truck, at least one with a muffler? At least he had the manners not to honk, she thought as she keyed the house alarm. Its reassuring light blinked from green to red.

*

Under the shade of an anonymous eucalyptus further down the block, two unremarkable, plain-dressed men in a gray Audi watched the woman smile a greeting and climb into the truck.

"You see that? Man, am I glad we saved her for last."

Both men dressed in L.A. casual, yet neither wore a tan—or sunglasses, for that matter; their expressionless eyes drank in the Southern California light in all its hues of harsh and soft. The driver started the car, but waited until the Bronco was nearly out of site before following.

"Sure," he said. "But that rack has got to be after-market. They're all plastic around here."

"Don't kid yourself. She's real. She could strangle a horse with those legs."

"Huh."

"At the gym the other day she did a pyramid set on the bench press.

Eight reps at one thirty five, six reps at one fifty, four reps at one eighty, and three reps at one ninety five."

"Huh."

"Leg press, too. Topped out at six hundred pounds. Telling you, could strangle a horse between those thighs." He was silent for a moment. "I hope she tries to run."

Chutes and Ladders

Paris
9AM

Why on earth hadn't she demanded they drive the car? Major Griffin glowered and quickened her pace to keep up with the two men in front of her. Flynn insisted upon strolling–practically marching—to the café, threading more or less straight through the crowds that grew thicker and thicker.

Paris was finally awake. Major had been assigned in the French capitol briefly during her second year in the diplomatic corps, though her schedule at the embassy offices had thankfully precluded her venturing forth before noon. Now, struggling to match pace with the two Americans, she was amazed at the volume of people on the streets. Vendors called out to passing mamans whose arms were full of the day's groceries. Taxis blared through clusters of pedestrians, leaving inky, staccato marks where they'd tapped their brakes. She passed a young man busy stapling *yet another* poster onto one of the cylindrical billboards that graced nearly every street corner. Such noise. A wonder the city didn't deafen itself.

Flynn led them around an aproned man who was positioning chairs around small tables at a streetside restaurant. Was this the one? Obviously not, as the American kept walking. Why a café? Her orders were elementary: collect Flynn and the others back at the hotel, then return to London. His Majesty *had* mentioned she'd be required to improvise considerably while assigned to Alonzo Noel, but Major Griffin had simply nodded and taken that to mean she'd be snared into acting as tour guide for the group if they ever actually arrived in London. Where they were to *consult* her superiors on the search for the Princess. Consult. A Hollywood actor and his ratty accomplice? Doubtful, but the mission had come directly from William, the king. Under any other circumstance—

First the girl selling flowers and now, off to a café for a late lunch. They were bloody wasting all this time.

Major Griffin closed the distance between herself and the two men in time to hear the shorter one make an exasperated noise. "Listen, Jack. I didn't want everybody to meet at your place. I got that itchy feeling, so I sent 'em all to Vincenzo's. Maybe I'm paranoid. Who could know we're in town?"

Jack Flynn didn't say anything. The man was far less than Griffin expected; unshaven, a bit listless and dissipated, though he looked to be in above-average physical condition–no doubt thanks to a personal trainer or some such. He seemed preoccupied, eyes darting apprehensively at the faces in the crowd. Flynn hadn't said more than two dozen words to the major at his apartment, and then she'd had to wait nearly two hours while he'd attended to who knew what on a lower floor of his suite. The Major sniffed. Actors. She'd never met a group more emotionally flat or uninteresting. The rest of the motley group would no doubt prove similar.

"Here, we should see them any minute. They took our old table at the edge of the balcony—"

Alonzo's phone chimed.

"Yeah, hello." He said. "Yeah. About another minute, I can almost see Solomon's big bald head. Good, tell Mama Spiranza I'd like an omelet–what?" He pressed a button on the folding phone and waited a few moments. "Encrypted. All clear." His tone changed instantly. "You're sure? No, we're just around the corner, by the river." He grimaced and rolled his eyes at Jack, who shook his head. "Okay. The minute I call again, clear out. Standard evasion, rendezvous at Jack's."

He snapped the phone shut and pursed his lips. "Just like old times, already," he said to Jack as the three of them pressed into a vacant spot between two street vendors. "That was Ian on the restaurant's special phone. Some of Vincenzo's boys spotted a surveillance nest right across the street. At least two guys three stories up in some kind of hat shop. It was set up in a hurry, but professional. Curtains didn't even move, that sort of thing."

Major Griffin shifted her briefcase and frowned. "What are you saying, that—"

"Sorry, Major." Jack leaned closer to Alonzo, his eyes hard. "Who."

"Couldn't be local intelligence; they all know Vincenzo." Alonzo glanced at Griffin. "Vatican agent, Major. His café is like a fortress, and well-screened. Ultrasonics, the works. He's got acoustic and infrared sensors set up in case of sniper activity, to tell where a shot comes from– that's how he knows someone's using a vibrational laser-listening device. Works the same as a laser rangefinder that a sniper would use to sight in on someone's head. Vincenzo's a genius." He looked at Jack. "A safe place, with a hell of a good cook."

"What else did he say?"

"Ten minutes after they sat down, somebody bounced a directional audial laser off the screen set up on the balcony. Vincenzo slipped a note to Solomon in his menu, and the four of them have been shooting the breeze for a couple hours, waiting for us. What do you think?"

"What do I think?" A long pause. Something like indecision crossed the American's face, then his eyes narrowed. "Hat shop, third floor?" He glanced around for a street sign, and said, "All right, how about this: going to be four exits out of the place. One in front, two in back–one'll be a fire escape–and a fourth through the attic, if they haven't had it sealed off. Shops in this district share an attic crawlspace, locked from the inside.

"That'll be mine. Give me, ah, a five minute head start, then tell everybody to get off the balcony and meet—where?"

"Your place?"

"Fine. Vincenzo's men can monitor the front entrance on the street. Major, if you wouldn't mind staying with Al and watching the back alley?"

Major Griffin took a breath. What were these two playing at? "I really don't see much point."

"You're right; it's probably nothing. Still," Jack's eyes glittered strangely. "Gives us a chance to practice, eh?"

The major nodded slowly. Something in Flynn's demeanor had changed slightly, though she couldn't put her finger on the exact inflection of voice or tone. He still looked flat and common.

Alonzo nodded sharply. "Good. You still want to meet at Vincenzo's?"

"Mama Spiranza won't like it if you let that omelet get cold." Jack said, then hesitated. A pained expression crossed his face. "This still feels a little . . . off."

His friend prodded his shoulder. "Like she said, Jack," he indicated the major. "Probably nothing. We'll see you inside or at the café."

Flynn leaned out toward the stream of pedestrians. With a single glance back at Alonzo and a still-dubious Griffin, he slipped into that river of moving humanity, plunging quickly towards the row of shop faces nearly a block away.

"Hey Major, watch this," Alonzo said as the other man departed. She looked from Jack to his grinning friend and back again, and almost missed it.

Amazing. It was the first time she suspected there was more to the two men than met the eye.

Approximately a dozen steps from them, Jack shrugged. Once, then again, and suddenly he changed. His stride shortened considerably, simultaneous with a change in posture and the angle of his whole body. He appeared smaller and more stout, slightly thicker through the neck and waist. The very manner in which he placed his feet altered as well. Another step, and Jack had shed his short jacket, then reversed it and began tying it about his waist.

To a casual observer, it might have appeared as though the man had briefly stumbled. For Major Griffin, it was as though a subtle yet absolute transformation had taken place. General characteristics were unaltered, of course. His hair and such were the same, but if she had glanced away or perhaps even blinked, the major was certain she'd have convinced herself she was looking at a wholly different man.

The crowd swallowed him as he shrugged again, and practical invisibility became part of the major's reality.

Alonzo looked at her. "Classic. I love it when he does that." He motioned for her to accompany him down a nearby alley.

"One moment." Griffin lingered at the entrance, vainly searching for the American. "That was bloody incredible." Perhaps this would make for an interesting assignment, after all. "And what was all that business about the entrances to the hat shop? A shared attic? Has he been there before?"

The small man raised his eyebrows. "I don't know. Jack never was much for hats. He probably came across the zoning plans for this block some time ago. Most of these buildings would qualify as landmarks back in the States."

"And he'd remember such an esoteric detail?"

Now it was Alonzo's turn to shrug. "Jack remembers all sorts of stuff. Let's go."

*

"Bonjour, mademoiselle. Où sont les toilettes s'il vous plaît?" Jack smiled and moved quickly through the store at the young cashier's direction, past racks and rows of headgear. It was a large shop, and customer flow had reached its peak. He wasn't sure why, but he'd never liked wearing a hat. Not that he was totally opposed to the idea.

He sidled past the doors to the restroom and silently ascended the stairs at the rear of the shop. The rooms on the second floor were well-organized, and he could move quickly. Between the rooms of neatly-spaced sewing machines were racks of raw materials–orderly stacks and squares of satin, felt, velvet, and grosgrain, and bins of straight pins and paper-covered wire.

He walked past two busy Asian women, their backs to the hall. Jack wove around a draft table littered with the equipment necessary to design and trim millinery, and found the door to the adjacent shop behind a bolt of stiff, gray, two–ply buckram.

Like many of the shops that altered or designed their own clothing, the manufacturing floors of the boutiques were linked with those of adjoining shops. The practical business of Parisian milliners allowed for their workers to move from station to station within each shop and, during the season when business flourished (thankfully for Jack, this *was* Paris), workers could move freely between the boutiques. Thus had the shop owners answered the equation of supply and demand and yet maintained a battalion of skilled craftsmen.

Only the storerooms above were isolated from the other boutiques, though each was accessible through the adjoining attic space. The fire escapes were another matter entirely.

Jack fought the urge to look up at the ceiling, towards the level where unknown men were spying on his friends. It didn't make all that much sense, given the security in place across the street. Local talent–rogue agents, mercs for hire, whatever—would be aware Vincenzo's restaurant had the tightest security and surveillance-detection equipment that Vatican superiors could provide. That left intelligence officers with an organized government behind them—no, too obvious—or rank amateurs.

Yet to set up an observation nest so quickly opposite the balcony, whoever it was had to be stone cold professional, not to say accustomed to the territory.

Jack took the staircase quietly, practically mincing up the steps to the storeroom of the shop adjacent to the one occupied by the watchers. He found the trapdoor in the ceiling–secured with a simple hasp from below—and eased it up and open.

The crawlspace beyond was wide enough for him to stand and spread his arms. There were sooty, thin skylights intermittently placed along the roof's peak, allowing narrow slits of sunlight to angle down. Jack followed their path, noting the swirling dust motes and footprints along the floor. Two men, moving fast. From their tracks, Jack judged them to be wearing soft athletic shoes. Comfort and speed. These two knew what they were doing.

Craftsmen.

Silently, silently now, Jack maneuvered up into the attic. The air was stagnant, numb, full of the smell of old wood and the tinny, metallic murmuring from machinery and artisans below. A line of insulation vertically in the wall marked where the first boutique began, and then he saw where the trapdoor lay open, swung up and back, flush with the floor.

Feeling for the weight of his handgun, Jack knelt down and placed his head close to the door. He barely breathed. On the floor below, sideways in his field of vision, two men sat with their backs to the trapdoor on either side of a mounted parabolic directional mike.

One of them, in headphones and a dark jacket that reminded Jack of the kind orchestral conductors wore, only minus the tails, shook his head and muttered something to the other, who bent over a phone.

"No sir, they're still talking about some kind of . . . fishing trip the fat one and the Asian took in the Czech Republic. The fat one is working at a portable computer, but we can't visually confirm what's on the screen. No sign of the other Americans or the British woman." The speaker was probably American–Midwest, Jack decided, though echoes in the empty storeroom made it difficult to make out. He was a pale man with a small, squarish jaw, a broad forehead, and sunken, fleshy eyes. As he listened to whoever it was giving orders on the other end of the phone he played with a double folding blade, the kind Americans called a butterfly knife, flipping it open and closed, open and closed. Jack licked his lips. In the Philippines, where such weapons were conceived, they were called bente nwebes–29's–and he'd seen the little knives thrown with enough force to drive through a silver dollar.

From the look of the youth on the phone, he knew just how to make that happen.

"No sir, no sign at all. No. The two Americans had some sort of disagreement in Flynn's apartment this morning, and that's the last we've gotten of them.

"Yes sir, we'll make that flight." He flipped the phone shut. Jack could see the man's natural expression was bleak, matter-of-fact. "Michael has reassigned us. Says the possible Flynn threat is a waste of time and he'll settle for monitoring the airports." He began dismantling the directional mike.

The other man, removed his headphones and sighed. He was much older, with a well-trimmed beard and a high widow's peak. "We just got here. Where are we to go this time?" He was French.

"Back to the land of the free and the home of the Braves." The younger watcher was brisk, almost mechanical in his economy of movement as he disassembled the microphone's parabolic dish.

His companion sighed again, and wrapped the headphones in their own wires.

Jack pushed himself noiselessly back from the trapdoor and chanced a deeper breath. Could he do this? From its holster in the small of his back he drew his Glock-22. It was a .40 auto, and he'd cleaned and loaded it himself barely an hour ago. All the safeties were internal; the outer plastic casing looked clean and starkly practical. One or both of those men below would come up through the trapdoor. He imagined a face rising over the sights of his pistol. Would he be able to take a life today?

The metal was cold and black-blue in his hand, the coarse grip clinging to his sweaty palm. He could feel perspiration gathering on his face, sliding off because the attic was too hot for sweat to bead, too stifling with risen heat trapped from below. The air held an oil smell, too; musky. He felt like gagging.

Barely a sound from below. The dry *click-click* of a steel case being closed and secured. Why were his hands so clammy? It hadn't felt like this in the past. Had it? Who were those guys, anyway?

The sound of a door opening and closing below. Jack wiped the back of his hand across his forehead.

Could he even do this anymore?

Shadows moved under the trapdoor. Jack raised his gun.

*

"This is as good a place as any to get shot," Alonzo said to the British government woman. He scowled. They were completely exposed in the mouth of the lane which ran behind the hat shops. Not a shadow or dumpster to loiter behind. And he was getting warm.

The clouds over Paris had been showing breaks all morning, and enough sunlight had made its way through to stir up some response from the old city's stones. Any hotter and he'd have to take off his coat and think of some other way to conceal his pistol. The local gendarmes took a dim view of open weapons on the street, and he knew feigning touristical stupidity wouldn't sail him through France's ban on proscribed handguns.

Then the door to the second floor fire escape of the hat shop opened, and a man in a long, black leather coat stepped out.

Immediately Alonzo moved, as if in midstride past the alleyway, smiling and pulling the major by her elbow. "That could be our boy," he said through his teeth, leading the woman at a leisurely gait past the other side of the entrance. Once out of sight he dropped her arm and produced a dental mirror on a rod, and used it to peer around the corner. Leather jacket was on the ground already. Alonzo swore. "This guy moves *fast*, man." He kept his eyes on the man's back as he retreated down the lane. "Okay, Major, get ready to—" But she had already pushed past him. Maybe Jane Austere was getting the hang of this after all.

★

It was the older of the two watchers. Jack exhaled evenly and put on his best poker face as the man's head and shoulders cleared the trapdoor. The conductor's jacket draped a form still angular and powerful, notwithstanding the amount of gray peppering his beard. His eyebrows jumped when he saw the younger man, though from surprise or amusement Jack couldn't tell. A smile played at the corners of the man's mouth, and his eyes went from Jack's gun to the cases in his own hands. He made an apologetic expression. "He of course leaves me to carry the equipment, eh?"

Jack squeezed the trigger just past the first safety in his pistol.

"I know what you are thinking, monsieur Flynn. Whether I will live or die, no?" He was calm, smooth, affable. "You could kill me with so much of a thought, though you're better with your hands than with that Glock you have there. So I've heard." He tested the weight at the end of his arms. "Just let me put this down first, before you begin. I was afraid that you would never show up, but then, how to go about this?"

Jack blinked. *He's actually delighted to see me.* The man before him looked to be on the brink of laughter. Jack shifted his grip on the pistol, and the Frenchman rose the rest of the way into the narrow passage. Under the jacket he wore a dark turtleneck, so midnight black in the attic's dimness he might not have existed at all below the face.

He sat at the edge of the trapdoor, the cases of surveillance gear at his back, and regarded Jack with a smile bordering on fatherly affection.

Jack wet his lips. "You know who I am?"

"I know that you are someone who spends the balance of your life trying to do the right thing. No, Jack Flynn, we've never met, you and I, but I think you comprehend what I am. Kill me and no doubt you'll save the lives of many people you'll never know. Perhaps a few you do."

Jack shook his head dismissively. "Why were you watching the café? Who is 'Michael?'"

The man ignored the first question. "I think 'Aleks Stefanovich' is a name you'll find more interesting." Before Jack could say anything, he continued. "If your computer expert over there," he nodded in the direction of the street, "is as good as he thinks he is, have him weasel into the newest de-classified intelligence vault at CIA headquarters. Your Freedom of Information Act can make things so much easier for people in our line of work, no?

"And this isn't your only occupation, is it, Mr. Flynn?" Despite his relaxed demeanor, the older man spoke rapidly, leaping from subject to subject nearly without taking a breath, as if his time was limited and he was fast approaching its end. "You make movies as well." The smile was becoming unnerving under the cold, intense eyes. "I had tickets to see one of yours, a premiere tonight in London, but it looks now as though I will have to wait." He leaned forward on the heels of his hands, allowing his legs to dangle over the floor below.

Jack motioned with the pistol. "Don't try to—"

"To jump? Or you'll 'fill me full of lead, pardner'?" The Frenchman had a passable Southern accent. "No doubt. But I've already answered your questions, Jack Flynn, and you've got to let me go. I've already stayed too long. If I arouse suspicion, we are both dead men, and you are not yet close enough to the little girl you are trying to find, eh?"

"What do you know about that? Why are you watching us?" Jack felt his face grow red.

The other man shifted back, out of the light falling from the stained skylight. Clouds overhead dimmed the dusty attic another notch. "If I turn up missing, the man I'm currently indentured to will know you are coming, and that will be the end of the little girl." He smiled, eerily

209

composed, calm. "Then again, if you let me go, who knows what will happen?"

Jack lowered his arm. The Frenchman obviously had no fear, and brandishing the gun at him was making Jack feel vaguely foolish. He might as well be flourishing a cucumber in the air. He worked his jaw and tried another tack. "And this is your idea of helping me? A few cryptic clues and some conspiracy innuendo? Why?"

If anything, the bearded man grew more intense. "Let's say I'm trying to be in the right place at the right time. Just like you." He swung his feet onto the stairs. "Now, I am going. You are either going to shoot me or let me go." He grunted under the weight of the two cases. "Remember: Stefanovich. Try the keyword, 'tesla.'"

And Jack watched the older man stride into the darkness. Faint nausea twisted inside him, and he looked again at his pistol. As he clipped it into the nylon holster in the small of his back, Jack's eyes fell on a sky-blue rectangle of paper where the older man had sat. He snatched it up.

It was a premiere-issue ticket for his latest film, *And Caesar Whispered*, redeemable at the Illuminatus Cineplex, in London.

*

Alonzo pressed against the crowd. *Nothing* on the street could move! The traffic had worsened along with the crushing mob in the past few minutes, and he hadn't seen the pale ghost in the black coat for nearly twenty seconds. Damn!

"Do you see him?" The major nearly had to shout in his ear above the cacophony of automobile horns and flatulent exhaust.

Instead of answering, Alonzo swore again and jumped onto a lamp post's base, wrapping a free arm around it and daring a blatant look in the direction of the vanished man. Nothing, nothing, *nothing* but a churning mass of irritable Frenchmen!

He shouldered off the streetlight and into the road, ignoring the withering insults of a pair of drivers as he rolled across the hood of their delivery truck and stepped up onto the roof of the cab. Alonzo saw an anorexic French woman with three children in tow; he saw a serious, bearded musician with a pair of metallic cases; he saw a pair of nuns.

But no pasty-faced cipher in a leather jacket.

The major was yelling something from the side of the street, and Alonzo heard the doors below him slam shut. Someone threw a red vegetable at him, probably a tomato. He glared one more time at the teeming street, then let himself down off the back of the truck and slipped into the crowd, cursing.

Further Up and Further In

San Jacinto State Park, California
6PM

The blond photographer with the unbelievable rack was the final target on the list. When they finished with her this afternoon, they'd be done before all the other teams, even those last-minute sweepers in Boston.

If things went well, maybe they'd finish tomorrow.

The two men in the rented Audi hung back far enough that those in the pickup truck ahead wouldn't know they were being followed, but found they had to narrow the chase distance considerably as the truck led them further and further up into the San Jacinto Mountains.

Both men dressed similarly; light brown slacks, pale yellow shirts, and comfortable shoes. They both wore simple expressions, simple expressions on forgettable faces. Both had been named for angels, but neither was in danger of making it to Heaven. The only thing remarkable about either was the level of sheer focus each brought to the task at hand.

The driver's eyes never left the pickup truck, as he slowed slightly around a turn. The other held a laptop computer on his knees and a booster antenna near the window. "The wireless is still having trouble," he said.

Same trouble with the cell phones. Signal had trouble reaching this far into the wilderness. On the ridgetops and upper saddles they'd have no trouble getting a clear signal back to L.A., but every canyon they entered put another ridgeline behind them, and the man on the computer had to reestablish contact with the company node and the hack that let him into a myriad of databases back in civilization. Scheduling reminders kept popping up onscreen.

They were at the end of their timetable. Company intelligence regarding Westen said she only possessed documents; she wasn't one of the chief scientists on the master list. Simply harvesting the files and loose documents wasn't enough for the higher-ups; for some reason, the woman was to die. Another suburban breaking-and-entering-that turned into assault, then rape, and finally murder. The two angels didn't care either way. The list was long, and the deadline for completion was reasonable. They'd both been doing little jobs like this for a long time.

"Why is it that the easiest target always becomes our biggest problem?" asked the driver.

His companion didn't look away from the screen. "Don't take it personally," he said. "How could we know she'd vanish off the face of the earth for so long?" He shook his head. "Idaho. Who goes on vacation to Idaho?"

The pavement gave way to a dirt road. "Good thing they let us take care of the others first, then come back for her," the driver said. He eased off on the accelerator, and the car slowed. The follow was always easier on dirt-and-gravel roads, with all the loose dirt kicked into the air by the lead vehicle. Even if the target pulled off onto one of the side roads, its dust cloud trail would be hard to miss. "We should have followed and done her in Idaho," he said.

"What?"

"We're going to end up in the woods, anyway."

His companion's expression didn't change. "I'm glad we saved her for last." The woman's file opened on the screen before him. Plastic

213

surgery or no, Southern California women exercised like maniacs, and this one was as toned as some of the women killers working for Raines and Lopez. "She's going to last awhile."

The driver didn't smile, but his voice turned jocular. "Thinking about a little dessert? What about the kid driving?"

"According to the DMV," he said. "The truck belongs to one of her employees. He's not a skilled climber, though, so either she's not taking him with her—"

"Or he's dropping her off and she's going to be alone."

"No." He closed the computer and began screwing a silencer onto his pistol. "She's not going to be alone."

"If he drops her off on a dead-end road and then doubles back—"

"We do him quietly, then her."

The driver nodded. "So how long before she's missed?"

"The studio isn't expecting her to check back with the office until tomorrow morning, but the birdwatchers she's supposed to meet might call in tonight if she doesn't show."

He shook his head. "The people she's meeting are forest-types, right?"

The other man consulted his computer. "Graduate students, they met while working at the California Raptor Center at U.C. Davis. Registered members of the Green Party. They both drive electric vehicles, and every year they max their credit cards at R.E.I. and Any Mountain."

"Tree-huggers. You really think they own a satellite phone?"

The other man shrugged. "The university expects them to stay in contact. Why not kill them as well?"

"Not unless you fancy a climb." They were dressed for an urban hit. The business-casual attire was perfect for blending into L.A., but beyond the suburbs both men felt exposed. Each knew they'd been selected for this mission based on their expertise in urban situations.

"Hold up, they stopped."—but the driver had already killed the engine and let the car coast to a stop in the shadows of a stand of pines.

They watched the woman exit the truck and begin strapping gear on. She wore thick canvas pants and a heavy cotton top, which she peeled off in the summer heat to reveal an aqua-colored sports bra.

"That's a very noticeable blue."

"We'll burn it with the rest of her stuff." It had already been decided that they'd bury the body in several locations, without teeth or clothes, to make post-mortem identification that much more difficult. Research into the target's background turned up close ties with L.A. homicide. Her cousin was a crime scene investigator who apparently kept close tabs on the Westen woman.

Most of her equipment, at least two cameras, went into a small backpack. Both men didn't move as she adjusted herself for the woods.

"Did she just put climbing shoes into her pack?"

His companion finished assembling the silencer. "Why?"

"What's she wearing on her feet?"

The woman waived to the driver of the truck, turned, and jogged straight into the forest.

"She's running?"

The pickup pulled cleanly away, and both men dashed up through the dust to the head of the trail, pistols out. The path lead down through pines, and then around a hill. The underbrush wasn't that thick, but everything was green, leafy, and growing. They heard a rhythmic *swish-swish* from somewhere ahead. Her pants legs brushing against one another.

Neither man flustered easily. Operational difficulties were nothing new, surprises in the target's behavior merely flavored the rich experience inherent to their profession. Neither had ever pursued a woman into

215

the woods before, certainly not while wearing new, stiff dress shoes designed for everything but running through the country.

She was already a good two hundred feet ahead of them, and moving fast. They caught a glimpse of bright blue, and a bouncing ponytail, and then she was around the hill.

"The rifle would work better here."

"You want to take the time to dig it out and put it together?" his companion replied. "Take the trail. I'm going to cut her off at the top of that hill."

They couldn't really see the top of the embankment; it disappeared past the tops of the nearby trees. Nevertheless, his companion started off, cracking and snapping loose bits of fallen branches as he did so.

The remaining man hesitated. He really was much more comfortable back in the car, using the computer. Nothing to be done now; he started down the trail as quickly as he could. At least he could get out of the dust.

Spring had thrown off any sign of winter, and everything was in bloom. He moved further into the deep green, twisting his feet around in the new shoes.

At least his job was easier; if the woman panicked and doubled back along the trail, the only route familiar to her, she'd run right into him.

*

Mercedes reached the bottom of the second slope and used her momentum to carry her up the next incline. The Forest Service hadn't spent much time maintaining the trails in this area; instead of the usual switchback style, where the footpath zigzagged back and forth up a hill to prevent erosion, these paths were more direct. She could make good time.

The two kids from the university raptor program, Eric and Sara Jensen, were scheduled to meet her at the cliffs, at the second level of ascension. They'd climb together to the Jensen's observation camp, and tonight or tomorrow she'd be shooting film of the baby golden eagles getting fed.

Three eggs—a nearly unheard of amount—had hatched in a nest in the top of a secluded, precariously balanced sequoia, and Eric and Sara J. asked for her immediately, before predators or the wind cleared the nest of life. Nature wasn't balanced in their favor—the male was nowhere to be found, and odds were he'd been killed due to mistaken belief that golden eagles are a danger to livestock. The female stayed close to the nest, and food was scarce after the harsh winter.

Mercedes paused a moment to stretch, and a crash sounded back along the trail she'd just run. It sounded distant, and the weave and weft of the hills made its source indistinct. A shadow of a sound.

A breeze carried the scent of new mountain sage across the clearing.

Mercedes' mind was beginning to relax as her body started to wake up and respond. Even with the light backpack, the run felt great. She started off again, inhaling as deeply as she could, lost in the beauty of the deep green. Only two miles to the base of the cliffs.

*

The angel tumbled down the bank in a shower of flinty, flat rocks and loose earth, pain from his ankle forking like lightning up his lower back. Immediately he shrugged off the twinge and concentrated on retained a grip on his pistol until he came to rest. This was becoming ridiculous. His breathing was the only sound he heard, crowded in and muffled by all the old bark.

Urban warfare was his specialty, his passion. He'd cut his teeth as a

217

contract man in Miami, built his portfolio of skills running with the old Cuban mercenaries, and operated for ten years in cities up and down both coasts of North and South America. But this damn wilderness—he was falling too far behind. Maybe his partner had already caught up with her, flanked the woman and brought her down.

He stepped directly on an old log to cross over it, and with a wet, rotten pop it broke open in pieces, further punishing his ankle.

According to his watch, they'd left the road twenty minutes ago, and still no sign of the woman or his partner. What had Mr. Raines' told them, something about never leaving your companion? The pain from a twisted ankle he could dismiss, but being forced to move so slowly was maddening. Why hadn't *she* turned an ankle?

He stopped. The area he was entering looked the same as the pile of logs and brush behind, and hadn't he come down the hill at an angle? What was that old trick about moss growing only on one side of a tree? He hobbled to the nearest tree and groaned; the spongy, greenish growth speckled the entire circumference of the trunk.

No signal on the cell phone.

The low foliage blocked the sun; he needed to get higher to get his bearings. Just needed to get a bit higher.

*

Mercedes stopped at the base of the cliffs to change shoes. Eric and Sara had left a safety line dangling for her, and a flashlight, but it looked like she'd make it up before total darkness.

Damn but this country was pretty.

She clipped in and started up, careful to move one extremity at a time. The crumbly rock face took all her attention, and it wasn't until the dying light on the rock turned red did she turn and look out over the

San Jacintos. Gorgeous. Not a road, television tower, or McDonald's in sight. Mercedes could easily imagine the world like this, an untouched series of rolling, rocky forest.

A warm breeze from below felt wonderful on her back, and she knew she should start moving again, while she still had the light, before evaporating perspiration could chill her.

A rock broke off explosively below her, a dozen feet down and slightly left. Mercedes hoped the safety line was well anchored. It could still freeze this late in the mountains, and cycles of repeated freezing and thawing water, working itself down into the rock, had killed more than one sure-footed climber. Frost reaving, that's what Grandpa Max called it.

Another heavy snap, and more rock trickled off the face. Closer this time. That was odd.

Mercedes looked upward for her next grip, and realized she was being watched. The sensation came over her quickly, the surety that a predator focused on her. The wind flowed up over the rock in a constant, mild stream. Instinctively Mercedes started to look over her shoulder, and felt vertigo crack around her.

The shyest whisper sounded behind her, very close, and another handful of pebbles broke away from the cliff.

Mercedes found a deep crack running through the granite near her left hand. Slowly she pressed her palm in as far as she could reach, nearly to her elbow, and made a fist. The makeshift anchor would fasten her to the cliff face as long as she held the fist. With her free hand she found her smaller camera, a digital, on its lanyard at her waist. Carefully, almost leisurely, she twisted enough to look back towards the valley below.

And looked right into the glaring eyes of an eagle.

Mercedes hands tensed, and she nearly lost her grip on the wall.

The enormous creature drifted smoothly before her, barely moving from side to side on the upwash of air. She'd never seen a live golden before, and Mercedes' practiced eye took in the dark brown plumage extending all the way to the toes, and the distinct gold bathing the back of its head and neck. While Mercedes remained for the most part in awe of the bird, the practical portion of her brain catalogued its wingspan at almost seven feet. *Of course, this is the female,* she thought.

It was big enough to pluck her off the wall, if it wanted to. *Mature females can carry whole deer away.* Now, how did she know that?

Its eyes flicked over her body; the head tilted quizzically, and when its gaze locked again with her own Mercedes was struck with how elemental, how uncommonly fierce they were. She felt helpless and at once exalted before the creature, and as her adrenaline spiked Mercedes felt a kinship with the mother bird, with the supreme predator spread majestically before her.

She almost forgot to take its picture, and took several until the eagle slid in front of the setting sun. Every outspread feather glowed pink, and the crown blazed with white-gold fire.

Something smacked the rock face just a few feet from them, walloped it hard enough for Mercedes to feel the impact through the stone, and for the first time Mercedes became aware of a whine, almost a whistle, that had preceded the hit. *Almost like the sound a bullet would make.*

The eagle glanced away, folded its wings, and sliced off down towards the darkening green below. Mercedes watched until she lost it against the pattern of the trees, and resumed her climb.

*

The damn pistol was no good at this range and angle, and the silencer deflected the shots past any hope of accuracy. His companion had been right after all; should have brought the rifle. Better not give him too much credit, he thought. The fool didn't have enough sense to stay on the trail, now, did he?

As long as the woman hung on the cliff, though, staring at the bird . . . he aimed again, then swore as the bird moved between them. He fired anyway, and saw that the bullet deflected a bit. Must be the same breeze the bird used. He raised the gun again—now where was the bird?

Dropping like a stone through the golden light, like some kind of screaming missle, like a sliver of fire, right for his position. He dropped his pistol and slithered backwards through the brush, suddenly, shockingly afraid

All the King's Horses and All the King's Men

Paris

10AM

Jack leaned back as far as the balcony rail allowed, considering the file before him. The three of them sat at his customary table at the corner of the terrace, where Vincenzo had long ago arranged the overhead canopy to block out any prying eyes.

Alonzo and the Major ate quietly, scrutinizing the boulevard below. The tagliatelle verdi and frittata were delicious, though Jack picked at them absentmindedly as he pored over the documents stamped with the seal of MI-5, the internal arm of British Secret Intelligence. Several small bottles of Sanpellegrino carbonated water turned double-duty, weighing the pages to the table. Jack lifted one and motioned to a nearby waiter. "Marcello? Another aranciata, per piacere?" His mouth had gone dry.

He shuffled the papers back into chronological order and skimmed once again over the pertinent details.

A week before, the Princess Christine, only child of Britain's Royal Family, had arrived with her guards at the family estate of Balmoral Castle in Scotland. She had traveled in a modified Sikorsky transport helicopter, what the American Navy was calling a Super Stallion these days. She spent the holiday with her parents, who left early for a press conference or to preside at the opening of some cheese factory or another. No member of the Royal Family travels with another, for obvious security reasons. In the company of fifteen security agents, plus the regular contingent of Scotland Yard detectives and other employees of the Crown, the Princess had spent two days "larking about with her ponies" under the direct supervision of more than one hundred people, according to the report. The last recorded contact with the security team at Balmoral occurred at one a.m. two days ago. A brief lightning storm and the resulting atmospheric disturbance made all contact with Balmoral's team impossible between four and four thirty the following morning. Radar coverage of the area had been blanked for nearly an hour. Jack skimmed over the transcripts of the attempts to contact the team by radio and phone, seeing nothing. *They knew exactly what they were doing,* he realized, *to have been* that *ready to act during the storm.*

At five o'clock three squads of marines from the nearby Royal Navy base converged on the grounds, to be greeted with utter silence. Only one man, an outer perimeter guard, had been found alive, wedged into a pocket of rock on a cliff overlooking the castle. He had yet to regain consciousness. Everyone else at Balmoral from the resident security chief down to the two stableboys had been coldly, efficiently murdered. They found the Secret Air Service guards posted outside Her Highness" door with their pistols drawn and readied, but not a shot fired.

It was as if Death had scythed through them like a wind.

The only thing missing from the grisly tableau was the Sikorsky, its pilot, and the Princess. Her personal kidnap recovery device, a microchip-sized telemetry burst transmitter hardwired into a bracelet she wore, was found in a saddlebag on one of the horses, where sufficient body heat would keep the alarm from sounding.

Jack skipped down through the details of the quiet, desperate mobilization of the Empire and the measures taken to prevent the news from leaking to the media. Anything to distract the slavering press from the Royals: A car bomb had exploded harmlessly but sensationally in the Whitechapel area of London, the government called an unusual, rambling press conference on the topic of the future of Welsh sheep cloning, and three sons of a tavern keeper had produced definitive recordings of the Loch Ness Monster. Jack shook his head. Misdirection was a hazardous game. Other news of the past two days had added to the confusion: four other little girls between the ages of five and nine had been abducted in the Greater London area.

Mid-afternoon the next day had heralded the discovery of the missing pilot, washed up on a beach near Bergen, Norway. He had suffered extreme exposure and was identifiable by the remains of his flight suit. An intensive search in the area produced part of the serial plate of the Sikorsky and oil particulate in the water characteristic of a high-velocity crash at sea. Current search and rescue operations were being conducted in radiating circles from the determined point of impact. Experts on sight could not agree whether the crash was authentic and verifiable, and the search went on—

Jack read over the details, noting the increasingly cold and professional tone in which it had been written. MI-5's progressive use of academic terminology masked a growing, palpable frustration. Several pages of theory and analysis followed on possible motive and identity of the kidnappers, all convoluted and improbable. Jack sighed and let the report fall into his lap. One fact lay unspoken in the entire file: the longer the kidnappers went without contacting anyone, either for ransom or political statement, the less likely the Princess would be rescued.

Of secondary importance, as the circling search patterns grew ever wider and more and more manpower was needed to maintain its intensity, the odds grew exponentially that news of the Princess' abduction would leak. The press would have a field day. All the governments in the hemisphere, to the best of Jack's knowledge, would fall over themselves in an effort to rescue her. Britain would be made a laughingstock in terms of security. Terrible things could happen to a country that has lost face. The door locking chaos out would be ajar, at the very least.

"Major Griffin," Jack handed the sheaf of papers back to the young woman seated opposite him. "Level with me here. How good is this intelligence?"

"That's the entire package, forwarded to me by His Majesty's private secretary this morning. Not much added from the information I was sent last night. The guard that was recovered from the outer perimeter remains in a coma, I'm afraid."

"Jack," Alonzo said, "Balmoral isn't all that defensible; wouldn't take too many men to get in."

"I remember. What's got me worried is the timing of the attack to coincide with the storm. Radio and digital communications went down about the same time the land lines were cut."

Alonzo's eyebrows shot up. "You think it's not a coincidence?"

"Look at the times of the attack and the atmospheric disturbance. What kind of a storm knocks out state-of-the-art radar?" Jack poured the last of his Sanpelligrino into a glass and drank it.

"So, you think whoever they were used something like a pink noise generator?"

The major broke in. "Excuse me, a what?"

"A pink noise generator," Jack said. "A machine that creates a random sound. Small ones are used to fine-tune a home speaker system. Because the sound from the generator changes randomly in frequency and amplitude, it is difficult to filter out. Build them bigger and you can mask conversations by, well, desensitizing a microphone or other type of listening device. Build them big enough and you can override microwave signals, pretty much anything on either side of the visible band."

"So you postulate that such a device was used?"

"It makes sense. I'm surprised none of your people thought so. "

Major Griffin shrugged. "Sounds a titch like science fiction."

The waiter came with two more of the small green bottles of carbonated water for Jack, and another bottle of Peroni beer for Alonzo, which he waved off. The smaller man was intently scrutinizing the blue movie ticket Jack had found.

Jack shook his head. "I seem to remember reading about the maser research going on right now in your country, Major. Microwave amplification instead of light amplification? A pink noise generator is just about the same thing."

"Could this machine be used to kill?"

He frowned. "I suppose. Why?"

Major Griffin pursed her lips. "Some of the Scotland Yard detectives assigned to the Princess were burned through. I mean to say, when they were autopsied, their internal organs and extremities showed an identical degree of scorching." In answer to his next question, she added, "Autopsy reports were deemed inconsequential, and not included in the report you read just now." She waved her hand. "The men and women were deceased, after all."

"Al, did William mention anything about a maser?"

Alonzo looked up. "He said something about an electric weapon being involved in that wacko plot to demoralize Western culture." He dropped the ticket on the table. "I'm more worried about this. Looks like an invitation to a trap, if you ask me. Any more ideas about the other stuff that guy said in the attic?"

"That name, 'Alex Stefanovich.' Except he said it harder, like 'Aleks.' Doesn't ring a bell. And I've never been to the Illuminatus Cineplex."

The major spoke up. "It's relatively new. I believe it's in the same building as the new Harrods."

"What I still don't get," Alonzo said. "Those two guys in the hat shop were so professional, but they didn't know about Vincenzo's countermeasures. And you say the older one was French?" he asked his friend.

"Yeah, he was. Maybe he knew about Vincenzo's security net all along. Wanted to get our attention. That makes sense when you think about all the clues he was so desperate to drop."

"But why should he be trusted?" The major asked.

They were silent for a moment. It was such a beautiful day in Paris. Despite the noise and fumes from the thoroughfare below, a special clarity held the air, a certain crisp freshness. A pair of pigeons alighted on the balustrade behind major, cooing; and Jack was tempted to smile at their warbling challenge. It wouldn't be Paris without legions of pigeons.

The city had become a refuge for him, a familiar fortress in which he'd ensconced himself behind walls of habit, of custom. Jack loved the fact that life continued to abide in the City of Light. Even before he and Victoria had come here to live, there had always been something vaguely comforting in the *idea* of Paris; of taking breath in the city where countless men and women had *also* lived and managed to make sense and civility out of generation upon generation of life; had sweat, sang, fought, prayed to a God in Heaven and then cursed each other by that god's name, had made peace, made war, made love, and then given birth to another generation that would inherit the ancient yet fresh walls of Paris. Borders of stone and mortar that framed the most exquisite living portrait of humanity Jack could imagine.

"Out of chaos, order," he muttered, his gaze aimless over the city.

"Eh?" Alonzo said, querulous.

"We won't make sense out of any of this until we go to London." Jack rubbed his eyes, passed a hand over his stubbly chin. Time to shake off a little of the stone and mortar.

Major Griffin was on her feet, the papers already in a manila folder. "I can make the arrangements right away, Mr. Flynn. The embassy has a special agreement with British Airways."

"No, ma'am." Alonzo made a dismissive gesture. "Jack overheard one of those spooks mention something about monitoring at the airports for us. We could all go in disguise, of course," he ignored her smirk, "but that would mean splitting up, making this all more complicated than it has to be—"

"And if it comes to that, we'll need some privacy and time in close quarters to plan together, Major."

Griffin was nonplused. "Perhaps you'd prefer an eight-man rowboat with which to cross the Channel."

Alonzo chuffed. "Through the Chunnel on the Eurostar, right?"

Jack nodded. "Have everyone check their tracks first. After this," he gestured to where the two watchers had set up their listening post, "we don't know who else might be paying attention to our comings and goings. Let's lose any tails before we leave town."

"That could take some time," the major said, frowning.

Alonzo shrugged. "It will take a few hours to prep the materiel. Anything else?"

"Get Steve to work on the name 'Aleks Stefanovich.'" Almost as an afterthought, Jack added, "And have Ian check in with his contacts in the FBI, just in case he's done anything stateside."

"What about you?"

"I'm going to need a little time to myself." He rocked back from the table. "I'll meet you all at the station."

The smaller man gave his friend a long look. Finally, "Don't take too long, Jack." He winked and added in a fake stage whisper. "You can do this, man."

Major Griffin snapped her briefcase shut. "Going to rain soon." A gust of wind tugged at her hair, rifled through the napkins on the table, and sent the pigeons fluttering.

She was right. Jack could smell the storm. "Okay, then. Anything else?"

Alonzo thumped his hand on the table and glanced around for the waiter. "Where's Marcello? He ever going to bring my beer?"

Hradek

London
12PM

T his will mean an end to hope."

He could feel night at the edges of noon. Alex Raines stood at the window of his London office, and flung the Sanderson toile drapes wide to let sunlight scour the room.

The onrushing radiance set his white suit aglow. He reveled in the light; soaked in it; drank it in as if it were a featherlight, intoxicating nectar. Or, better yet, a kind of nourishment. Raines savored the sunlight like the heavy aromas of the Italian cuisine he relished preparing personally, meticulously, lingering for hours in the kitchen of one of his homes. Steam from risotto, just after you poured the seasoned broth over the rice. Freshly baked ziti drowned in virgin tomato sauce. He wet his lips.

His entire adult life he'd been thrust into the role of the connoisseur.

Raines stood in the very center of the window, the streaming light turning his pale linen suit to pure gold. He touched his long fingers to the glass. London at noon in the early spring was deliciously luxuriant. Raines counted it one of his life's greatest blessings that he was able to see the joy in his life, more specifically, in this particular day, with such completeness and overpowering depth. In his forty-five years he'd met no one capable as he was of savoring the daily slices, the tartness, of reality. Perhaps he alone among men looked down on the London of this particular moment and *tasted* it, tasted it as sure as if it was a dessert of zabaglione, made with a touch of Marsala wine from his own vineyard.

Delectable. He considered bowing his head briefly and offering thanks for the clarity granted him, but his chosen deity had never required that particular obeisance.

And the moment was passing. Already the sun overhead was sliding on toward a twilight that waited like a patient leviathan under the waves to the west. Raines could feel the day dying, and he relished that, too. Below him spread Hyde Park, and beyond that the Royal House at Kensington Gardens. The long, narrow lake they called the Serpentine shimmered like a giant tear between the two. His office was almost too far up to see the people milling about. The parks below teemed with Londoners on their lunch break; sojourners, tourists, quite possibly the odd provincial visitor come to explore the city. Blissfully unaware. Not one of them could feel the darkness coming. He closed his eyes and gasped gently at the pressure of the subtle juggernaut, the utter blackness bearing down above the illusion of a blue sky. He looked up, and saw the marred blueness, heard the distant, tenebrous unraveling. The edges of the day were tattering into night.

Behind him, slightly to the left and just beyond the reach of the light, Miklos Nasim stood with his hands folded across the knife-like pleats of his impeccable grey suit. Miklos was a tall man, but nothing about his posture or build seemed to suggest height. He was all angles, from the abrupt vee of his eyebrows to the lines down along his cheekbones, pitted slightly by sun and a frantically adventurous youth, to the precise jut of his frown. Long, lank, colorless hair fell past his collar.

Motionless, he surveyed the room, letting his awareness sift past the expensive art and lavish decor. He noted the bulletproof Lexan glass, the stance and posture of the man before him who so arrogantly leaned back on his heels in the light. Miklos noted the various bulges in the suit of a third man, an enormous, powerful Chinese, also dressed with improbable fashion, who sat typing at a computer terminal a few meters away, and knew instinctively what weapons the larger man had secreted on his person.

Bah. Armed or not, Miklos had no patience for accountants.

His gaze returned to bore at a spot between the shoulder blades of Raines as the other man motioned to him, never turning from the window. "Look, Miklos, and remember it while we still have the chance," Raines said.

"You put that in an interesting way, 'an end to hope,'" Miklos said. He shifted his head, as if looking out the window, but kept his focus on the older man. He was able to meet Raines' gaze as he turned.

"What would *you* call our wondrous project? We are about to purify the entire human race–at least, that portion which believes itself capable of coherent thought–through despair." He motioned with his thin, spidery fingers at the city beyond the glass. "And tomorrow, by the time these people wake up from the shock to realize that their lives are over, we'll be ready to begin the Cuba phase."

Miklos raised an eyebrow. The phase of the project that would be fulfilled in the Caribbean had bothered him from the beginning. The overall goal was clear: destroy and humiliate as many world leaders as possible; after the operation in London, they'd unmake the symbolic heart of what was fast being seen a succeeding democracy. Their allies, however— "You know my people report that Armand Lopez is unreliable. Probably unstable in the extreme. His vendetta against the Cuban president has led him to commit tactical errors in the past—"

Nothing could spoil Raines' appreciation of the bright afternoon. "But can't you appreciate the irony before us, Miklos? Laundering the profits Lopez funnels toward us from his sales of illegal narcotics in the

United States and Western Europe helped us construct this building and its counterpart on Rockwell Island. Or do you simply dislike the fact that Armand's money bought your freedom from the Albanian authorities?"

It was true; Miklos would still be awaiting execution if not for the bribes cast on his behalf. "Caution is all I advocate, sir," he said, deferring to the older man. "Lopez is a psychotic."

Raines smiled, disquietingly. "Exactly what we need."

"And everything else is ready. The actors," he made a face, "are rehearsing in the studio below. We'll actually use the apparatus itself to broadcast our message tonight, shortly before you return the princess. If you have any further preparations, I suggest you see to them."

He knew a dismissal when he heard one. Miklos nodded curtly and stepped out of the room.

As the door shut, Raines' assistant cleared his throat. "Sir, I have an item requiring your attention." The giant Asian in the pinstriped suit nodded at the screen before him. "Regarding the copy of the Hradek file. The network at MIT was wiped, but we believe a copy was forwarded to someone in California."

Raines steepled his fingers. The project was too far along now to be checked. Still . . . A copy of Hradek, the complete files on his apparatus, not to mention the blueprints of the office building in which he now sat? Discovered? Probably by some idiot at the plant in Czech–but then why send the file to MIT? And California? Odd.

"We still have angels in California. Have them do whatever is necessary. Stay on top of this, Michael."

The Asian called Michael busied himself at the keyboard.

Raines turned back to the sunlight. Whoever had unearthed the Hradek file, odds were they had no idea what they'd stumbled across, and even less likelihood they'd be able to alert anyone who could do anything about it.

The project was too far along now, too perfect. Nearly done.

*

Miklos swore quietly to himself as he spiraled down through the darkened stairways and halls. The project was flawed, faulty, and much too reliant upon unstable elements–unstable *fools*, there; he'd thought it as loudly as he dared. Sometimes he swore Raines could read his mind.

Alex Raines was a genius: that much he'd seen from examining the machine in the basement and on the roof, but the man's quiet, unnerving faith in the overall project struck Miklos as empty and arrogant as belief in the absentee Christian god. Yet Alex Raines and Miklos Nasim were not markedly different. Of Serbian descent, Raines could conceivably be connected somehow to Miklos's own noble Albanian ancestry.

The man intrigued Miklos. Nothing in the whole of his experience could have prepared him for someone like Raines, not even the years of abbreviated childhood he'd spent behind the Iron Curtain. Miklos had been one of a handful of Albanian children deemed worthy of special training, selected by local KGB officers to attend a school located not far from the main headquarters at Number 2 Dzerzhinsky Square. There they were painstakingly trained in the arts of covert war, destined by the State to return to their homeland and impart their knowledge and leadership to others. Miklos excelled; pummeling himself toward perfection. He'd begun the preparations for his first assignment with an inkling of awe, a certainty of his destiny. It was a great thing to make a difference in the world.

Then one day, a Wall fell down.

Before they cast him aside, the Soviets taught Miklos that most of his fellow human beings were inherently weak-willed, led as easily as sheep when the right amount of pressure was brought to bear in the form of a bomb or a bullet. Terror was nothing more than a goad. Mankind exists to be controlled through fear, to be compelled and coerced toward a realization that ultimately, there was nothing else. Nothing. Even the so-called "holy books" named fear of God as the greatest motivation.

There was nothing as pure. Nothing but fear, and the man who controlled the fear eventually controlled everything. History had already proven Miklos right.

Occasionally, of course, the sheep would rally around a person or an idea which, by its novelty, would captivate them and lull them into forgetting their reverence for terror. This anomaly in the true order of things had many names–love, brotherhood, joy, esteem, faith . . . useless, worthless concepts, made up out of scrabbling desperation in the face of the truth. The people needed someone to remove these distractions– gently or not—to cleanse their lives of examples of such empty ideas, and thereby lead them along the path toward humble subservience. Individual self-realization was an illusion, a distraction, a paper grail. To feel alive, men and women needed fear. Only then could they order themselves according to their individual paranoias, and realize their potential.

For more than twenty years Miklos had considered himself something of a dark shepherd, ranging over the fields of the earth, tending to the flocks of whatever lord and master could meet his price. Bombings in major population centers, gradual poisoning of water supplies, explosions aboard airliners in flight, carefully orchestrated mishaps involving biohazardous materials. His resume was his contribution to mankind.

The Soviet inculcation had wedged another truth into Miklos's psyche: Westerners were utterly unpredictable, completely without culture, and pitiably mad in the pursuit of their mass delusions. If there were any truer evidence of this fact, it surrounded him now. The

Illuminatus Tower, as Raines had christened his new building, was a monstrosity.

Who in their right mind would mix Georgian and medieval architecture, then gild it over with the mirror-and-steel-facade common to office buildings worldwide?

Who but a genius or madman could envision and then create the nightmare machine hardwired into its walls? Miklos stepped lightly through the dark halls.

*

Raines stood at the window and pulled at the corners of his pale linen suit. "History will call this terrorism," he said.

"What was that, Mr. Raines?" The massive Chinese looked up from his desk.

"The systematic use of terror, violence, or intimidation to achieve an end. Not very poetic, is it? That is to say, for the glorious ends we will accomplish tomorrow, eh, Michael?"

The other man's broad Asian face creased with a grin as he resumed typing.

Just then there was a rapping knock from the door. Another man, coiffed and dressed as impeccably as the other two, entered. Raines smiled. "Yes, Chomriel?"

"It's our young guest, Mr. Raines. She's taken to crying again."

The thin man in the pale suit turned back to the window. The clouds had begun to crowd back in over the city. London was already wrapping itself in shadows as thick as cobweb. Below him, to the south, lay the Thames and an unsuspecting Buckingham Palace. "Let her cry, my son. Such a cleansing sound, wouldn't you say? Enjoy it while it lasts." He smiled at the reflection of himself. "I'll show them terror."

Raines turned his consideration fully back to the unusually bright London day, the radiance pooling in shimmering lakes on the rooftops and burnished byways below, the brilliantly blue sky splashed with sunlight. He devoured it whole.

Lessons in Flight

Paris

11AM

The second pay phone downstairs at Vincenzo's was fairly safe; it used a randomized algorithm to encode messages over a power line that fed directly into the central switch, a few blocks away, where it was re-encoded as pieces of a random MP3 from the Beatles catalogue. A second, hard-to-notice program "followed" the MP3 down the line; only a phone with a SIM chip incorporating a special hardware key could decode the original message. It was entirely original, and it was entirely Alonzo's idea, and he was completely proud of it every time he used Vincenzo's phone. Too bad the French government was catching up with the technology; in a few years he'd have to think of another way for Vincenzo to get free phone calls to his uncle at the Vatican.

"The Eurostar, right. Repeat the time." Alonzo paused for the response, then added, "No, 'Stefanovich'. Pull whatever you can find and dump soft copies onto everyone's phone." He sighed. "No, I'll comp you for the train tickets, just like before. SOP applies. Nothing's changed."

Nothing's changed. As he hung up the phone, Alonzo spotted Jack walk slowly out the restaurant's side door, making way for a middle-aged couple headed in. Alonzo glanced once at the stairs, and wondered about the woman. The major could take care of herself—frankly, he admitted, they'd be better off without an outsider once they really started to move, if Jack's little club still functioned the same.

And that hinged on the man himself, which is why curiosity pushed Alonzo himself out the door and into the Parisian foot traffic.

He kept his distance as Jack wandered, staying across the street, taking care to always fall in step with anyone around him—a myriad of tricks to mute his presence. Jack kept his head down, hunched a bit, stiffer than he'd remembered—stiffer than he'd moved after any of his injuries, that's for sure.

Victoria would know what to do for Jack now. She could've figured it out. Jack always liked women smarter than he was, and he had loved Victoria. There were ways to engage him, focus his mind and his abilities by distracting him at opportune moments, but for the life of him, Alonzo didn't know what magical buttons to push that would snap Jack back into himself. The group needed him, not this somber, un-Jack little old man with a furrowed brow.

Alonzo trailed, wondering if Jack could follow his own orders and lose a shadow. Jack slowly entered a WH Smith's, and vanished in the fiction aisles. Alonzo felt the smile on his face grow as he strode back and forth through the store. None of the clerks had even seen the American enter.

The major was already gone from Vincenzo's. Alonzo wondered if Jack paid the bill before slipping out, or if they'd stiffed the major. That thought entertained him all the way across town, until he arrived back at Jack's apartment.

Jack was on the balcony, moving quickly in the wind that blew ahead of the storm. It was close to T'ai Chi Chuan, or looked similar, but Alonzo figured the stretching-striking-flexing exercise was something Jack had cobbled together himself, drawn from any number of martial arts. He breathed deeply as he moved, and Alonzo knew better than to interrupt. Jack believed that stuff was good for the soul. He found a phone and checked up on everyone's progress.

Jack snatched a towel off the back of a chair near the balcony door.

"How the hell do you keep getting in here?" He watched Alonzo as he mopped his face and torso. If Alonzo read his expression right, it was almost a joke.

He covered the phone's receiver. "Get a shower and some deodorant, or have you lived long enough in Paris to evolve beyond that kind of thing?" He ducked the thrown towel as the other man left the room.

*

When Jack returned ten minutes later, Alonzo had collected enough info for a rough readiness report. "The thing that worries me is the connection between Espinosa and whatever is going on with William's daughter."

Jack shook his head. "We'll have to let London play out first, before we can focus on Cuba. Don't you have the Tanner twins down there right now, training up the new Cuban army?"

Alonzo grinned. "You *are* paying attention. Vern and Mack had a whole platoon at Herefordshire up until last week, training with the SAS; that would have been some welcome help."

"But when does timing work out in our favor?" Jack perched on the sofa opposite. "You're eating again?"

The smaller man glanced down at a plate of eggs on the low table between them, next to his glass of Foster's and the crystal bird—it was some kind of predator, a hawk or a falcon. "We've got a good three hours. You ever eat the food on the Eurostar?"

Jack yawned and stretched, relaxing a shade. He stared for a long moment out through the open balcony doors over Alonzo's head, at clouds already beginning to glow with the coming night.

His friend certainly looked better, more himself than he had a few hours ago. The dark hardness under his eyes had nearly vanished, and

Jack had steadily become more expressive, more voluble while he'd worked. It was only a matter of time, Alonzo was certain, until Jack would be . . . Jack again.

There was still a lingering wistfulness about him that defied release. What would Victoria have done to break the spell? Sitting there in what had been her home, the answer came to Alonzo in a rush, almost as if she'd whispered in his ear. *Get Jack to tell a story. Get him to use that fat brain.*

On the cushion next to Jack, taken from one of the shelves above his head, lay a framed picture of Victoria. Taken–what, almost a week after she learned to waterski. It wasn't that good a picture; for instance, the lighting was way too bright, she was slightly out of focus and not even centered properly, and she'd just gone across a wake, scattering up a rainbow. She was gorgeous, her already dusky skin burnished nearly into chocolate by the summer sun. The femininity of Irish women in general had always been more apparent to Alonzo in their overt intelligence, attitudes, and sensibility, rather than in their physical appearance. Meeting Victoria, more pointedly, meeting Victoria in her bathing suit, had caused him to rapidly rethink that philosophy. He remembered then that the picture had been taken just before she'd lost a ski and fell, and how mock-mad she'd been when she thought her undignified wreck had been caught on camera. Alonzo smiled at the thought. He'd taken the picture himself, from the deck of his parents' boat.

He allowed his eyes to drop to Jack, who suddenly furrowed his brow in thought. The movement only added to his expression of melancholy.

Alonzo leaned forward, plucking up the wrought-crystal bird from the coffee table. Jack's gaze shifted downward slightly and he raised his eyebrows. The smaller man met his gaze.

"I miss her, too," he said softly.

241

Jack nodded, his frown reversing itself gradually into a smile. He looked briefly again at the picture in the golden frame, then stood and returned it to the shelf. "She sure got dark fast that summer."

"Well, she might have been Irish, but she grew up in Asia. She was used to a lot of sun."

"Yeah. Toria had a head start in just about everything."

Alonzo emptied his glass. "You always did date the ones that could tan," he said around a mouthful of food. He lifted the crystal bird. "When'd she give this to you?"

Jack looked down over his shoulder. "What? Oh, the falcon? Toria didn't give it to me."

Alonzo took a closer look at the crystal. It really wasn't carved that well. Although a special care had been taken with the details of the eyes and wings, overall the piece was substandard. "Who, then?"

"Remember that girl, when we were seventeen, and you'd just gotten back—"

"Back from Australia, yeah, I remember. Oh, that's right! What was her name?"

Jack sat and reached for the falcon. "Mercedes."

"Yeah. Hey, you got anymore Foster's?"

"In the fridge, behind the fruit cake-thing your mom sent me last Christmas." Jack studied the crystal as Alonzo stood. Flashes of coruscant light played across his face, refracted from deep within the translucent falcon. "She was really amazing."

Alonzo raised his head from the refrigerator in order to yell back. "Sheeze, Jack, my mom's still alive you know." He took a bottle of springwater for Jack and a thick can of Foster's for himself, then reentered the library. "Bad luck to speak of the living in the past tense, man."

242

Jack snagged the bottle thrown at him. "Not your mom, you moron. Mercedes."

Ensconced once again in the sofa's cushions, the smaller man popped the tab on the can of beer. "That's right. She was—Diane Bergstrom's cousin, or something. You really had it going on that summer, amigo. State Champs coming up, you were finishing that chemistry assignment for Mrs. Riley for fall semester, working on your tan guarding pool honeys all day, then, wham, in walks this chick."

"In walks Mercedes."

Alonzo poured some beer into a glass, then drank straight from the can. "So what ever happened to her?"

Jack took a long pull on the water bottle. "I never told you the whole story, did I? 'Bout how she showed up at the pool at four in the morning, and all that."

Alonzo blinked. "Four o'clock? No way! What, when you were doing one of those crazy workouts under the spotlight? Why'd she come to the pool at four?"

"Couldn't sleep, I guess. This was the day after she ran into Kyle."

He sniffed again. "Dremel. That guy. So what happened?"

Jack set down his water and the crystal, so as to have his hands free. *His hands are half the story,* Alonzo thought, but he kept his mouth shut. It had been months since he'd seen Jack this animated. His friend leaned forward as he spoke, grinning unselfconsciously. Points of green and blue light gathering in the falcon found his face, and Jack paused, an expression somewhere between guilt and amusement rippling out of the silent, dark waters that made an island of his soul.

"First off, I about break my leg when I see her . . ."

*

Forge
5AM

He felt like an idiot, but he offered his hand anyway. "My name's Jack."

"Mine's Mercedes. Nice to meet you Jack." She had a firm, no, a *hard* grip; almost like she was trying to cement him to her. Her hand was calloused from much use. *What is she, some kind of spot welder?* Jack thought. No, not this girl. Couldn't be.

He'd simply never seen anyone as beautiful as—what was her name, again?

"Mercedes," he said agreeably, taking a step forward. Without warning, Jack went down hard, landing with a grunt on the concrete deck. Grimacing, he noted that his foot had become tangled in the black, ropy cords of the electronic time clock. *Brilliant*, he thought. *Yeah, Jack, this is a great impression.*

He untwined himself, stealing glances at the girl, who was trying valiantly to hide her laughter (and almost succeeding, he noted ruefully) behind a feigned cough. She was wearing an old denim jacket over white shorts and pink t-shirt. "How'd you get in here?" he pressed.

"You left the door open. Hey, you're bleeding a little." She pointed.

Jack looked down at his knee. Sure enough. It wasn't much of a wound; merely an abrasion, and the chlorine and other pool chemicals would probably be antiseptic enough, but you never could tell. He kept his eyes firmly on the blond girl as he walked over to the shower and yanked the chain. "Not a mass-murderer or anything, are you?" he asked as he rinsed his stinging knee. "Come in here to, um, add another felony to your list of crimes, maybe strangle me?"

Her reply was quick. "I think you're doing a good enough job of that on your own."

Now it was Jack's turn to laugh. He slipped a pair of cotton shorts on over his suit.

Mercedes continued. "My grandparents–do you know the Adams'?– live a couple blocks away, and I couldn't sleep."

He was incredulous. "Couldn't sleep–what, in Greater Metropolitan Forge? Holy cow, Mercedes, that's a first." He sat, crosslegged, on the lower diving board. Watching her talk, Jack surprised himself by wondering if her mind was as flawless as the rest of her. Careful, buddy, he told himself. She was perfect for him at that moment. No nicks or chips marred his perception of her, which was only a few minutes old. Well, that wasn't exactly true.

"I saw you at the pool yesterday afternoon. All those kids were with you?" She nodded. "Any of them yours?" She looked confused, so he added, "I mean, do you have any kids?" Now, why had he asked *that*?

He got another laugh in response, and she joined him on the board. "Are you kidding?"

Mentally, he backpedaled fast. What was wrong with him? He found himself almost wishing she'd go away, just vanish back into the soft summer night she'd conjured herself out of, or something.

On some deep level, Jack realized the longer they spoke the more he could very well be getting himself into, well, what?

She was saying something, something about walking to the pool . . .and Jack suddenly wondered what it would be like to sketch her face. If he had a good piece of charcoal and a little bit better lighting, he could probably capture her wide brow and straight nose. The full, sleek lips and strong jaw might be a bit hard for him, but he didn't doubt he could do it, given a little time. She's Italian, he thought abruptly, surprised at

245

the flash of insight, despite her Nordic hair and body type. If he only had a pad of paper and a good pencil–

Jack brought himself up short. In his entire life, he'd never drawn a single thing.

This was getting a little too weird. He needed to move.

"—and then I saw you start your little race, Mr. Aquaman, and there we have it." she summed up with a smile. Jack nodded amiably, sucked his eyes away from the dimple that had appeared in her right cheek, and lurched off the diving board towards the pool building.

"I need to do a few things to get the pool ready. Want to come? We open up for earlybird swim in about an hour."

"Sure," she said, following. Gesturing to the Ziplock bag with the CD player in it, she said, "So you're not afraid of electrocuting yourself?"

Jack tapped the buttons through the plastic, then pulled the speaker off the pool bottom by its cord. "Not really. It's insulated. I kind of made it myself."

"Oh," she said, and left it at that.

She followed him into the lifeguards' lounge, which adjoined the front office. He stowed the CD player in a mesh basket on the wall with his name on it, then grabbed a handful of keys off a peg near the cash register. Jack was dying to ask her more questions, but for the life of him, he couldn't figure out what they were. "Ah, I've got to get some stuff out of the basement." She nodded back at him, then continued to examine the pale blue room. Jack watched her gaze linger over the six shelves of swimming trophies. "A lot of those are left over from the old pool," he said.

"They're dusty," she replied.

Not having much else to say, Jack nodded and walked past the dingy white linoleum counter and out the front door, then around to the lower side of the building where the combination of large white double doors and his keys gave him access to the machinery that ran the pool. He looked at the gray, chugging mass of pipes and tubes for a moment before checking the gauges on the surge tank and the cannister of chlorine. Everything was covered in a dusting of fine white grit; concentrated around a stack of bulging brown paper sacks in one corner. As Jack was about to heft one of the hundred pound bags of soda ash onto his shoulders, he paused. It seemed he could finally think straight. His head was beginning to clear, despite the dust which filled the air and clung to the rumbling, churning esoterica of the filtration system.

As he crossed the threshold with the big sack, Jack started to laugh. The girl, Mercedes, had found a moth-eaten feather duster and pushed a chair over against the bank of shelves. She grinned down at him through a small cloud. "Regular dust bunny farm up here," she said, squinting.

Again, Jack didn't know what to say. He continued through the pool building and dumped most of the grainy powder into the pool, carrying the trickling bag along the edge to help disperse the soda. Now for the fun part, he shuddered. He'd already rolled back the other sheet of plastic insulation, and a thin layer of steam was beginning to rise above the water as Jack began his ascent up the diving platform. He kept his eyes riveted on the steps ahead of him and moved up the ladder gently, gingerly.

He took great care to only move one arm or one leg at a time, sliding his hands upward around the rails which led to the top.

There was already a growing pale of light along the eastern rim of the great canyon by the time Jack had worked through half the knots which affixed the spotlight to the platform's edge and the adjoining aluminum rail. The sky had gone from velvet blue to pearl. He was sweating profusely in the cool breeze.

"How'd you rig up the light?" she asked from thirty feet below.

Jack started and nearly swore, clutching at the grainy surface of the platform. He brushed a sheaf of hair out of his eyes and peered cautiously over the edge. The girl was standing, arms akimbo, at the edge of the pool. He wondered if she'd really dusted all the trophies.

"I mean, how did you get it to make a narrow beam?"

Jack stretched his fingers, and continued working at the knots. "Easy. I borrowed a scrim from the high school drama club before school was out. Here, catch this and I'll show you." He lowered the heavy spot by its rope until she caught it. Then, as cautiously as before, he walked backwards down the long ladder.

Mercedes was moving the adjustable shutter over the light. "I see how this works. Hey, why don't you just dive off?"

He was more than halfway down. Half-a-dozen quick responses came to mind, but as Jack jumped the last few feet to the ground, he decided to stick with the truth. "I never really learned," he said. "I've mostly stuck with swimming. You were pretty impressive yesterday, though. I thought you were going to hit your head when you did that, um—"

"Inward dive? You saw that?"

"Everybody saw it." He indicated the spotlight, pointing to the hinged shutters. "This is a scrim, so you can sort of shape the light."

They stood there for a few seconds, smiling at each other. She'd coiled the nylon rope they'd used to lower the spotlight. Jack could see thoughts racing, shark-like and shadow-quick, behind her eyes. He wet his lips. "Think you could teach me that sometime?"

"Teach you what?"

"Inward dive."

"Right! Um, sure." She looked down at herself. "I'll need to run home and get something to wear."

Jack took the spotlight from her hand. He'd left it turned on too long; the black metal was hot. "I can loan you a suit of mine," he said, forcing himself to keep a straight face. "You know, we could get started right away."

She blinked, then her eyes widened. "I think I need a bit more . . . comprehensive coverage, if you know what I mean." A snatch of cloud over her shoulder, above the valley's lip, blushed a rosy red. The sun generally came up quickly out of the mountains around Forge.

Jack let his smile break through. What had gotten into him, he wondered. "Could you come back at noon? That's when lessons get over, then there's an hour break before open swim, when all the kids get here. Just some ladies doing water aerobics and one or two triathlon maniacs, but we can dive. If you're not busy." Quite a speech there, Jack. You've got a great future marketing pre-driven automobiles.

"I'll be here at eleven–my cousins have lessons."

The sun trembled at the edge of the world. "Great, that's my break. I'll try and be ready." She followed behind at a distance as he carried the spotlight and coiled rope into the lifeguard's lounge. Jack turned to catch her yawning.

"Guess I'd better go," she said. "I wouldn't want to get you in trouble, or anything. For having me in here."

She paused in the doorway. "See you in a few hours, Jack."

"See you. Mercedes."

She looked like she was about to say something else, but just smiled and then was gone. Jack listened for a moment to the sound of her tennis shoes on the wooden deck, then grabbed a pair of goggles from his mesh basket.

He hung his loose shorts on the back of a chair near the timing clock, and lobbed his goggles far out towards the middle of the pool.

The sun breached the wall of trees arrayed along the eastern frontier, and shadows were born into the new day. One sprang into existence, elongated and pincerlike in its exaggerated proportions, clawing across the smooth water toward the tiny ripples made by his goggles. I can't do this, he thought, staring with more than a little trepidation at the diving platform. It dominated the pool, a gleaming gargantuan poised in mid-lurch like some existential Godzilla as written by Orson Scott Card.

The door banged shut behind him, and John Gessner ambled out onto the deck, clutching a styrofoam cup of coffee. "What, here again?" he muttered in Jack's general direction, wincing even behind his sunglasses. The older man, tanned even darker than Jack, blew gingerly at the cup's steaming rim, then took a sip. "Too early. Going to stunt your growth, Jack." He sat in the chair recently vacated by Mercedes.

Jack grinned. He'd often wondered if fifteen more years would turn him into the man now stretching languorously before him. Mr. John Gessner—pool manager, high school biology teacher, local basketball coach, single parent—but just plain John to a few lucky students during the months they were employed at the pool. He was the ultimate authority within the boundaries of the pool's fence; a benevolent monarch in Jack's experience, but one who was able to conjour up visions of formaldehyde and partially preserved corpses of cats or frogs in the minds of any potential rulebreakers. He wore his usual early-morning uniform: a purple and gold Lakers tanktop over baggy shorts and Tivas. Even in the weak light under the pool building's shadow, the steel bracelet around John's right arm–a memento from Peace Corp days in India—matched the glint off his reflective Randolph Aviator sunglasses.

John shuffled one foot out of his faded, laceless deck shoes and prodded the deck, shivered, and swore at the chill. He took a too-deep sip of the steaming coffee and swore again. Jack turned away before his boss could see his widening smile. The things some people have to do just to wake up.

He should probably tell the older man about the diving lesson he was scheduled to receive in a few hours, but there was just no talking to Gessner until he was nursing at least his second cup of coffee, no cream, extra sugar.

She was something else, though, wasn't she? Oh, man. And one look at those eyes and you knew she was thinking fiercely, nonstop, and there was no telling what was going through her head.

Jack knew he should have felt intimidated by her beauty. He'd watched yesterday, amused, as no less than three of Diane's and Alice's friends–guys he'd run track with the past few years–had struck up conversations with her poolside, then quickly retreated under the frank combination of her emerald glare and turquoise swimsuit.

But he couldn't *wait* to see her again.

He ran to the edge of the pool and launched himself across it, into the angling sunlight, keeping pace with his phantom reflection on the water below—

*

—and Jack hit the water hard, harder than anything he'd imagined. He'd tried to aim for the reflection of the sun, which hung almost directly overhead, but something had gone wrong, he'd over-rotated too much or something during his ten meter controlled fall, and the water slapped his back brutally. He swore and choked underwater, cringing at the sting. Breaching the surface, he clawed his way feebly toward where Mercedes hung on the edge of the pool. She guided his hand to the wall.

Grimacing, Mercedes touched his shoulder. "Mi scusi–I mean, I'm so sorry, Jack. Are you okay?"

Jack gasped for air. "Feels like somebody's been using a sander on my back. Is all my skin still there?"

She looked. "Ouch. Maybe we should stop for a while. It's like you keep going over too far. You're getting better, but—this can't be good for you. Do you want me to go again?" Mercedes bobbed in the water next to him, a hand on his arm for balance.

Jack had almost gotten his wind back. "No, that's okay. Just give me a sec. Catch my breath." He dragged himself up the aluminum ladder. The pool area was mostly quiet; Gessner and another lifeguard were herding a Mom's & Tots class around in the shallow end. Straightening up to catch Jack's eye, John smirked and shook his head. Kate, who had worked at the pool as long as Jack had, assumed her patented pained expression and turned back to her class, which included at least two of Mercedes' little cousins. The pool was otherwise vacant, all the other guards at lunch. Aside from a cluster of little girls left over from Jack's last class, he and Mercedes had the diving well entirely to themselves.

One of the little girls, her face nearly covered by an oversized pair of wraparound sunglasses, solemnly handed a towel to Jack. "Thanks, Thea," he said, wiping his eyes. He could see the redness of his chest and shoulders in the funhouse reflection off her eyewear.

But the sting was fading fast. "What did you say a sec ago?" he said to Mercedes. "'Me skew-?'"

"Mi scusi, it means I'm sorry in Italian. It's what I am. Italian."

Jack sat on the edge of the pool. "But aren't the Bergstrom's Swedish?"

"That's right, I'm a mix. A real mutt. A Swedish wop–that means thug." She pushed off the wall and started treading water.

"You should meet my best friend, Al. He's Swedish-Mexican, but could pass pretty much for Swedish except he's only about 5' 5'. Kind of a thug himself. He's coming home in a few weeks—he did the exchange student thing last year."

"Swedish, hunh? Maybe we're related." She took a deep breath and ducked her head under the water.

Jack waited until she'd bobbed back to the surface. "Wouldn't be a surprise. Not a lot of people in Forge, you know. Got to be careful who you date." He moved his feet so she could grab the edge and rest. "Maybe five thousand people on a Saturday night—"

"–if a good band is in town." she finished, pulling a laugh from Jack. She laughed too, for an moment, then swatted him lightly in the leg. "Hey, *we're* not related, are we?"

"Gosh, I hope not," he said instantly. Then the smile dropped from his face. "Actually, I'm not from around here at all."

Mercedes stopped laughing at the curtness of his tone. She frowned slightly, as if sensing a chill through the water around her.

She opened her mouth to speak, but Jack cut her off by jumping to his feet. "Once more unto the breach, dear friends, blah, blah, blah." He went to the ladder and started climbing. "Tell me some more Italian," he called down, eyes firmly on the rungs before him.

"Really?"

Anything to keep my mind off how high up this is, he silently replied. "Yeah, like how do you say this thing I'm on?" He reached the top and clawed himself onto the grainy platform.

"How high are you? Thirty feet?"

"Feels like a thousand." He chuckled nervously.

"Then that'd be 'la piattaforma dei dieci metri.'"

"And if I dive off, what do you call me?"

She'd left the pool and was half reclining on her canary yellow towel a few feet from the pool's edge. "You're definitely a 'tuffatore', Jack. Is this helping at all?"

Mercedes was pretty much the only thing Jack could bear to look down on from this height. He stood, loosening his shoulders, forcing himself to breathe evenly. "Keeps me from thinking about—how do you say 'good luck?'"

Mercedes thought a minute, pulling a pair of sunglasses from her bag. "My grandmother would say something like, in bocca al lupo! 'Into the mouth of the wolf.' Is that close enough?"

"I guess. Your grandmother sounds like a lot of fun. So how do you say "scream my head off?"

"Grida molto, you big sissy," she laughed, shaking her head.

"How about—"

"Respiri a fondo!"

Jack stopped swinging his arms and looked down again. Mercedes chuckled. She had a throaty, if hesitant laugh. "'Take a deep breath!' I swear, you're going to pass out up there!" The crowd of younger girls, now crowding around Mercedes with thick cotton towels of their own, joined in, clapping for Jack to dive. Mercedes beckoned them in, whispering. They all looked up at Jack and giggled.

Muttering under his breath, Jack edged toward the gulf of empty space at the end of the platform. The whole concrete slab looked marvelously smaller than it had from below. He was standing on a toothpick, for crying out loud! How many Jacks can dance on the head of a pin?

This wouldn't do at all. He closed his eyes, picturing the water below, mentally *feeling* the expanse of air he would fall–no, *move*–through. He imagined himself smoothly jumping back and up, folding over himself in a somersault, then landing perfectly vertical against the water, as if he was sliding through a circle just big enough to–but that was it! A circle–no, a parabola. He was thinking about this all wrong; his trajectory off the board would be a finite parabola, and as such could never be truly vertical! No wonder he was turning too far. Sometimes he was a complete idiot. He could do this. He inched backward until his heels were over the edge. "Okay, wish me up a little luck here, okay?"

Almost in unison, the mob of girls screamed, "Break a leg, Jack!"

Startled, he fell.

But he got it right.

Jack shoved hard with his feet against the lip of the platform as he tumbled from it, got enough momentum to begin the rotation of his body back toward the platform, then, as gravity plucked him from the sky and the cement stage slipped past, he had a terrifying sensation that he wasn't turning fast enough; that he'd pancake down *hard* against the uprush of water.

Then the parabola flashed through his mind again, and he snapped into a dive position nearly a quarter of a second before his fingertips touched the water.

Ha! Jack broke the surface, buoyed upward by the billowing, surging relief that he'd managed a thirty foot dive–an inward dive!— without further injury. The crowd of little girls clapped their hands and squealed with delight.

"Not bad, Aquaman. Fenomenale," said Mercedes, grinning, running to the ladder. "My turn!"

Literally. Any newfound sense of confidence in his diving ability was definitively erased the moment the girl's feet left the platform and she curled into a tight, twisting two-and-a-half.

Later, as Mercedes and her cousins were getting dressed, Jack caught up to Gessner as the older man tested the pool's chemical balance. Jack had found a tank top and another pair of faded shorts.

"Hey, John, can I take second shift later?" He stood awkwardly on one foot, attempting to tie his shoelaces and maintain eye contact at the same time. The white canvas shoe felt odd around his foot; he really did need to wear shoes more often in the summer.

"I don't care; whatever. Going to have lunch with your new friend?" Gessner was inscrutable behind his aviator glasses. "Ah, will you look at this? Too many kids using the pool as their own personal toilet!" He shook the plastic vials angrily. "There're going to be beatings today, Jack!"

"Unh-*huh*. I'll be back in about an hour, but Mercedes has never eaten at Medley's, and—"

"–You're taking her to Medley's, and you're dressed like that?" Gessner snorted derisively. You're a novice, my friend. Take the whole afternoon off, go put on something nice, wash the chlorine out of your brain. We're covered for today, and you spend too much time here for your own good. You smell like the surge tank, you know that?" The older man shrugged and added a few drops of base to the vial. "There, that's better. More soda ash. No, I'll get it," he roared at Jack, who was nearly out the door. "You clean up the books you littered all over the lounge. Scott, Dave, and Andy are going up on the towers today, and the place is enough a mess as it is."

He looked at Jack over his sunglasses. "Mercedes, hunh? Nice to see such good genetic material at work."

Jack grinned. Sometimes he forgot the man was a biology teacher. "Yeah, she'll be pretty good looking in a few years."

"She's pretty good looking right now, you cretin!" Gessner made as if to slap his forehead. "Novice!" He shook his head. "I swear, I was never this—Just be sure and invite me to the bachelor party, you amateur, when you finally decide she's gorgeous enough. And tell her not to pee in the pool!" Gessner stormed out, ranting good-naturedly under his breath.

A few minutes later he returned, directing the efforts of three other boys as they attempted to manhandle one of the hundred pound bags of soda ash out onto the pool area. Jack was on his knees fishing his other shoe out from behind a scratched-up desk when the three newcomers boiled back into the lounge, stripping down to their suits and reaching for sunblock.

"The Gez says your not working today, Jack," said Dave, the tannest and skinniest of the three. "What up? I heard Alonzo's parents got a new boat, you going up on the lake?"

"Naw." Jack found his shoe. "Water's not quite warm enough to ski. Maybe a couple more weeks. He's not back home from Australia yet, anyway." He slipped into his shoe and started working on the laces.

"Who's not working today?" asked Andy, smearing bright blue zinc on his nose. "Jack, man, you're going to miss the show! I heard that new chick is coming back today with the kids she babysits!"

Jack looked up. Though Dave, Andy, and Scott would be seniors with him when high school started up again in a few months, he'd never been particularly close to any of them. He knew they talked about him behind his back; made fun of the textbooks he left in the lounge–even switched him to the hottest, most hectic shifts when they got hold of the upcoming week's schedule. To the best of his knowledge, Jack couldn't recall ever having an eye-to-eye conversation with any of them while either of the other two were present. The exchange usually turned towards their expertise vis-a-vis the opposite sex, or more often, kiddingly, Jack's lack thereof. Each had that special talent for mockery that could insidiously insert itself into any discussion. Jack was noticing it more and more lately, as if many of his classmates had all signed up for an AP course in hubris. Dave, Andy, and Scott were almost bullies. Jack didn't really care; their cumulative respect for his size and speed kept the playing field more than even. "The 'new chick?'"

"The honey in the green suit." Andy had finished with his nose and now spread twin streaks of blue under both eyes, like warpaint. "The blond." He turned to Dave. "You know who I mean, bro!"

Dave rolled his eyes. "Diane's cousin. Totally stacked 'til Tuesday. Hey, Earth to Jack; anybody home?"

Scott joined in the conversation. "I dunno, guys, I think she's a little cold. She wouldn't give me the time of day. Rick neither. And you saw what she did to Kyle–he's probably still berserko. Brrrr."

"Cold," Dave agreed.

"Regular ice queen."

"But man, is she ever built," returned Dave.

"Bet she had to jump out of a tree to get into that suit." Andy said.

Jack started to stand, keeping his face down, trying not to make eye contact with Gessner, who stood behind the three sweating young men, as close to open laughter as Jack had ever seen him.

Scott scooped his whistle off the desk. "I'd crawl over hot coals just to get—"

"Well, guys, got to run," Jack broke in. "Got to pay her back for a diving lesson." He pushed past them. As if on cue, Mercedes and her two youngest cousins walked around the corner from the women's locker room.

Maybe Jack's heart actually skipped a beat at the sight of her, or maybe he just didn't notice it thumping away for an instant, but he was dead sure he could hear three pairs of eyes bulge behind him as he headed for the door.

This is perfect, he thought. Just like in the movies.

Gessner touched one finger to his tongue and tapped it on Jack's chest, making a hissing sound as the younger man passed him. "Whew! Careful, Andy, leave your mouth open like that and something greasy could fly in. Multifaceted eyes. Yum."

*

It was nearly ten o'clock by the time Jack got back to the pool, fumbling for a moment under the yellow porchlight for his key to the pool. He found he couldn't wipe the smile off his face.

The two of them had gone to Medley's, one of the slightly exclusive restaurants ringing the reservoir's marina that catered to Forge's seasonal tourist flow. Except for a few of his classmates who were bussing tables, Jack didn't recognize a soul. It would be an expensive date–okay, payback, but Jack figured, what the heck. It's not like he was trying to impress her; he just knew–instinct, he realized—there was no use pulling punches with a girl like Mercedes.

They'd found a table on the balcony overlooking the stretch of lake. Mercedes seemed taken with the view, a good ten mile stretch of dark green-blue water rimmed by an even darker border of Douglas firs and pines. The breeze off the lake undercut the bright afternoon with the mild, earthy smell of pine needles. At the far end of the marina, a young couple in wetsuits were unloading a pair of shiny blue jetskis. The three wooden docks were already beginning to fill up for the summer; over half the slips were occupied already by pleasurecraft and houseboats. At least a dozen bright pennants snapped in the warm air. "It looks so peaceful." she said.

Her eyes had widened slightly when he explained how she was only seeing a tiny piece of the reservoir. She's putting me on, Jack thought. I'm boring this city girl to tears.

But Mercedes was either genuinely interested or an incredibly good sport. She'd managed to keep a straight face when he ordered escargot, and in return, Jack had pretended not to be surprised when Mercedes balanced her soupspoon on her nose.

259

He'd thought for a moment they'd actually be asked to leave when she drew several startled glances by loudly crunching her ice. One man in yuppie-green golf pants two tables down almost choked on his veal cutlet, then on the glass of water with which he attempted to wash it down. As he blotted himself off, Mercedes whispered to the man, "Too much ice in the drinks, if you ask me."

And that had elicited a laugh from the three tables around them. One silver-haired man on the opposite side of Jack and Mercedes was particularly appreciative, and offered to pay for their lunch. "You see, I know who you two are," he said, eyes twinkling. "I'd ask you to join me, but then that'd make me something of a fifth wheel, eh? Besides, I'm supposed to meet Max here in a few minutes." He lifted his cup to his smiling mouth, and looked to Mercedes. "He's always showing off one picture or another of you."

She mirrored Jack's bewilderment, but before he could think of any kind of a reply, her frown broke into a grin. "You're Sean Lyons, aren't you?" To Jack, she said, "This is my grandpa's friend, Mr. Lyons. He's a famous architect–so my grandpa says," she amended as the older man laughed again.

Jack rose out of his chair far enough to reach the other man's hand. "Nice to meet you, sir." He wasn't much past fifty, if that, and from all appearances was quite the clothes horse. Jack didn't know that much about expensive clothing, but even under the shade of the building's awning, the man's white mercerized cotton t-shirt nearly blinded him. Then a thought struck Jack, and he cursed himself inwardly for his lack of manners. "Thank you for building the new pool, Mr. Lyons. Everything works great now. Mercedes, he donated the plans, the equipment, everything."

Lyons shrugged. "To be honest, it gave me something to do after

I moved here. Retirement can be such a—well. I should be the one thanking *you*, Jack, for putting it to such good use." He considered Jack as he spoke to Mercedes. "Did you know you were sharing a table with the future Idaho state swimming champion?" He looked sideways at her. "*You'd* better eat those snails for him. This boy's in training."

Jack's cheeks grew warm at that, and he'd managed to parry the conversation away from himself until Max arrived. He'd never met the tall Swede, but Jack was instantly struck by the man's resemblance to his granddaughter, especially their unusual green eyes. The four of them ended up eating together, and it was strange for Jack how comfortable he felt around them all. He actually managed to hold up his end of the conversation, answering questions about swimming scholarships and what did he think of the upcoming high school wrestling team. Strange how well he fit in, considering he'd never met either man before and every time he stole a glance at Mercedes—

—his mental train completely derailed.

Her love for her grandfather was obvious. Sitting across from her, Jack could feel it, almost warm against his skin. He was admittedly a little envious of the total attention she gave Max whenever the older man spoke, but it was understandable. She almost seemed to be the kind of person who was more at home with adults than people her own age. And both Max and Mr. Lyons returned her attention, listening actively whenever she spoke. With their eyes and rapt expressions, they showed Mercedes that center stage was hers, and she glowed for it.

Here was a lesson worth remembering. He'd only known her a day—less, really—but Jack was certain he was seeing another, more relaxed Mercedes. Last night, earlier at the side of the pool, and especially yesterday afternoon, she'd kept her distance, almost imperceptibly, from everyone around. There was a certain abruptness, if not outright coldness to her, even when she was smiling that glorious smile. She had a still, sad thing like a stone held tightly inside somewhere that she only released in the honesty of the older men's attention.

It was at that moment Jack knew that he'd never have noticed the sadness without the contrast he'd stumbled upon, like a photographic negative, in Mercedes' admiration for her grandfather. He was surprised at his insight, and suddenly more grateful than ever to the old gentleman.

There's a lot more to Mercedes than meets the eye, he had thought, looking back and forth between the girl and her chuckling, big-jawed Grandpa Max.

*

10PM

A whole lot more than even she realizes, he thought again under the watery yellow light, rummaging through his duffel bag for his pool keys. Nothing. Jack shook the bag, tumbling the books inside against one another hollowly. No jingling clatter of keys.

Jack bit off an expletive, then shrugged. Not like this hadn't happened before. He took a quick look around. The moon was already setting, and the park below was empty of life. A car glided by on the street bordering the park, its headlights washing the trees with dusty light, and then the night was his alone.

This portion of the pool building was built against the slope of the hill; by virtue of that steep slope, the entrance and wooden deck stood a good 12 feet above the grass at the base of the building. Jack lowered his bag to the deck, then stepped up onto the top rail, arms hesitantly out for balance. If he did this quick, he wouldn't have a chance to think about how far up he was.

Jack turned and grabbed the lip of the roof, reaching for a firm hold before swinging himself up and over the eaves. The roof was flat and sloped slightly back towards the pool; if it had been peaked, Jack doubted he'd ever have discovered this secret entrance. Serves Gessner right for making him clean the skylight every spring.

He loved this. Creeping along the roof, which had finally cooled down and now only served to absorb his footfalls, Jack felt like a thief, or better yet, a spy. Near the skylight, tethered to an exhaust vent, lay a loose coil of rope, thickly knotted at regular intervals. Jack wondered as he gathered up the cord if spies or secret agents had the time to plan for such contingencies as misplacing their keys.

He reached the mullioned skylight and swung it up on its anodized aluminum hinge, then dropped the rope into the dark, empty space below him.

Jack held tightly to the line as he lowered himself through the vent, breathing only when he felt solid flooring beneath him. He sighed and sat heavily into one of the wide, overstuffed couches. Jack smiled against the darkness. If not for a slight problem with heights, there was still time for him to run away with the circus when it next came to town.

He coiled the rope again, then tossed it up through the skylight. Later, probably tomorrow morning while Gessner was still fixated on his daily two-hour coffee break, Jack would close the overhead window by tapping gently on its hinge with a telescoping dust broom.

Kate and the other two college girls who worked at the pool loved to see him lurching around with the dust broom, anyway. They got a special, practically vindictive pleasure out of watching the *boys* do the housecleaning. Jack didn't care; the girls kept the lounge looking good, toning down the stale, black-and-yellowing-white posters of lifesaving techniques by adding half-a-dozen potted plants with thin, frothy leaves to which Jack had never bothered to learn the names.

He retrieved his bag from the deck and flipped on the reading lights he'd installed in the lounge. A trip to the fridge the city had donated, and Jack had a carelessly thrown-together pastrami sandwich from his brown paper bag of supplies. He briefly considered turning on the radio, but he had studying to do and had never felt comfortable trying to learn while music was playing. Something about introducing new knowledge to his brain cells along with the weekly top 40 bothered him. Jack liked to concentrate fully on things. He'd read once that Einstein had kept a closet full of identical suits because he didn't want to waste any brainpower on unnecessary decisions, like, does this tie go with these socks? Jack was no Einstein (he snickered at the thought), so all the more reason not to confuse his mind with DJ lingo-bingo as he held ideas up to the inquiring light of his meager wits. Wouldn't want to imprint the wrong stuff.

He selected the more comfortable of the two worn couches, then carefully arranged the night's reading material on the cushions around him and took a bite out of the sandwich. Good thing you could never max out a library card, he thought. He'd spend fifteen minutes apiece on each book before deciding if it was worth his time, then go back at the end of two hours and read until he felt sleepy. Not like he had anywhere else to go. Mercedes had gone off a few hours earlier with her cousins to shop in Lewiston, an hour's drive down the river and the biggest town in over a hundred miles. Jack smiled as he imagined her expression upon seeing the Lewiston mall. You could throw a frisbee from one end of the "mall" to the next.

Jack mentally tore his mind away from the girl's smile and stared at the books in front of him. Ugly. *Beginning Italian*, by Annalisa Lavecchia, Ph.D. *Italian for the Real World*–hey, that one came with a CD-ROM in a sleeve in the back. Cool. Too bad Jack didn't have a computer. *The Gift of Fear*, by Gavin de Becker. *The Insight City Guide's* book on San Francisco. *Strange Highways* by Dean Koontz. Odds were, he'd end up reading that one until he fell asleep. It sounded a lot more fun than *Tracing Your Scottish History*. Jack sighed. He'd also picked up a few books on comparative religion that no doubt would cost him a few dollars in overdue fines before he got around to them. You just couldn't do everything now, could you?

"Best thing I can do is try," Jack answered aloud as he hefted the first book. "Alright, Annalisa Lavecchia, Ph.D. You don't scare me."

—and Jack's eyes opened at the grating breath of wood on wood, immediately noting the slight change in air currents that stirred the leaves of the plant a few feet from where his cheek rested on the open page of a book. He always came awake like this; he couldn't explain it. One second's worth of the sensation that he was swimming upward towards consciousness, then the next, fully alert.

A papery taste in the back of his mouth told him he'd been asleep at least a few hours, though darkness still pressed against the big windows that looked out on the pool area.

More wind now, lifting the pages of another open book on the floor, scattering a damp scent of —new-mown grass? —from the park below. Jack wished he could see around the corner of the lounge, into the darkened front. The cash register was up there.

A foot scraped against the front stoop.

Jack sat up.

There was a hinged section of the white countertop that ran the width of the reception area, right in front of the door. You had to unhook it and push it up to get into the pool's main area, or to reach the cash register. Had he left the countertop down and locked? If so, he'd hear it squeak as it was pushed up. What an *idiot* I am, he thought, looking around sharply. Not a thing in sight he could use to defend himself.

Another whisper-thin footfall on the concrete floor. Up there in the dark.

Suddenly, Jack was sure, positive, that whoever'd broken into the pool would investigate the lounge. He'd fallen asleep and left the lights on. Idiot, *idiot!* With no cash in the register *of course* they'd come back and look around the corner, down into the lounge. Whoever it was had to already be able to hear his heart slamming away against his ribcage. This was bad.

He felt exposed. Paralyzed. Nothing around he could use as a weapon–wait, what about one of the trophies? Sure, they'd be big enough, and most had either a hard wood or a marble base. If he swung one of those–

But all the trophies were set up high on a shelf above the doorway between the two rooms, and what was worse, the shelf faced out towards the front counter. In order to get his hands on a potential weapon, Jack would have to enter the same room as the intruder, turn around, and jump up high enough to grab a trophy. Not likely. He licked his lips. But if the trespasser was busy trying to open up the till, with his back to the door, maybe Jack could pull it off.

He brought himself up short then, wondering if the intruder had a baseball bat.

Almost two years before, during Jack's sophomore year, the body of a girl his age had been discovered on the local sheriff's lawn. He shuddered thinking about it. The details of the autopsy had so captured the town's collective morbid interest–no one living could remember such a monstrous crime. She'd been beaten with a baseball bat, raped repeatedly, and then dumped, broken, practically on the sheriff's front stoop. Cecilia Montgomery had been alive, technically, when she was discovered the next morning, but died before she could regain consciousness. Jack and his best friend, Alonzo, had been on their way to lift weights early at school, had jogged past the policeman's house in time to see the shrouded body being loaded into the coroner's van by a solemn group of white-faced, thin-lipped, uniformed paramedics.

No one really knew Cecilia. Her family moved in right before school started, and she had been fairly shy. Both the boys had danced with her at the End of Summer Bash, and Jack had been particularly taken by her auburn hair, like a sheaf of dark fire, and her open, slow smile.

—that had been broken by an aluminum baseball bat. How could the police tell such things? Where was the justice in the fact that they could determine the exact weapon used but utterly fail to find any trace of the maniac who'd swung it? The police had all looked grim and ferociously busy for a few months afterward, and the parents of the town imposed an unofficial curfew which lasted almost the entire school year before Cecilia's family moved away and it was forgotten.

There'd actually been some mention of the FBI, but the case slowly seemed to just go away. The only clue besides the body fluids typed B positive and A negative was the presence of wet red clay under Cecilia's fingernails–clay found abundantly in any of over a hundred abandoned mines in the area.

The final conclusion deducted from the evidence was that the young girl had fallen victim to a couple of drifters unassociated with the town, a couple of psychopaths who'd picked the sheriff's lawn and rosebushes by sheer chance.

Another idea, though unpopular, pointed an accusing finger at the college students returning in droves to any of the three universities within a hundred miles. Classes were scheduled to begin soon, and the highways were conspicuously full of out-of-state license plates. But ultimately, the authorities had nothing.

Jack and Alonzo had slowly walked the rest of the way to school that day shunted into a mute, impotent daze. Sure, the world was filling up with madmen perversely intent on chaos; yeah, the last few years before the turn of the millennium were turning out to be a barrage of howling senselessness, but that was T.V. That was CNN. Surely evil could not wander far enough off the beaten track to show up in Forge, Idaho. Surely.

But that had been the day Jack looked up the meaning of the word 'misogynist.' It had been the first time in his life he'd felt any sense of mission, of purpose. He'd been struck by a wild sort of idea, as he looked up from his suddenly meaningless homework and across the oak breakfast table at Alonzo's house into his friend's indignant black eyes, an idea that the two of them could someday make a difference. Jack had *never* been so pissed.

He felt a dim stirring of that anger now as he rose to his feet in the lifeguard's lounge. He flexed his hands and prepared to move.

Patron Saint of the Unlikely

Gare du Nord station, Paris
7PM

Jack stood in a quiet pocket of air, just beyond the reach of the Parisian rain, alternately flexing and relaxing his hands. He stood by himself at the train station, as alone as he had ever been. Left solitary, a man can become as wretched as a sailor shipwrecked on a frozen, silent sea. Jack held the laminated photograph away from his body, catching enough light from the sodium vapor lamp a hundred meters away to make out the image smiling up at him. The rain beaded quickly on the hard, plastic square, sliding off too quickly to imagine it as tears on his wife's face.

Was he *ready*?

Jack stood unmoving, barely in the shadows, barely inside the semicircle of dry ground defined by the overhanging roof of the Gare du Norde. Parisian rain fell solidly on the low buildings around him, thrummed against the skin of the steel train he stared at so intently. If not for the barest hint of steam as he breathed, if not for the occasional fleeting blink, he might never have been there. No one else stood on the deck beside him; this was a departing train, and the departure platform was one story below. The five men and one woman alone in the cabin had no inkling they were being observed. Jack studied each in turn, watching expressions, taking note of body positions and angles, of gestures both intentional and otherwise. He knew these men as well as anyone could, as well as they knew him. They were family of a sort.

269

Alonzo, hands clasped pensively before him on the table, sat next to the British woman he had met earlier in the day. The major was no doubt bringing the rest of the group up to speed on the latest kidnapping information; at least they were paying attention as she handed each a dossier. She looked fit enough. Not the kind of woman who'd ever need to wear much makeup, or want to, for that matter. Strong, obstinate jaw. Auburn hair cut in a short fashion like uncounted businesswomen and bureaucrats the world over. She sat rigidly, almost uncomfortably, on the edge of her seat, not resting her elbows on the table as she elaborated on the sheets of data each of the men had before him. The major never smiled. And why should she, Jack asked himself, considering the nature of the mission? Most likely she had her own set of personal misgivings about the little group before her.

Brad, for once without his ever present Stetson, sat across from her. With the opening of the mission folders he'd given up his mild flirtation with the major and lowered his eyes to the information before him. His black case of catburglar tricks lay at his feet. Jack watched his eyes as they flitted down the page. He was also on the edge of his seat, but more relaxed, calm. Brad was ready. He looked once at the huge man next to him, pointing at something in the document.

The other man smiled and flexed one enormous hand as dark as the mahogany on which it rested. Solomon, the bald giant, looked slightly out of place in his canary yellow jacket and red bow tie. He was listening keenly to the woman. Jack stared at his face. Solomon's eyes were shimmering and alive, even in blank repose, the eyes of a wanderer, both geographically and intellectually. Was the man ready? Jack caught himself in the question. With Solomon, he never had to ask.

The man seated between Solomon and Alonzo shook his head at something the major said and pointed to a line on the page before him.

Ian had grown a goatee since Jack had last seen him. The eyes of the stout, hard man were bright behind gold-framed glasses. Ian wore a plaid chambray shirt and jeans, contrasting sharply with the two men on either side. Jack bet he was wearing boots. Ian was not only ready, he looked to be already on his way.

The last man, Steve, sat apart from the others, typing almost feverishly at a modular computer. He never changed. For the past ten years the heavyset fellow had looked to be on the verge of going bald. A half-eaten Snickers bar lay wrapperless, melting beside him next to one of two nondescript black boxes cabled to his main computing unit.

Jack watched as the major excused herself and left the men to pore over the documents on the desk. She retrieved a polka-dotted umbrella from a nearby window seat and stepped offstage.

The lone man on the balcony glanced at his watch. About two minutes until the train was due to depart. Jack's eyes sought out each man's face one final time, then he turned deeper into the darkness. He found his small knapsack without any trouble, and stowed the photograph inside.

Jack swallowed, suddenly chilled as a wind gusted across the stairs he descended. A middle-aged woman, one of the many vendors on the lower platform, offered him a biscuit or something from a covered basket which smelled delicious. Jack silently refused.

The major stepped down from the train, umbrella raised against the gusting rain. A polka-dotted umbrella. She looked ridiculously like a circus performer who'd run away to join the army. Her government insignia was mostly obscured by a dark green rain slicker. "We've gone over all the material we discussed earlier in your flat." She spoke loudly so as to be heard over the hum of the train and the gusting wind. "They seem surprisingly capable fellows. Not what you"d expect from, ah—"

"Mercenaries, Major?"

"Let's say 'walk-ins,' shall we? That's how you Americans put it, is it not?"

Jack shook his head. "Those men inside aren't with CIA, Major, A couple of them work for the U.S. government, but for the moment, we're all on vacation. We're just here to help."

"Yes, well. At any rate, if you yourself are prepared, Mr. Flynn, we'll be off. Your computer man, Fisbeck, and the Chinese (it wasn't particularly obvious what Brad did for a living; Jack could see this irritated her) have come across something interesting; combined with what that mysterious fellow told you this afternoon, we could actually have an idea about the little girl's whereabouts. If we might board?" The major stepped back and held the umbrella up against the rain.

Jack hesitated, then glanced to his left, down the length of the depot's platform. Simultaneously the wind brought the sounds of scuffling feet and a woman's muffled cry. The major breathed in sharply as Jack seized her umbrella.

The older woman with the basket was struggling against an unkempt youth barely out of his teens. The major watched as the young man took a firmer grip on the woman's handbag and heaved it out of her mittened fingers. Laughing, the young man ran a few steps with the bag, then turned to yell something deprecating in French. He spun back to make his getaway complete, then shouted in fright at the rushing explosion of polka dots that blossomed suddenly a few inches from his face.

"Eh ben, me voici!" said Jack, his face grim. He darted the major's umbrella at him a few more times, working the catch and lunging like a swordsman, until the young man dropped the bag and swore. From his ragged pocket the would-be assailant pulled an old-fashioned switchblade, instantly bringing it around between himself and the American.

Jack spun along with the young man's arm, catching his wrist and bringing the blade past himself with one hand, the other hand knifing in and under the mugger's chin. The young man instantly gagged and sagged halfway to his knees. The switchblade fell with a clatter, and Jack kicked it under the train.

The young man found himself spun around instantly, his free hand clutching his throat, as Jack seized him by the arm and scooped up the purse. Jack dug his fingers into the soft flesh behind the youth's elbow, squeezing viciously. He handed the purse to the woman, who smiled.

"Maintenant, donne-moi ton portefeuille, voyou." said Jack to the young man.

He switched to English. "You took hers, now I want yours. Dépêche-toi." Major Griffin watched as the young man reluctantly handed over his wallet and loose change. He started to whine, but Jack only tightened the grip on his elbow. "Viola, madam. En fait, j'aimerais bien du pain."

Jack took his time digging a few bills out of his pockets, pointedly ignoring the squirming youth next to him. He pressed the francs into the woman's grateful hands, and took her basket in return. He waved as she retreated into the depot, spouting thanks in the name of several legitimate saints and a few the major wasn't sure of.

The sound of muted cheers reached them. Jack turned to the train and found several men and women in the adjacent cabin all standing behind the glass, clapping. Further back in the train, Brad gave him a thumbs-up as Alonzo grinned and pounded against the glass.

Jack turned and marched the young man down the platform towards the major, who suddenly realized the rain had nearly soaked her to the skin. She stepped back into the train, watching as the American bent his head low and said something to the young man, who grimaced and nodded. Jack released his arm, and the young man ran down the platform, disappearing into the darkness beyond the lights.

Jack retrieved the umbrella, then vaulted the distance between the platform and the train, stepping up beside the major as the train began to pull away. "I think I'm ready now, Major."

The two of them stepped up into the gangway as the major said "Where did you learn that? If not in the CIA." Her tone was curious, but not accusatory.

"Oh, the elbow-grip thing? Red Cross Senior Lifesaving Certificate. Releases the grip of a drowning man, but I've never had to use it." Jack shook the rain from his hair, shifting the basket to his other hand. "I was a lifeguard in high school, Major. Lucky thing I remembered it, yeah?"

She stared at his back as he turned to enter the cabin. "Hey guys. Want some bread?"

*

London

"Really my child, you can have anything you want to eat." Raines said, smiling broadly at the young blond girl sitting inside a miniature toy castle. She hesitated, tapping one patent-leather black shoe on the floor.

"I want my mum," she said again, resolutely.

"And you'll see her tomorrow morning, right after breakfast. Just as we planned." Raines intoned assuringly. "But tonight you really must eat. Really, all this screaming. What do you think your mother will say if she finds out you've been blubbering about all afternoon?" He waited, watching her eyes grow larger at the thought. "Now, what does she always tell you to do when she talks to you on the phone every night?"

The little girl responded instantly. "She tells me to be good and eat my greens."

Raines' smile grew even broader. "That's right! And aren't you a

274

good girl who does just what her mother tells her? Of course you are!" He turned to go.

"And then I'm allowed to help feed the pony Jack gave to me! He's coming to get me so we can go riding next week." Raines looked back at her, catching the eye of the guard on the other side of the toy-strewn room. The other man shrugged.

Leaving the room, Raines paused long enough to speak to the guard in the hall. "See that she's dressed in her special new clothes by eleven o'clock."

"Sir, what was that about someone coming to ride with her?" His grip on the submachine gun never relaxed.

Raines waved his hand in dismissal. "Nothing of importance. The man she refers to is in no position to help anyone. The patron saint of the unlikely.

"Give all our little guests a shot of Ketamine with their meals. Only a half-dose. We want them docile, but still breathing." He smiled once again, that sly, eerily compelling grin, and strode off down the hall.

*

The Eurorail shot through the falling darkness like a steel comet. Rising pastures, liquid green oceans in the twilight, slid by on either side as the train neared Calais and the tunnel. Dinner was being served inside. Seven of its passengers, however, were too busy to even consider the gourmet meal.

Jack turned to the heavyset man behind the computer. "All right, Steve, what have you got?"

The chubby man was completely in his element. "Most of the files on Aleks Stefanovich are public domain. Got the rest from a buried file. Some spook analyst back in the States wrote it up and it got sent to the info vault as worthless intelligence. Stefanovich. Name means 'son of the crown.' U.S. emigration shows him and his parents getting out of Eastern Europe in late 1980, right when the Cold War was turning crispy. Official record shows his father as a high school janitor, but this guy never banged any erasers. According to the CIA central net at Langley—" he ignored the raised eyebrows—"his parents Stefan and Tereza were Tesla scientists before they jumped the Wall."

"How's that again?" Brad said.

"Tesla," said Ian. "A genius in the field of electromagnetism, lived around 1900. I read where he once caused a controlled earthquake in an abandoned section of New York City. Leveled nine square blocks."

Steve cleared his throat. "Stefan and Tereza were pioneering the field of medium- and high- energy weapons. Directed radiation. You know, focused microwave beams that can knock out a satellite, ultra low- and high-frequency explosions that can burst internal organs at extreme distance. Armageddon stuff. It looks like CIA got the family out just in time. Their Soviet sponsors had decided that the couple's research had achieved its end, and the project was to be terminated." He paused long enough for everyone to understand the implication. "They got out with most of their research, but hell, what the Soviets slapped together afterward managed to keep them in Afghanistan for another seven years or so.

"They built a little capitalist empire before the turn of the century, mostly servicing the U.S. government and military. Both Stefan and Tereza passed away a few years ago from natural causes, this report says. Get this: Their son, Aleks, changed his name before studying at Stanford, and has made himself quite well known on this side of the Atlantic as a philanthropist and entrepreneur. In the field of electronics alone—"

"Wait a minute." Jack broke in. "You're not going to say that Alex Raines, the 21st century's version of Donald Trump, is the son of Cold War defectors?" He sank back into his chair. "I met the guy at the opening of the Planet Hollywood London a few years ago. He had maybe a half-dozen bodyguards with him, all Eastern European muscleheads. If I remember right, Raines was pretty good at showing off his money, but something about the guy—like a part of him wasn't there. Lots of teeth but never really smiled, know what I mean?"

"According to the CIA report, he hires bodyguards heavily from the old KGB network. Even names his closest men after angels–you know, Raphael, Gabriel, that sort of thing. His personal bodyguard-trainer-secretary is a big Chinese he calls 'Michael.'"

"What could a stuffed shirt like that have to do with the Princess' kidnapping?" asked Brad. "Wasn't he in Newsweek a little while ago?"

"That's right," said Solomon. "He's building a chain of mini-malls in the Ukraine and Bulgaria, or something like that, employing thousands. The article had a picture taken when he attended the public trial of Miklos Nasim, the Albanian terrorist who escaped last week."

Now Ian spoke up. "Here's something else that doesn't figure: what would he have to do with a kidnapping? Ransom? Nobody does that anymore. In the States, at least, there hasn't been a successful abduction for ransom in over twenty years, despite what the movies say."

"So you think Raines is in the clear?" Alonzo asked.

"That's the funny part. The Bureau has a file on Raines as thick as any. I checked with my supervisor, and he says we've got three separate investigations underway right now. I guess somebody thinks he's laundering money for the drug cartel; Armand Lopez in particular."

"How does he go about that?" Solomon asked.

"Raines donates heavily to several political action committees in the States." For the benefit of Major Griffin and Brad, both non-American citizens, he added, "these committees lobby heavily, trying to influence our government. They also provide funds to certain candidates they think will support their agendas."

The major was curious. "Isn't that simply a method of buying out your government?"

Ian shrugged. "In reality, it's much more complicated than what I told you, but that possibility exists. Anyway, one theory is that Raines shuffles the money around within his various PACs, then passes it through a few charitable organizations he chairs. Charitable organizations *can* interact with political action committees, but they have to walk a fine line. In the end, the money is funneled by Congress right back to projects Raines has going in South America and other places. He's smooth. No one can even guess how much money went into his new digs in London."

Brad crunched some ice between his teeth. "Are you close to nailing him?"

"No," the FBI man seemed reluctant to admit. "We're not. Every time we start building a warm case, the Bureau gets pressured to divert our resources somewhere else."

Jack nodded at Ian. "Did any of the PACs he supports donate to the campaign fund of the President who had so much trouble a few years ago?"

Everyone knew who he meant. "Raines donates heavily to both Republicans and Democrats; liberals, conservatives, moderates— though just a little more to the side that wins, it seems. Why?"

"I just keep thinking about the plot that King William told Alonzo about," Jack said. "It doesn't seem so far-fetched now, to think that someone would go to such elaborate lengths to 'undermine national trust,' especially if they could gain influence for themselves by setting up and then ridiculing the President of the Unites States. More chaos, more distrust. Makes a country unsure of itself, easier to manipulate."

Brad pushed his cowboy hat back off his forehead. "Raines' company might be getting into stranger things than that, Jack." To Steve he said, "We'd better show them what we found in Czech."

The others made various expressions of disbelief when the blueprints came up on the screen. Bit by bit, Brad and Steve explained the items they'd come across in Czech, the next-generation nanotransistors, the fiber optics fabricated from synthetic diamond filament that made the microscopic transistors look archaic by comparison. Steve then related everything his former teacher at MIT had said about electromagnetic radiation. "I sent a copy of the file to Dr. Gale, and he told me he'd contact a man in California who could tell us what it is." He looked sheepish. "All I really wanted to know was who I could sell it to, to tell the truth."

Ian frowned, twisting his goatee into an angry knot. "This is dangerous, Fisbeck; you're in violation of national security. And you were worried about making a buck?"

The major leaned forward, on the edge of her seat. "Raines may not be involved at all," she began in a low voice. "He might just be a pawn in this, or rather, something he owns might be taken advantage of. Have any of you actually seen his corporate headquarters?"

"Major," said Alonzo, "What are you trying to say?"

Steve spoke up again. "The Illuminatus Tower. Raines' newest masterpiece. European headquarters of Raines Dynamic in London." He pulled the laptop close again and began to type.

"I'm afraid I haven't been to London in a few years," said Solomon. "What is this 'tower?'"

Alonzo turned toward him. "Ever been to any of those wild shops just north of Hyde Park? Raines built a commercial complex at the Park's northeast corner. It's about 40 stories high, easy the biggest thing in the whole West Side. Like someone wanted an office building to look like a castle, only smooth on the outside. Ugly as sin, if you ask me. He's got glass and stone together, with statues all around the outside of the thing. Yuck."

Steve turned the screen to face the others. "O.K., here's what we've got." An image spun into view of a massive, three-tiered building. "Raines says in a press release I've got here that he was trying to 'combine ancient and future Britain in one edifice, showing the past as well as the glorious destiny, blah, blah, blah.' I'm with you, Al; this thing stinks. Can't imagine the Londoners think much of it, eh Major?"

"If I remember correctly, there were demonstrators all up and down Oxford street when construction began. Bloody thing won't be done for another year."

"What's the layout, Steve?" Jack asked.

The portly man's fingers did their staccato dance once again over the keyboard. "Like all the new commercial buildings in London, the blueprints are registered—There we go. Okay, we've got the new Harrods on the first ten floors or so, then some corporate offices, a theater, and restaurants on the second tier, and the third main part is scheduled to be all apartments, maybe a few offices. About a third are already tenanted." A smaller section of the screen expanded into a list. "By the names, it looks like mostly women renters.

"This looks like a miniature television studio, with a soundstage." A floorplan began scrolling by on the screen. "Still in the final stages of construction, like the major said. The new BBC transmitter was put up about three months ago." Steve sat back and rubbed his eyes.

Alonzo started. "Did you say a theater complex?" He held up the blue ticket. "The Illuminatus Cineplex?"

"That's the one."

"Son of a—"

280

"Is there a show at 10:45 tonight?" Jack snatched the ticket.

"Well, according to today's schedule, that's when the main cinema on the twelfth floor lets out." Steve blinked at the screen. "They're showing one of your movies, Jack. The MacArthur flick. It just opened this week."

Ian snapped his fingers. "That means there'll be a crowd. Betcha that's how they're going to move the little girl."

Brad grinned, nodding. "And then we snatch her back."

Jack looked at the little team. He could already feel the momentum. Enthusiasm glimmered across the back of each man's eyes. Even the major looked excited, which was a stretch. "At least we've got a place to start. One more thing. Steve, can you superimpose the blueprints you got in Czech–the hradek file–with Raines' complex in London?"

The stout man complied, intent on the screen. He paled, gave a low whistle. The others crowded around the little screen, except Major Griffin and Solomon, who merely looked at Jack and nodded. "Exact match, eh, my friend?"

Ian cleaned his glasses on his shirt. "Fits like a glove. All the blank spaces in the government copy of the blueprints are taken up in the Czech plans by electronics work, mostly those fiber optic cables. The stone work, all the statues–they match exactly."

Steve swung the laptop so it faced Jack. "And it goes a hell of a lot further underground than the government specs say it does, too, Jack."

Silence fell over the little group. The wind was suddenly preternaturally evident, gusting against the smooth steel shell of the train. "Well. Well, we can figure that out as we go. Al, what is the full situation on Cuba right now? Anyone in place who could get in and talk to President Espinosa?"

"Funny you should ask. The Tanner brothers have been working with their anti-drug corps and specwar team since February. The whole outfit was in England up until last week, training with the SAS at Hereford. We just missed them. Espinosa isn't an idiot: Cuba is hosting the Goodwill Games next week, and wanted his security trained up."

Jack considered. Vernon Tanner and his brother Mack had been DEA officers longer than they had been part of his collection of friends, and had been working against the cartel nearly all their professional lives. Both men could be doubly trusted. So they'd gone ahead and helped Espinosa organize a training operation, like many governments had, between Cuban military and the British Special Air Service? He grinned tightly. Smart move. The SAS were the best in the world. Espinosa's men would be well trained. Still . . . "When you've got a minute, contact Miguel directly and ask him if he'd like us to be around for security during the Games. Like always, we don't want an official role."

"Sure. I went ahead and called London. We'll have transportation ready at Waterloo station."

"Then let's break out the equipment. Only a few hours left."

*

London

The man was livid, nearly raging, as he spoke to the camera. "And we, the true representatives of the combined peoples of Eastern Europe, further demand the immediate withdrawal of British and American military forces from Sarajevo and Budapest." He was nearly frothing, Raines observed from his vantage point next to Miklos, behind the spotlights.

"We will no longer stand by like sheep at the slaughter! The

United Nations will no longer make our homeland a laboratory for the fashionable social theory of the day, or play at games with our region's governments." The actor stepped closer to the camera, the hate in his voice nearly boiling over. "You have not asked us to enter our land, for you to walk in our streets. You have not asked us for permission to rape our natural resources with your capitalist knives."

A bit obscure, thought Raines, but the scriptwriter *did* know how to convey an image.

"You have not asked yourselves if we could defend ourselves. Now, we give you our answer! Your cherished Princess Christine will be deposited in exactly one minute at the gates of Buckingham Palace. This is a warning to you, you who can hide no longer! And we will rain fire on all who oppose us. On your children and your children's children. Fire." He glowered into the camera lens.

The diminutive director clapped his hands and slid off his chair. "That's a cut! All right people, let's have this wrapped and ready to edit within the hour. Craft Services! Get Mr. Miklos and Mr. Raines something to drink, some Evian! Let's move, move! I want this set taken down and everybody done with lunch by two o'clock." He raised his sunglasses above the single line of his eyebrows. "Nice job, eh Mr. Raines? Really positive work here! I can feel the karma." The director slapped Miklos on the back and jaunted off, bellowing for an assistant to bring him a cigarette, yesterday.

Miklos turned to Raines. "I absolutely hate that little man."

"A necessary evil." Raines smiled and nodded approvingly at the actor, a man he'd recently had hired off a Cairo soap opera. "With an exorbitant fee. Let's hope he's staying within the blast shadow tonight, eh? Now, Miklos, we have much to prepare." Raines turned, gesturing toward the door.

Miklos waved off the young man offering him a water bottle. "There is still much to be done before the morning. We must keep all of this as simple as possible."

*

The northwestern edge of France

"All right, Jack, you wanted the basics so here's what we've got." Ian, the group's weapons master, began arranging items on the low table between Jack and Major Griffin.

"First, for your Glock," here Jack set the pistol on the table, "Three fifteen-round clips of subsonic hollowpoint. One clip of Magsafe." Here he smiled. "I hand-loaded those myself. Here's a silencer, should be good for twenty or so shots.

"When we were in Rome you had that idea about body armor that wasn't so intrusive, so here you go." Ian laid a sleek black jacket on the table. "Looks like leather, doesn't it? This is a new slant to the military fragmentation vest–should stop anything lower than .45 caliber. *And* you can wear it in the rain." Next he pointed to a cardboard box. "Those are all the grenades you get for this trip, unless we open the caches in London. You know what to do with these." He removed one of the smallish black disks. "Same as last year. Basic polymer adhesive on this side; should stick to anything but human flesh. Three flash-bang and three incendiary.

"Don't mix them up."

Steve set a phone next to Jack's gun. "Everybody's batteries are all charged, boss. I re-keyed the scrambler, too, just to be on the safe side. Remember everybody, in England it's 999 for emergencies, not 911. Major," he handed a phone and a tiny earbud to Griffin. "This is set for a conference-type call with all our phones, but just in case I programmed all the individual phone numbers in as well–oh, and this little guy's set so he doesn't ring, he vibrates for about thirty seconds, so, ah, put this where you'll feel it." Steve blushed. "Also, Jack, this is new." He set a tiny green square on the table.

"Looks like a chicklet." said Jack.

"Fireproof, waterproof, shockproof. We've all got them now, just give it a good hard press if you're in over your head and I or Alonzo will find you."

Jack pocketed the tiny device. "Anything else for this trip?"

*

While the men about her busied themselves for their arrival at Waterloo Station, Major Griffin watched. They were turning out to be much more than she anticipated. Consultants was not exactly the appropriate word for what they were planning to do.

They decided to proceed directly to Raines' corporate headquarters, on the chance that they were making a mistake they didn't particularly want to share with the London police. If the princess was indeed there, the major would place a call to D-11, the section of London's Metropolitan Police outfitted for counterterrorism, then call King William directly. Major Griffin would stay close to Steve, helping him set up an information hub–or 'crow"s nest,' as he'd termed it–somewhere that would give him a chance to crack into the building's security and other automated systems.

Just then Alonzo appeared, lugging a massive black case, almost a trunk. He dropped it in the aisle next to Jack and looked at him expectantly.

Jack came close to a smirk. "Is this what I think it is?"

"The makeup is a year old, but it should still be good, right?" Alonzo smiled. "You said next job I'd get a disguise too, remember?"

285

Alonzo had finally revealed his background, that he'd joined the military soon after graduating high school and spent a tour of duty in Asia and then in the Gulf and as a naval flight officer, a helicopter pilot, of all things. "Yankin' and bankin', Major," as he described it.

Major Griffin sniffed derisively.

"Was that a snort, ma'am?" The small man raised an eyebrow.

She shook her head. Flynn and his friend seemed to be changing by the moment, coming alive with animation and barely-contained exuberance. "I was just wondering about the two of you. Have either of you ever been normal?"

Jack seemed to consider her question seriously for a moment. "Once, I think. I'm pretty sure. The summer I was seventeen." He eyed Alonzo. "My associate here is a different matter. Al used to own several sets of red satin underwear. Hideous. Had 'Home of the Whopper' printed on 'em."

Behind him, his friend snickered and pulled up the waistband of his undershorts to confirm that, yes, it was indeed red. His other hand held a magazine. "Our cabin attendant wants to know if you'll autograph this." It was a copy of a recent Entertainment Weekly.

Jack's mouth twitched. "Not like I wrote anything in there. They just used my headshot." He looked at the Major as he signed. "This is what passes for normal, these days. Don't know why they need my signature."

Major Griffin considered her words carefully. "Perhaps she wants proof that you are a real person, more than just ink on a page."

Things were quiet for a few minutes. Alonzo flipped through the magazine, then dropped it on the table. After a long look at the Major, he fixed Jack with his gaze and said, "So what happened next?"

"What are you talking about?"

"That night, at the pool, when there was a break in, and you thought it might be the maniac that killed Cecilia Montgomery. A girl in our class," he added for the Major's benefit.

Jack shuddered. "Remember how it felt when we saw the—when we were running to school that day?"

Alonzo's hand went to the back of his neck, and he huddled into himself.

Ben English

Breaking Her Fall

The two boys slowly walked the rest of the way to school shunted into a mute, impotent daze. Their world had suddenly filled with madmen perversely intent on chaos; the last few years had twisted into a barrage of howling senselessness, but that was T.V. That was CNN. Surely evil could not wander far enough off the beaten track to show up in Forge, Idaho. Surely.

Forge
3AM

Jack felt a dim stirring of that anger now as he rose to his feet in the lifeguard's lounge. Grimacing, he grabbed up a metal folding chair and leaped into the doorway, clumsily brushing at the wall with his shoulder where he knew the light switch would be.

Mercedes started laughing even before the cold flourescent light came on. "Jack! You should *see* your face!" she said. She raised her hand to her stomach, panting. "Ow, that hurts!" Then she doubled over again in another fit of laughter.

Jack mentally went down the list of swear words he knew as he let the chair fall the length of his arms. He needed the right weapon! He dropped the chair with a clatter and snatched up a purple featherduster that was poking out of Kate's locker. "Why, you—" he began as he beat her over the head with the bright feathers.

Still laughing, Mercedes looked up long enough to push back her

288

hair and cover her head in the same motion, then she came in for a clinch, shoving her shoulder into Jack's ribs hard enough to push him backward, down the single step into the lounge.

He staggered, surprised. "Hey, you Swedi—whoa?" The back of his knee hit the edge of a sofa and folded, dropping Jack down hard into the cushions with the girl on top of him. Mercedes' ponytail hit him in the eyes. Mmm. She smelled great–some kind of apple-pear sort of shampoo, maybe. He cudgeled her a few more times with the feathers, but she'd tucked her head down–then he was in serious trouble, as her thumbs dug into his sides right above his first rib. Jack yelped and convulsed with laughter. "Stop it!" he choked. "Quit! I'll, —yaah!" She was merciless. Jack threw the featherduster up in the air. "I give, I give, you win, stop, pla—hah! Please!"

Finally she raised her head. "Thanks for breaking my fall." She pushed off him and stood up, grinning. "Mercedes one, Jack: zip." She was flushed. "Whew! Got anything to drink in here?"

"Check the . . .fridge." He could breathe evenly again, but man! "Just to the left of where you assaulted me." He was weak. Nobody had tickled Jack in years. He'd almost forgotten about that spot on his sides—his particular Achilles heel.

She returned with an unopened bottle of water. "Is it okay if I drink this?"

He nodded. She was even more beautiful, if that was possible, than she had been that afternoon. Her hair was mostly pulled back, but a few pale chestnut locks–dislodged during their struggle—fell across her face. She was wearing a green collarless men's shirt tucked into a pair of faded jeans, and the same denim jacket as the night before. No makeup, but wow anyway.

"How'd you know to tickle me there, hunh?"

She lowered the clear plastic bottle, and leaned against the doorway. "'Cause that's where I'm most ticklish. Oops, maybe I shouldn't have said that!" She eyed Jack, who was still reclining. "You'll forget I said that, right?"

"No way," he said, and sat up. "But thanks to you I'm a little too gone to do anything about it right now. Sheeze, what time is it, anyway?"

Mercedes looked at her watch. "Just past four." She kept her other hand on her stomach. "So do you sleep here or something?"

Jack blinked. "Sometimes. Could I have some of that water?" She handed it over. He eyed the bottle's opening before drinking. "You don't have any weird disease or anything, do you?"

Even her sneer was pretty. Watch yourself, Jack, he thought, taking a sip from her bottle. This is a little crazy. Common sense goes to bed at midnight, and all that. He handed the bottle back. "How about you? Couldn't sleep again?"

She shook her head. "Must have been all those snails for lunch. Plus, you promised me a tour of the town, remember?"

Now it was his turn to laugh. "That should take all of ten minutes." He stood. "Want to go now?"

"What, right now, at four in the morning? I wasn't serious."

"Not a whole lot of difference traffic-wise between now and rush hour."

She finished the water and sat on the edge of a nearby desk. "Are you sure? Look, I'm really sorry for waking you up and all." Jack raised his hands to ward off the apology, but she was already looking down at his pile of books. "What are you reading? Hey, Italian, cool!" She smiled lopsidedly. "Learn any so far?"

"I can ask where the bathroom is. Is this right? 'Lei e molto bella.'"

Her eyes twinkled. "Thanks. I was expecting you to say something corny like, 'spaghetti,' or 'bread sticks.'

Jack laughed, leaning into the door jamb near the desk. He brushed his hair away from his eyes. There were all number of ways to simply get physically closer to her. New territory. It was a bit surreal. "This is getting a little weird. You want to go?"

He pulled a cotton shirt from his basket and shouldered into it, leaving the buttons undone over his T-shirt. "How'd you manage to get in here, anyway, city girl? Pick the lock?"

Mercedes held up his keys. Jangled them in front of his face. "You left 'em in my car."

*

Jack and Mercedes walked down from the pool through the park, threading their way between the trees to the main thoroughfare. Michigan Avenue ran the length of Forge, from the small end of the valley to where Oro Fino Creek spilled into the Clearwater River. As Jack had said, the road was all but abandoned, leaving the sodium vapor lamps to cast a grainy amber veil over the striped macadam and the dark, inanimate houses to either side. They walked southwest, toward the river and the city center about eight blocks away. Jack figured they could walk to the gas station near the interstate, then maybe buy some ice cream or hot chocolate, whatever Mercedes felt like.

He seriously considered trying to hold her hand–should have done that back in the lightless park before the road, you dope, he thought. Maybe he *was* still partially asleep. That would go a long way to explain his lightheadedness and the disconcerting urge he felt to laugh like a buffoon at every little thing she said. He couldn't believe he was actually walking down the main drag of his home town in the still of night with a girl who seemed more fantasy than real. Hopefully he'd be able to make sense of how he felt when he looked back on the night as memory.

291

Yet for the peculiarity of the moment, there was something exceedingly precious in these seconds flickering into the past. Life and time had taken from him most of the things that were supposed to be eternal, but at that moment Jack found himself grateful for whatever power or fate provided that he could be walking down Michigan Avenue at four in the morning with a girl as bright, as beautiful, as—*unexpected* as Mercedes. He looked at her arm, a few inches away from his, and stuck his hand firmly into his pock–but his cotton shorts didn't have pockets. Man, this was awkward. He walked more slowly.

After a few blocks they drifted to the center of the empty road. Jack pointed out the local landmarks to Mercedes: the elementary school made from the same red brick as every other elementary in America, the theater, the twin flashing ruby lights on the ridge above the town that marked the local radio station. Most of the buildings they passed were residential homes, so when they spoke they whispered, heads together. Jack was proud of the neatness and order of the sleepy streets. Four blocks of neat, one- and two-story homes lay between Michigan Avenue and the steep slopes marking the edge of relative civilization.

For her part, Mercedes was impressed with all the trees. Elm and ash, and occasionally an oak spread their boughs over the streets, obscuring the streetlights and sinking the sidestreets into soft green shadows. "I can sure see why my grandparents wanted to move back here," she said. "This place is like living on a golf course, only more trees."

Jack could only nod at that. He'd run out of interesting things to say, and didn't really trust himself all that much to wax extemporaneous about the little town. He had a premonition of himself articulating the finer points of the architecture of the VFW building, and shuddered mentally.

Mercedes squeezed his arm and then passed her hand through the crook of his elbow. "Jack, you've known my cousin Irene for awhile, right?"

"Sure, we've had a couple classes together. We'll graduate next spring." She was close enough for him to smell her hair again.

"Um, how long has she been going with Kyle Dremel?"

Jack felt her uneasiness behind the question. He thought a moment, then answered. "Oh, it's got to be like half a year. I think the first time we all noticed was at the New Year's Eve dance, when he spilled beer all over her."

Mercedes wrinkled her nose. "He really bugs me." She was silent a moment. "I hope you don't think I—what I mean is, yesterday—I don't usually yell at people like I did. He just made me sick, you know? His hands all over her–eew! And you know what else?" She stopped and thumped Jack dead center in the chest. "When I took Irene home afterward, there was already three voice messages waiting for her. Creepy." They started walking again, Mercedes hugging even closer. "What do you think?"

"About what? Kyle, or the two of them together?" They were nearing the junior high, where an asbestos tile from the ceiling had once fallen during an English class and missed Jack by mere inches. He'd been saving that story for this particular moment in the tour, actually, but he sensed Mercedes' need to know about the older boy.

"Kyle's always been a jerk, but he's not that bad."

Mercedes gave him a look that could have laid frost over oil.

"–Compared to the rest of his family," Jack was quick to amend. "His older brothers were worse, believe me." Jack didn't want to go into detail. From what he knew of her already, Mercedes would understand. Every town, every school has its bullies. "They're pretty typical, I guess. They all kind of run wild. The family's lived in Forge forever, and their parents don't care what they do." (And are buzzed-out alcoholics, he silently added). They own a logging company; live on a farm. Kyle's the youngest. The next oldest, Merrick, he's always hated me–well, you don't want to hear this, do you?" He looked at Mercedes.

She returned his gaze. "This guy is pretty much stalking my cousin, so, yeah; if you want to tell me. Secret's safe," she raised her hand.

"Okay, but let's sit down first." They'd reached a spot in front of the town library where a squat wooden bench had been set under a willow tree. Jack normally tried to avoid even thinking about Merrick Dremel, but if Mercedes wanted to know . . .

"He's got a way with people, especially adults. Everybody loves him—the total opposite of Kyle—but Merrick's—dark. He's a psycho. I mean, when I was littler, you know, just a little kid, he was always slapping me around, chasing me. He's the kind of guy who makes childhood a miserable experience if you're a boy. He'd round us all up before school even started. Forget about guarding your lunch money. Merrick'd just go straight for the lunch. He'd really torment all of us. Be glad you're a girl," he added.

"But you learned to take care of yourself, right? You got bigger and stronger than him, and stood up for yourself, didn't you, Jack?" She patted his biceps absently.

Jack chuffed and cleared his throat. "I was a lot fatter back then, and he was always huge. That whole family must have an extra chromosome or something." He looked askance at Mercedes. "Mostly I stayed out of his way. 'Sides, all the grownups liked him a lot by the time he got into high school. Three years in a row we took State in all four sports because of the guy."

"So what happened to him?"

Jack made a wry expression. "Pride of the town. Full ride scholarship a couple of years ago to the university. Good riddance." He gripped the bench's seat and leaned forward. "Yeah, Mercedes, Kyle's a lightweight compared to his psycho brothers. You really think he's a problem for Irene?"

She looked surprised. "Of course! What would you call a guy who leaves three messages on the phone within five minutes, just so he could play through some sick black metal song? What would you say about a guy who buys a girl underwear on their second date, then, that time she was going to break up with him, he sent her a picture of herself with the eyes all sliced up? Jack, he's a few fries short of a Happy Meal. Irene says he talks about guns and things all the time. He even got her a cell phone so he could keep tabs on her."

"Wow. I didn't know all that stuff. I thought he was just being persistent. You know, to prove himself."

Mercedes shook her head urgently. "Jack, the only thing that persistence proves is persistence. Not love. Not even close." She shuddered, shrugging and grimacing into herself, prompting Jack to place a steadying hand on her back. "I talked to her about it all day, even though maybe it's none of my business. Then, know what? When we got back home he was waiting outside their house! She can't seem to shake him off. He's so gross!

"I swear, sometimes it's like you guys just don't understand how nuts it is when a girl says no and you just keep on going. It's like that old movie, you know, where Dustin Hoffman keeps proposing to Katherine Ross and she keeps telling him 'no,' then right after she's married some other guy he breaks into the church, beats everybody up with a cross, and carries her off. She doesn't get much say now, does she? Stupid show. What was it called?"

"*The Graduate.*" Jack knew the movie well, even had some of the dialogue memorized. His favorite part was when Benjamin, Hoffman's character, impersonated a friend of the groom, then a family member, and finally a priest in order to get the girl. But after what Mercedes had just said—the contemptibility of Benjamin's actions was something he'd never considered, though he *had* thought the romance a little screwy. Come to think of it, the whole courtship was awfully like a series of weird stalking encounters.

"Why doesn't she just tell him it's over, then ignore him? It's not like she has to get a restraining order or anything. She's got enough friends to watch out for her if anything should happen. Chad, Ryan, Mike—"

"Yeah, I met them the other day at the pool. Well, I'll tell her." Mercedes took a long, deep breath. "This is so beautiful." she said after a moment. "Too nice tonight to talk about jerks like that. Hey, a shooting star!"

Jack began to look up, and his eye was caught by a growing pair of headlights farther down the road. He'd already explained to Mercedes that they'd been walking down the middle of Forge's eight-block cruising strip, though he didn't think anybody would be driving it so late at night. There'd probably been a party somewhere up in the hills. Jack had always considered cruising to be one of the more useless fads. Most of his friends had grown out of it within a month of getting their license. He wondered if it was a police car behind the bright lights.

The vehicle drew closer, and they saw it was a white Ford pickup, tricked out with all manner of accessories in the way of extra spotlights lined across the extended cab, a roll bar, and chrome wheel rims to match the grill. The owner neglected it, though. Dirty red rust specks spattered the hood, and a crack zigzagged across the windshield on the passenger's side. The truck's hoarse roar filled the night, advertising a worn-out muffler. Jack couldn't see past the tinted glass, but he felt eyes on them from within, and the truck slowed to a growl as it passed on the street. Its undercarriage was jagged with rust.

Mercedes was unimpressed. "That probably looked really cool when it was new. Too bad the owner doesn't know how to take care of his stuff." She leaned out, elbows on her knees, like a man. "Whose is it?"

Jack had seen the truck before in the high school parking lot, but not since he was a freshman. "I don't know. Hasn't been around for a while. Serious, Mercedes; just tell Irene to forget about Kyle. We can look out for her. Besides, she'll have all those college guys next year." Jack yawned. "One thing's for sure; Kyle won't graduate with us, least not in the spring."

"You—" Mercedes began, before she was blindsided herself by a yawn.

Jack smiled. Even with her mouth wide open, she was beautiful. She noticed his scrutiny, and laughed. "Thanks a lot! I hate it when someone makes me yawn. Hey, they're coming back."

He looked. The white Ford was just completing a wide U-turn at the intersection a block away. Its front wheels didn't quite clear the curb, and as they watched, the Ford took out a clump of shrubbery at the corner. Mercedes sniffed. "Nice try."

The passenger window slid down and acid rock crashed out, filling the street with grinding guitar. Jack saw the raised bottle an instant before the leering owner threw it, and ducked to the side over a surprised Mercedes. His quick reaction was unnecessary, however, as the bottle rocketed over their heads and shattered against the bole of the willow behind them. There were at least two other people inside the truck that got off a couple of shots each as well, though the container that landed nearest Jack and Mercedes actually was an empty aluminum can

297

that fell far short of its target, then bounced into the gutter. From what they could see of the murky interior of the cab, the truck was crowded. Someone was swearing loudly and incoherently, and the truck leaped forward. With a clink of bottles being readied and a snarling clatter of heavy metal, the truck lurched toward the next intersection, a scant fifty feet away.

Jack's heart pounded, and he threw a quick look at Mercedes. She hadn't been hit. Instead, he was surprised to see the expression of fierce anger that gritted her teeth and trembled down through her shoulders. She moved, and Jack followed Mercedes around the edge of the sign towards the library. They could run around behind it and lose themselves in the yards of the residential section. Who were these guys? Would they come after them if they ran? He'd have to take the lead before they got too far; show her the swinging board behind Weller's house, and then the little alley that ran behind the post office toward Gessner's old apartment, but–

And he realized Mercedes wasn't running for the lawn that led around the library. She'd bent down and retrieved one of the unbroken bottles of beer. The red and silver Miller logo rolled over in her hand, and with a yell she launched it at the retreating pickup.

It wasn't that difficult a shot, but Jack had trouble believing it fell so perfectly together, or that the girl's arm was that good. The heavy, thick glass end of the bottle whipped right through the rear window and sent a shower of keen splinters into the cab. An incredulous, bearded face appeared briefly against the harsh illumination from the streetlamps, then vanished as the brake lights flared on. Jack heard the thud and the resultant howls as whoever it had been was thrown, backwards probably, against the dash and driver.

He gaped as Mercedes threw another bottle, which shattered against the upper edge of the tailgate, dashing glass against the truck bed and throwing a few heavy pieces through the broken window. The passenger door opened and Kyle Dremel stumbled out in a miniature avalanche of beer containers. He glared, sputtering, at Jack and Mercedes, who was looking around hard for an unbroken bottle. Kyle slipped and fell against someone behind him who was also trying to exit, as the driver's side door opened with a screech and clatter of accompanying bottles hitting the pavement.

The heavy metal song ended with a long, drawn-out chord from a base guitar, and another began, saturating the street with steel drums and what sounded like a number of cats being shaved. Jack bowled into Mercedes as she raised another bottle. "Come on!" he said, pulling at her jacket. "There's at least four of them in there! Let's *go!*"

She whipped around towards him, and for an instant Jack was dead sure she'd use the dark bottle against his head, so vicious and violent was her expression.

He grabbed at her shoulders, more in reflex against a possible attack, and she blinked, then bit her lip. Mercedes looked wordlessly at him for another split second, then ran for the shadows at the back of the library.

Swift on her heels, Jack looked over his shoulder at the street. An instant's glance showed him four grown men milling around the truck, and another clambering out. Three had bottles in their hands and were peering at the shattered window. Two had been in school with Jack but had dropped out. One Jack recognized as a scraggly, older version of a boy who'd graduated a year previous. Floyd.

He was grinning at Jack.

Bad to worse.

Floyd Heaton had gone on to college on a track scholarship, then had been kicked out for drug violations the next year. "Best Smile" in the school yearbook, voted in by the graduating class two years previous. They'd caught him taking speed meth. Floyd gave Jack a nastier version of the same smile, wiped his mouth on the collar of his stained T-shirt, and took off running for the corner.

Mercedes stopped in the narrow alley behind the library annex, unsure. "Keep going," Jack whispered, jerking her as he passed and moved to the right, away from the alley's entrance where he was sure Floyd would appear. Strung out or not, drunk or not, Heaton could outrun them easy.

The alley was defined by fences of varying height and construction. They ducked through a backyard gate pursued closely by shouted expletives from the library's side yard. Jack was still in the lead, and guided Mercedes low to the ground as they ran back to the left, toward a lower picket fence and another back yard. They crossed without difficulty, Jack practically hurdling it then turning to lend Mercedes a steadying hand. Her face was stark white, and Jack could feel her shaking slightly.

He knew the neighborhood well. They were in the McDades' yard, a freshly-mown plot bordered by walnut trees, and on the side facing the alley, a ten-foot cedar fence. The edge of their yard came just up to the sidewalk on the nearby street, and Jack half expected to see Floyd Heaton step around the corner and smile at them. His stomach churned.

On the other side of the fence, a half-whispered conference was taking place in the alley. Jack edged up to it, then peered between the slats, instinctively taking care to keep some distance between himself and the fence, so that their peripheral vision, focused only to the depth of the cedar planks, wouldn't pick him up. For a fraction of a second Jack paused, wondered how he knew that trick, then mentally cast the abstraction aside. It just made sense, and there were far too many other thoughts occupying his mind.

He could see the layout of the entire block in his head.

Their conversation only carried in snatches beyond the tight circle of shadowy, huddled forms, and Jack could make out only a few words at a time. They were all too drunk to really manage a whisper but still cautious against waking up the neighborhood, despite all the raucous music from the truck. The steel drums had completely given up to the electric caterwaul.

Next to a pair guys with goatees Jack had never seen before stood Kyle. The fourth member, a head taller than the rest, had his back to the fence and was wearing a letterman's jacket. Heaton ran up noisily.

The smartest thing to do would be to just go up to one of the houses on the street and ring the doorbell until someone came. Easy enough; the mere presence of an adult would probably work to scare off Kyle and the others. Their problem lay in evading the others long enough to pick the right house, one where someone would be quick to answer the door. The more Jack considered it, the more he realized the plan was flawed. Who would be anxious to open their door to strangers at four-thirty in the morning? Who would even hear them knocking at this hour? Kyle and his friends would have plenty of time to grab him and Mercedes; maybe pull them right off somebody's front stoop.

Jack had played in the area since he had been a little boy; had ridden his bike up every trail and down every alley in the neighborhood. There was a trail–barely a deer track, really–that led up into the woods at the edge of town, over a steep bench that changed quickly from hill to mountain, and it began only about three blocks away. He suspected that only himself and a few other cross country runners on the track team knew and used it regularly. That made him think of Floyd--but no, he'd been mostly short course and had never gone on long runs through town.

301

They were silent on the green carpet as they crept toward the street. Jack pulled Mercedes close into the intersecting shadows of the wall and the walnut tree nearest the sidewalk. They stood hip-to-hip as Jack explained his plan.

He breathed a quick version of their route into her ear, and she nodded, then yanked him even closer to her at the scrape of footfalls on the sidewalk. As Mercedes pressed herself into him, Jack covered her blond ponytail with one hand, leaning out slightly to get a better view.

Kyle and one of his goateed companions stalked by on the other side of the tree, looking warily into the gloom between the line of houses and back fences. Goatee had a flashlight and was playing its thin beam into the yard, discreetly. The two were obviously in a hurry though, and Goatee kept the light low, ahead of himself and Kyle. Jack prayed they hadn't counted on him doubling back.

And he wouldn't have, either, if Mercedes hadn't been with him. Jack had been running from the Dremel kids in one way or another since childhood, but always alone. It occurred to him now that he hadn't even considered leaving Mercedes or striking off on his own. This went way beyond any male-dominance version of Hide and Seek, however; far off into the land of the unsettling and bizarre.

The silence was stifling. He had the oddest urge to let out an Indian whoop at the top of his lungs. Jack had no idea what Kyle and the others would do if they caught him and Mercedes—

—and the thought turned into ice as Kyle turned back and looked *straight at him.*

The thin ochre light from the lamppost on the other side of the road opposite the tree clung to Kyle's bright yellow T-shirt. It drew cruel lines down around his arms and the thickness of his farm boy muscles. His black hair, matted wetly against his forehead, nevertheless parted sufficiently for some of the light to catch in the edge of his eye and gleam dully like some kind of night-glowing mold.

He looked straight into Jack.

Jack didn't move, pressing Mercedes and himself into each other slightly as if they could shrink. He'd read about this in books; how the naked eye could be fooled into thinking it saw something else if the thing observed acted differently than was expected. People saw what they wanted to see.

Kyle expected Jack to run.

Jack didn't move.

Didn't breath.

And Kyle's weird phosphorescent gaze wavered past them along the cedar fence, while his companion made a great show of shining his flashlight into the shrubs along the base of the dark house.

Further down the block, a dog started barking.

Mercedes lifted her head enough to take a shallow breath. Jack could feel her heart beat all the way through him. In pretty much any other circumstance—but the strange rage that possessed her at the street had fled, and she was beginning to lean into him more and more in nervous exhaustion. Jack could tell she was scared, and wished fervently there was something he could do in the way of reassurance. Not that he was feeling all that confident himself!

Slowly, he lowered his free hand to her shoulder. Watching Kyle carefully, Jack then began brushing his fingertips through the fine hairs on the back of Mercedes' neck, gently stroking the tension out of her fear-tangled tendons. Her skin was velvet-soft.

It seemed a strange thing to do, but it worked. Her body slowly relaxed. Mercedes sighed, a sound he felt more than heard, and rested her forehead against the crook of Jack's arm.

By the time Mercedes' heart had begun to slow, Kyle and his companion had reached the McDade's front yard. They continued onward to the next corner and split up, one taking the new street in front of the house and the other jogging up the increasingly inclined blacktop to the next block. As soon as he was able, Jack eased himself and Mercedes around the base of the walnut tree.

They crossed the street on quiet feet, eyes riveted on the back of the retreating Goatee. Mercedes' feet scuffed once on the bottom of a dry mud puddle that heralded the entrance to an unpaved alleyway, and then they were out of sight.

But not out of danger. *Loud enough and they can still get you, Jack,* a dry voice whispered in the forefront of his mind. He and Mercedes raced as quickly as they could up a paved path that ran between two cement walls. Their footsteps echoed loudly around them, thunderously loud to Jack's ears. He stole a look at Mercedes, and she grinned back, tired but fierce. It must have been the adrenaline, but he had to admit he was having *fun!*

They entered a driveway cluttered by the skeleton and approximations of a disassembled Army Jeep, and stopped in front of another cedar fence. "Friend of mine lives here," Jack said. "Kind of eccentric." As he spoke he pushed hard against the upper end of the fence, and a three-foot section swung up from the bottom, pivoting soundlessly on hinges that gleamed in the diffused light.

Mercedes put her hand out. "Wait. Does your friend have a dog or anything?"

"No, well; yes. Sort of. It's a Yorkie."

He led the way into the darkness beyond, then let the fence down slowly. On the other side of the small yard, they climbed up the stones of a rough rock wall, pushed over the knots of ivy at the top, and stood on the hillside. They could see over and between the nearby roofs all the way to the main street, where the white Ford still sat at an angle in the intersection.

The foliage was thicker along the base of the hill than Jack remembered, but he had never run the footpath in the dark. A lighter line of dirt against the grassy slope marked the trail, and he beckoned Mercedes into the trees. More light from the town actually reached them over the roofs of the houses, but they still had to pick their way with care upward through the thickening pines. Mercedes was soon breathing deeply. Somewhere between when Jack stepped sideways on a pinecone and when Mercedes tripped on a protruding rock, they started holding hands. Funny. Jack couldn't remember the trail being wide enough to accommodate two.

A pleasant breeze bent the heads of the long grass and carried with it all the fragrance of the midsummer night. Even in their haste, Jack took a moment to point out a bed of wild evening primrose to Mercedes, and smiled as she squealed and bent over the butter-yellow blossoms with delight. Their sweet scent mingled with those of clover and Indian paintbrush that grew in the shelter of the pines on the south-facing slope. Jack took a deep breath. The air was so sweet and clean. Everything in that night was sharper.

The trail leveled out at a flat area several hundred feet wide where the trees were sparse. In the center of the meadow stood two great bull pines, thrusting up royally into the star-bedecked sky. A third pine lay in the curve of earth where it had fallen, its prodigious bole held in a cluster of boulders. Wordlessly they clambered over the rocks to the tree. Wind and a season on the ground had managed to strip away much of the beautifully fissured bark, but the iron-colored trunk was still sound.

"Think they'll look for us up here?" asked Mercedes as they sat.

"I doubt it," Jack replied. "But even if they do, by the time they climb up this far they'll be too tired to do anything about it."

The wide canyon spread the city out below, and Jack and Mercedes had come far enough to be able also to see several miles up the Clearwater River. The enclosing mountains were quilted in fields and forests, tan and blue under the starlight.

Jack looked over at Mercedes. The faint town lights cast her features in a pale glow. She reached back and removed the tie holding her ponytail in place, and her hair slid back in an unbroken, argentine wave past her shoulders. She flexed her fingers inside the elastic tie, still gazing down, absorbing the vast panorama. "Isn't this view incredible?"

"Yes," he blurted without turning away, and grinned. She started at the speed of his answer, then returned his grin shyly. Jack wished he could tell if she was blushing. He ran his tongue over his lower lip. Now would be the time to say something romantic, if he could just decide what that might be.

Mercedes snapped the hair tie around her wrist, and said, "Did I hear you right at the library when you said you used to be fat?"

He blinked. This was an interesting turn in the conversation. "Yup. You wouldn't believe it–and we're not just talking chunky, Mercedes. I had dreams I was the round kid from Willy Wonka and the Chocolate Factory. I've been wearing the same size jeans since I was ten."

She laughed. "That's nothing. Just be glad you didn't grow up with my grandmother feeding you. Everybody used to call me the Pillsbury Doughgirl."

"You? No way!" Jack tried to imagine a younger, mega-chinned Mercedes and failed. "What did you eat?"

"What *didn't* I eat? My cousins were the worst. They got this weird kick off of seeing how much I could hold. Ack!" She held her side, remembering. "They even made me put peanut butter on pizza."

Jack thumbed his chest. "*Slathered* butter on saltine crackers." This was fun. "Sometimes I would sneak slices of bread to bed by hiding them in my pajamas."

She arched an eyebrow. "Hah! Poptarts instead of bread. In my underwear."

"Yuck! All those empty nutrients? How about this: three big bowls of cereal as an afternoon snack? Can you top that?"

"Sure. Butterscotch-flavored toothpaste."

"So?"

"I used to eat it."

Jack started to laugh, then caught himself. "But can't that kill you?"

She leaned toward him. "Depends on how much chocolate milk you need to wash it down." Mercedes started to laugh.

"Drank maple syrup straight from the bottle," he shot back.

"No!" She squirmed with laughter, and Jack chuckled at her hysterics. She nearly fell off the log. Heh. Mercedes one, Jack one.

"You have an odd way of saying things," she said at last.

"I watch a lot of old movies." He looked pointedly at her grin. "When you smile, you look a little bit like Stanley Laurel."

"Stan Laurel? Black-and-white movie Stan? Thin guy, crazy hair, wiggly ears?"

"Can you wiggle your ears?" he asked.

"That would make you Oliver Hardy."

"The fat man's fat man," he agreed.

They sat on the log for a while then without speaking, and found the lull in the conversation had become a companionable hush. Slowly the sounds of night stirred up from the trees and long grass around them.

Crickets began to sing. A bat breathed by above, flapping twice around the two bull pines before heading off to hunt field mice. Jack rarely came here at night; he was struck by how vivid and crisp the stars were, despite the upwash of Forge's streetlights and candy-neon signs.

A shooting star sliced by overhead, and Mercedes pointed to it before it vanished over the horizon. Jack rubbed his eyes. She sure was quick. They grinned at each other with childlike excitement, then turned skyward again.

Jack took a deep breath, hesitant to break the cricket's music. "So, how come you learned to speak Italian so well?" he whispered.

Mercedes smiled faintly. "My mom's family, back in San Francisco, is pretty much all Italian. Do you know much about the Bay Area?"

He shook his head.

"Well, if you go into North Beach, be careful. You can't hardly turn around without falling over one of my cousins. North Beach is full of my relatives from Florence; they've been coming over a few at a time since, well, since the city got started. Have you ever heard of A.P. Giannini?"

Again Jack shook his head. "Nope." He remembered the name from one high school textbook or another on American history, but he didn't want to interrupt. Jack didn't think he could stand it if Mercedes got the impression he was a bookworm. Besides, he didn't want to say or do anything that might stop her from talking; if her face was beautiful in repose, it was *alive* with expression when she spoke.

This time she smiled at him. "You're so cute, Jack. So this guy owned a bank—he just loaned money out to Italians and other poor people, even the Irish immigrants, and everybody made fun of him and his 'little dago bank in North Beach.' So when the big 'quake of 1906 hit and flattened almost everything, nobody had any money. Giannini stole all the gold and cash out of his own bank and hid it underneath his fireplace. Then, when his customers needed money, he loaned it out to 'em, but never had anybody sign any paperwork, because he knew them all personally. Cool guy. My grandfather says North Beach was rebuilt because of A.P. Giannini, his godfather."

Jack shifted slightly. The log seemed to be getting harder under him. "So what happened to your godfather's grandfather? Did he go broke after he gave all his money away?" It sounded a bit like something out of a Frank Capra movie.

"It's the other way around. Grandfather's godfather." She laughed. "He did all right in the end. Everybody who borrowed money gave it back, with interest. Ever heard of the Bank of America? Biggest bank in the world?" When he nodded, she continued. "That's what happened to the 'little dago bank in North Beach.'

"Anyway, our family's really close back home. My parents worked at the same place since I was a baby, and they'd have to leave me for a couple of months at a time when they had a special project. So my mom's family took care of me. They didn't mind at all–heck, they're still convinced my dad's going to win the Nobel Prize and prove himself worthy at last to marry my mother. They spoke nothing but Italian at home all the time I was growing up. Boy, do they know how to talk!"

"Not like you at all, though, right?"

She smiled, suddenly shy again. "Right!" She ran her hand along the steam-colored surface of the old tree. "Actually, I don't usually talk this much."

Jack patted her arm. "Sorry if I'm sarcastic. I like hearing about stuff like this. How come your parents left you for so long when you were little? What do they do?" Jack didn't want to pry, but he had an idea where the conversation was beginning to go, and he wanted to let her do the talking.

"They're–they were high-energy physicists. Most of the stuff they did was for the government, really hush-hush; they could never talk about it. They'd been doing it since before I was born. I think they were at some base in Nevada for a while, because they took me to Vegas for vacation and showed me some cool stuff, you know, out-of-the-way kinds of things. And they would teach a little at Stanford. Dad's a good teacher. They made a great team." She looked out over the town. "That's what everybody says. My dad always says how Mom is the smart one–you know, the old joke about how the girl's got great legs but she's no rocket scientist? In this case, she was." Jack barely caught the catch in her throat, but by the time she turned back to him, Mercedes was expressionless, ice-smooth, distant as the moon. Her tone was dead even as she spoke. "My mother died a little over a year ago."

Jack's mind went suddenly numb and fiery, as if he'd brushed up against an electric current. The back of his neck iced over, and he winced, scorched by the coldness of the sweat between the middle of his shoulders. She must have heard him gasp or something, because the next thing he knew, she'd slid across the log and placed her hand along his arm.

Before she could say anything, he gulped quietly and asked, "Did you get to know them? With your mom and dad being gone a lot? Did you get to know them very well?"

Concern for him etched her face, and she answered hesitatingly at first. "They were . . . great. Never spoke to me like I was a dumb kid, or too little to understand. They hated it when people spoke to me in baby-talk. I was a part of their lives. Parties, birthdays, promotions, whatever, I always got to come along."

He smiled so she would know he was fine, a-okay, nothing amiss, just some bad escargot.

Mercedes continued. "They went out of their way to show me neat things and places, and they'd play with me. All the special occasions you'd think they would have celebrated on their own, even their wedding anniversary, they included me." She paused. "What about your mom and dad? What are they like?"

He stiffened. They were barely more than a foot apart, but the silence that descended was more palpable than it should have been; more like a pane of glass miles thick, distorting and destroying his view of her, waiting to be shattered.

Jack bent and picked up a rock.

"My very first memory is seeing the stars through the front windshield of my parents' car as we slid backwards down the hill or cliff or whatever towards the river. My dad was driving, and I heard him yell something to my mother, probably "get out," as he twisted the wheel and tried to brake, but the gravel under the car was too loose, and sounded like scrabbling hands.

"The car stopped sliding once, and Mom pulled me out of my carseat in the back. When she pulled me around into her lap, I saw headlights up at the top and the silhouettes of people looking down, then they just went away. The car moved again, and it felt like we were floating up out of our seats, then we hit and I landed on my mom. She made me look at her, and I did, even though she'd gotten a little scratched when the glass from her window exploded. She was really calm and she said, "Jack, we love you. Remember us. Remember, remember." She said it a couple of times, and then the water was all around her, and it was really cold. They couldn't get out because the roof was really low, but my dad grabbed me and held me up above the water. He had a big jaw, like mine is now. I can still see him, sticking his arm straight up with me on the end, this sort of grim, determined look on his face. He wasn't scared, I'm sure.

The water was past his elbow by the time the paramedics ripped the windshield off the car and dragged me out."

Jack looked over at Mercedes, whose lips were parted as if in a long, silent cry. "My parents were killed when we were run off the road by three drunk guys out hunting. They sent me around for a few years, and I ended up here with my uncle Bill."

Her hand was warm where it touched his face. Mercedes brushed at his cheek, then seemed surprised to find she was the one weeping. She quickly wiped her eyes and re-arraigned herself next to him, smiling shyly again. Jack noticed a single vagabond tear, a spot of silver-gold against the city lights, track down her smooth face. It dropped, and he caught it against his fingers as Mercedes turned away on the log, as if to leave. Then she settled back slowly against his arm and side, laying her head against his shoulder. She shook softly.

At length she cleared her throat. "How much longer 'til the sun comes up, Jack?"

"Maybe an hour."

"Can you just, ah—hold onto me for another hour?"

He brushed aside a bit of her hair. "I should think so. Unless my arm falls asleep and I have to have it surgically removed."

Mercedes laughed, a sad-happy sound heavy with unshed tears, and pointed. Jack looked up in time to see another shooting star silently roar by.

*

The northwestern edge of France
8PM

Alonzo slapped his knee. "Whoa! I can't believe you told her about your parents." He tipped his water bottle back. He thought about getting a beer, but that was just reflex; he'd stay sharp and frosty until the mission was over.

"I don't know what I was thinking. We'd known each other for, what, a day?" Jack shrugged. "I just—felt different around her. Mercedes had a way of bringing out the weird in me." Alonzo laughed, and his friend continued. "I mean it, Al; it was *good* to be around her; *I* was good. Smarter or something, I don't know. I actually told jokes that made sense when she was around."

Alonzo shook his head. Jack had always been funny, he just never realized it until Mercedes. "You were seventeen. A girl like that fills up your world."

"She made me want to howl at the moon is what she did."

Alonzo cut Jack short with a guffaw. Recovering, he said, "Yeah, I bet. Hah! So then what happened?"

"The next few weeks—before you got home—were amazing. I was getting ready for the State meet; you know, swimming about 10,000 yards a day, trying to get more sleep. The teachers kept on me pretty hard about that chemistry assignment; the liquid-to-solid polymer thing—"

"–your Jell-o experiment for Mrs. Riley."

"Right. We still saw each other every day. Mercedes . . . was still really angry inside after her mother passed away. We talked about that a lot.

"She was so fun to be around. She helped me with my dives and we tried to learn tennis together." Jack smiled.

Alonzo chuffed out a long breath. He was getting the Clif Notes version. "Come on, Jack! Details, buddy, details. What about the first time you kissed her? Taste?"

His friend stretched his neck, grin widening. "Orange-pineapple frozen yogurt."

Alonzo whistled. "Your memory always amazes me, amigo." He finished the water. "And that was the summer it all came together. Funny to think, if it hadn't been for her we might not be sitting here. You and me, on a train in France. Riding with this crew, into—who knows what." He picked up the bottle of water and shook it. Empty.

"The thing of it is, she changed me. She changed who I was."

Alonzo shook his head firmly. "No, Jack; Mercedes just uncovered what was already there. You've romanticized her all these years because she was drop-dead gorgeous, maybe a little mysterious, a little eccentric, and, well, 'cause all the dead spooky stuff that happened later that summer. Mercedes opened the door, sure; but everything that came through from the other side was you, man." Alonzo pushed his hair out of his eyes. There had to be a more elegant way to express this.

Jack leaned forward and ran his hands through his own hair. "And what is that? What do you mean? After all these years–the people we've helped, so much of my time playing the actor," His expression soured. "Playing at being a D'artagnan, a knight errant—whatever, after all this life and these damn crystal-clear memories, who am I supposed to be now?"

Alonzo considered a moment, then picked up the copy of Entertainment Weekly he'd been flipping through earlier. "You are 'the great Jack Flynn, hyperbole in the vocabulary of Hollywood,'" he quoted grandiosely.

"That's not what I mean."

Alonzo paused, dropped the magazine. Against the quiet in their end of the cabin, he spoke. "You're Jack Flynn, my *friend*, the smartest, strongest man or boy I ever knew. In the end—for me, at least—it comes to that."

Major Griffin, who'd listened to the entire exchange, was suddenly startled by the appearance of Steve Fisbeck, seemingly at her elbow. She hadn't realized Jack's story had captivated her so fully, and she smoothed her clothes as the chubby man handed over a tablet computer. "This just came for you on the secure email address. Forwarded by your service in Paris."

Flynn set the computer down next to his equipment. The major watched his eyes flit back and forth over the message as he filled the pockets of his new jacket. "Something the matter, Mr. Flynn?"

"Please, call me Jack," he said absently. In a moment, the mercurial man had grown distant, quiet. He paused, staring blankly at the blur of lights as the Calais station flew past in the night.

"This is from my sister-in-law. She wants me to come for dinner Sunday, in Geneva." The man across from her was actually surprised, thought Griffin. "I never expected to hear from her again," he went on, half to himself. The banks of earth outside began to rise.

"You're married then?" the major asked.

Jack's eyes snapped up to meet hers. They were soft but direct. "My wife died on a trip like very much this one, nearly a year ago," he said. "And it looks like," he held up the paper, "her family's beginning to forgive me." He shook his head. "They'll forgive, but never forget, that's for sure."

"And yourself?"

He laughed quietly, mirthlessly, and began to arrange his equipment. "I suppose I'm the opposite, Major Griffin. At least, sometimes I can almost forget." He worked the action on his pistol, then released it with a metallic snap.

"Almost."

Jack looked sharply around at the other members of his team. "Listen up, boys, here's how we go in. You're going to love this."

The train sped on, leaping headlong into the gaping vault of the tunnel, and the fields of liquid green rolled back over in the wind like breakers on an empty sea.

Up the Beanstalk

9PM

London

His feet were almost soundless as he brushed across the roof of the Illuminatus Tower. The instant Jack found firmness under his feet he released his parachute's harness and jerked it, billowing, out of the sky. Above and behind him, Major Allison Griffin snarled, pulling hard on her parachute rudders as she spiraled about the steel tower. Steve landed in much the same way, grunting as he hit the roof.

"I love the BBC," he growled at the transmitter. Its red airplane warning signal glowered down at him from another hundred feet above the craggy tower.

The three moved across the roof, staying well away from the slowly pulsing aircraft warning lights. "You never said anything about a low altitude jump, Flynn," hissed the major for the third time in fifteen minutes.

Jack was almost smiling as he looked around the roof. "Unless you want to make another *right now* we'd better get out of this wind."

They looked down on an unfinished section of the new building, a maze of pipe and aluminum two-by-four skeletoning at least three partially-constructed floors. Jack was the first one to the ladder. The adrenaline rush he'd used to talk himself into the drop was fading, and the wind bit into him with teeth and claws of ice. Darkness awaited them below, but at least it was solid. "'Once more unto the breach, dear friends,'" he said.

*

"Is this your first time shopping at Harrods?" asked the uniformed woman several hundred feet below.

The kindly—if garishly dressed–African man before her glanced up from the display of ties. "Why, yes, as a matter of fact, it is." He held up a green silk Gino Resillio. "You wouldn't happen to carry shoes that match this?"

The saleswoman turned, gesturing past a service entrance and an exit to the stairs. "At Harrods, sir, we carry everything." she said confidently. "If you'd like, we can have those fitted for you while you wait." But he was already gone.

*

The Asian with an accent out of the American South pushed the wide brim of his hat back and eyed the antique silver coins shimmering in the velvet case. "Pirate's treasure, huh? From Sir Francis Drake? You say they're how much?" He drawled heavily–almost exaggeratedly—over each syllable.

The floor manager straightened his monocle. "One hundred and twelve thousand pounds, if you must know." He was becoming entirely fed up with this inane Asian-American and his endless questions. It was nearly time to re-wax his mustache, at any rate. "Now see here, my good fellow, it's a quarter to closing and I really must insist on locking up this section of the store."

The other man didn't move. "I wouldn't know about all that, Jimmy-boy. I made my money in oil and natural gas. You know anything about gas?" His attention never left the doubloons. "Must have a hum-dinger of a security system in this dump to protect all this shiny stuff."

"Harrods is protected by a Fortress security arrangement, yes. Now I really must insist we—"

"I'm-a goin', I'm-a goin. Which way to them Baluga fish eggs I heard about?"

*

The young concierge manning the desk near the private elevators gaped openly at the man who stepped in out of the fog. "What are you looking at, sonny?" said the clown, chomping vigorously on a huge plastic cigar. One flaring, rainbow eyebrow arched dangerously. "I'm here for the bachelorette party on the 29th floor, so buzz me in, chop chop." He honked his bicycle horn twice for emphasis.

The concierge remembered himself and pressed the button, opening the elevator. The clown paused as he flopped his enormous shoes past the desk. "Here you go, kid," he said, handing the young man a balloon poodle. The clown pulled absently at the red and blue cloth "buttons" fronting his outfit. "Ever want to kill your boss?" he asked.

*

Steve had to labor to keep up with Jack and the major, forcing himself to breathe as quietly as possible as they rushed through a labyrinth of half-formed walls and dusty two-by-four frames. The night jump had been enough of an ordeal; he'd be lucky to make it through the next few hours without a major cardiac infarction. Worse, he knew his stentorian breathing would give them away in an instant, should any sentries or daytime laborers be lingering about. At least the air conditioning's already been activated, he thought. "Wait up," he wheezed. *They* didn't have to carry all of his equipment.

319

*

"Just here to examine your building for any possible threat to the water table, fellows," said the blond, bespectacled geologist. "Whitaker's the name. Mr. Raines' office called me down just this morning from Edinburgh." He eyed the building's foundations, oblivious to the scrutiny of the three janitors whose pinocle game he'd disturbed. "Don't mind me, I can find my own way about. Dreadfully high water table you chaps have here in London, what with the Thames and all." He peered closely at the concrete wall, apparently following a minute crack with his finger as well as his eyes, and shuffled off down the tunnel.

*

The three figures in black skidded to a stop before a doorway to a huge, vaulted room full of workmen's equipment. According to the construction timetable (available to anyone over the net) and the registered blueprints (available to anyone capable of decrypting seven layers of net security at the architectural firm), this space was destined to serve as an auxiliary circuitry room. "Chokepoint." said Jack. Half-laid walls and exposed ductwork obscured all but a portion of the cavernous area. "Power's on, Steve."

He gestured at an electrician's box between a stack of drywall slabs and a support beam. The finished part of the room looked like a giant walk-in closet, with a switchboard full of switches, plugs, fuses, lights, wires, and shunts. Translucent plastic sheets hung from beams crisscrossing the ceiling, dividing the room up into mismatched sections. Fine dust and bits of wood covered the floor. Jack began stripping out of his black Nomex flight suit.

The major rested her pack on an overturned pail. "This isn't the most defensible position, but I agree." Underneath her insulated coveralls she wore a form-fitting black bodysuit similar to those worn by the two men. Hers was also short sleeved, and Jack caught himself watching the play of muscles along the back of her arm as she hunted in her pack for one of the armored jackets. He sped up his own preparation, tightly packing certain items into a smaller knapsack. The required attention to detail, he found gratefully, forced him back to the task at hand.

The three of them stashed their extra equipment and spare parachutes under a pink snowdrift of insulation and began arranging a small level area on which to set the computer. As she hefted a 10 pound bag of drywall powder, Major Griffin said, "I must certainly admit, I for one never thought your people would get nearly this far."

"Like I said before, Major, we're here to help," said Jack as he laid a wooden board atop the stack of drywall bags.

"Afraid that should be my line, Mr. Fl–Jack." She found her armored jacket and slipped into it. "I never anticipated my assignment from His Majesty would involve more than my acting as tour guide."

Jack looked pointedly at her handgun. "You just show me you can use that .45, Major, and this could be the beginning of a beautiful friendship."

The other man finished connecting the cables from his laptop to the various boxes on the walls marked *Danger! High voltage,* and booted up his hard drive. "We're in luck, folks. I can get us direct video freefeed from the surveillance cameras. As soon as Brad finds out which brand security system this place uses, I can access our database and override theirs. No one will ever know we're here."

"That takes care of that," said Griffin. "What about Raines' offices?"

Steve shook his head. "No good. Looks like he may have his own setup in there. It's a complete stand-alone; I can't get in." He fished a minuscule headset out from a pocket and plugged it into his computer.

Jack and the major activated their tiny wireless earbuds and married them electronically to the phones they carried clipped to their belts. He grabbed up his knapsack. "Give me about fifteen minutes to get into place, then we'll run a check on everybody."

The major checked the numbers she'd programmed into her phone. "And as soon as you have ascertained that Her Highness is actually here, I'll make the call to D-11."

Jack nodded. "It's good to know that at least some of the police in London are allowed to carry firearms."

The major returned his gaze dubiously. Before she could speak, he closed his mouth into a grin and walked off into the darkness, swinging the small duffel bag.

Steve set a Snickers bar next to the laptop, and opened a long, narrow case strapped to his thigh. Stealing into Raines' sound would be a trick.

*

The Vienna Boys Choir and the Stuttgart Philharmonic Orchestra were praising light and truth from several recessed speakers in the main office as Raines scanned the security report, then handed it back to the tall Chinese called Michael. "Very good. Call Raphael and Gabriel in here, would you please? Now, my friend," he said to the man who stood pulling himself into a gray trenchcoat. "The van and other cars are in the basement garage."

"Yes, yes, we've been over this," snapped Miklos. "You and I rendezvous in two hours. My men and I drive around London until the broadcast, then deposit the child at the gates of Buckingham Palace."

"–the press will be there," Raines gestured as if urging Miklos to speed up.

"The press will be there. As soon as she's picked up or on camera, we—"

Raines finished for him. "You make our *real* political statement."

Miklos smiled. It never reached his eyes. "And the *whole world* will shake."

Raines waited until Miklos had left, then walked to his desk, switching his computer on before settling into his brass-studded, leather club chair. Pity. The chair was just beginning to feel right. He should have had it removed before tonight's activities made such an activity impossible.

Raines had prepared and tested the Hradek program months before, and now only needed a simple systems diagnostic to make sure everything was proceeding properly. As the diagnostic began, he activated another program, a custom-built teleconferencing suite that made use of the cluster of special instruments on the roof of the Illuminatus Tower.

Within moments his system was shaking hands with a similar communications setup at a villa outside Cartagena. Lopez's secretary answered, her English unmarred by any trace of accent. "Good evening, Mr. Raines. How can I serve you?"

Mmm. The three million he'd spent perfecting the video feed was money well spent. Raines had always enjoyed blond Latina women. Further proof that European blood, even a few generations old, carried well through the tangled ancestries of South America. "Please tell Armand the project is well underway, and to proceed with matters at his discretion. I shall join him tomorrow or very likely early the next day. Also, my dear, this will be the final transmission from London."

"Very good, sir."

Raines terminated the call and then activated a final program from his workstation. He then transferred certain data and control protocols from his desk-mounted system into a smaller, hand-held computer, just finishing as two of his suited and impeccably-coiffed men paused outside the door.

"Gentlemen," he said, pocketing the miniature system. "After you complete your assignment this evening, you'll have twenty minutes to join us above." They nodded, the smaller one with the beard grinning viciously. Raines rounded his desk, tapping the lacquered finish. Gabriel and Raphael, as he enjoyed calling the two brothers, were two of his most bloodthirsty recruits. "Tempus fugit, my sons."

*

Elbow-deep in wires and cabling, Steve swam through the electronic physicality of the Illuminatus Tower. Everything forgotten beyond the tangle of colored lines. Smiling faintly—music?—he spliced into another cable, tying the new line off and pulling another from his vest pocket. Got to talk to Jack about going totally wireless. His favorite wireless gadget still had a patent pending: the spider.

Steve hooked the tiny mechanism—it was black, antennaeless, and about half size of a match head—into a conduit and checked a receiver clipped to his arm. Grunted to himself in satisfaction when he saw the strength of spider's signal. Where was that Snickers?

*

Solomon lay nearly prone on the roof between the two windows, screwing the special attachment onto the barrel of his rifle. He didn't exactly harbor a love of heights, but the bright light streaming upward from the theater lobby gave the illusion of definition to the wide, yawning space above and behind him. He definitely didn't want to turn around to enjoy the scenery. The entire roof was canted slightly in that direction, anyway. He shuddered, and adjusted his headset. At least this wing of the building kept him out of the wind.

Leaning a foot to either side gave him a perfect view of the theater lobby and the wide, mall-like hall the moviegoers would walk down to reach the public elevators. That was fine. He could shoot equally well from either shoulder. All the shops were closed now, of course, but a few restaurants remained open, and some young, wild-haired punks still hung around the lobby and surrounding area.

Solomon knew the feel and temperament of his McMillan M-88 sniper rifle like he knew his left arm, and he'd been a lefty since Pony League on the Big Island. The .50 caliber repeater was accurate up to 2500 yards, and in addition to his routine ammunition he carried additional magazines of incendiary and armor-piercing shells in various pockets of his black ninja suit.

All told, it looked to be an easy mission. Solomon lay under a hundred meters from the targets, which made accounting for windage and height simplicity itself. After they blew the windows and provided suitable distraction, he would switch to his infrared sight and clear the area using specially-prepared Magsafe ammo Ian had loaded for him. The crowd below would be panicky around the cell of killers, and Solomon had no wish to accidentally deliver a deathblow to an innocent bystander. Hence the Magsafe: lethal, frangible ammunition that would not penetrate the human body. Solomon's sidearm held the same type, though in smaller, more conventional shells. Magsafe was best for close quarters battle, but Jack had suggested they come up with a form that could be delivered via sniper rifle for situations like this.

Jack placed great faith in preparation.

Laying supine on the cold concrete, a slight breeze tugging at his black cap as he continued to survey the kill zone, Solomon allowed a few of his thoughts to return to a particular student left behind in Germany. The Hopkins poem had been the right move, though the school board would have collectively scowled had they known Solomon told Carl he was a Baptist.

Solomon sighed. In his professional career as an educator—he refused to think of his job as just a "cover"–he'd always shrugged off discussions about separation of religion and scholarship, though he held tightly to his personal religiosity. Most of his life he'd been a sniper, trained in the twin arts of killing at range and psychologically manipulating enemy troops into sheer terror. Yet if he could make room in his worldview for belief in hope and a higher power, why was it that the teaching profession recoiled from the concept as if it were a form of leprosy?

He never would have seen the movement off to his left if he hadn't been watching for it. Several meters and three gaping skylights away, Brad gave him the thumbs-up. Like Solomon, he too was making the final adjustments to his weapon, a cannister rifle, and like the other man, Brad wore a ninja suit and one of Ian's jackets. Far above and behind him, the edge of a curtain billowed from one of two open windows, either of which had given him access to the roof.

Solomon settled down to wait out the movie, thinking fleetingly of the green tie as he adjusted his sights. Six more minutes.

*

Ian's gaze swept from his wristwatch to the multiple concrete corridors. Where the hell am I? he thought. According to the blueprints, I should be coming up on the service elevator. Nobody said anything about all these branching tunnels. And I've definitely never seen *this* before.

He eyed the bundle of thick, dark wires snaking along the ceiling of the tunnel. They weren't threaded through in any piping, nothing to protect them as they wound along next to the naked flourescent bulbs. He could be mistaken, but weren't those microchips embedded every couple of inches in the wire? This could be the special fiber optics. Now, what would they be connected to, he wondered.

Ian began to jog through the narrow, sloping corridor.

*

Steve was inordinately proud of his communications equipment. He'd designed the bone microphones himself, tiny flesh-colored microdots that nestled quite nicely in the ear. Voice was picked up by vibrations in the bones of the user's face, so the bone mic was practically invisible. Each mic piggybacked off of the user's cellphone, so as long as nothing interfered with the phone signal, the hardware was solid.

Software was another matter. Steve knew he was good—hell, great, but he also knew there wasn't a single encryption scheme that couldn't be broken. As an added security measure, the team used codes and codenames to communicate in the field.

For some damn reason, Jack was partial to classic comedy star and famous fat man, Oliver Hardy.

"Ready for check, Ollie," said Steve into his headset. The screen before him was taken up primarily by a patched-in view of the building's security system. Even as his computer sent doctored images to the building's security force, he was permitted an untampered perspective of the theater lobby, while six smaller windows on his screen rotated through views of various hallways throughout the building. Beside him sat Major Griffin, eyes riveted on the small computer, the huge .45 Combat Magnum in her hand.

Jack cleared his throat over the line. "Groucho?"

"Check," said Steve.

327

"Gummo?"

"Lock and load," said Brad.

"Zeppo?"

"Ready." intoned Solomon.

"Chico?"

Ian's voice crackled and warbled strangely over the connection. "Yeah, I'm a little behind, but I'll be there."

"Harpo?"

Honk, honk.

"That's nice. Okay people, two minutes till *our* show starts. Safeties off, everybody. This is what we train for."

*

Steve looked over his equipment, set his pistol next to his keyboard, then sat back. The editing software was running smoothly with the surveillance camera interface, he saw. He'd routed all video feed from the building through the computer before him. The current program would selectively cut all signs of the team out of any scene before relaying it on to the building's security net. Steve sighed, pleased with his work. He pulled a small serviceman's Bible from his breast pocket, and began to flip through the worn pages.

*

Funny, according to the blueprints this was a parking garage. The tunnel down which Ian had been running had gradually taken on the look of the type of mortar he'd seen in blast vaults and bomb shelters, and three steel doors and two broken lockpicks later, he found himself in an enormous circular room heavy with the stink of ozone. Alcoves sat in the yellowed walls, and Ian had the initial impression he'd walked into a mausoleum, though the niches were filled with electronics–

"Holy Mary," he breathed, looking down from a steel gangway at the machine.

It dominated the room. Not physically, no; the contraption wasn't much more than ten feet tall and half again as thick. The whole of it sat on an enormous black base–insulation, Ian realized. But why? It had no definable symmetry. More of the thick, steely wires snaked into the machine from five other corridors. A single, glossy pipe of some kind extended from the apex up through the ceiling. Machine is the wrong word for this thing, he decided, squinting as the entire surface lit up. It's more like some kind of animal.

Twisting silver cables and solid, seamless steel housing wrapped themselves in a lattice around a center core at least four feet thick. The glass or crystal core pulsed with an inner light, and indistinct shapes moved liquidly just underneath its glossy surface. Ian found he couldn't get a clear look at what they were. Every time he focused his eyes on the tube, its silvery brilliance pulsed yet again, leaving blue and red afterimages dancing on the backs of his eyes. The inner movement gave the eerie impression of life, alien life, to the entire apparatus.

"Steve, Jack, guys," he spoke into his mike. Nothing. Must be too much interference. Ian turned down the steel gangway and sprinted for what he prayed fervently was an elevator. The thing behind him began to vibrate and pound. Someone had turned it on, and it sounded as though whatever was inside was just waking up, and waking up angry.

*

Miklos yawned. He wasn't sleepy in the least; the reflex had been with him since he was a child, a precursor to any activity which excited him. Sound and distorted shadows played across the expressionless faces of his men. They stood silently behind the great white motion picture screen, some looking intently at the enormous images of Douglas MacArthur, the little girl swaying slightly between them. She'd been given just enough narcotics to keep her docile and unaware of her surroundings, though from time to time her eyes tracked the action on the back of the screen, lingering particularly on the face of the young MacArthur.

The movie was winding up; he'd just gotten his call from the President of the Philippine Commonwealth, played by Antonio Banderas, to return to that country he'd loved as a child and organize its military. *Hah!* thought Miklos. Wait a few years. The Japanese have a surprise in store for you, you arrogant American meddler.

But that would remain for the sequel. Already the end credits were rolling, and as the score boomed out from the speakers around them, Miklos signaled his men into motion. The plan was simple; mingle with the crowd and keep the little girl's face down. He sat on his haunches and looked her in the eye. Still dazed, that was acceptable. "Move," he said simply. He hated American martial music.

*

Almost in position, thought Alonzo, waddling down a darkened hallway. He couldn't wait for the chance to shed his second skin and assemble the weapons he'd brought along. Alonzo could probably get to his HK, but the grenades were beyond his reach.

He hated the shoes most of all. "Some disguise," he muttered. Without warning, a door opened, and light spilled into the hall.

"Who are you?" asked the man in the pale suit, obviously puzzled.

"I'm fine, thanks, who're you?" Alonzo said, shuffling by. Nobody's supposed to be in this part of the building, he thought. What gives?

"Stop right there," the other man commanded, lifting a radio.

*

Solomon returned Brad's thumbs up as the murmur of the crowd increased beyond the glass. "Remember, we wait for Jack," he said, fitting the rifle snugly against his shoulder in the spot weld, the surest position. The first two rounds were hostage duds, he reminded himself, special pellets that would shatter the glass before him and let it fall straight downward, instead of spraying it all over the civilians. He looked over at Brad, who stood, feet firmly planted and rifle aimed almost straight down.

Below both men, the lobby and surrounding shop fronts were filling rapidly. If all went according to plan, the crowds would drift toward the main elevators and, as those filled, move on to the other elevators, tiled catwalks, and escalators which zigzagged down between the shop levels.

Solomon wiped the back of his hand across his forehead. He was sweating rivers despite the chill air. This was always the most difficult part, the waiting with every sense alert, with every nerve screaming. Waiting until–

There. "Targets onstage, gentlemen." he whispered into the headset.

"Got 'em." said Brad and Steve simultaneously. Six, no, seven men in gray suits all stepped out of a theater exit and began sifting through the crowd. Each man carried an air of indifference and walked at a different speed, but there was something strange about the way they moved, never straying more than ten feet from each other. Solomon could see a child in a blue coat and hat between them, holding the hand of the biggest, a huge blond Slav with craggy, scarred cheekbones like axe heads. The same face he's seen on CNN only recently.

"The one in the middle is Miklos Nasim, the Albanian terrorist." Major Griffin's voice across the digital connection carried an unmistakable note of disgust. "KGB-trained and one of the first to turn against his own people when the Soviets fell. As deadly as they come, fellows." The man was devoid of expression–not merely relaxed, but utterly empty. Solomon imagined more than saw him expertly frisk each member of the crowd with his eyes as he steered his small charge purposefully toward the elevators.

They were about halfway across Solomon's line of fire when he saw a bushy-haired Asian woman in a voluminous military jacket and sunglasses sweep around a corner on rollerblades. She slid, oblivious, through the startled theatergoers, pirouetting and bouncing to whatever beat throbbed from her headphones. And she was headed full-out for the ensemble of Slavic killers.

Solomon winced as the young Asian woman came out of a spin backwards and collided clumsily with two of the goons from Eastern Europe. The one closest to her made to step aside and brush her away from the little girl in blue, then folded over sharply in pain, clutching his abdomen.

Solomon didn't even see the strike.

Was that the signal?

"Now!" whispered Jack's voice over the headsets, and instantly the windows above the milling crowd shattered. The egglike shells that pounded down around the suited men exploded noisily on impact with the tile and filled the air with a reddish-green haze. The suits stumbled back uncertainly toward their leader. A ratcheting whine filled the air, and the entire crowd stampeded for the exit. Several had their hands pressed firmly to their ears.

Steve's chortle sounded over the digital connection, then was itself drowned out as he activated every single fire, smoke, and burglar alarm on the floor. The jets in the ceiling opened up full, then closed, then began spurting water sporadically, showering the multitude below.

In the middle of the chaos the huge Slav leaned down and jerked the shrieking little girl back to her feet, more dragging than carrying her as he made for the hall leading to the stairways. He whipped a machine pistol from his jacket and aimed it at the mob before him. Before he could pull the trigger and carve an escape route for himself, the Asian woman, still fumbling, suddenly somersaulted over the back of his doubled-over comrade, in the process raking the huge man across the face and neck with her skates. Miklos barked a curse in his native tongue and swung the barrel of his gun towards her, but was engulfed in the crowd. Someone else ran into the backs of his knees and then his legs were knocked out from under him entirely. Briefly, he went down, under the crowd. Scrabbling upright, he found he'd maintained his grip on the blue jacket, but the little girl inside was nowhere to be found. The cloying smoke continued to rise. Miklos gritted his teeth against the cacophony and staggered towards one of his men.

*

"I'm here for the bachelorette party on the 29th floor," the clown said again.

Cassiel backed away from the advancing jester. "You're a bit off track, old chum." He pressed the button on his radio. Something just a tad unsettling about stumbling across an elaborately made-up clown in the dark.

He never got the chance to complete the thought, as the other man's white-gloved hand, blocked from view by the radio, prodding him in the stomach.

"No funny stuff," said the clown, jabbing again with the machine pistol.

*

Brad hooted and fired the last of his noisemaker bombs down into the tightly-packed clutch of suits. Time to switch to real munitions.

He shucked the special grenade attachment from his rifle and slapped in a clip. The boys below would never know what hit them.

Across from him on the roof Solomon switched to infrared. They'd worked like this together in a dozen different countries, in at least as many situations. He'd already selected his first target, but Solomon hesitated. Something was amiss, something he couldn't quite grasp. The fine hairs on the back of his neck stood up, and the skin began to twitch. He didn't like the sensation. Of course something's wrong, he thought crossly. I can look over my shoulder and set my watch by Big Ben if I care to! He shrugged it off and returned to his task. He pulled the trigger and shifted his crosshairs over another suit. He'd already squeezed the trigger again before the first man knew he was dead.

*

The Asian woman, her prize clutched tightly to her chest, sailed around a corner far down the hall opposite the screaming mob. The little girl clasped her arms tightly about her rescuer's neck, sobbing groggily. The two of them rolled in that manner around a few more corners, then spun to a stop near a janitor's closet flanked by two elevators. "There-there, dearie, we've got a bit of a surprise for you we do." The Asian set her charge on an upended garbage pail and spun back towards the hall, listening intently while she drew a knife and sliced cleanly through her shoelaces.

The little girl continued to whimper behind him as Jack threw his coat, wig, and sunglasses into a nearby barrel. He scoured his face with a specially treated towel, and stuffed that and the remnants of his disguise into the barrel. Scant seconds had passed and things were going almost according to plan. He set his pistol on a drinking fountain and reached into the trash barrel, retrieving a small knapsack.

"Come on, Ian," he muttered at one of the elevators as he slipped into a pair of black running shoes. "Don't worry, your Highness, we're almost in the clear." He spoke into his headset. "Groucho, this is Jack. Where the hell is our ride out of here?" He glanced back at the girl and did a double take.

It wasn't the Princess.

*

Solomon's finger was just tightening again on the trigger when he realized what it was that caused his scalp to twitch. *Two* open windows? He raised his head to shout at Brad, forgetting his headset.

Just in time to see his friend go down under a flash of fire from the upper window.

*

The two bearded men leaned back from the casement, laughing. The smaller one shifted his automatic rifle enough to reach his radio. "The boss was dead on, Michael. There is at least one more on the roof, I think Raphael and I can take him. Yes sir. Where can he hide?"

His companion nudged him and handed over another clip for his Kalashnikov. "Look, the black one is running." They both laughed and leaned out the window.

Nyet, ya Amerikanyets

Brad, Sol?" **Steve blinked** uncertainly at the streaming video on his screen. He could see Jack and what was obviously the little girl, but smoke obscured everything else. "Major, let's see if we can—"

But she was already ahead of him, running over the debris-strewn floor to a window. "Your men are under fire! Pull them out, get them out now!"

Halfway to the window himself, Steve nodded and spun back to the computer, then halted abruptly. "What are you doing?" yelled the major.

He pointed wordlessly across the hall to a monstrous, shrouded shape. Behind several layers of plastic, it had been hidden from view, just another silent tangle of steel and drop cloth. But the outline of the huge turbines and the fanlike rotor blades was unmistakable. Peering through the gloom at the surrounding area, Steve's swirling brain noted disposable fuel bladders and various mechanic's tools corresponding to the upkeep of a military helicopter. A set of thick cables ran from either turbine to a pair of machines about the size of ice coolers. Each machine hummed softly. It's being kept warm, Steve realized. Drawing closer, he and the major could see the pulley-and-wheel system on the nearest wall: the entire section was nothing but a pair of rollback doors.

Steve scrambled over his workstation, groping for his headset. "Chico, Zeppo, get out of there. Jack, we've found the missing Sikorky. It's right here with us! Do you have the package? Jack?" The security cameras on screen showed nothing.

"I'm here, Steve. We've got the wrong girl."

"*What?*"

*

Jack held the drowsy child awkwardly in one arm, eyeing the hallway. "It was a setup, a double-blind." Might as well forget code names, now. He paused to shift the little girl to one side, then tapped the elevator call button with the barrel of his gun. "Her name's Flora Clark, she's one of the kids that disappeared the morning after Christine was kidnapped. Decoy. Hey, where's Alonzo?"

Steve was beginning to hyperventilate over the digital interface. "No—word, Jack; we need to pull out. Solomon and Brad may be down. We've lost the—element of surprise."

*

"Steve, I doubt we ever had it. Any clue where the princess is?"

Before he could answer, Major Griffin pointed over his shoulder at the screen. The two of them watched as a security camera tracked several blurry images down a long corridor. Steve typed feverishly on his keyboard. "Oh, my. They're moving, Jack. From Raines' office on the thirtieth floor. Looks like they've got the little girl with them. And I'm reading some kind of fire on that floor."

Jack's voice was utterly calm. "Alright, Steve; now: Are you plugged into the elevators? Got any control there?"

"Uh, I'll work on it." Steve practically dove into his rucksack, yanking out coils of cable. "Major!" he hissed. "Help!" He thrust the tangle of cords at the British woman.

Jack kept talking, his voice still level, "as soon as you can, see if you can lock out all the elevators on their floor. Keep them moving up to you, away from the crowds down here. Did we set off enough alarms?"

"Yeah, firefighters at least will be here in a few minutes. But if that other fire is for real—"

"Good. Might as well trip any other alarms this place has. Make Raines' security think the whole place has caught on fire, or something. You can do that, right? Piece of cake, isn't it?"

Steve was beginning to relax. "Yeah, uh, should be." He began to tap out commands to the central computer.

Jack chuckled across the digital connection. "Practically nothing compared to the time you set off the sprinklers in the Oval Office—"

"Hey!" Steve smiled despite himself, typing faster.

The major spoke. "Listen, Flynn. We've called in the cavalry, as you Yanks say. SAS and D-11 will be here in less than fifteen minutes. Get the little girl to safety, then meet me in—" she yanked the blueprints straight. "The thirty-fifth floor hallway. Take the central express elevator. If you hurry we can cut them off."

*

Jack grimaced. "This is getting much too complicated. I'm on my way." Just then the elevator door slid open and Ian staggered out. "Here!" Jack passed the little girl over to the other man. "Get her out on the street and call a cop."

"No, Jack, wait! This thing downstairs—" Quickly Ian related what he had seen.

"Beats the hell out of me, Ian. Maybe one of those Tesla things you saw on T.V. I'll ask Raines about it if I see him." Jack ran back down the hall, gun in hand.

Ian looked at the little girl. She yawned and closed her eyes.

*

Solomon threw himself into motion, standing and firing at the same time. A bullet gouged a nick into the edge, an inch from his left foot. This was insane.

The enormous black man dropped his rifle and began to sprint across the roof, toward the oncoming fire. He wondered if this would surprise the gunmen long enough to buy him some time. Just a few seconds.

He leaped over the first window with nearly a foot of roof to spare. "Hold on, Brad!" he shouted.

*

Jack ran through the abandoned lobby, taking note of the four suited bodies and where they lay. Steve had killed the sprinklers and turned the alarms off, though colored lights still flashed in shops further down the promenade. Someone was shouting above him, and he turned just in time to see Solomon sail overhead, bathed in the golden light of the theater's marquee. If any of them lived through this, he thought as he exited the lobby, this was going to make one hell of a story.

*

Solomon exhaled hard as he hit the other side. One more hurdle to go. He kept his head down, expecting any moment to feel a hot explosion rip across his chest or legs. One more skylight. He was close enough now to see that Brad was still moving, still conscious, and surprisingly little blood had run down the window on which he lay. Still sprinting, Solomon drew his pistol and fired into the glass above and below his friend. The maniacal chatter of gunfire from the window sent him into a full-out dive, and Solomon slammed down onto his friend, shattering the window on which he lay.

They fell through the darkness, shouting, in a shower of sparkling glass.

*

The major securely fastened her handgun in its holster at the base of her spine and checked her tightly-knotted hair. Watching her from behind his laptop, Steve noted what a decidedly pretty woman the major was. He snapped the last cable into the appropriate port and began typing, his thoughts awhirl. *Great timing, Fisbeck.* "Good luck, Major."

The programs which ran the elevator operated on a completely different platform than the building's security. Access to the elevator would be difficult–no, it would just take a bit of time, he corrected. This is what he was good at; he knew exactly what to do. Steve glanced up in time to see the resolute line of the woman's shoulders as she walked away. She looked lethal, pantherlike.

Steve found himself wondering what he would have to do to gain a bit of access to Major Allison Griffin. "Living through tonight would be a good start," he muttered.

*

The two bearded men sighed. "Too bad," said the one called Raphael, delicately wiping his mouth with a paisley handkerchief. "Now we will hunt them like rats, eh?"

His companion chuckled, swinging his AK-47 back inside the room. "These ones fall too easily. They couldn't be SAS." Then he brightened. "Perhaps we can find a few more scurrying about."

He paused in mid-chortle. Light from the window fell on a large, bulbous red shoe. The red shoe was half-on a polka-dotted sock.

Alonzo flipped on the lights and kicked a shoe at either man's face. In the time it took for the two terrorists to blink and bat at the unwieldy projectiles, he had barreled across the room and slammed into Raphael hard enough to knock him off balance. His companion seized a handful of Alonzo's baggy shirt, and yelled in surprise as the smaller man grabbed his own hem and whipped the shirt off himself and over his opponent's head. Alonzo slammed his forehead into the terrorist and then turned back to Raphael.

The bearded man lunged, knife in hand. Alonzo slapped the knife away and caught his opponent by the wrist and armpit. Spinning, he sent the other man sailing into the window frame. Alonzo shoved the stunned man halfway out the window, then slammed it nearly shut with his shoulder, trapping the other's head and knife hand outside. Bending, he slipped one handcuff around Raphael's ankle, the other he fit over his unconscious comrade's wrist. Raphael was beginning to struggle, so Alonzo opened the window wide enough to shove the unfortunate terrorist the remainder of the way out.

His scream was cut short as his foot jerked against the handcuff. Alonzo shut the window as far as he could and then drew his pistol. Oblivious to the groaning man below him, Alonzo leaned back behind the window frame and shot twice point-blank into the gears governing the window's opening system. Before the twin roars had completely died away he was testing the hinge. It wouldn't budge.

He looked one last time at the terrorist known as Raphael, who was swaying slightly in the wind. Raphael looked back in time to see Alonzo drop their two radios past him. The small man waved.

Cursing steadily beneath his breath, Alonzo wiped a small trickle of blood from the underside of his arm. He'd been cut after all, but nothing a Band-aid and some bourbon wouldn't fix. He tossed the remainder of his clown suit on the floor, and turned the lights off on his way out.

*

Jack caught sight of another group of Miklos's men in the wide atrium that opened up on the top floor of Harrods, below. There was no mistaking the three men, smooth and lethal in their gray suits like a school of sharks, one carrying a little girl in a green coat. Their manner suggested nothing of the disorientation stirred into their ranks by the earlier attack, and Jack wondered then if Miklos had survived.

The atrium was a vast space topped by a light rig, crisscrossing balconies, and the occasional banner hung from the lowest balcony to the level below. A few theatergoers still struggled down the descending stairs and across the catwalks that led to the escalators and elevators below. Their cries of alarm upon seeing the suited men and their unconcealed machine pistols echoed eerily up to Jack like the despaired, lost half-whispers of ghosts.

He ran along the edge of the balcony, eyes on the unfolding situation below, dodging potted plants and abandoned vendor wagons offering Pizza by the Pound. Reaching a stairwell to the floor below he leaped down it five steps at a time, passed two floors as quietly as he could, then slid to a stop a scant thirty feet behind the cowering Londoners. They were halfway across a raised walkway, one floor above darkened racks of coats and scarves. Miklos's men were just beginning to cross the span that separated them from their potential hostages. They'd left the little girl behind, asleep and mostly out of sight on a vendor's cart, which gave him an idea. She probably wasn't the Princess but, well. Someone's daughter.

Move, Jack, move faster, the silent voice within him urged.

Two men, older, a young woman and a white-haired grandmother dressed as a beatnik, attempting to hold their own against three suited,

342

fairly clean-cut young men with automatic weapons. A year ago, Jack would have found a sort of gallows humor in the situation. *At least we outnumber 'em!*

He took a flash-bang in his hand and, crouching low, crept closer. His dark jacket helped him blend into the shadows somewhat. With the civilians blocking the gunmen's line of sight and his footfalls barely a dry whisper along the blood-colored, fired-brick tile, Jack eased out onto the walkway. "Run," he whispered, and lobbed the disk over their heads at the oncoming men.

Although he'd clapped his hands over his eyes and shut them tightly, Jack was standing so close to the blast he could clearly see the outlines of his fingerbones. Though he expected the sudden, rushing explosion of sound and light, he was still a bit stunned by the grenade's ferocity. It blew one of the men clean off the walkway; the other two fell to their knees in pain and shock. Rolling back to his feet, Jack drew his gun and fired, putting one of Miklos's men all the way down and ruining a perfectly good suit. The other suited gunman skittered back along the span, and Jack lost him in the residual wash of smoke from the grenade.

A chanced look over his shoulder informed Jack that the group behind him was clearing out fast, though not fast enough. He charged forward, thinking to at least draw the other man's fire, and slipped in the first man's blood, going down hard as his opponent seized the opportunity and rushed in, kicking his gun from his hand, then stomping down hard.

Jack took the blow on the meat of his forearm, which was already flush with the floor, minimizing the damage. He was still slippery from the first man's gore, so he gripped his adversary's planted leg and spun into him, wrapping his foot up and around for a blow to the groin.

The suited man left the floor, and then abruptly crashed back into it in a heap, choking. Jack shoved off him and gained his feet, then planted a low side kick squarely across his opponent's forehead. It was inelegant and poorly delivered, but enough. Jack went to his knees, holding the sprawled man still while he felt for his handcuffs, and then shackled him to his dead companion.

From the time he'd thrown the grenade until he clicked the handcuffs into place, perhaps fifteen seconds had passed. It seemed more like—

–the click of metal-on-metal above and behind him drove a deep wedge of panicked energy from Jack's heart to his legs, and he dove from the balcony, snagging the edge of one of the banners as he tumbled over the edge. The sagging cloth broke his impact with the floor somewhat, and he rolled under the walkway, jostling through a coat rack and knocking over a display of running shoes. Bullets thudded thickly into the carpet near his hands. Again from behind, he thought, and ignored the irrational impulse to cast around for the oversized thug who'd accosted him in the Parisian alley. He had the presence of mind to look down, and quickly found the unconscious form of the gunman that had been knocked off the walkway earlier, groaning in the darkness.

"Very fast," someone said from above, and Jack heard the impact on the walkway of someone jumping onto it from a higher level. From further above, someone barked out a series of commands, most likely in Russian but too indistinct for Jack to make out. He found the supine man's gun–happily, a Glock fairly close to the one he'd lost–and checked the magazine. At least three bullets left.

It would have to do.

"Do you know what my superior just said, whoever you are?" The voice from above was high-pitched for a man, but full, not feminine. Slightly haughty. Jack placed the man about halfway along the walkway, near a potted plant he'd almost collided with earlier. He slipped under the span, staying close to it, pistol fully extended before him. He caught a glimpse of the back of the speaker's full head of hair before the man turned to hunt for him. "He says you have real *yaytsa* for an Englishman. I think you are a member of your Secret Air Service, no?" Without warning, he loosed a spray of bullets into the shadows below, raking the carpet, shredding the hung suits. Hangers clinked and clanged like chimes in a gust of wind.

Jack backed under the walkway. It appeared that he and the huge Russian were alone in the shop turned shooting gallery. He could see a corner of his opponent's overcoat. "Nyet, ya Amerikanyets," he said, and fired a shot of his own. Got you now, he thought, racing under and along the length of the walkway, keeping his pistol extended, the sights tracking along the line where he knew, he *felt* the other man to be.

*

No, I'm American. The voice was naggingly familiar to the big Slav. He'd heard it before, and recently, though not speaking Russian. The accent was even Moskovian, though the vicissitudes of that fact were lost on him as he ducked under the clap and whine of a bullet. A glimmer of movement from below, and he emptied his magazine into the shadows, then stepped quickly away from the edge of the walkway as he ejected the clip from the MAC-10 and withdrew another. He backed all the way across the width of the narrow bridge, wondering fleetingly if the man below had any chance of tracking him, of guessing his movement. None, he decided in less than a second. His footfalls were silent; he wasn't even breathing loudly. Following Miklos' example without fail. Sasha had never felt so calm, so completely in control in his entire life. Just to be sure, he glanced behind and down as he ran the clip into his weapon.

And looked straight over Trijicon night sights into the American's eyes as the other man slid smoothly out of the shadows.

*

Brad's injuries weren't as grave as Solomon had feared. He'd taken at least two bullets clean through his thigh, and another had grazed his lower abdomen. It was when he tried to remove his friend's jacket that Solomon received his biggest shock of the night.

The two shooters had been excellent marksmen, lapping almost all their hits over what would normally have been vital areas. The leatherlike material had taken several bullets before finally shredding, but the inner lining itself had stopped nearly a dozen rounds. They had lodged between disks of metal Brad had roughly glued into the jacket's lining. Most of the disks had bent or broken under impact, but they looked to Solomon like—no, they couldn't be. But that"s what they were. Antique silver doubloons.

Brad cracked open an eye and moaned. "Saved by a life of crime."

Solomon smiled for his friend's benefit, and yanked open his medical kit.

*

Miklos and his companion strode down the shadowed hallway. He was furious. Raines had betrayed him! *Him!* Inwardly, Miklos cursed himself. How could he have not seen the duplicity for what it would become? He had assumed the decoy maneuver was for the crowd's benefit, so that someone would recognize him in the morning when his manifesto was broadcast. Of course Raines had known there would be men above the theater with rifles. He sneered indignantly into the dark. Instinct and training demanded that he run, that he mingle and

346

vanish into the mindless herd that even now was stampeding down the stairs and escalators. Once out on the street it was only a few meters to an entrance to the Tube, and the two men would be untraceable. They could even make Belgium before dawn. But how to balance this, this—

Betrayal! His mind still reeled from the possibility. Then, like an eagle wheeling in the sky, Miklos' thoughts came fully about. The man at his side, at least, he could trust. "Tovik! We're not going to leave just yet. Raines owes us a soul. Blood for blood, eh?"

Tovik's impassive frown remained unchanging. "You know he will use the Sikorsky."

"And we'll be there to greet him," said Miklos. The two checked their weapons. Each carried an American-made MAC-10, a fine piece of deadly art that fired over forty five rounds every second and a half. Its design was not necessarily to kill, but to wreak shattering havoc on the human body—as different from a regular revolver as a sledgehammer is to a surgeon's scalpel.

"We'll use the service lift in the back of the building, the one used by the workmen to reach the construction site." Miklos explained to the other man.

"Blood for blood."

*

The little girl asleep on the vendor's cart bore a striking resemblance to Christine Windsor; she was a closer match than the girl at the theater had been. Same height, same hair, different nose–another one of the four abducted girls he'd read about in the major's file, no doubt. Jack ran a fresh clip home and then stowed the Glock before picking her up.

There were still a few people left at the top of the escalators leading to the next lower level, and Jack whistled to get their attention when he drew close enough. "Hey," he said, slipping automatically into a West End accent. "Would ya mind getting the little miss down below with ya?"

The couple he approached looked at him, dazed, and Jack realized he was still half-covered in blood. "Not to worry, I slipped into one o' those demmed American hotdog wagons up top." They took the snoring little girl, still eying the stains on his black clothing. "Right then, be down m'self in two shakes. Just see her to a bobby, will ya?"

He spent half a minute in a men's room cleaning himself off and checking his equipment. His headset was still in his jacket's inner pocket, and he put it on immediately. "Steve?" The lift had to be around here somewhere.

"Jack, where've you been?"

"I'm on the floor above Harrods, in the big atrium, facing north. The window's behind me. Which way to the elevators?"

Papers fluttered over the digital line. "'Kay, go straight until you come to the wall, then it should be 50 meters to your right, near an information kiosk. Hey, Al and the Major are going to meet you on the 35th floor. Raines is moving."

Jack found the kiosk, a touch-activated show-and-tell of the whole building, hard-wired into a black plastic pillar with a slanted face, in the general three-tiered three-winged shape of the Illuminatus Tower itself. The bank of elevators–three in all–sat behind it, obscured slightly by a BBC display on easels. Jack stabbed at the call button, then glanced again at the plastic-faced BBC announcement.

Intense Broadband Capability–Tower Transmits Crystal-Clear Images Using New Technology.

Above the fine print was an artist's rendering of the transmitter Jack had parachuted past only an hour before. Light refracted off the ad, however, and he had to tilt his head slightly to block the glare and see the huge, electronics-laden disk at the tower's summit. As he moved, the weak light behind him played out over the plastic laminate covering the poster, casting an illusion of energy coruscating over the disk.

The elevator chimed and Jack entered, pressing the button for the thirty-fifth floor. Staring at his vague, streaked reflection, Jack cast his thoughts upward. He hoped Christine wasn't too frightened. There were myriad tortures that could be inflicted upon a child–though Jack quickly locked his imagination away from such possibilities. No, she would be fine. If Raines wanted her for ransom, he'd keep her safe; as intact mentally as physically.

Yet ransom made no sense. There'd been no demands made, no price allotted for her return. Besides if there was any truth to the plot William had mentioned to Alonzo–to weaken the collective British resolve?– the perpetrators of the kidnapping must have taken into account that they'd be running for the remainder of their lives, once the ire of the people stirred against them. Nothing was more cherished in any given nation than that country's children—and Princess Christine was the embodiment of the entire extended British Family. The kidnapers would have nowhere to–

The elevator shuddered to a halt. Jack looked up; he was barely above the twentieth floor. Before he could move, the lift began moving again, but now descending. Rapidly. Jack touched his headset. "Steve?"

*

Rain was beginning to fall in irregular, fat drops on the street and the gathering crowd. Ian exhaled in relief as he handed the little girl off to a paramedic, turning his attention from the looming building above to the approaching police vans. Behind them, he could see flashing lights of the fire truck variety, with accompanying sirens. A mounted officer reined in between the gathered crowd and the vacant lobby. "Here now, what's all this?

"And where would you be goin'?" He pressed his heels into the horse's flanks, moving to interpose himself between Ian and the entrance.

Before the other policemen in the crowd could react, Ian patted the horse on the neck, then took a firm grip on the halter. It wouldn't do to pull FBI credentials here; besides, nobody was supposed to know he was even in the country. "The King's business, mate," he said, jerking the horse's head. The animal shied and reared slightly, and its rider had to struggle to keep his seat.

Ian jogged into the lobby and pressed the call button for the elevators. There were five banks of them at this level, not counting the service lift he'd used to bring the little girl down. If he remembered right, the middle three went all the way to the top.

"You there, you!" Two of the bobbies he'd seen in the street entered the lobby, their batons loose and ready at their sides. Except for the truncheons, they reminded Ian unfailingly–like every other first-time American in London, he supposed—of Mack Sennett's classic Keystone Kops.

He looked back at the elevators. At least one would surely–

Ian swore in dismay as the backlit numbers above the door diminished. First one, then another, then a third elevator passed him on its way to the basement. He heard the fourth descend past the lobby, then turned in dismay.

Only to be rushed by four big policemen who hammerlocked his arms before he could get a word out. Someone punched him hard in a kidney, and he collapsed, gasping, into their collective grip. "Jack," he blurted into his headpiece, and then it was ripped from his ear.

"Jack Scratch is what you'll be getting, my friend," said the burliest of the officers. "'Ere Charlie, look at this! Bloke's got a gun!"

*

"Steve, what's up with the elevators?" Jack swallowed hard. Shouting would not do just now. "I thought you had control." He flipped open the emergency call box.

The voice on the other end was pinched, irritated. "I was trying to find Raines or Christine on the security cameras. The elevators sort of got away from me."

"Sort of got away?" There it was, a list of notices and operating procedures printed in light red on the backside of the call box door. IN CASE OF FIRE, LIFT WILL PROCEED TO BASEMENT. USE STAIRS, it supplied helpfully. Jack worked a kink out of his neck, then calmly kicked the little door from its hinges.

"You alright, Jack?" Steve asked. "The system's acting like there's a real fire somewhere in the building."

He was already pushing at the ceiling escape hatch. "Here's one you won't see in the movies, Steve," he said, and dropped back to the floor as he pulled his gun. Three shots rang out like one-note thunder in the confined space, and the hatch tumbled back with a clatter and a crash that sounded tinny and far-off to Jack's ringing ears. He planted a foot on the waist-high rail that ran the inner circumference of the cabin, and levered himself onto the roof.

"Any chance you can get control of this again?" he shouted. The noise in the shaft was tremendous. He couldn't see any sort of ladder built into the wall, like those in movies used by the hero to escape and rescue the damsel in distress. Well, hell.

And it was lighted, which surprised him. Besides the cables and the bolstering lines for the other two elevators, a bright, almost glossy column ran up one wall, half hidden by iodized piping and sectioned, segmented steel wire casing. It embraced a sharp white light, much, much brighter than the conventional phosphorescent flame. No, he decided. Fire was the wrong analogy. He could feel a chill radiating across the gap. What lay before him was something even more elemental. This was heatless, liquid energy, almost plasma. Though it was cris-crossed with cables, its unchanging brightness lent it the illusion that the glossy pillar was keeping pace with Jack as the rest of the shaft flew upward around them both.

Ghostly blue-tinged light played just under the surface of the glass, and Jack felt a ripple pass over his skin. The small hairs on his arms stood erect.

Jack stared at it for a long moment, possibilities unraveling across his mind's eye. Ian had found some monstrous device in the sub-basement.

—Intense Broadband Capability–Tower Transmits Crystal-Clear Images Using New Technology—.

Weak light behind him playing out over the laminated poster, an illusion of rising, furious energy coruscating over an enormous, electronics-laden disk—

Tesla.

The elevator halted, started moving upward again. Steve's voice was a mixture of exasperation and fatigue. "There, is it working yet?"

Jack wiped his lips and checked the load in his pistol. It was a Glock-24; nearly identical to his lost -22, though a touch heavier. More importantly, the -24 also accepted a 15-round magazine, so his spare ammunition would fit.

Then, music sounding faintly through the wall. Someone must have left a stereo playing in their haste to obey the fire alarm, he mused.

It was a song he'd listened to during swimming workouts, years ago. Pride, by U2. "One more, in the name of love," he murmured absently along with the music, eyes upward. The glowing tube, the malevolent pillar of frigid fire, was a bright line through the abyss above him as far as he could see.

The elevator's speed doubled, leaving the song behind. Jack soared upward, into the gloom.

Heights

Ian leaned back into the bulldog cop who'd shackled him, feigning weakness. If he ducked his head he could see his gun amidst the pile of equipment the bobbies had removed from him and dumped on the hood of the police cruiser. Several of them stood around it, one was shaking the phone they'd yanked from him, trying to get a dial tone. Splashes of red light cast each man's face in an expressionless, deathlike mask. They'd been so interested in his collection of gadgets and gimcrackery they'd left his wallet untouched.

Ian gritted his teeth as the constable yanked him to his feet. Should've removed the Bureau ID. They'd get to it soon enough.

"This bloke's done up right proper," said one of the policemen at the car. "He's got as many weapons as one of Lopez's couriers." That got him another round of dirty looks. Boy, were they in for a surprise when they looked in his billfold—

While Ian made apologetic faces at the glowering bobbies, his hands were busy behind him. Bit by bit, he worried his last lock pick from a concealed pouch under the back of his belt. He wondered who he should thank for shackling him in the old-fashioned, sawtooth handcuffs–the new, seamless rubber ones were nearly impossible to pick.

"Look at this, boys." The same cop who'd spoken before held up a packet of cigarettes. He'd peeled back the wrapping enough to expose the heads of six mini-missiles packed inside.

Ian pushed the slender rod into the path of the ratchets, inserted it delicately like a shim under the teeth of the cuff, began to press–and then lost his grip on the pick as the cop shook him. "I said, what do ya think yer doing with this kind of contraband, mister wee beard-man, if you please?" He thrust a grenade under Ian's nose. "And what the 'ell is this thing?"

It was obvious they hadn't seen military grenades yet, at least this particular packaging. Ian frowned and stammered, knitting his brows together while his concealed hand groped for the lock pick. He almost let the relief explode across his face when he found it still jammed in the handcuffs.

Now the hard part. He pushed the pick as hard as his curled, cramping fingers allowed, squeezing the cuffs even further closed with his free thumb. Metal bit into his flesh. Pain knifed up his arm–

And then the narrow rod slipped past the locking ratchet and triggered the release. He awkwardly shoved the pick back into his waistband.

"Look you bugger, we'll get the truth out of ya one way or t'other, now—"

Ian spoke, startling the red-faced constable. "You know, there's just one thing I don't like about you fellas finding out who I am and where all the special gear comes from."

"What might that be?"

"Because then I could probably never bring my wife here on vacation." He drove his heel down hard, scraping the shin of the cop who held him, feeling the skin grate away. As the man screamed, Ian stepped forward and snatched the flash-bang. He looked the senior officer dead in the eye. "We mean no harm to your planet," he said, and triggered the grenade.

Ian was already ducking into a crouch as he tossed the disk straight up, covering his ears and opening his mouth wide. The explosion knocked him flat anyway, and he tasted cold, wet macadam flavored with his own blood. It sounded like someone had ripped open a portal on the threshold of a howling Hell barely a meter above their heads.

As soon as he was able, Ian drove himself back to his feet and looked about. Thankfully, his glasses had not shattered. A wave of shock and panic rippled out through the crowd from his epicenter, and he noticed immediately that those policemen not blinded or knocked flat outright had immediately turned out to the crowd, some obviously searching for him, others seeing to the needs of the staggering mass of Londoners.

Ian threw himself across the hood of the police cruiser, scooping up what he could of his equipment, including his gun and wallet. He shoved past a stumbling officer and dodged into the crowd.

*

The sweat running off Steve's palms was so cold and greasy-thick he was tempted to wring out his hands. He activated one after another of the surveillance cameras, searching in vain for the cluster of men he and the major had glimpsed. An old-fashioned paper blueprint lay spread out on the floor next to him; he constantly glanced back and forth from it to his screen. It was apparent that Raines had made at least more than one last-minute alteration to his building's design. Down this hall? No, nothing that way but construction; no egress there. What about this one? No, it lead straight out onto the roof. Steve swore. The interior of the Illuminatus was straightforward enough, but all the slanting, canted roofs and connecting walkways on its exterior bothered him.

And what was with the statuary? Workman's sketches along the borders of the blueprints showed the positioning of some of the most obscure images Steve had ever laid eyes on. According to the notes on the border, Raines himself had sculpted the original models of what now stood guard outside the building. Steve saw one or two that actually looked uplifting. All the rest were grotesque. A few of them looked almost human, but normal men and women were never designed to live through such agony as was evident by their posture and expression. The portly man shuddered involuntarily. What could Raines have possibly seen in his life that would conjure up such warped creations?

The phone hummed briefly.

"Hello?"

"Steve? This is Ian, thank God I got the right number this time! I just called some lady in Sussex!"

"What?"

"Never mind. I'm calling from a pay phone in the park. What's going on up there? Two fire trucks just pulled up and the place is lousy with cops. Least I think they're cops; nobody I can see's got a gun. What's going on?"

Steve wiped his hands on his shirt. "That's a little complicated right now. " His fingers resumed their dance over the keyboard as Steve activated set after set of surveillance cameras.

"Raines and whoever is with him are moving, and they've got nowhere to go but up. Alonzo just tripped a motion sensor on the thirty-fifth floor; he and Jack and the major are going to meet up there. No contact from Brad or Solomon–they may be down." Steve gritted his teeth and continued. "The Sikorsky is up here, all prepped and warm— looks like somebody's going for a little trip, and tonight. Can you get around the police?"

Ian frowned with his voice. "What kind of a question is that?"

"Then get up here as quick as you can. Listen, there's a service elevator in the back of the building, it comes straight up to where the construction starts. Hurry! I don't need to tell you how badly we're outnumbered."

*

The D-11 squad moved fast and quietly up through the darkened hallways. "Looks as though nearly all of Harrods is clear," the team leader whispered into his helmet-mounted radio, then turned, sweeping slowly over the dim racks and shelves of sporting goods for the benefit of the anascopic camera, also mounted on his headgear. Modeled after their SWAT counterparts in America, the officers of the D-11 carried the best array of anti-terrorist equipment available to law enforcement. "Proceeding to the next level–hold up. Blake, right ahead." A huge figure advanced toward them, resolving out of the dark like some ponderous juggernaut.

"Put up your arms and come forward slowly!" He shouted at the enormous man, lifting his sidearm and taking aim.

The large, black male–nearly half as wide as he was tall, held a smaller man in his arms. At least one of them was bleeding, most likely the small Asian, as he was covered by a profusion of bandages.

Oddly, the bald giant held a dignity about himself, a strength and an assurance reserved for nobility. He might have been a member of the ruling class addressing an embassy from a distant court as he said, "I assume you gentlemen are skilled medics as well as sharpshooters. My friend requires expert attention, instantly."

*

Jack, Alonzo, and the major came together in a tight, black knot on the thirty-fifth floor. "Talk, Steve," whispered Jack into his mouthpiece as he glared up at a camera. Alonzo and Major Griffin were quickly,

358

professionally checking their guns and loosening extra clips of ammunition. This would have to be quick.

"Uh, uh, okay, I got it!" Steve breathed excitedly. "There are three groups of guards moving on your floor. Raines and more than half-a-dozen guys in light-colored suits are headed parallel to you, in the third corridor to your . . . right. They've got about (he counted under his breath) a hundred yards to go until they get to the corner, then another hundred to the north stairway. They'll walk right past your hallway." Jack looked at his two companions. Their expressions confirmed they were getting the feed as well. "I can't make out what—wait, Raines and two other guys are walking about fifty feet behind the others, and one for sure is carrying a little kid!"

"No time to do this by the book." said Jack to the other two. "Get ahead of them and cause a diversion, I'll make the grab. Meet me in the wing that shoots off the other section of the building, this same floor." Without a word they dashed off, running silently. Jack slipped around the corner and ghosted through an unfurnished office. The smell of new carpet enveloped him. If the plans he'd studied on the train were correct, beyond where he would intercept Raines would be a balcony across the face of the central tower that connected the two main wings. He prayed the construction workers were on schedule.

Near the stairwell to the north, Alonzo and the major worked on opposite sides of the hall, lightly slapping their flash-bang grenades against the corridor's wall and then waiting the fraction of a second it took for each to adhere. Thanks to Steve's timely heads-up, Alonzo figured they could trigger the flash-bangs and then hose the goons in front before Raines and the princess even rounded the corner.

The beat of disciplined, hard footfalls approaching them was maddeningly close.

Alonzo took an instant to look over the major's work and nodded admiringly; she knew what she was doing, setting her three charges high, medium, and low on the wall so as to create the widest possible flash. He was surprised to catch her scrutinizing his own placement. They traded tight grins and stepped back into doorways on either sides of the hall. "I'll go high, you stay low," she whispered across the digital connection.

Alonzo ran his thumb around the detonator stud and wondered briefly if the Eurotrash they were facing had anything better than his Heckler and Koch MP-5 submachine gun. He'd soon find out.

*

Ian left the steel cage of the construction elevator and quickly got his bearings. Much of the top several floors lay uncompleted–but he managed to find a path through the joists and support columns to the more finished hallways and chambers near the building's center. He'd overshot the thirty-fifth level by at least one floor, unable to judge correctly in the unmarked cab of the construction lift.

Further down the hall, the elevator chimed. Ian immediately took a defensive position in the doorway, training his weapon on the slanting block of light. He waited a long moment, evening his breathing, sweeping his thoughts clean, even smiling a little to help himself relax, waiting, waiting for something to enter his kill zone.

Solomon stepped out of the elevator, his face a mask of concentration. He looked right at Ian, then nodded.

Ian felt like yelling at the top of his lungs, but choked the stress deep down inside, blocked it off. "Hey," was all he said.

"Where's Jack and the others?" Solomon asked, sidestepping quickly out of the light. He held a long, heavy rifle in one hand. In the movement, Ian noticed the wetness–blood?—covering the front of his friend's ninja suit. Solomon followed his eyes downward, and said, "It's Brad's. He's being cared for right now."

Quickly, they traded information. Solomon was at a loss to explain why the elevator worked for him. "It was the only one to respond after I pushed the call button. The rest are evidently in the basement. Fire's taken three floors below, in the east wing.

"D-11 has surveillance and sniper units in position on some of the surrounding buildings, scanning the surface with infrareds. They won't be of much help; the Tower is much too tall, and the wind is picking up. More clouds, more rain."

Ian smoothed his beard. "Take up a position near the main stairs?" he offered.

"Tactically risky. Four stairways, remember? We'll need to sweep them all." He pointed.

Ian fell into place at his side. Motioning to the long, thick weapon, he said, "Plan on hunting some Cape buffalo or rhinoceros tonight?"

Solomon lifted the elephant gun. ".410 caliber. 'At Harrods, sir, we carry everything.'"

*

Raines laid his hand on Michael's shoulder, slowing the big Chinese and the other bodyguard. Michael shifted the limp child to his other shoulder, then looked quizzically down at his employer. Raines stared intently ahead as the last of the advancing men rounded the corner. His teeth gleamed in the half-light from the single florescent bulb before them, and he cocked his head, as if listening to something.

"Wait," he said suddenly. "We'll have to take another route, my sons."

Unquestioningly the two other men turned back, and blinked in surprise at the face that seemed to carve itself out of the blue shadows behind them. Raines gasped.

Jack clicked his tongue, winked, and spun into a blur, his foot driving upward and into the smaller bodyguard's Adam's apple, actually slamming the man up and backward into Raines. In the same motion he lashed his other foot sideways into Michael's knee, folding the huge man toward him and pitching Michael's burden directly into Jack's arms.

Then a bright light flared behind them, and a shattering, palpable roar sundered the hallway. Raines shoved Chomriel's limp form to one side and grappled at Jack, but lost his balance. He wrenched himself to his feet in time to see Jack Flynn, eyes seething, toss something small and black and round into the hall from the room he'd entered.

Then Michael heaved into Raines with enough force to knock both men back through another doorway as the hall exploded into a blindingly white fireball.

*

Take no pleasure, feel no regret, just move. From his supine position on the floor, Alonzo watched the six men die. The two million-candlepower *flash* combined with the 185 decibel *bang* had caught them totally off guard, and he and the major had opened fire immediately. Alonzo didn't relish death; he'd never come to terms with actually enjoying killing as had most of the professional shooters he'd met. He didn't wonder what thoughts choked through each man's head as he fell, or what metaphysical reasoning process the major–a woman–was engaged in behind her own blazing, cannon-like gun. He didn't mourn the passing of Raines' hired killers, or contemplate what marks their cries–pitiably weak—left on his soul.

He simply squeezed the trigger, and lived with the memory.

As the last man—he'd actually managed to draw his gun—stumbled to the ground, a second explosion shuddered through the floor. Alonzo rolled to his feet and slid another clip into his gun as the brief heat washed over him. Incendiary grenade. Jack.

Major Griffin stepped over him, giving him the thumbs-up and waiting for his in return before continuing down around the corner. In the center of a growing circle of billowing black smoke and flames lay a single body. Around the grenade's blast radius lay globs of searingly white hot liquid. Belatedly the sprinklers on the ceiling activated, covering everything in a fine mist.

"No Raines. No Jack, no princess." Alonzo said, scanning the empty doorways. He and the major retreated to the hall and Alonzo watched as Griffin quickly examined each of the dead man's faces before gesturing for him to follow her to the stairs. He looked back at the fire; it was growing steadily but slowly. They wouldn't have much time. He shut the door. "See anybody you recognize back there?" he asked the major as they began to run up the stairs two and three at a time.

*

Jack locked the double doors behind him and flipped the lights on in what he supposed eventually would become an executive office suite. Bending to the floor, he fixed another grenade against the crack where the two doors came together, then activated it. There. Anyone opening either door and breaking the adhesive connection would get a nasty surprise. Princess Christine Windsor clicked the backs of her heels against the desk where she sat blinking, watching him work.

Jack faced her and breathed a sigh of relief. She was groggy and confused, but past the stage where she had screamed incoherently at the explosions. He looked about. The office held another desk and two high-backed swivel chairs still sheathed in plastic, but nothing they could use. The balcony doors were locked; leaning against the glass Jack could see the balcony proper remained, as he had feared, incomplete. In its place between the two arms of the building stretched a narrow, suspended scaffold. It looked as if it would sway under any considerable weight. This was going to be interesting.

"Jack?" The child on the desk rubbed her eyes and made to sneeze. Jack crossed the room, pulling a handkerchief from his inner pocket in time to catch the sneeze and the immediate snuffle that followed.

"How are you feeling, your Hi—" he began, then more slowly, "How are you, Christine?"

"Rather like a small animal's been sleeping in my mouth," she answered. She beamed up at him. "I knew you would come."

It was ridiculous in the face of their situation, but for the first time in as long as he could remember, Jack found himself grinning like an idiot.

*

Ian and Solomon nearly drew on Alonzo and the major as they cleared the next floor. "There's guys with Russian-type accents all over the place up here!" Ian whispered ferociously at Alonzo as the smaller man inserted a long, narrow rod into the lock of the door he and Major Griffin had just come through.

"They won't be using this door," the smaller man said through gritted teeth. He leaned hard on the narrow lockpick, producing an audible snap from deep within the door. "Jack's got Christine, I guess. We'll meet him in the other wing, one floor down. Where are your phones?"

"I think I found one of those Tesla electric machine-things downstairs." The major looked at him quickly. Ian ignored her. "Now I can't even get a dialtone."

"I fell on mine." Solomon frowned.

"Did you say 'Tesla machine?'" Griffin asked.

Ian nodded, then looked sharply down the hall. "Whatever it is, somebody's turned it on."

*

Jack hated heights in the first place.

He scooped up the little girl and pulled the edges of his coat firmly around her. The scaffolding they had to traverse was less than a hundred meters long, and firmly anchored at either end, but the wind was bitingly cold. Holding the princess would prevent him from maintaining any kind of grip on the thin handrails. Better do this as quick as possible, he thought. The gridwork of streets far below cast a surreal light up against them, and Jack couldn't shake the sensation that the entire building was swaying slightly. It had rained earlier in the day, and wind whistled up between the slats of the darkly slick gangway, through a shiny rime of ice. He fleetingly remembered his backup parachute, stowed several floors above under a stack of insulation. Just look over at the building, he thought, the nice solid building. Focus on the other end, look where you're going.

The wind gusted again, and the entire wooden structure along the building's face breathed out a long, eerie moan. "What was that sound, Jack?" The princess asked from the folds of his jacket.

This was no place for a child. "Hold on now, Christine. Hold tight." He gathered her close and stepped out onto the platform. It *did* sway under his weight.

"Ooh! Look!" her voice was muffled by the coat, but Jack glanced down long enough to see her eyes were locked on something above and behind them. He turned, and momentarily forgot the yawning chasm below.

Wings and arms outspread as if in supplication or flight, the Herculean statue of the angel loomed over them. It had been completely worked, Jack noticed; sculpted down to the most minute detail. He took it in for a moment, wondering why Raines would set it and the other stone-and-mortar figures so high on the building, above the scrutiny of anyone. "Wow," he said, more for the little girl's benefit than anything else. The wind shuddered along the wooden planks once again, and he braced his legs wide on the scaffold. "Tell you what," he said, sure she could feel his heart slamming away. "You just look really hard at that gargoyle, sweetheart, okay? Can you describe him to me?" He took a few hesitant steps toward the gaping hole at the other end of the gangway. "What does he look like?" Jack slid his feet along the sopping boards. Further out, where the gangway hung in the constant wind, he found the dampness had frozen deep into the wood, turning the entire middle section of the scaffold into a heavy, icy deathtrap.

Jack hated heights.

"He looks a bit mean, but that's just because somebody stuck him up here all alone. I think he's too big and strong to be cold."

Jack was beginning to shiver. "Lucky for him. Keep looking at the gargoyle, Christine. What else do you see?"

*

Steve could see he was in trouble. Even rotating his feed from the cameras as fast as he could, he still only saw so much of what was going on a few stories below. The first warning that someone else had entered the warehouse-like room where he hid was the muted voices coming from behind the layers of insulation and plastic. Something metal a few dozen feet away clanged against a long I-beam he sat next to, and Steve could have sworn what was left of his hair stood straight on end.

366

He disconnected all the attachments to his computer as fast as he could while slowly rising to his feet. His hand found his Glock as he eased the screen down.

Shadows and indistinct shapes loomed beyond the plastic barrier as the footsteps grew louder. One roughly resolved itself into a bearded face.

*

A stray ribbon of plastic snapped in the wind at the ice-sheathed entrance to the other wing. Jack staggered in, shivering, through the triple-layered plastic sheets, stomping his feet to force circulation back into them. At least the air was heated. Jack glanced quickly around for a safe place to tuck Christine, and settled for an empty wheelbarrow. Then as quietly as possible he set about stretching some warmth back into his arms and legs. He and the princess were safe for the moment.

They were in a workman's area, a section of bare wooden two-by-fours bracketed with steel casing. Cold, impersonal light issued from a florescent bulb hung in a jumble of cords above them. He checked the load in his pistol. Seven bullets left and one more clip, stuck horizontally in its clasp on the back of his belt. He slid the first clip home and let the bolt slip forward slowly, deliberately. A Hollywood-style lock-and-load (*Chack-chaack!*) let too many people know where you were. Wouldn't do to attract that much attention.

Jack set the gun down and worked two grenades out of their padded scabbard in the small of his back. He never knew how to check if the smallish, dark disks were fully operational or not. The contours along their edges identified them as flash-bangs. Lastly, Jack checked his most important weapon: the phone. He'd lost the remote headset somewhere in the other wing, automatically disconnecting the conference call option. He speed-dialed Steve's extension, smiling at Christine, who was regarding him curiously. The Ketamine or whatever they'd given her was beginning to wear off, he saw by the clarity of her eyes. Their little jaunt out in the wind had helped too, no doubt. Steve's number rang on; no answer.

"Jack, where do they come from?"

"I'm sorry sweetheart, what?" He laid the phone aside and hunkered down close to where she was stirring in the coat.

"The gar-, the gar-"

"The gargoyles?" She nodded. "Well, they've been around for hundreds of years. People make them, mostly, and then they put them around where they live to help scare away bad things." She seemed unimpressed. He lowered his voice to a whisper. "Have you noticed how some are really scary?" She nodded again, eyes wide. "The scarier they are, the better job they do of frightening away all the evil stuff."

"But they are good?" She was dreadfully serious, Jack noticed. He smiled, brushing a few stray hairs back from her face.

"Oh yes. They keep the evil away. They watch over us at night when we sleep." He paused. "And you know what else they do?" She shook her head. "They do whatever they have to in order to take especially good care of little children."

Christine sat back in the wheelbarrow, pleased. She yawned. "Do you think I might take a little nap before we go home?"

He couldn't help but grin. "I think that would be the very best thing, if we had a little more time."

Then something made him turn; an almost imperceptible noise, a shift in the air. His hand found the gun while his eyes tracked a group of deeper shadows within the darkness. Jack spun towards it, leading with his pistol, when a whisper seethed out of the darkness.

"For crying out loud, Jack! It's us!" Alonzo, Solomon, Ian, and the major melted in from the darkness.

Immediately Major Griffin rushed to the little princess. As Jack, Alonzo, and Ian reprised each other of the night's events, the major quickly examined the girl from head to foot. "Hello, your Highness, I'm Allison. Your mummy and daddy sent us to look after you, did you know that?" She continued, speaking in soothing tones as she worked. Everything looked all right, in fact, the princess was even wearing new– wait.

"Jack; gentlemen; what do you make of this?"

The major held a section of cloth from Christine's jacket. The princess looked up at the three men. "They said the new clothes would help keep me warm."

Ian hunkered down, squinting at the material. "They did? Why, this looks like–get it off her, *get it off her now!*" He reached over and nearly tore the jacket off the suddenly frightened little girl.

"What?" demanded Jack, turning away with the two other men as the major comforted Christine.

Ian was cursing a steady stream under his breath as he held the small coat up to the light. "Look at this." He indicated a thicker-than-usual portion of padding underneath the blue fabric. "This is a detonator. This whole thing is made of high explosive, Jack." Ian whispered. "Remember that stuff we used to blow the doors in the embassy in Norway?" he asked Alonzo.

Alonzo breathed in sharply. "The really thin stuff we slipped between the—" His eyes widened. "This is bad, Jack." He took a step back, away from the coat. "That's ammonium picrate, bad medicine. If this is it, or close," he pointed at the jacket, "she was wearing enough to kill her."

"And I doubt Raines would want to stop there." Jack knelt back down in front of the princess, She stared distrustfully over his shoulder at Ian. "Sweetheart," began Jack, smiling confidently. "We need to look at the clothes those nasty guys gave you."

Nearly five minutes later the four adults had accumulated a small pile of the bottlecap-sized detonators. Ian knifed a final one out of the top of a sock and threw it on the pile. "Ammonium P in cloth form is really stable–requires a lot of heat to set it off. She should be okay wearing it until we can get her out of this funhouse."

Major Griffin worked the last of the princess' shirt material through her fingers. "That's the third go for the lot of it. She's clean."

"And her shoes are regular leather," said Alonzo. "What kind of a sicko would dress a little girl up in a bomb?"

Jack tipped the pile of detonators into an empty trashcan and fastened its lid. "They wanted to make a statement, probably catch the whole thing on CNN."

He helped the heir to the British Empire on with her socks. "I don't get it, though. What about the machine Ian found down below?"

Griffin regarded Ian. "The wires you describe, with the miniature computer chips embedded, sound like some sort of elaborate grounding mechanism. And you said that your phone is nonfunctional?"

Ian nodded. "That's not all. The tank of goop in the middle of the whole thing, maybe a power source, or whatever–looked like nothing I've ever seen. Like it was alive."

"Some kind of bomb?" Solomon wondered. "Chemical?"

"Maybe as a catalyst for the whole system, but in form it's electrical," said Jack. He told them about the power-engorged conduit in the central shaft.

"We can only assume the bloody thing is going to go off," said the major. The first rule in dealing with a bomb.

Jack thought a moment. "Steve's all alone up there." He ran his tongue across his lower lip. "So. We'll split up. Ian, you think you can remember how to get to the machine from below?"

The stocky man nodded, and Jack handed him his earbud and phone. "You and the major get Christine out of the building first, then try and shut it down, short it out, I don't care. The three of us will go with you as far as the elevator you used to come up. Solomon, you and Al and I will get to Steve." To the major, he said, "Do whatever you have to do, but get her Highness back to her family. New clothes as quick as you can manage."

As if to punctuate his statement, there was a muffled *chuff* from the covered trashcan, and greasy-gray smoke instantly boiled out from under the lid.

Everyone moved.

Like Shining From Shook Foil

Once they reached the elevator, Jack passed the child over to Major Griffin. "Here you go, Christine. I'll see you later." The little girl gave him an almost perfunctory peck on the cheek and laid her head against Griffin's shoulder.

The major squeezed her sleepy burden tightly. "Thank you, Jack."

"No, thank you, major. I feel," he traced a line across Christine's cheek. "This feels *good*."

Jack moved for the stairs. "Come on."

Alonzo had to sprint to keep up. "Here we go," he muttered.

*

The footprints on the floor lacked any semblance of symmetry. A lunatic's checkerboard in grime and dust.

They'd just reached the top floor when the first tremor butted up through the building. It was a minor jar; not much more than a whisper, but it made Alonzo's blood run cold all the same. There was something odd about the way the building's walls and floor trembled. Something not right. Jack paused also, and Solomon ducked his head as if he thought the roof might fail, squinting against the fine dust that trickled from the exposed beams.

Around them, from at least two directions, echoed brief, surprised murmurs. The three companions remained motionless in the shadows of a half-formed room as a group of three men walked by, not daring to breathe. Each of the pale, suited figures carried an automatic weapon and scanned about themselves as they patrolled, but too sloppily in Alonzo's opinion. They'd been startled as well by the sudden, curious quake. Uneasiness showed in each face as the men made hasty, perfunctory sweeps of unlit spaces grown opaque in the falling dust.

When they had passed, Solomon placed a hand on Jack's shoulder and whispered. "If you were Steve and this place was full of unfriendlies, where would you hide away?"

*

They found him huddled under a mound of pink insulation near the access to the roof, the light from his computer screen doubly shielded under a plastic bag. True to their guess, Steve had spliced into a communications panel and was attempting to phreak a call for help.

"None of this works anymore," he wheezed, jabbing at the cluster of splayed wires. "Everything's down. No dial tone, nothing. Raines had a state-of-the-art system up here, maybe as good as the array the NSA's got set up in Alice Springs, but now it's just so much platinum wire." A vein bulged across Steve's temple. "Some of it works, but I can't figure out how."

Behind them, in the direction of the makeshift helicopter hanger, something crashed to the floor. "Sounds like someone dropped the silverware," Alonzo said. No one laughed.

"Al, can you fly the Sikorsky?" Jack asked.

"I've got 400 hours in something similar; yeah, I should think so. You thinking that's our way out?"

"It may be, if Raines has put together a Tesla machine."

Steve gave him a blank look.

"The high-density fiber optics and the other stuff you and Brad

373

found in Czech, remember? What would something like that be used for?" Jack continued at a whisper. "Ian found what's got to be a battery or a charging system down below, when he came in through the sub-basement. In the middle of the main elevator shaft there's a solid conduit, like an optic line, or—"

"Like one long lens!" Ian clicked open another program on his computer. "Well, not really a lens, but a solid-state magnification system."

"What?" Alonzo squinted at the screen, at the blueprints for the Illuminatus Tower.

"Raines built a maser, Al."

"And he's used this building, with its steel superstructure—"

"—and the network of diamond fiber optics wired into every major support structure," Solomon added.

"To build one big-ass weapon." Alonzo finished.

Jack licked his lips, eyes narrowing. "What about a power source? Steve, do you still have the city blueprints you downloaded back in the train?"

"Right here." Steve clicked twice more, opening a screen superimposed by the title Greater Metropolitan London Power Grid.

Jack frowned at the schematic. "I don't know how to read this." It resembled nothing so much as a road map of freeway interchanges, though with hundreds of alternating junctions and over-and-under crossroads, all in different colors. Steve zoomed in on a particular section.

He pointed at several intersecting stripes. "These all come together underground at Oxford Street. Not much runs under Hyde Park, so the major lines lay right under this building. Raines could have tapped into—well, *all* of them if he wanted."

"Can we shut it down?" Jack nodded to Alonzo, who started dialing on his phone.

Steve pursed his lips. "If I were building this, I'd set up failsafes with the electric company–the substations here," he gestured, "and here. That's where I'd control the flow of electricity from, if something went wrong when I needed power. Raines could be carrying a remote-control device. Oh, and there should be a final switch at the point of delivery." He looked momentarily bewildered. "I can"t believe we're even talking about this. An entire building as a weapon? Something so big can't really exist, can it?"

Alonzo cleared his throat. "My phone's gone out."

Lightning played somewhere above them, refracted oddly through the nooks and crannies and billowing, snapping plastic sheets, casting each man in a liquid blue, speckling light. It continued for several seconds, eerily silent, peculiarly luminous, turning the walls into shimmering, blue fields of dark-bright-dark, like arctic light off turbulent, chaotic waters.

"Solomon and I will get up to the transmitter: maybe we can figure out a way to shut this contraption down from there. Al, you and Steve see what you can do about securing the—" Another tremor shuddered up through the floor. "Helicopter."

*

"Stand your weapons down, men, stand them down." The D-11 commander raised his own hands to show that they were empty as he backed into the street. Behind him, eight other policemen lowered their weapons. "Here now," said the commander. "You've got what you want, now take the car and go."

The bearded man in the gray suit stepped guardedly onto the loading dock platform, his four companions immediately behind, equally deliberate. At this range, the MAC-10's constituted as formidable a weapon as anything the men from D-11 carried, made even more so by the fact that one was directed at the back of a little girl in red, which the lead terrorist prodded before him. The commander winced, as perspiration burned into his left eye. If he could just get the muzzle of that weapon off the back of the little miss' head—

"We will need two additional guests." The first terrorist smiled and nodded towards the car. "Perhaps you will volunteer yourself, constable?"

He grimaced inwardly. They'd read the response booklet. "You'll never make it out of London, mate," he said. "Hostage attempts are always unsuccessful these days; you must have read that in our tactics book as well."

The bearded man dropped his smile. "I don't believe we'll take you with us, actually." He raised his machine pistol–

Crack, crack, crack! The commander dropped to his knees as the snipers on the roof opened fire, dropping the first three men instantly. As the little girl stumbled woozily to the ground, the commander drew his own pistol. "Drop your weapons!" he boomed at the two surviving suited men.

They were professionals, even so they complied, no doubt aware that the three snipers had already acquired new targets. As his men swarmed in to cuff the two terrorists, the commander gently examined the little girl. Activating his collar mike, he said, "Sir, this is Walters at the north entrance. We have a fourth young lady and two survivors in custody. Requesting instructions."

*

The same constable who'd nearly throttled him an hour before now merely grunted as he handed Ian two steaming cups of coffee. Most of the policemen had left the crowd to take up positions around the Princess Christine, who stood with her hand in Major Griffin's. Ian handed the coffee to the major and looked up with them at the face of the Tower. An odd, sort of shimmering light played through the clouds directly over the central tower. It had begun the moment the rain stopped.

"We're lucky to have gotten out of there alive, is what I'm thinking," the major said. Ian nodded soberly.

"Sir, we've rounded up some equipment for you," one of the agents from D-11 said to Ian. "Bulletproof vest, a helmet." A group stood ready to assault the underground portion of Raine's machine.

He took the helmet. "Thanks. My jacket will be enough." He zipped up the jacket made of leather and more-than-leather. "Your men are doing a good job of keeping the press back." So far, no one had gotten close enough to take his picture, or for that matter, get any kind of hard look at the little girl he'd carried off the construction lift.

"That's according to a direct order from His Majesty, King William, sir." The burly man swelled with pride as he spoke the name of his monarch. Acting on the king's business was much more engaging than writing parking tickets, Ian decided.

"Good enough. Let's get this over with." He patted Christine's head and got a sleepy smile in return. "Your Highness, you take good care of the major 'til we all get back, okay?"

She nodded. "I'm a gargoyle."

Ian let that one pass, trading looks with Griffin.

The D-11 man cleared his throat. "Right then, let's be off."

*

The sky that greeted Jack and Solomon as they made their way to the roof held a kind of incandescence neither man had seen before. Clouds varying from slate-gray to lustrous pearl roiled in the heavens above and to either side of the Tower, themselves a distortion of the light below. Upward and before them, through the overlapping configuration of beams and posts, the aircraft-warning signal throbbed like an eye of molten steel.

Stray lightning played all around the roof: arc-blue, fiery green, arterial-red, turning the gusting rain into a single-minded squadrons of fireflies. Both men watched as a ruby-colored ball of lightning orbited the central tower, spinning wider and wider as it dropped, finally circumnavigating the entire Tower at their level and exploding into a shower of dim sparks.

Solomon cleared his throat, eyes wide. "'The world is charged with the grandeur of God,'" he said plainly.

Jack nodded. "A poem." There was a mundane explanation, of course. The earth sought equilibrium in all its systems; the tremendous charge building up in the Tower, both on or just below the earth's surface, would naturally call up an opposite charge gathering as energy in the atmosphere above. Nature simply responded, seeking balance.

A hundred feet from the ladder to the upper platform, Jack and Solomon spotted the figures of the two men at the base of the wall. The two guards were holding their weapons carelessly, trying without success to light cigarettes in the gusting wind. Solomon and Jack crouched low, though their outlines were broken up considerably by the honeycomb of unfinished steel forms and aluminum molding. Jack drew his pistol.

"Wait." Solomon had to speak in a normal tone of voice to be heard above the wind. He pointed.

Two more figures, wearing rain slickers and hunched against the wind stood sullenly at the top of the ladder, the barrels of their weapons protruding from the wide sleeves of each man's overcoat. Solomon pulled the elephant gun from his shoulder.

"You can make the shot, in this wind?" said Jack. It felt odd not to be whispering.

Solomon nodded grimly. "I'll need a few moments to figure angles. Give you time to get close to the fellows at the base of the ladder. I'll wait."

The big man had noticed Jack's replacement pistol was not threaded for a silencer; for surprise to be on their side, the assault needed to be up close. Jack left the "hallway" and headed into the construction, keeping the bulk of ductwork and angling I-beams between himself and the sentries at the ladder. The wind made a warbling, bleating whistle as it gushed about the braces and girders. For all the adrenaline he was beginning to feel the cold again, and moved faster, casting his thoughts ahead to the men at the base of the wall.

The raised section, upon which rose the transmitter with the disk-like apparatus at its peak, extended the width of the building. They'd be right about over the center here, he noted. Right about dead even with the central elevator shaft and the conduit of energy.

Seventy feet from the ladder, Jack abandoned the shadows and stole to the wall. Gun in his hand, he crept closer to the guards, who'd finally managed to work their lighters. Twin points of glowing orange marked the embers of their cigarettes, barely twenty feet away.

Lightning flared again all around them, a ghostly strobe silhouetting everything in a lambent glow. Thunder followed immediately, only it was a flat, sullen sound, as if the raging powers of the storm were being kept at bay, caged. For the first time Jack became aware of a deep hum, suddenly loud in the silence after the thunder.

And they'd seen him. Jack tracked back up the path of a falling cigarette and squeezed off two quick shots, then threw himself forward and to the ground, ducking his head against the chatter of the automatic weapon. He hoped the darkness would provide enough cover to shield him from the 9mm slugs tearing rough holes through the air above his body.

A resounding *boom* rolled across the escarpment, simultaneous with a scream from the top of the stairway.

Jack rolled up and into a run, aiming for the guard as he lowered his machine pistol to scrape the pavement. The sentinel's head had jerked towards the sound of the elephant gun. He just began to look back as Jack's foot caught him in the side of the head. For the most part the blow glanced off, carrying a piece of headset, and as Jack sailed past he followed up with a quick punch to the inner arm, sweeping the machine pistol to the ground.

The guard recovered quickly, flexing into a classic tiger stance and snapping a clawlike hand at Jack's face. Jack pushed the hand harmlessly up with his rising elbow, then shifted to the side, slapping his opponent. As the man fought to recover, Jack accepted a weak punch, then followed his slap with a brutal elbow strike to the underside of the jaw and a kick to the back of the guard's knee. As the man fell backward, Jack stepped in close and brought his elbow down with all his strength into his opponent's sternum and throat. The *pop-crack* of snapping bone was drowned out by a second roar from the elephant gun.

A spurt of fire chattered up into the sky, the death reflex of the second guard at the top of the ladder.

Jack's opponent hit the ground solidly, breath whooshing from his lungs. When he struggled to twist to his feet, he screamed in pain.

"You're collarbone's broken," Jack said, bending to hold the man still. "You'll be fine if you don't try to move." The man began swearing in Russian, and Jack repeated himself in that language as he took a pistol and knife from the broken man's belt.

A few moments later Solomon joined him. "The rifle's going to draw some attention," he said to Jack. "We'd better get up to the transmitter. Is he secure?" he asked, gesturing at the writhing guard.

Jack nodded. "We'll let D-11 clean up when they get here."

The other guard was dead, one of Jack's first two shots having taken him in the head. Luck, he reflected. He retrieved his Glock and began climbing the ladder. Solomon was already almost to the top.

The third tremor was the worst of them all.

Jack felt it build beneath him, heard a rising clatter from a nearby stack of aluminum rain gutters, *tasted* the rough, thick ozone in the air before the tremendous jolt passed up from the foundation, from Hell itself for all he knew, and shook him from the ladder.

He tried to angle onto his feet but the wrenching shift of the roof threw him to the side and spun him about like a rag doll. The wounded guard shrieked as a few loose boards and one actual rafter thudded down heavily. Loose wood and steel, nails and bits of aluminum, and even a dozen irregular chunks of the building *itself* stuttered and skittered along the surface of the roof near the two men, like pebbles on a drumhead.

Jack covered his head and rolled from the wall as bits of the upper platform chewed themselves loose and rained down around him. He heard the ladder crackle loose and clang down.

Everything slid a few feet to the side. Piles of aluminum squealed and chittered towards the edge.

Laying there, Jack felt his stomach plunge and winced—sure the building had begun its final sway, had started a long, sheering, final drop to the ground.

Another internal lurch, then everything settled. He lay there for a long moment before daring to breathe. When he opened his eyes, he saw that a great portion of the building had given way and splintered off, falling onto tiers below or onto the street. Huge cracks had appeared in the stone and steel walls–but from his vantage at the peak of the artificial summit, he could see a symmetry to the destruction, an evenness. Jack's stomach plunged again as a growing sense of dread swept him. Raines' weapon was functioning perfectly. Already, light filtered from those crevices and crannies, flickering out over London.

Worst of all was the approach to the transmitter platform. The ladder was gone, probably over the edge. Though the wall had taken damage and patches had fallen, it was still smooth and unclimbable; too high to use some of the building materials as a ladder–

Solomon leaned his head over the edge. He looked unshaken, as always. "I've found a cutoff switch, must have been what those four were guarding." The great black disk of the transmitter loomed behind him like a negative halo. "There's a problem, Jack."

"What's that?" Must be a way to get up there. A second ladder; something.

"Just like Steve told us, two big levers connected by a grip, though it's all I can do to pull it down. Like a circuit breaker. Keeping it down is easy enough, but there's some sort of spring device inside that snaps the whole affair up again as soon as I release it."

Jack looked around the roof, then back at Solomon. "Can you hold it down?"

"As long as it takes."

Both men spoke at the same time.

"You'll have to—"

"I'll stay and—" Solomon smiled. "I'll stay. You go." His eyes shone.

Jack looked at him a long moment, then spun and raced into the darkness.

*

Solomon shrugged and worked his neck. The access panel before him lay in tatters; he'd ripped it off to get to the breaker. There were other controls on the board; a bank of digitized numbers and touch commands, backlit for easy reading; and three ports for cable and network access.

He ignored them. His task was simple. Solomon gripped the enormous lever in an equally large fist, and forced it down.

The reverberating hum, which he'd noticed upon climbing the ladder, quieted to a droning hiss.

*

Either the architect never intended the top floors to be completed, or they were predestined to be part of a model for a madhouse, Alonzo decided. There seemed to be no point to the rambling passages and mismatched floorplan, though Steve assured him the way was clear to the makeshift hanger. "Fine. I'll check out the helicopter. See what you can do by way of diversion–here." He handed over his last grenades. "Be careful with the remote detonation."

Steve agreed. "The stray radiation in this place is really messing up radio frequencies. So I plant the grenades. Then what?"

"Just meet me here. If Jack and Sol aren't back by then, we'll think of something."

Alonzo ascended an unworked staircase, senses straining. Very few of the rooms were lighted, and he stayed low, moving cautiously from room to room. The maze of two-by-fours and half-laid drywall gave way to a wide loft overlooking the main room below. Ahead, the voices of at least three men were accompanied by the clatter of mechanic's tools. The loft evidently served as a temporary rough work and storage area, piled with drywall slats and spare wood of various dimensions. Alonzo crept up behind a moveable rack of power tools and peered over the edge.

Raines stood below, in heated conversation with a long-haired man in a grey suit, who held a machine pistol. They stood near the helicopter; sure enough, a three-bladed Sikorsky. Three 7500 shp General Electric turboshaft engines, gaping open to receive as much air as possible. Usually they required a three man crew, but he'd do fine without a navigator or a flight engineer–the transports couldn't fly themselves, but each Sikorsky carried a state-of-the-art avionics package which included a weather radar, radio navigation gear, Doppler radar, and a moving map display. He'd flown birds similar enough.

The suited man turned his head, and Alonzo got a good look at his face. Miklos Nasim, and he was furious. Raines offered a cigarette to the gesturing man, then lit one himself before continuing the conversation. Alonzo strained but couldn't make out their exchange over the noise of the three mechanics and the increasing thrum of the turbines on the Sikorsky. Have to get closer.

He mentally noted the positions of five other guards in the room, then retreated from the edge. No sign of Raines' personal secretary/ bodyguard/whatever, the burly Oriental he called Michael.

Another minor tremor passed, rocking the sixty-watt bulbs in their hanging cages. Alonzo circled through the loft, moving clockwise. If he could get closer to the helicopter he'd be able to see exactly how many guards watched the room. The loft extended around half the vault; providing a view of the entire lower floor. He clung to the darkness, skirting the open rooms and stealing along the walls.

Only a few more minutes and the Sikorsky would be fully flight-capable. Alonzo wondered how they planned on leaving the country. Getting to a private airfield wouldn't be difficult at all, he supposed, considering the chaos that Raines' weapon would spawn over London. He had no conception of the exact manner in which the maser would detonate, but his mind's eye filled briefly with images of an unearthly crater, a mile wide and deep, filling rapidly with gushing, acrid seawater.

Alonzo turned the corner and came face-to-face with the huge Chinese in the Saville Row suit, standing there, silently, in the dark. Before Alonzo could bring his machine gun around he found himself lifted in one oversized, manicured fist. The man's other hand neatly covered the grip of the MP-5, and Alonzo winced as the frowning man tore it from him. Breath hissing from between clenched teeth, he groped blindly for his other gun, but felt that hand also immobilized.

"Roaches, capering in the dark," Michael whispered, squeezing Alonzo up against a support. He began grinding the air out of the little man.

Then Michael bellowed as Alonzo's free hand rammed a combat knife hilt-deep into his elbow. The razor ridges on the blade's spine cut as well through flesh as they did the expensive fabric of the suit.

Alonzo writhed out of the weakening grasp and dodged to the side as his opponent surged, growling, after him. Backpedaling, he breathed in as fully as he was able. His chest ached hideously where Michael had pressed his knuckles, though he cut the pain off before it reached his face. Michael slowed, favoring his wounded arm, eyes riveted on Alonzo. The knife still stuck horrifically from his extremity.

If the man's abilities had any roots whatsoever in the old Soviet doctrines, this was not going to be easy. Spetznatz hand-to-hand training was never completed until the student was able to deliver over one hundred and fifty potentially lethal blows in under a minute.

Both men circled sinuously around the room, measuring, judging, defining. The battle was joined.

*

Ian noted the dumbfounded look on each face in the squad as the D-11 men filtered into the vault and took their first look at the machine. No one was quite sure how to proceed.

"How do we get down to it, then?" asked the lead man. He had to shout over the grating din which echoed all about them. It was as though they'd entered the nightmare heart of a colony of demon wasps.

The single massive tube extending through the ceiling, which had been glossy before, now shone pure white, and Ian saw the inner core had turned a hellish gold-red. The indistinct, wraithlike shapes within were all but beating themselves to pieces. "I think we'd better leave," he said.

Another tremor began, prompting the men to clutch at the platform railing. The crystal core abruptly went from gold-red to pure white, accompanied by an infernal shrieking wail, as if something unearthly were being racked with unbearable pain. The officers nearest Ian began backing toward the door. The walls and other surfaces shivered all around them. A terrible crashing preceded the growing network of luminous cracks suddenly cris-crossing the walls and ceiling. "Back!" the commander shouted needlessly. His other words were drowned out by a tumultuous rending peal, a thunderclap of solid cement.

Ian shoved men ahead of himself as he ran. Raines' property was shaking itself to dust.

*

Vibrations passed up from the steel floor through Miklos' boots as the helicopter engine warmed. Miklos sat next to Raines in a cushioned seat of the Sikorsky and considered the digital sweep of numbers on the other man's computer screen. The Hradek program was operating exactly as the tests at Rockwell Island predicted. The palmtop was shielded, like the systems in the helicopter, to withstand certain microwave frequencies. Hradek would not disable their technology.

In one corner of the miniature screen, a colorless CCD-type video rotated through the various approaches to the hanger. Raines could continue monitoring the security cameras and access any of the building's programs as long as they were within 12 kilometers of the Tower. As Miklos understood it, every component of the maser was preprogrammed and functioned perfectly without the input of the creator, but Raines seemed to enjoy the ringside seat that his computer provided to each process. Either he would execute the final command from the helicopter as they left the city, or allow the maser to activate on its own.

Miklos regretted they hadn't been able to televise the mock demands they'd prepared, set to broadcast one minute before CNN would televise the footage of the princess killing everyone on the steps of Buckingham Palace. He'd been forced to endure the presence of the diminutive, fascist motion picture director for nothing, not even the pleasure of killing the man. Nothing to be done about that now.

An assistant approached the open cargo door. "Everything is done, sir. Computer records are clean and the hard copies of all your personal records in London have been destroyed as well."

Raines nodded. "Very good." He painstakingly lit a cigarette. He flicked his lighter shut, then leaned forward abruptly, staring at the tiny video screen on his computer. He pressed a series of keys, frowning.

Miklos regarded his employer intently. Was this a trace of dismay?

Raines turned to him. "Flynn is coming." He spoke in a soft, distant voice, cool, absent of all emotion but amusement. Almost as if he were trying to encourage or reassure Miklos.

"Who?"

"Jack Flynn. I saw him a moment ago. He's coming here to stop us."

"Same name as the American actor? What—" This was absurd. The older man seemed on the verge of giddiness, though he remained quiet.

Raines continued, still speaking gently, the damned sly Cheshire grin unearthly beneath his dead eyes.

"Alert your men." He exited the helicopter, engrossed in the video streaming through his computer.

Miklos joined him. "Tovik!" he barked. He looked to Raines, finding the man grinning expectantly and looking up at the storage loft on the opposite side of the helicopter from where they'd descended. A brief yell, and then a shriek of mismatched metal giving way heralded the appearance of two struggling figures.

*

Alonzo hit the drywall with his shoulder, and let his momentum carry him all the way through to the other side. The shallow laceration on the underside of his arm opened up again, and he was bleeding from at least three other minor cuts and abrasions. Alonzo grunted as he landed next to a loose stack of short, narrow beams. He only hoped he didn't look as bad as the raging behemoth who barreled after him through the shards of drywall. Michael's expensive suit hadn't proven an adequate defense when Alonzo threw a bucket of nails in his face. One eye had swollen completely shut.

The huge man continued past Alonzo, snatching a thin beam from the pile. Alonzo twisted himself to his feet, slapping the end of one of the thick stakes so the other end flipped over in the air and into his waiting palm.

Though their staves were equal, the Chinese had a longer reach, and pressed his advantage. Alonzo backed away along the edge of the loft, doing his best to avoid meeting Michael's massive swings and blocking two-handedly when he was forced to. Each time the rods met Alonzo's entire frame quivered. He wouldn't be able to take much more of this.

*

As each man below turned towards the opposite loft, Jack adjusted his grip around the Glock. Raines stood barely twenty feet away, the back of his head a ripe target against the dark metal of the helicopter's hull. Jack took a deep breath as he lined up his front and rear sights, then paused, recognizing his friend's pained breathing.

Michael battered Al back; pursued him around a stack of sawhorses, then kicked the entire mass at him, closing in immediately with the staff. Though he returned each blow with his own, Jack could tell Alonzo was tiring in the deadly, whirling pas-a-deux.

The others in the room stood watching, nervously idle. Jack lined his sights with Raine's skull. Logic, strategy, hell, any and *all* his training screamed for him to pull the trigger and end Alex Raines. Cut off the head and the body will fall. Remove the leader and you diminish the whole.

Alonzo gasped in exertion. Michael's tattered suit made an easy target. Raines stood below, rapt with concentration, all senses turned towards the unfolding action.

Cut off the head and the body will fall.

Your friend will die unless you move now, *Jack.*

Bright Wings

Miklos spun as four rapid shots rang out in the enclosed space of the vault. An *American actor*, sheathed in a dark jacket, leaped from the rail-less storage space and jumped towards them, touching down only briefly on a stack of drywall powder, then soaring again, somersaulting over the heads of two of his men, aiming for Raines, who, for once, stood in shock.

An ammunition clip hit the floor beneath the loft even as Miklos grasped his weapon and interposed himself between his employer and the newcomer. The man twisted liquidly in the air, landing on his feet within reach of the three guards and backhanding one to the floor with a closed fist. He moved so *fast*, seizing the closest man's gun and slamming him into the third. He dodged to one side and down, as if evading the bullets Miklos had not yet loosed, and came up with one of the MAC-10's.

Interesting. Miklos began to squeeze the trigger just as another quake clutched the Tower in a shivering grip. Everyone around him lost their feet, including the new man, and Miklos's aim was ruined. Barrels of supplies crashed down from the loft. A long rack of power tools toppled to the floor as well, sending loose circle blades bouncing and chipping across the floor. Miklos alone remained standing.

He closed in on the fallen outsider as the tremors subsided, kicking the weapon from his hand. Such a temptation to take the other up by the throat, to break him apart with his bare hands. He could practically taste the blood fountaining and sluicing from the corpse.

Instead, as the newcomer began to move, Miklos stepped back and leveled his own machine pistol at the fellow's head. A few of the other guards, shaken as much by the newcomer's arrival as the shuddering floor, raised their weapons as well.

Miklos met the grim stare. "Think you're faster than a speeding bullet, my friend?" he asked.

*

Alonzo countered, fell short, and used his momentum to push into Michael, kneeing the man in the groin and managing an elbow strike to his armpit. As the Chinese stumbled back, Alonzo continued forward, past his opponent, further away from the central hanger, and found himself in a corner room, without walls.

Why wouldn't Michael fall? He'd been shot at least once, taken a grazing bullet across his back from whoever had fired. The larger man's defense was becoming ragged; basic mistakes became more and more frequent, though for all the blood he'd lost, he seemed as powerful as ever. Even now, he drew himself up, grinning weirdly, the bright wooden stave a smear of lighter color across Alonzo's clouding vision. The harder I strike, the stronger he becomes, like some sort of vampiric—

The cold wind snapped over his body, enlivening Alonzo as Michael suddenly pressed in, hammering from two angles at once. As the other's guard fell, Alonzo was able to get in a half-dozen solid hits, but his opponent's double-sided attack worked the inevitable.

Michael's staff slipped past that of the smaller man. Alonzo's scream nearly masked the *crack* of his breaking rib. He spun with the impact, and realized the motive behind his opponent's reckless attack: beyond a thin sheet of plastic and five bare feet of plywood hung empty space.

Michael shouted incoherently and swung at Alonzo's fingers. He managed to jerk them out of the way, but his staff went flying. Michael stood back, eyeing the cornered man.

391

Alonzo grimaced. There would be no Jack to pull him up from *this* drop. If there was only something he could–

–His opponent shuffled his feet.

Alonzo reacted without thinking, crouching to the floor as the other man's foot ripped through the air over his head. Michael's other foot lashed upward in a snap kick, and Alonzo dodged back and to the side, ribs on fire. It was just a matter of time, now. He couldn't watch the other man's feet forever, and even as the thought ran through his head, he felt his heels hang in space.

Michael laughed, bubbling through the blood on his lips. "Goodbye, cockroach." As he rushed forward Alonzo crouched and let himself fall. The Chinese began another devastating lunge with the staff, and when it did not meet the expected resistance, he overbalanced and fell forward. Alonzo caught the rough edge of the roof, nearly dislocating his shoulder with the jolt. As he swung forward into the building, he felt more than saw the huge bodyguard sail past him, gasping with astonishment.

Alonzo hung there for a moment, arms and shoulders quickly numbing with pain. It seemed the simplest idea in the world to let go, to let the blithe darkness swallow him whole. It hurt so much.

Then, groaning, he levered himself slowly back up over the edge. He lay gasping for a long moment, his ribcage a shapeless, blinding fire against the cold, cold floor.

*

"I'm afraid you're all out of allies, Mr. Flynn," said the gaunt, smiling man in the white suit as he lit another cigarette.

Jack forced his face to remain expressionless; kept his eyes on Raines while his mind roamed the hanger, working furiously. He sat crosslegged with his hands on his head. The four remaining guards all watched from positions safely outside his reach, except for the gloating, pacing Miklos. As he walked he adjusted the angle his machine pistol accordingly, keeping it even with Jack's head. He supposed it was some sort of terror technique. It was a good one. The empty blackness at the end of his MAC-10 seemed impossibly large.

"You mean this man here led the assault tonight? *He* was with them?" Miklos scoffed.

"Mr. Flynn apparently hires a cell of mercenaries from time to time to help with—certain humanitarian projects he fancies."

Miklos sneered. "But he's an actor. Hollywood. An American sham."

"That's just my day job." Jack said amicably. It was bloody hard to concentrate with that gun a few inches from his face. He had their attention, however, and Raines grinned again. How can one man smile and show so many teeth?

The Albanian terrorist was the real professional, he realized. The man would have already shot him if Raines hadn't desired a diversion as the last few men returned. Three men in flight suits approached dispassionately and entered the helicopter. The metallic tap-click-tap of their steel briefcases against the zippers on their flight suits sounded like three misaligned clocks ticking. If diverting Raines would buy him a few minutes—

"What's that down in your basement, Alex? Looks like a giant lava lamp."

"A bit more than that, I'm afraid." He chortled good-naturedly. "Would you like to see exactly what it does?"

Jack looked him dead in the eye. "You built a maser."

Perversely, this seemed to entertain Raines even further. He finished his cigarette and spoke. His voice was crystal clear. "Lightning is an amazing thing, Flynn. Pure chaos.

"When I was a teenager, growing up on the unfashionable side of the old Iron Curtain," he continued, "I saw a man, a political prisoner, tortured and cut into little pieces by electricity in my parent's laboratory. Fascinating. Sterile–not a drop of blood, as all the bits were instantly cauterized. My mother and father were quite horrified, you can imagine. They'd simply followed an eighty-year-old recipe left behind by another scientist, one who'd managed to harness more raw power during his life than any other man ever has, living or otherwise."

"Nikola Tesla," said Jack.

Raines looked up, surprised. "Tesla." His eyes narrowed. "Do you know what happens if you pump enough energy into a steel rod? It magnetizes, yes, but as it continues to increase in power, you can set up an electromagnetic resonance that gives you even more power—"

Jack cut him off "You're talking about the photoelectric effect. Are you saying this Tower is some kind of photovoltaic cell?"

Raines mouth twitched. "The device does considerably more than convert light into electrical energy. Tesla found a way to span the entire spectrum, produce so much more in terms of frequency."

"So the reaction gives off energy. Starts simple enough, but eventually you pass upwards through the visible light spectrum and into ultraviolet light, then eventually x-rays, then eventually—"

Raines' dead eyes gleamed in the light. "The raw power rippling off *breaks things* on a molecular level. Molecular bonds separate, atoms crack away from one another. The very air itself turns to fire. Heat stress fractures everything into splinters, and the wildly fluctuating magnetic fields force everything further apart."

"Just like a nuclear bomb." Jack's blood turned icy.

"Exactly like a nuclear bomb. And this entire wonderful structure you see around us is nothing more than a giant electromagnetic resonator."

394

Raines paused as another minor tremor rattled up through the building. Weak, it lasted considerably longer than any of the others. The lights dimmed. A look of puzzlement struck the older man's face, and he withdrew a miniature computer.

"No, these levels are all wrong. Insufficient power is reaching the array." The look of dismay that fell across his features had a curious effect on the Albanian. As Raines began typing and clicking one-handedly, Miklos stepped close and glanced rapidly between the small screen and his employer's face, his own countenance shifting from boredom to annoyance to concern to frustration. The gun on Jack never wavered, though Miklos shifted his grip on it several times.

He doesn't trust Raines, Jack realized. Before he could think how to turn this new fact into any kind of advantage, the lights completely failed, and darkness swarmed up around them on velvet wings.

Even as darkness fell, even before he realized instinct was taking over, Jack moved. Jerking his feet, he rolled backwards and shoved into the legs of a guard. Using the man's bulk for resistance, he quickly stood, found the MAC-10, and fumbled for the trigger as his opponent blustered and flailed with his free arm.

A series of explosions just off the hangar entrance cast a reflected strobe effect through the room. Miklos, now a silhouette against the interior cockpit lights, reeled back, pushing Raines with him toward the helicopter. He kept his weapon close.

A guard screamed, his suit suddenly in flames and his face liquefying under glowing, white phosphorus. The others fired past him at the entrance, raking their weapons right and left. Sparks flew as their bullets glanced off machinery and piping. Jack wrested the machine pistol from its owner, nearly dislocating the other's shoulder, and brought the gun up just as the nearest suited man turned towards him.

Jack emptied the clip into the man and his companion behind him, then dove for the stack of drywall powder he'd used earlier as a stepping stone to reach Raines.   Light from the explosions now lit the room. The mountain of baled, bound bags of grit proved ample protection as he considered his weapons. No gun, no grenades, and down to his last magazine of 9mm ammo.

Above his head, slugs tore through the thick sacks and sprayed colorless powder over his entire field of vision. Through the thickness at his back he felt the impact of dozens and dozens of rounds.

The angle meant he was being fired on by someone right outside the helicopter, maybe even inside the transport bay. He heard the rotors begin to spin up.

*

Steve fired again from his position behind the ductwork near the entrance, cutting the last man down as he ran for the Sikorsky. A strange haze filled his vision, abnormal in that he seemed to see everything with an added dimension of clarity and sharp definition. He could feel the rough, raspy surface of his pistol grip on his bare hand as he fired it; felt the keen pressure as each bullet drove itself from the Glock.   He threw another grenade and watched it tumble slowly through the air, noticing the unmistakable, shiny edges on the disk and the markings which identified it as a concussion grenade. *Crrrump!*

The oddest detail was, he didn't have to consciously consider any of what he did. It was as though he'd lost the ability—or perhaps the need—to weigh his actions, to deliberate the pulling of a trigger and the ending of a life.

The bay doors began to slide open on their rollers. Incandescent light blasted in from below and then vanished: spotlights below scoured the building's skin.

*

Major Griffin held the Princess' hand tightly, kneeling as both of them looked up. The little girl had gasped when the cracks appeared in the building, shedding their sickly illumination. The major desperately wanted to secure Her Highness in more protected surroundings—something told her there must be more of Raines' lackeys about in the night. Nothing stronger than a patrol car offered itself at the moment, however.

More spinning lights could be seen on the streets bordering the Tower. A jangle of red, blue, and gold flashed against the shops and apartments on one side of Oxford Street. On the other, the reflected light shine like fire through the new leaves of the trees and gates bordering Hyde Park.

Two of the spotlights halted their scan and fastened onto a growing spot of darkness near the very top of the central tower. Major Griffin stood, glanced at the enraptured princess, and reached for her binoculars. That's about where the hanger doors should be.

She blinked the weariness from her eyes. Odd, so much illumination at the top of the structure. The indistinct radiance around the BBC transmitter had to be more than mere St. Elmo's Fire.

Abruptly, all the lights went out.

*

Solomon acknowledged the burgeoning power under his feet, nodded mentally at the raw energy surging up from the infernal depths under the Tower. The panel before him glowed brightly, bathing him in multicolored light from its many digital dials and esoteric displays.

He'd set the elephant gun down, so as to be able to switch hands occasionally on the circuit breaker. Actually, he doubted that was its true function, as a great deal of energy seemed to be passing into the electronics above his head no matter how hard he pressed the lever down.

An ominous snapping filled the air, accompanied by a deep hum from the machinery above. He felt it through his entire body. A rivulet of perspiration ran down the middle of Solomon's back, and he looked back over his shoulder at the city, then started in dark shock.

In a growing radius from the Tower, lights were going out. Whole apartment buildings, extinguished. Colonnades of streetlamps supporting a contiguous arch of light, doused. Commercial billboards, traffic lights, neon and flourescents; all smothered. The flat circle of inky black lay relieved only by the headlights of vehicles moving on the streets. It spread uniformly, distorted temporarily by the angling line of the Thames, then assumed congruity again. Moving along pathways of electric cables, Solomon supposed.

The purring drone increased sharply in volume. Solomon nearly lost his grip on the lever, then slapped both hands down over it.

The sky was incredible. He was high enough to actually see mist and vapor slide together in the clouds. The luminosity had become more defined, drawing shapes fantastic in the sinuous, piling billows. Forks of electricity played crosswise in the air above, and Solomon looked up to see the clouds press together, forming whorls and creases not unlike the fingerprint of a transcendent finger, attached to a larger almighty hand.

"'The world is charged with the grandeur of God,'" he said again. "'It will flame out, like shining from shook foil.'"

A bright filigree of blue energy danced over everything in his field of vision. Solomon took another deep breath and smiled, calmly, placidly holding the lever in place. "And for all this, nature is never spent; there lives the dearest freshness deep down in things.'"

Raw electricity began to play over the black surface of the disk above. Below, a piercing wail that was almost human. The chaos and havoc of Raines' weapon stormed up at him.

*

Another suited man crouched at the end of the hanger, squinting in the cold wind. Before Steve could train his weapon on him, he jerked and folded straight down, a marionette with cut strings.

Alonzo limped-ran into the hangar, gripping a smoking pistol. Jack dodged out from behind a stack of drywall bags. They had the great beast roughly surrounded. Steve, the closest, ran and took up a position in front of the helicopter. He and Alonzo were firing steadily, scattering sparks off the gray fuselage.

The blades above were merely another shadow now, the hanger a black hurricane tunnel. The Sikorsky wavered on its landing gear. Turbines roared, and the massive helicopter began to ease forward towards the open doors.

Jack yelled something to them but the rotors sliced and tore the words even as they left his throat. He didn't appear to have a weapon. The machine cleared the floor fully and began to gather speed. Its gaping entrance would slide right past him.

Steve assumed a classic Weaver stance, firing directly at the pilot, but the bulletproof glass sent his rounds screaming away from the 'copter. White streaks appeared where the glass compressed under each bullet.

Alonzo, grimacing and holding his side, scooped up a ten-pound bag of drywall mix and hefted it into one of the turbines as it advanced past him. He was blown from his feet as the turbine exploded, billowing black smoke and pale white powder.

The Sikorsky cleared the rollback doors. Alonzo watched it drop-jerk down and to the left, losing power on the side of the damaged turbine. He swore and pumped the air triumphantly. "See how far they get on one engine! Suppose we can leave it up to His Majesty's Royal Air Force, eh Jack?" He looked across the hanger to where his friend stood scant seconds before. "Jack?"

"Jack?"

*

He slammed Raines up against a flight seat, then stumbled as the floor of the Sikorsky jerked down and to left. Miklos lashed out with a kick, missed, and struggled to bring his weapon to bear. As he moved forward, Jack dove underneath him, then came up behind before his opponent could get a steady foothold to turn about. Gripping the hands that held the machine pistol, Jack heaved the gun back into Miklos's stomach. Fire blossomed out into the helicopter, spilling into the cockpit and rebounding bullets off the dark green steel.

Miklos dropped the gun and twisted, smashing Jack with an elbow and a fist simultaneously. Jack spun along with him, snarling with pain even as he locked Miklos' arms with his own and threw the man headlong into the rear portion of the transport deck.

Jack spared a glance to where Raines crouched, and saw to his dismay that the older man held a pistol in his free hand. Miklos came in again, palms darting. Jack kicked the MAC-10 out the door and raised his own hands to defend himself.

The pilot made an odd gurgling sound from the cockpit. The three in the midsection turned enough to see the uniformed man slump against his smashed and sparking controls.

Alonzo and Steve watched the helicopter's flashing lights descend into the darkness below, then slide off rapidly to the side until they vanished around a corner of the building.

The sky around them was a frozen maelstrom of pigments. Alonzo had never seen such radiant crimsons and tints of pearl-touched indigo in his life.

A humming buzz pervaded the room. He realized it had always been present, but now suddenly surged into a throbbing, resonant tone, and the lights came back on. They were weak, fluctuating sparks.

The floor on which the two men stood began to shake.

The air around them began to take on a strange hue.

"We've got to try to make it to the elevator!" Alonzo shouted.

Steve shook his head. "In an earthquake? Deathtrap." He seemed strangely shaken, and blinked his eyes repeatedly. He glanced apprehensively about at the trembling building. "We'll never make it down that way."

Alonzo began to wish *he'd* been on the helicopter. "Then what–"

"Wait!" Steve lurched toward his concealed equipment. "The spare parachutes!"

Alonzo limped after him. "Steve! I broke a rib or something. I need," He struggled for breath. A cold weariness washed over him. "I need your help."

*

The entire flight crew was dead, ripped to pieces by the ricocheting eruptions of the machine pistol. Jack tried to fall away from the yawning door as he, Raines, and Miklos were thrown about inside the 'copter like dice in a tumbler.

It dropped rapidly and sheered left, weaving unsteadily in a nearly-complete circle around the Tower.   Jack was the first to recover his balance and landed a solid right fist on Raines' jaw, then snatched up the miniature computer that slid along the floor.

Time to abandon ship.

He slid into the pilot's chair, shoving the dead man toward the rear. Miklos dodged, seized Raines, and slammed him into an empty flight chair.

Alonzo had repeatedly shown him the rudiments of flying, though Jack had no hope of being able to pilot the machine. He could barely hear himself think over the whine and shriek of bending, buckling steel, over the hard metal groan of rivets tested to their limit. Jack found the collective without any trouble, leveling out somewhat at a hundred feet and descending above the street.

He ran his hands and eyes over the instrument panel, increasingly desperate.

The crippled, flaming Sikorsky cleared the fence surrounding Hyde Park and sheered through the top of a tree. Jack belted himself in with one hand while the other skittered over the controls. Damn, it had to be here somewhere!

Ever catlike, Miklos slipped into the co-pilot's space. Jack saw the knife at the limit of his peripheral vision, and managed to duck down and to the left, catching three inches of steel in the thick folds of his jacket. As he dodged, his hand came in contact with a lever over a central button.

He looked down, ignoring Miklos. The helicopter began to veer right and forward, blurring the passage of scenery. Perhaps three seconds until the blades hit the ground and they pinwheeled, in fire and bloody slag, across the middle of the park.

The button was large and red. Practically a circus clown's nose.

Miklos dropped the knife and reached for his safety belt. Raines was shouting in the background, somewhere behind them in the shattering helicopter.

"I'm sorry," was all Jack had time to say as he punched the eject button and the 'copter's rotors blew off. His chair erupted through the rapidly fragmenting canopy and Jack screamed as he blew past the other two men. The world spun, and he watched the blackness of the ground rotate below, as if time was speeding up without him, only to be replaced by dim blurs that had to be stars. But he was too low.

The Sikorsky plowed into the earth, digging a furrow thirty meters long before exploding into a police shed.

He heard the parachute billow open above him, but he knew he was too low for it to do much good. Jack felt strangely disappointed. He'd always expected to see bits of his life flash before him at the end. "*Victoria*," he began, then felt a tremendous, chilling impact, and all went black as a starless night.

*

Alonzo glided downward ten meters above Steve, aiming for the rooftops on the south side of Oxford Street. Above and behind him, the Tower suddenly flared a brilliant white-gold, shining through the thin silk of his parachute and painting his giant, magically suspended silhouette on the buildings and crowds below.

Far to his right, in the middle of the lightless green fields of the park, a lesser fire burned at the end of a swath of glowing metal. Flaming shreds of steel still rained on the grass.

Alonzo spiraled back over the street and came down near the gates of Hyde Park. The crowd below scattered out of his way, squinting up against the growing light.

He tried to land in a run, had to settle for a slow, injured lurch, and cursed his lost knife. Alonzo struggled with the straps of his parachute, finally surrendering to the assistance of a pair of middle-aged men in rain slickers. "I have to get into Hyde Park," he said to a nearby policeman.

Then an explosion of light drew their attention back to the Illuminatus Tower. "Everyone get back! Back now, clear the area!" An officer on horseback was motioning for their retreat, all the while taking nervous glances over his shoulder at the building.

The light filled the sky with an incandescence as pure and strong as a single, perfect musical note.

*

The black water shattered upward as Jack surged to the surface, clawing for air. He was covered in mud from a skidding stop on the lake's bottom, and water gushed from his clothes as he dragged himself onto the far bank. "Smack dab in the middle of the Serpentine," he said, coughing.

Slowly he rolled to his back and sat up. Half a mile across the park, the brilliance at the crown of the Illuminatus Tower was just reaching full bloom. The top ten floors consumed themselves, their molecules burning into ambient light energy.

Long shadows blossomed under the noonday light from the Tower. Nearby, in a muddy groove of the river lay the conjoined co-pilot and navigator chairs, empty. There was no sign of Raines or the Albanian.

Jack opened Raines's computer, and managed to shut down all the currently running programs. He had no idea if deactivating the miniature computer would have any effect, but he did it regardless. If Solomon had managed to curb much of the discharge, the power would most likely burn itself out before going much above the harmless visual spectrum.

Solomon.

Spreading plumes of energy raised themselves high, silently triumphant in the heavens over the Tower.

How did the rest of that go?

"And though the last lights off the black West went

Oh, morning, at the brown brink eastward, springs—

Because the Holy Ghost over the bent

World broods with warm breast and with ah! bright wings."

Jack bowed his head and let his vision blur. His blue reflection over the calm waters of the Serpentine looked back stonily, steadily, softened by scant tears.

The very top of the tower erupted in a solid blaze of light, and Jack crawled from the cool lawn to his feet. The light was warm, soaking through his clammy clothes. After a moment more, he fished the chicklet-sized transmitter out of his front pocket and pressed it firmly. He looked up once again at the Tower. The light would burn for a long time yet.

He took a deep breath and walked toward it.

*

By the time Jack reached the edge of Hyde Park the streetlamps and other sources of illumination were beginning to flicker on. As he greeted Ian, Alonzo, Major Griffin, and the little princess, a gleaming Rolls Royce Phantom IV pulled up. "Right this way, if you please," said a uniformed driver. He introduced himself as a Special Security aid to Buckingham Palace, and shooed them all inside.

Alonzo explained that they were waiting for the last member of their party. "Steve is probably still trying to get off the roof," he said, pointing to a nearby office complex on the south side of Oxford. "I should think he'll be right along.

"Afraid that's not quick enough," said the man after consulting his timepiece. "We can send another car back for him. His Majesty is most anxious to see his daughter."

They entered the limousine as three ranks of D-11 and SAS closed about them. Exhaustion painted every face in long shadows. Jack sat across from Alonzo with the princess between himself and the major. Christine patted him reassuringly on the knee as the Phantom IV hummed to life.

"You are all dreadfully dirty," said the princess, solemnly. Alonzo chuckled.

"And what about you, Your Highness?" Jack asked, pointing to her hair. "You're so dirty you've started a garden in your hair."

"I have not either, I–oh!"

Jack pulled a tulip from her unruly blond mop, smiling as she trilled with delight and clapped her hands. "Just like you did in the movie!"

Major Griffin leaned out, puzzled. "What on earth?"

"I had a small role as an American entertainer, Harry Houdini, in a film a few years back." To Christine, he said, "Can you believe I fell into a flowerbed over by the statue of Peter Pan just now? Maybe you can give that to your mother. I'll bet she's missed you."

"Oh, yes, sir." She grinned. "Mum likes flowers. Does your mother like flowers when you come home, Jack?"

She was an innocent. "My mom and dad are in Heaven, Christine."

"Oh." She seemed a bit puzzled by that, then her eyes found Alonzo, seated across from her. "Are your parents in Heaven too?"

He smiled back at her. "My parents live in Sun Valley. It's a suburb of Heaven." As the princess turned her attention to the little flower, he nodded at Jack. "What now?"

Jack considered. "Raines and Miklos are probably still alive, thanks to me. The Sikorsky was built to protect all the occupants, and I ejected us all before it hit," he said, before Alonzo could ask the obvious question. "Best to contact Miguel Espinosa and let him know we're on our way to Cuba."

His friend agreed. "He's next on the list of targets, according to William. I started a case file on all this yesterday, but it's sloppy. Think we should rewrite it?"

"When we all get back to Paris. Steve mentioned he's got some contacts back in the States that can help us figure out Raines' maser. One of his old professors at MIT, and maybe a guy over on the West Coast."

No reply. Jack looked over as Alonzo's eyes closed and his head tilted back against the dark plush headrest. He was snoring before they reached the gates of Buckingham Palace.

Night Run

Studio City, California
8PM

By rights she should have been bone-ache tired after the helicopter ride out of the San Jacintos, but Mercedes felt incredible when the birdwatchers from UC Davis dropped her off at home. She bent and waved to them as the garage door descended. Weird. Could've been the photos—the pictures of the baby eagles had really turned out well, definitely worth the chill they'd felt last night on the climb. Another instance of her being a mere spectator, but *still*. Eagles were her new favorite bird.

The way the chicks had fought for the outside air, pecked, hammered, and thrashed their way out into the world, drew a reverence, a kind of internal hush out of Mercedes. The little birds didn't know, did they? The world they broke out into had already decided to roll the dice against them, that the jig was up and the fix was in for their entire species. And yet they fought.

Briefly she hugged herself in the garage. She felt so good. She felt like redecorating the entire dining room tonight before bedtime, instead of watching the highlights of a rugby game on the DVR.

Mercedes stowed her equipment in her studio, the first spare bedroom down the hall that intersected with the dining room, the living room, and the sunken room she thought of as a library. "I'm home," she said to no one, and flipped on the lights. The motion sensors in the corner of the ceiling clicked from red to green, and from her bedroom in the far end of the house a stereo chimed to life.

She smiled. No pets, no noisy family, but at least the house was glad she was home. And no redecorating tonight, either. Mercedes looked to her plants, first the big jade plants in the pots near the front door, then the ivy she'd hung in homemade latticework underneath the skylights in the living room. Months ago Mercedes decided that the wide rafters that ran the width of the house, though painted white to match the walls, looked naked. She felt like she was living in somebody''s barn, despite the sturdy, comfortable furniture she'd filled it with. Mercedes avoided the temptation to sit down or brush up against anything as she checked her plants. Most of the dust and bits of bark from the shoot still stuck to her, clotted her hair, and grimed her nose.

Mercedes walked from plant, watering each with a little teakettle she kept for that purpose. The lattice was her favorite, and she saved it for last. She'd designed it herself, suspending thin strips of teak from anchor points in the rafters, then arranging a series of simultaneously fired flower pots all networked together so she could water one—the highest—and each would get water in turn. She'd gotten the idea from while shooting native clothing in the terraced, northern mountains of the Philippines. She'd done a real job on the house.

She stood on a wooden chair to reach the uppermost plant, but her reach was short. With barely a thought, Mercedes took the teapot handle in her teeth and swung herself up onto a rafter. If the ivy was grateful for the water, she couldn't tell. It struck her as she let herself down that any normal person would have fetched a stepladder, but she'd seen a quicker way.

"You're an odd one, Merc," she said.

The stereo had found its place and was starting a Buddy Holly song she'd forgotten she'd put on the hard drive.

From the mantle, the picture of her parents gleamed in the low light. She wondered what they'd think of their daughter now, dangling from the architecture and climbing around the hills. They hadn't lived long enough to see just how strong she would become, or see the first few years of the illness that, perversely, made her so strong. She knew the battlefield of her body.

Since the onset of health problems at the close of her teenage years, Mercedes had taken any measure she thought sane—and a few she had her doubts about—to regain control of her body. To stop the bizarre spread of tumors, cysts, and rogue cells within her.

The first batch of doctors diagnosed her with *endo*—classic endometriosis—and of course the only way to really discover the presence of the painful, internal lesions was through exploratory surgery, making diagnosis and hasty treatment somewhat simultaneous. She'd undergone five hard surgeries in three years, and three years after that, two more.

There were always doctors willing to pump her full of danazol, Demerol, or Depo-Provera. She shuddered. The latter had been prescribed by her parents' doctor, a woman they had trusted for years, and Mercedes had been shocked to learn the injectable form of progesterone was definitely linked to breast tumors, though doctors were still encouraged to recommend it. Sometime it felt like Mercedes was waging a war on two fronts.

So they'd thrown medication after medication at her, thoughtless of the psychological typhoon accompanying each new chemical. The most horrible aspect of endo lay not in the extreme pain or the danger of infertility, but in not knowing the cause for the growths within her body. No one knew. Mercedes couldn't bring herself to work through the idea that her health problems were related to whatever really killed her parents, but those records were spotless, simple, and suspiciously brief. The official ones, at least.

The raw, tender edge of the present was enough to worry about.

For nearly half her life, endo had taught her to regard her body as something never to be trusted fully; at best, a trapdoor that might open up at any moment over a chasm of pain.

For all the battles lost in this particular war, Mercedes regarded her body in a surprisingly—to her—positive light. She only weighed herself four times a year, during her visits to Jeff Hansen's office. Doctor Hansen was the first professional who'd actually done Mercedes some good in addition to being properly sympathetic. His wife had collected a sizeable library on the subject of endo, and the Hansens practically gave Mercedes a key to their house.

There was simply no way endometriosis was going to beat her. She took vitamin B supplements. She alternated vitamin E and selenium with a number of herbal teas. As much as was possible and practical in a professional environment, Mercedes eliminated caffeine, refined sugar, and alcohol from her diet. At Hansen's recommendation she began seeing Shawn Munk, a chiropractor-physical therapist who introduced her to yoga and helped design an exercise regimen that provided intense aerobic activity and much muscle stretching and motion. She'd caught on quickly. According to the cherubic Dr. Munk, the only thing Mercedes needed was a lover trained as a masseuse, one with hands big enough to work themselves around her thickening sheathes of muscle. "Cowboy muscles." She'd laughed at that.

She'd read an article by someone on the board of the British Endometriosis Society extolling safflower and evening primrose oil, and she'd gradually worked that, too, into her diet. Mercedes made sure she always lived near a good farmer's market, a whole grain bakery, and (she grinned) a real Italian deli. She snatched up the phone and keyed the speed dial for Arnaldo's All Night.

411

"Hello?"

Hey, Arnaldo!, This is Mercedes. Siete aperti?"

The man on the other end exhaled sharply through his nose. "We would not be working at Arnaldo's All Night if we were not open for business, Scimmia."

She'd taken the family photo that hung above his cash register. Big, Catholic family. Arnaldo's Italian smacked out in that odd accent from the northeast corner of Italy, but it was so nice to speak with someone. No matter how black her mood, Mercedes only needed to hear the ebb and flow of that sexy, liquid language and she was a chubby little girl again, sneaking scraps of her grandmother's torta in the kitchen in North Beach. Italian would always be the language of her heart.

And the language of her stomach. One hand on the phone, she quickly took inventory of her kitchen. "I need a one-pound package of Penne, some oil-cured olives, some oregano, maybe three cloves of garlic, and some Graffeo coffee. And a pack of Slim Jims."

"Ah, and it is 'Mercedes' Day Off' already, neh?"

"Tomorrow, Arnaldo. Tomorrow is Mercedes's Day Off."

Most days, for weeks at a stretch, she made herself eat like an austere, ascetic warrior monk with an almost gleeful penchant for self-denial, but not on Mercedes' Day Off. "And a Ghirardelli's chocolate bar, if you have any. Whatever flavor." Part of the Hansen-Munk regime. Mercedes Day Off, she ate whatever she felt like.

The two doctors were geniuses. Mercedes skip-grooved through her bedroom to the bath, grinding and singing along with her stereo as Sting crowed about breaking down the clock of time. Her fleece top and thick canvas pants hit the lid of her clothes hamper as the sound of rushing water overlaid the jaunty music. Her climbing shoes, yellow Boreal Stingers, were the most comfortable shoes she'd ever worn. Like somebody had poured a shoe mold around her foot. She wasn't tired at all. It was a perfect day.

She measured a handful of mango-scented salts and threw them in the tub. It was *damn* good to have a day off.

*

She knew she would dream that night, even in anticipation of the next day's feast. Sometimes on Mercedes' Day Off, she'd eat something *way* off her diet, like spicy pork rinds or gyros and champagne, and then pay for it through the night, dreaming away like an Alice down the rabbit hole. It helped when she had the time for a light workout before bed, of course, but that she still couldn't shake the presentiment of night visions. Hours before she locked up the house and retreated to her chilly bedroom, Mercedes knew she would dream.

She loved to run at night. Running at night meant trading the next day's ugly morning jog for free weights and jump rope. Her personal marathons through the canyons and hills of Southern California were fun, and some nights she even went out without any pepper spray.

There were still some neighborhoods where you could be safe at night, running.

The park she angled through was bordered by ash, elm, and an occasional oak. Night runs *were* the best, and the cool air felt satiny-slick against her skin. Mist sprayed across her as she cruised past a stone fountain. She'd run for some time, long enough for her breathing to settle into its accustomed metronomic pulse; her entire body a familiar rhythm.

Night birds cooed weirdly from the dark spaces under the surrounding boughs. No one else in sight. The park felt empty. If this had been a dream she might actually be the only woman left in the world, and the whole world a series of finely-manicured lawns and groves.

But at last she drew near its edge. Though the same trees and grasses extended beyond its boundary, the hillside was untamed. Trees crowded further inward, brush clogged the spaces between the huge boles, and all sorts of weeds and grasses tangled the undergrowth.

Mercedes ran on.

A staircase led up out of the park, complete with a polished steel handrail and bordered by a low, clipped hedge. She never broke stride, taking the stairs two at a time, leaning up into the hill.

She probably could have managed three steps at a stride, but Mercedes didn't want to wind herself before reaching the end of the trail, wherever that might be. She'd run through the park before, though never at night, and she'd never taken the stairs.

The stairway led on, upward. Lights in wrought iron globes lit the way every few dozen feet, and Mercedes could see the steps beneath her were ornately worked. Each vertical surface was scalloped, bordered by a relief of half-circles. The iron railing was vermiculated as well.

She ran on, upward through the green gloom.

Slowly the staircase took on a more weathered aspect. Each connecting step began to look increasingly worn. Aged. In places the concrete was pitted, chipped, cracked, or notched. Moss and lichen sprouted up through some of the fissures.

Mercedes stumbled once on a canted step, reaching for the handrail. She regained her balance and drove on, intent on the uneven, slanting surfaces before her. Wisps of fog coiled sinuously in the brush to either side. It occurred to Mercedes that the very existence of the stairs implied that something interesting and important must lie at its terminus, though why the owners of whatever it was didn't take better care of the long concrete flight–

And two of the lights ahead in their opaque globes went out. She remembered where to place her feet, but Mercedes slowed anyway, trusting to instinct.

Sure enough, a splintered stair shifted under her weight, sliding right and back under her. Mercedes caught herself, then pushed beyond the unsteady level. The jagged paving growled stonily and tipped off the path altogether, then rolled several feet through the brush.

The hill had become steeper; the handrail ended.

She righted herself in the darkness, and ran on. Wouldn't do to let her heart rate drop. Mercedes pumped her knees higher, driving herself up, up.

Only one in four frosted globes glowed brightly now. Ahead in the gloom, Mercedes heard a faint, atonal chime, and then another. She slowed, then stopped altogether as she realized she was nearing the summit. Another chime sounded through the trees, this time accompanied by a vague metallic ring. The chimes had no regularity; they rang unevenly and as unbalanced as the stairway behind her.

For she stood at a sort of landing, not at the crest of the hill but at the top of a ridge. A deer trail led further up the mountain, into the darkness filling up the spaces between the trees. To her left lay another section of the stairs, headed down the opposite side of the ridge. They descended gradually and were well-lit. From the bright illumination she could see they were in perfect repair, unlike the long flight she'd just navigated.

Mercedes wiped a hand along her forehead. Leave it to her luck to pick the worse set of stairs to run. Her hand came back slick, soaked in perspiration. The run up the stairs had taken more out of her than she realized, and she knew the easy descent would give her climbing muscles a sort of rest. Thanks to her self-inflicted torture-by-exercise, she was resistant to shin splints, and–

Another chime, faint but insistent from somewhere up the unlit path.

Without another thought, Mercedes turned and jogged away from the stairs, off the bright landing and into the dark.

She had to slow almost immediately in order to pick her way along the animal track. What was she doing? She hated following these trails, anyway. Deer paths always disappeared after a few dozen yards. She paused, waiting for her eyes to become accustomed to the dark. Couldn't have been even a sliver of moon in the sky, could there?

It never occurred to her to fear the darkness, the lightless undefined order of the woods. The time she'd spent photographing wild animals in their own territory had given Mercedes a healthy respect for the habits of predators, and she'd even been stalked once by a cougar on a shoot in British Columbia. Then as now, she'd found safety in trusting her instinct. "Lions and tigers and bears, oh my!" she whispered to herself. Most injuries and nearly all fatalities in the timberlands resulted from stupidity. There was nothing on this particular mountain that would hurt her, unless she inadvertently strolled off a cliff or into a tree.

After at least a minute of stumbling upwards in the gloom she paused near a yellow bed of evening primrose. The chime had grown louder, closer to the actual toll of a bell. Around a curve of the ridge her wide pupils picked out a soft gold-red glow against the trees. Emboldened, she continued towards it. The ringing had taken on a vicious tone, still bell-like but harsher; strike after strike close together now, almost overlapping. An indistinct, constant roar accompanied the urgent knell.

Mercedes left the fading path and clawed up a mossy bank that came away in her hands. Raising herself up, she saw a natural clearing, framed by granite boulders and smaller, smooth stones left behind by the last ice age. At the center of the bowl-like space, a fire was raging in the mouth of a man-sized furnace, dwarfed by the shadows leaping off the blocky figure that stood before it, swinging a hammer.

She hesitated, then stood and began circling the clearing. An oversized bellows rested near the man, and from time to time he took it up and coaxed the embers before him until they were white-hot. He wore a thick, stiff apron and a faded work shirt, scorched and holed by many hours in front of his anvil. Mercedes noticed his rough appearance from behind was due partly to his thick clothing, though he was an enormous, broad man. His graying hair and beard came nearly to his collar, wild and singed, and his eyebrows were full, heavy, and black. The effort rolling through his wide shoulders reminded her of Grandpa Max splitting firewood.

Mercedes slipped cautiously from boulder to stone. The giant–he swung the hammer with hairy arms that bulged and swelled with each stroke against the steel–seemed completely intent on his work. She couldn't think of him as old, for the portion of his face she could see was smooth, and he wielded the hammer and bellows with immense strength and an almost casual control, despite the quick pace he sustained.

A single piece of steel occupied the anvil before him, and again he brought the sledge down in a gloved hand, full force. The metal sang, and Mercedes heard–felt–the peal from the hot, red-gold iron.

She halted across the anvil from the young-old man, watching him work for several moments. He glanced up from time to time, noting her presence with the hint of a smile but staying focused on the long steel before him.

Heat washing off the furnace dried her perspiration quickly.

The man's smile grew. He paused a moment and seemed about to speak, recognition evident in his face and posture, but then just chuckled and shifted his grip on the sledge. As he returned to work, the man grinned at her almost sheepishly and raised his eyebrows, as if possessing a special secret he wanted to share with her, a mysterious truth. Affection and tenderness shone in his eyes every time he looked up. Again she thought of her grandfather; though she knew the smith couldn't be Max, she had the feeling she should recognize him, that she *did* know him, and that their relationship was somehow more precious and infinite, and—*familial* than she was capable of comprehending.

And she could almost remember it.

The smith returned fully to his anvil, driving and folding the iron into an ever smoother, more resilient form. He turned the metal and renewed the pressure, intensity creasing his face. Pounding. Battering. Hammering his own strength down into the metal with every resonant stroke.

Mercedes drew closer to the singing steel.

"Careful," said the titanic blacksmith, pausing. "It's going to get much hotter before he's ready." He rolled his shoulders and turned back to the steel.

Mercedes abruptly awoke, rolling into motion, astonished to find herself in bed. "Jack," she said, startling herself further.

Her silk sheets lay in disarray, twisted by her dream of the night run, kicked from her. Back in her Studio City bungalow. Her arms were still warm, as if actual heat had washed off the furnace onto her skin.

The night around her held pure with silence. The dim darkness beyond the three walls of glass was quiet, cool. It was the time of night Mercedes usually loved best. No birds, no breeze, nothing to mar the stillness before the new day was born. There was something almost holy in these calm hours.

She folded her arms over her knees and sat like that for a long minute, thoughts awhirl. The dream had been so vivid. She hadn't had a dream that sharp and clear since—well, in years. Bizarre. Eerie.

Jack?

Good thing sleepwalking hadn't been a part of her imagined run. Mercedes couldn't imagine what the neighbors would think of her dashing around the block in her underwear. Then again, it *was* California.

Softly, not wanting to break the quiet of the night, but also partly because she wanted to keep the dream as intact as she could, Mercedes slid out of bed and walked to the kitchen, where she opened the refrigerator and poured herself a glass of water.

But— "'Jack?'" she said, rubbing her arms. A car passed by out in the street, and from the darkness she watched it flicker past her wrought-iron gate.

Still several hours until dawn.

As she walked down the hall to her darkroom, Mercedes tried a yawn. No good. She'd be lucky to fall asleep again before the paperboy came, and she wasn't going to spend a couple hours tossing and turning, pretending to rest. Working on the pictures of the baby eagles would help shake off the weird dream.

Since her first day at college—almost since her first real camera— Mercedes hadn't used a photo-processing company. Under the amber light in her darkroom, she could make magic. The slow, sometimes painstaking process of developing her own pictures always made her think of alchemy, conjuration, creation. She loved the esoteric equipment, the chemicals, and the sheer ritual of making a picture.

Three of the prints of the eagle's feeding were amazing, and amazingly flawed. Sunlight falling through the tops of the trees had cast uneven shadows over the birds, and the part of the nest on the left-hand side of the picture was overexposed, not too murky to be distinguished but enough to throw the picture out of balance. Mercedes frowned and crumpled the prints into the wastecan. Returning to the enlarger, she prepared to reexpose a sheet of paper to a negative. The negative was still in the negative holder, set to the correct focus. She put a sheet of eight-by-ten-inch printing paper into an easel, and checked the timer on the enlarger lamp. This portion of the spell was always accomplished through trial-and-error, determining the exact amount of time necessary to achieve the proper contrasts of lights and darks and density of detail. Light shining from the enlarger lamp through the negative would paint the picture onto the printing paper. The timer had been set for twenty three seconds, just right for most of the picture but enough to overexpose the left-hand side.

Mercedes again set the timer for twenty three seconds and activated the lamp, but this time, when the timer reached seventeen seconds, she slowly waved her left hand between the paper and the negative, preventing the enlarger lamp from projecting onto the left-hand side of the print for the final five seconds. By lessening the exposure over that area, she was able to bring out the detail, almost beckoning it out of the paper. The gesture of an alchemist.

When the sheet was fully exposed, Mercedes set it into the developing tray and watched the image reveal itself. Then she transferred the print to a tray filled with stopping solution. She gently moved the print in the solution, careful to rotate it from top to bottom to make sure the chemicals touched it evenly. Finally, she shifted the print to a tray filled with chemicals that fixed the image on the paper, making it permanent. Again she gingerly rotated the print, then placed it in a tray filled with slowly running water that would rinse the chemicals from it.

It worked. Mercedes realized she was smiling. Technically it was a good shot. Crisp. Composed well, yet there was something else. They'd made a picture together, she and the mother eagle. The mother gently coaxed her babies to take the strip of meat, held daintily in her fiercely hooked beak. Under the curve of her wings the baby eagles, jostling, straining to stand on tiny legs, demanded life. This was more than mere existence. The picture seethed and beat with something elemental.

Mercedes found it hard to look away. At last she washed her hands and wrists, then padded down the hall to her office.

She tried another yawn.

In contrast to the overstuffed style and form of her bedroom, Mercedes always picked very Spartan furniture for her office—it wasn't an uncomfortable room, but she felt the least distractions she had about while doing the paperwork, the better. A few tiny art prints, a bird-of-paradise plant, and a palm-sized glass globe of the world, which she rolled into her hand as she sat at her desk and woke up her computer.

There was an email from Eric and Sara Jensen, excited about the pictures and their forthcoming thesis. They wanted her opinion about some of the text they'd written to accompany the pictures.

She hadn't known that golden eagles usually mate for the first time when relatively young, at around four years old, and paired with the same mate for their entire fifteen- to twenty-year lifespan. Mercedes thought about the mother eagle, and the wild, warrior expression in the creature's eyes. She found herself wondering what sorts of things attracted one eagle to another.

Mercedes looked through half-a-dozen invoices, checking dates and payments, then logged into her bank account. Everything was fine, set to go smoothly next month when she moved the last of the paperwork needed to completely regain her last name. By mid-summer—near the end of celebrity wedding season—she'd be sending out invoices with her own name—Mercedes *Adams*—on the letterhead. The next few months would be a lot of work, and maybe she could go ahead and hire a fourth photographer. There were two kids she had in mind, both recent grads from UCLA who had great eyes for shadows and light. Better, she had to admit, than she had been a few years ago, right out of school. Why not hire both and take a little break?

She sat back, wrapped her hand around the frosted globe, and smiled. A few birds were stirring in the trees outside her window. Dawn still hours away. When the stores opened she could do some shopping for her next shoot.

What was a dream, anyway? Fantasy? Fear? A psychic tease—or scraps of self-doubt, wrapped in something familiar and intimate, say, a memory? This last explanation makes sense. The subconscious demands order, meaning. Mercedes worked very hard to keep an even tenor to her life, a routine, a dependable arrangement. Who's to say her subconscious wasn't engaging in a little housekeeping, tidying up bits and pieces of misfit information? Groping to find order in barely-perceived sensory data. Sure. That feeling of heat on her arm as she drew close to the fire? Nothing. Dreams mean nothing.

Tell that to Joseph in Egypt.

What did Thoreau write? She affected a British accent, purely for the fact that it made her sound more intelligent than she knew she deserved. "Dreams are the touchstones of our characters." There, that was profound. Mercedes firmly believed all dead intellectuals sounded most credible when quoted out loud in BBC English.

But *this* dream, in particular, meant nothing. She might still be half-asleep, the way it hung before her mind's eye.

Jack.

She found herself surfing over to the Internet Movie Database and typing his name into the site search engine.

It was her favorite site to check out basic movie info—Mercedes often clicked through to Amazon (usually to buy the book the movie was based on, get right to the source of the goodness). The section on actors was sparse, giving basic info like date of birth (which in this case she knew already), a list of movie titles and television appearances, and occasionally a snippet of biographical data.

As far as she knew Mercedes had seen all of Jack's movies, some on cable, though the only one she'd ever bought for her own collection was one of his first, a Dean Koontz miniseries called *Strange Highways*. She'd caught the beginning on TV with no idea who was in it, and Jack had scared the hell out of her. The sight of his familiar face was chilling, but the performance—he played the part of the protagonist's older brother, a local sports hero, the laurelled golden boy—and thorough psychopath.

—she shivered.

She knew where he drew the character from.

Before he could be typecast, Jack appeared as the comic relief character in a Kenneth Branagh film called *Storming the Castle*, and then as the romantic lead in *Xanthippe*, an independent film that had done well in broad release for reasons Mercedes never understood.

According to the bio she'd read on a fan's website, it was around this time Jack had been taken aside by John Cusack and Kelsey Grammer, of all people, and counseled against trading his soul to Hollywood. Five of Jack's movies released the same year; playing a young Jack Ryan in *Without Remorse*, (in her opinion, coming off more believable than Harrison Ford had as a mature Ryan—Mercedes had inherited the Tom Clancy books from her father), another Koontz miniseries and two movies opposite Bruce Willis and Daryn Tufts where all three had played wildly different characters.

Jack fit in everywhere, but managed to stand out at the same time.

His first starring role—and the last time Mercedes had seen a movie in a real theater—was in *The Walking Drum*, a historical Celtic story set around the turn of the first Millennium. Directed by Ridley Scott from an original novel by Louis L'amour, it had been a monstrous success, one of those films to come along unexpectedly and do better business every succeeding week it stayed in theaters. Tired Hollywood had surprised everyone with *Drum*; it was widely thought that swashbuckling adventure movies were a dead franchise. It was a star-maker, a breakout. Mercedes decided she really liked it after her third screening.

During breaks in filming, Jack occasionally wrote pieces for Premier and Variety. Rumor was Jack had helped tighten *Drum's* screenplay, and that rumor led to others, one fingering him for being the adventure novelist Fletcher Engstrom.

Mercedes had to laugh. During the brief media flurry, Engstrom himself had emerged a few days later from his apartment outside Farmington, New Mexico, blinking and looking concerned for the cameras. *Entertainment Tonight* had exposed the odd little man, a chemist by vocation, who had written a string of fair-to-decent thrillers and a few sweaty bodice rippers.

Problem was, Engstrom had been writing for years before Jack Flynn stood before a camera, and the shiny, coiffed network spokesface had a hard time drawing enough sound bites from the chubby closet-writer to fill a 2-minute segment.

Sales of Engstrom's books rocketed, the world went on, and by the time attention turned back to Jack Flynn, he was gone. Vanished into vacation. He'd never been sought so fiercely before, and at the time his publicist explained that Flynn had simply done what he did several times a year, gotten an itch to travel and look around. His last words in front of a camera, it would turn out for several months, had been, "I think I'll round up some old friends and hit the beach."

The Flynn disappearance was a minor thing as far as Hollywood was concerned, and in a day was quickly swallowed up in the headlines by the outbreak of another conflict in Iran and the failed peacekeeping mission headed by the European Union.

And there was his picture, top of the web page. He'd aged well; lines appeared down either side of his face when he smiled. The sadness in his eyes could be a photographer's trick.

There was even a quote by an actress, a glittery, fluttery thing barely out of her teens, who'd described Jack as "a man in a world full of boys.

He's got a craziness to him you wouldn't expect." The backstory went on to describe the shoot they'd been on together: she'd fumbled a valuable prop, some kind of antique watch, off a 30-ft pier into the South China Sea. Before the watch hit the water, Jack was in the air, diving after it. Mercedes forced her way through the puff journalism.

There was the inevitable comparison of Jack to any one of a dozen "rugged, old-fashioned movie stars. If this was the '50s, he might have changed his name to Rock. This is a man who doesn't own a hair dryer."

Mercedes skimmed the list of Jack's other television and movie appearances, paused for a moment over a review of his latest, *And Caesar Whispered,* then stopped herself. Frowning, Mercedes pushed herself back in her chair until she could rest her feet on the keyboard, and smirked. She'd joined the ranks of wackos and wierdos who stayed up all night worshipping the virtual world, sitting in their underwear and stuffing their brains to overflowing with nonsense. Jack's life should be his own, and she felt guilty enough for the time she'd spent ogling him across the 'Net.

The trees outside postured in the wind, and their posing shadows swam on the walls of her office. In a few minutes the sun would be up in earnest and she'd be back to a much harder world, where she was a grownup and couldn't pretend to be a kid in front of a movie screen, with a mouth full of popcorn and a head full of lunacy. A world, honestly, that she enjoyed more most of the time, where meaning and purpose could be found, where friendships for her were few but *real.*

"Jack," she said, trying to force a note of disgust into her voice, and failing. "Jack," she said again, softer, as she tossed the glass world into the air. The crystal caught the day's first light, and sent whorls and points of brilliance through the room.

The phone rang suddenly, and she hiccupped, plucking the crystal out of the air with one hand while the other groped for the phone. "Jack?—I mean, hello?"

It was her cousin, Irene. She was hoarse, insistent. "I need you. I need what you can do. Do you feel up to a double murder?"

—Epilogue Part One—

Paris
4AM

Alonzo leaned his elbows against the bridge, patiently staring at the widening ripples beneath him. The Seine murmured quietly by, whispering to him in the voices of ghosts, in snatches of an old, old song he was supposed to remember. It always went like this, he reflected. Hours and hours of waiting–and for a woman, nonetheless. He slid closer to the leering statue that shared his vigil.

She would come. He suspected that she thought she loved him, and so he would wait.

The sun had yet to touch the eastern horizon when he saw Eliane stroll around the corner. She was wearing her blue cardigan and the Detroit Tigers baseball cap he'd given her. Joining him on the bridge, she snuggled close.

"Ow! Watch that rib, darling," he murmured. "How did it go today? Any luck in the flower business?"

Eliane shrugged. "Enough to pay for us to see a movie tonight. Is that American-style enough for a date?" She was laughing behind her eyes, he could tell.

"Only if I buy us breakfast first! Have you ever eaten at the Jules Verne restaurant, in the Eiffel Tower?"

"Oh, non, non. C'est impossible!" She blushed. "They do not serve breakfast, and also, you need reservations for at least three months in advance."

"Well, see Eliane, I've got this friend . . ."

As they stepped off the bridge, Alonzo paused and turned one last time, looking across the Seine and up, up into the darkness gathering over the city. Against the angular line of night stood the gargoyles as they had for ages, as they would for ages to come, watching, waiting. As if ready to burst into ferocious action.

One of them moved.

It was Jack.

Ready for more?

The story continues in Jack Be Nimble: Tyro.

Available now.

Acknowledgements & End Notes

Thank you for buying and reading this book. I sincerely hope you had a blast reading it & would be thrilled to hear from you about your experience! I hope you'll consider visiting my website at www. BenEnglishAuthor.com and connecting with me through Twitter, Facebook, carrier pigeon, owl post, Patronus messenger charm, message in a bottle-tossed-in-a-wormhole, whatever. Twitter's fine. Would be a huge honor to hear from you.

A quick note regarding the technology mentioned in the book: While the events of **Jack Be Nimble: Gargoyle** obviously take place a few years in the future (after the coronation of William Wales to the British throne and the peaceful democratization of Cuba, for instance), you need to know that all the tech in the book is either real or within the easy reach of likelihood, given a year or two of applied science. I've worked among the mad genius-nerds of Silicon Valley long enough to experience many amazing technologies that either haven't yet been fully developed or merely lie within reach but down the road not taken. Humans are amazing. Get this: a hundred and fifty years ago, the United States Patent Office was ready to close its doors, believing at the time that everything necessary and possible had already been invented—but look at us now. Imagine what we'll see tomorrow.

There is a ridiculously high number of people whose efforts made this book possible, whether by offering technical advice, military information, scientific instruction, ice cream, or other manifestations of selfless love and support. So many friends read the manuscript in various forms and stages and gave suggestions and encouragement throughout the adventure of writing it. It was a wonderful avalanche. Some sort of special recognition must go to Gilen English, Eric and Sara Jensen, Terry Gorton, Kate Piersanti, Mike and Debbie Schramer, Douglas Thayer, Barbara English, Clark Seaman, Erik Swanson, Dan Brownlee, Bonnie Barnes, Kristeen and John Cantillo, and Daryn Tufts. Titanic friends, every one.

Thank you!

Ben

P.S. You really should get the next book in the series, *Tyro*. It's out already. Go ahead, treat yourself. Treat your friend. Treat ten friends!

Made in the USA
Columbia, SC
20 July 2017